A Wreath of Lilies

Miss Gascoigne mysteries: book 2

Caron Allan

A Wreath of Lilies: Miss Gascoigne mysteries: book 2

Dedication

To my family

And to anyone who has ever worked in customer services: you are seriously awesome.

A Wreath of Lilies

Prologue

The door of the church was standing open, like it was when Bet left the church on her previous visit that morning.

She came up the aisle, as she had twenty-eight years earlier as a bride, although today she was wearing her flowered apron and a pair of good strong brogues, not her mother's wedding dress. And the only man waiting at the altar for her was the Reverend Kenneth Riley, and everyone knew he had no interest in women whatsoever.

As Bet approached, her eyes flitted from here to there. So much to think about, so many tasks she absolutely mustn't forget. Not to mention, things to pack. The vases. The pruning shears. Even the teacups and the kettle on the tray in the corner of the vestry. The tray itself, of course. The matches. The packet of tea, the spoons, the sugar. The apron she'd left hanging up behind the door in case she ever needed a spare.

She gave the Reverend Riley a curt nod, unable to forgive him, as any good Christian should, because after all, surely it had been his responsibility to keep the church thriving, to keep its doors open. And now, here they were, just...

She got no further, her thoughts interrupted by the sounds behind her. A clumping of feet, coming closer, but something else too, something almost melodic.

A most unChristian rage took hold of her as she bolted about to see them coming into the church in her wake: the Seekers of Light. She clenched her hands at her sides and took a deep breath.

Kenneth Riley was coming forward now, and beyond him, Miss Marriott, an elderly villager, was leaning heavily on the arm of her maid, Doris, and looking extremely upset. Doris herself was looking terribly shocked and upset by what was happening. Nearby another elderly woman, Miss Didsbury, was quite clearly furious, her thin lips pressed so tightly together that the flesh was white at the corners. Clive Barton and several other villagers were standing near the door to the vestry, also watching as the group approached.

Inside the door now, and still moving came the invaders, waving their sticks of incense and their tambourines. Their robes brushed the ground as they came, garlands of flowers swathed their necks, with beads too, in all manner of shapes, sizes and colours.

They were already singing, but not a song of Godly origin, but a song of the earth, of the depths and the seasons and the stars. Somehow the villagers fell back, making way for the group to approach the altar, where they set aside their instruments and sat, cross-legged before the altar itself, as if it was their space and no one else's. Then, their leader, Tristan Summers, came forward to stand there, holding up his hand. As one, the seekers stopped their song and fell to humming a single pensive, low-keyed note.

And he began to proclaim:

'A guilt is here that has never been cleansed. A soul is here that has never been mourned. A spirit, unreleased, broods in the portals of the between-world, unable to leave or to enter but trapped, for years of our time, and times unknown. Let the unclaimed one be freed, let the unclaimed one be brought back into the fold.'

*

Chapter One

Dee Gascoigne was the only person in the train carriage. She had a newspaper in case she got bored, as it was a long, slow journey to Hartwell Priory, a village close to the North Essex coast. And if the newspaper was not enough, she had a novel in her handbag: the Agatha Christie book that she had wanted to read for some time and that she'd been given by her cousin Jenny as a birthday present. Next to the brand new copy of *A Caribbean Mystery* was the envelope Monty had given her. She had better not lose it. It contained some cash to cover any expenses, and a couple of sheets of paper that outlined her new 'case'. She used the word in her mind, and it thrilled her to the core: she was actually *on a case.* In addition to these she had a letter of introduction and a handful of business cards so that she could be confident in the face of any challenge to her—call it what it was—nosy questioning.

If there was something that could be called a 'gift'

in Dee's character it was her ability to ask far too many questions, and it was pleasing to know that these could now be asked officially on behalf of *Montague Montague of London, legal services*.

Only yesterday, Thursday September 2nd 1965, Dee had been sitting in Monty's office, hoping almost against hope that he could help her.

It had been six months since she had left—or been asked to leave—her job as a modern languages teacher at a very nice school for very nice young ladies. Since then, she had found herself at a loss over what to do with her life.

Then, in the Spring, she had been sent off to the seaside to convalesce after an illness and had stumbled into a murder mystery exactly like those she so dearly loved to read. (Here she glanced with fond anticipation at the bit of the cover of *A Caribbean Mystery* that she could see nestling in the top of her open bag). She had helped her dratted sort-of cousin, Inspector Bill Hardy, to clear up the mystery, risking her own life and limb to do so, but had he been grateful? Not at all.

'You really must keep out of police business in future,' he had murmured to her at her mother's birthday party, grabbing her and steering her away from the celebrations where she had been enjoying discussing the case with her aunt, his mother, who also loved to 'dabble' in mysteries. He had then spent three minutes explaining why civilians shouldn't mess about in police matters. She had rolled her eyes, stalked off and left him to it. He had a bloody cheek, Dee grumbled to herself, still irritated about it.

Anyway... Where was she? She had lost herself in the midst of feeling angry with Bill. She certainly wasn't going to think about how handsome he had looked in his formal dinner suit, nor about how much she liked the way his dark hair crinkled behind his ears and at his neck now that he was wearing it slightly longer as many young men did these days. And the slightly longer sideburns too. So sexy.

She had been out of work for some months now. Oh, she had been invited to several interviews for positions at other schools, but it always came down to the same thing: she just didn't want to go back to teaching.

Yet what else could a recently separated woman do? People were so sniffy about the idea of a woman leaving her husband. It was this scandalous action on her part that had cost her the job in the first place.

And then, seemingly from nowhere, when all hope was lost and the money she had borrowed from her parents was dwindling to a pitifully tiny amount, dear sweet Monty had asked her brother Rob to get her to come and see him.

'I've got something in the way of a job idea that might interest you,' M'dear Monty had wheezed at her across his vast oak desk. Eighty if he was a day, and about to start his fifth retirement, Monty's legal expertise had saved Dee's family on more than one occasion.

She had been all ears. Could he really be serious? She held her breath waiting to see what he said. Even if it was a typing job, she'd have to take it. Not that she could type, not really. But she could no longer pretend that she wasn't desperate. Her pride—that thing that goeth before a fall—was now in tatters.

'Most law practices engage investigators to find out things for them. To carry out research, or to go to speak to people, that sort of thing. Montague's is no different. But the fellow I have been using for the last two or three years has, er—shall we say—found it advantageous to his health to quickly move to South America. Therefore I now have a vacancy.

'Dear Rob has kindly given me full account of your exploits down in Porthlea—delightful place—in the spring, and I think you could be just what I'm looking for. I know your inquiring mind, (he means nosiness, Dee told herself) and that you are an intelligent woman. Resourceful too, (crafty, Dee amended) and I know that I need have no doubts whatsoever about your moral integrity.'

She was on the point of speaking, but he held up a hand to halt her. He added, 'Oh I know this is rather new to you, M'dear, but I feel you have a certain bent for investigating. In any case, if I may be blunt for a moment, I need someone right now, and you need the money. Can I persuade you to give it a try? If it doesn't suit you, M'dear, no harm done on either side. What do you say?'

Well, what could she say?

'My goodness, Monty dearest, I'd love to!'

And so here she was, on a painfully slow train that seemingly stopped at every rabbit hutch and milepost, heading to a place she'd never even heard of: Hartwell Priory.

She knew it was a tiny place, barely more than a halfway point between the busy port of Harwich and the town of Colchester in the county of Essex. She was to find her way to a guesthouse and rent herself a room for the week. Monty seemed to think it could take her several days, perhaps a whole week, to find out the things he needed to know.

She had money for her expenses, and the promise of ten pounds in wages, whether she was successful or not. Oh, she prayed she would be. The last thing she wanted was to let Monty down after his kindness.

The guard peered at her through the window of the

connecting door to the next carriage. He'd already clipped her ticket and was checking to see if any new passengers had boarded into her carriage. They hadn't of course, it had been almost an hour since she'd seen anyone other than the guard.

The business cards Monty had so clearly had printed *before* he even knew what she would say, stated simply: *Miss Diana Gascoigne, Associate, Montague Montague of London, legal services*. And the letter of introduction, was exactly that, short, to the point, impossible to quibble with or gainsay:

'To whom it may concern,

I confirm that Miss Diana Gascoigne is an associate of this company, Montague Montague of London, legal services, and that she is employed by myself and working under my instructions.

The Honourable Montague Montague QC, Bart.,'

The connecting door now opened. Dee glanced up. The guard, a young man in his twenties, said, 'We'll be there in two minutes, miss. Watch your step getting down, it's quite a drop to the platform.'

'Thank you.'

'Do you need help with your suitcase?'

'Oh no, that's quite all right, thanks.' She beamed at him.

He blushed and left, and Dee closed her handbag with a snap, got up, grabbed her raincoat and hat, and hefted her case down off the luggage net and began to make her way to the corridor. The train slowed and the long narrow platform appeared beneath the window.

She had arrived.

Mrs Padham was a sour-faced unfriendly sort, the exact opposite of the kind of person one would expect to run a guesthouse, Dee thought.

It was only after she had already agreed terms and been shown to her room that it occurred to Dee that she ought to have gone to the village pub first. Pubs often let rooms. As she looked about her at the gloomy, cupboard-sized room, sparsely furnished and with a view of a blank wall, she could have kicked herself. Oh well, it was probably only for a few days. Or nights, rather. She had told Mrs Padham three nights. She had been informed that breakfast was served between half past seven and half past eight, and that dinner—five shillings extra—was between six and seven o'clock.

'I'm afraid I shan't be wanting dinner,' Dee had said, hoping that she could find somewhere else to eat than this dreary establishment. Mrs Padham huffed crossly at this and began to walk away.

'And no men!' The woman's parting shot was confusing.

'You don't allow men in the guesthouse?' Dee called after her.

Without turning back, Mrs Padham responded crisply, 'I don't allow men in the room of a single girl.'

Fat chance of that happening, Dee thought. She sat on the side of the bed and gave it an experimental bounce. The mattress was lumpy and the bed frame squeaked horribly. She wrinkled her nose then reminded herself again that she was only expecting to be there for a few days.

She unpacked her suitcase, hanging up the tree dresses, three blouses and one skirt she had brought in case she needed to look smart, then threw her underwear, slacks and tops in the first drawer of the chest. There was no chair, so she returned to the bed, and sat there to read through Monty's instructions.

It all seemed quite intriguing.

The local church diocese had decided that declining attendance meant that the church in Hartwell Priory was no longer viable to maintain. The church had been closed, and the plan was for the church and its churchyard to be sold off to developers who wanted to demolish the church and build three hundred new houses on the land.

Of course, this had led to all sorts of outcries. Many local residents did not want new houses built practically on their doorsteps, suggesting that these 'modern eyesores' would encourage the 'wrong' kind of people to descend upon lovely Hartwell Priory.

Other local groups, such as the Village Association, the Hartwell Priory and District Local History Society, the Save Hartwell Priory Church Group, the Christian Mothers Group and the Save Our Heritage Group had all bombarded the town council with protests, complaints and—according to a local news report—even rotten eggs and squashy tomatoes.

But it had been an old client of Monty's who had asked for his help. Miss Dolores Marriott had written to report that a new group calling themselves the Seekers of Light had arrived in the village a month or so earlier and had been holding séances in the churchyard at midnight, in itself the subject of a debacle, and proclaiming that several of the 'passed over ones' from 'beyond' had 'come through' (the quotation marks were Monty's) to declare themselves unhappy with the proposal to move them from the churchyard to a 'new resting place'.

Miss Marriott was not a member of any of these groups but a village resident with ancestors buried in the churchyard. She had asked Monty to find out if the 'paranormal people' were genuine, (and how could they be, Monty had scrawled in parenthesis), and whether it had been her ancestors who had come through in the séance to protest the move. Because, she said, if they had, she would have no choice but to throw herself in front of any bulldozers that came to dig up her great-great-grandmother and sundry other relations.

'Probably nothing in it but a load of silly local excitement, but Miss Marriott is begging me to find this out for her. I don't want to offend her by refusing, and the poor woman is genuinely concerned. However, I have neither the time nor the inclination to take charge of this myself. So, M'dear, how does ten pounds plus expenses sound for three- or four-days' work?'

It sounded really good, and Dee's curiosity was aroused. She put the papers away once again in her handbag. She put on some good strong walking shoes. And a less outrageously modern blouse over her navy slacks, and grabbed a jacket, a hat and her bag.

First, she decided, she would take a look at the church and the churchyard. Then, she would go and find this Miss Marriott, introduce herself and hopefully have a chat. She checked her handbag for pen and a notebook. Satisfied she had all an investigator might need, plus a lipstick and a clean handkerchief, she went downstairs. Mrs Padham was in the hallway.

'Going out already?'

Dee was rather taken aback by this. 'Oh yes. I thought I'd have a look around the village.'

'Meeting a man?'

Dee's polite smile froze a little and she said firmly, 'I shall see you later, no doubt. But, erm, which way is it to the churchyard?'

'I'm not a signpost.' Mrs Padham turned and removed herself to the rear quarters of the house, through a door marked, 'Private'.

Reflecting that the landlady did not improve on acquaintance, Dee left the guesthouse and stood outside in the lane, looking about her.

It was almost three o'clock, and as the pub would be closing at any minute and would not reopen until half past five, it would be no use going there now, though as far as she could tell, it looked a much more welcoming sight than the Belle Vue Guesthouse *(No Vacancies)* behind her.

As she glanced in the other direction, Dee saw the spire of a church peeking out from amongst the trees. Aha! she thought with a satisfied grin and headed that way. It was a neat church built of grey stone, a replica of possibly thousands of churches up and down the land, with no ancient quirks or features to give it importance. It had probably only been in existence for sixty years or so, if that, and yet it was already deemed unnecessary. Dee felt sad about that. Not that she was in the habit of going to church, but she nevertheless liked to know they were there.

The grounds at the front and sides of the church were terribly overgrown, and as she entered, the gate grated on its hinges, the sound setting her teeth on edge. She found a path leading to the church itself and followed it past the notice-board which was blank now, and the name board which announced the church was called, or rather had been called, Saint John the Apostle. The incumbent was displayed as Vacant.

She couldn't help wondering how this came to be the case. Had the minister already moved on to a new parish? Both the front door and the side door proved to be locked when she tried them, so she continued along the path which skirted around to the back of the church, where she could see several large stone tombs rising up out of the waist-high swaying grass and buttercups, and at the end of the path there was an archway of strong yew hedging.

Stepping through this archway brought her into... it would have been a meadow but for the leaning and broken stones scattered here and there. Clearly then, this meadow of wildflowers, dancing butterflies and contentedly humming bees was the condemned churchyard.

*

Chapter Two

She didn't have the place completely to herself, however. Amid the tall grass, she caught sight of a trilby hat, and assuming that the hat was not out adventuring alone, Dee headed over to see who was there.

The man, perhaps in his early fifties, straightened up on seeing her, turning a beaming smile to greet her in addition to his outstretched hand.

'Good afternoon, young lady. Haven't seen you here before. Dare I suggest you're a visitor?'

'Indeed I am.' Dee took the offered hand in a brief handshake and smiled at him. 'I'm spending a few days here, just arrived from London.'

'Ah.' His expression became cautious. 'Not one of those newspaper bods, are you? We've had quite a few, coming down here to salivate over our little problem.'

'I'm not a journalist, no,' Dee said. 'But I am down here about the 'little problem'. At least, I imagine we're talking about the same thing.'

He nodded, still cautious, but inclined to listen, she thought. She might as well tell him, he might be able to help, or at least offer her some information.

'I'm Dee Gascoigne,' she said. 'And I've been sent here by my boss, a top London barrister, who wants to know what's going on. One of his clients has written to ask for his help. Our help, I should say.'

He nodded again. 'Clive Barton, village resident and chairman of the Hartwell Priory and District Local History Society. I believe I may know who your client is. Would I be right in saying it's Dolores Marriott? I know she has a London-based lawyer.'

'You may well be,' Dee admitted. She turned to look at the half-hidden gravestone he had been tending.

He held up a small wire brush. 'I'm trying to get the worst of the lichen off, then I'm going to weed the front. I'm afraid things get out of hand very quickly here—we've had wild weather of late, with plenty of alternating sun and rain. But that's perfect for the weeds of course, and they grow at a terrific pace.'

'It's almost as if the whole place is reverting to nature. And they may be weeds, but they're lovely. It's positively heavenly here. So many insects and birds.'

'Oh, yes, it's very heaven, as they say.' He gave a gentle rub at the lichen with his brush.

'It's a shame there's going to be a brand-new housing estate on this spot,' she ventured, to see what kind of response she provoked.

He frowned, looking back at the gravestone. 'Over my dead body. Local peoples' ancestors have been buried here for over two hundred years. I intend to join them when my time comes.'

'But the church is modern, isn't it?'

'The previous church was damaged by fire just before the First World War. This one was built on the same site, reusing many of the remaining stones and even much of the wooden interior that was still sound. On the inside it's a far less modern building but a very tasteful reconstruction of the old. The original one was the priory from which the village get its name. Which is another reason we are so passionate about it, and determined to keep it up and running, regardless of what the diocese or the town council may say about its suitability as a building site.'

'Is either side showing any sign of relenting?' Dee asked.

He shook his head immediately. 'Not in the least. In theory, ground is to be broken this coming Monday, the 6th. There will be plenty of us to give the developers a headache if that goes ahead. There's another public meeting tonight, in the back room of the pub. You'd be welcome to come along, it starts at eight o'clock.'

'Is it true some druids or beatniks or something have been here trying to communicate with the dead?'

'Oh that lot!' he scoffed. 'Bloody time-wasting, drug-taking layabouts. Excuse my French. Well, I'm sorry, I really have to go. Very nice talking to you, Miss Grayson.'

'Gascoigne,' Dee said.

'Sorry, sorry. Miss Gascoigne. Do come along this evening if you can. You may find it interesting.'

As he hurried away, Dee stared after him, wondering why he'd abandoned his idea of tidying up the grave of his ancestor. She carefully smoothed away some of the worst creepers and moss to reveal the inscription on the gravestone.

Sacred to the memory of
Maureen Barton
Beloved wife of Clive and mother of Barry and Jane
Born Sept 1915
Departed this life July 1957
Always loved, never forgotten,
Treasured in our hearts forever.

Dee stood there for a moment deep in thought. Why hadn't he just said it was his wife's grave? Why say it was an ancestor, implying an ancient burial? The only answer she could think of was that perhaps, even after eight years, his wife's death was still too painful a subject to speak of. You heard of such things. And it might be especially difficult to speak of it to a total stranger.

A few yards away, she found a low brick wall that formed an almost-hidden perimeter around the churchyard. She sat there for half an hour, captivated by the natural beauty of the spot, until eventually realising it was time to brush the dust and grass seeds from her slacks and go in search of Monty's client's house.

Dolores Marriott was at least seventy, if not closer to eighty, Dee decided as she made her way across a vast expanse of highly patterned carpet towards the elderly woman waiting regally in an armchair to receive her.

Dee smiled as pleasantly yet politely as she could, but it was not until her letter of introduction and her business card had been carefully scrutinised through a lorgnette that she received any answering warmth from Miss Marriott.

Dee said, 'If it's not convenient, I can come back some other time. I don't want to disturb you.'

Miss Marriott appeared to waver, the temptation to send Dee away again seemed to be considered for several moments. Perhaps she had changed her mind and regretted sending the letter to Monty now, Dee thought.

But then the elderly lady smiled, and said, very warmly, 'Not at all. This is perfectly all right, I am delighted to meet you, Miss Gascoigne. Do sit down.'

'Do please call me Dee.' She sat.

Again there was a short silence, but then Miss Marriott said, in a perfectly friendly way, 'Is Dee short for something?'

'Oh yes, it is. It was my nickname as a child. Short for Diana.'

Now the old woman smiled. 'How sweet. I was always known as Lola by my siblings, two brothers, both older than I and now sadly, no longer with us.'

'I'm sorry to hear that,' Dee said in truth. 'I have brothers. We are very close.'

'Gascoigne. Gascoigne. Let me see.' She adjusted the lorgnette. 'Are you by any chance related to the Hertfordshire Gascoigne de la Gascoignes? It used to be Piers and – er - Evangeline, I believe.'

'Oh yes, that's right. They were my grandparents. I'm afraid they passed away when I was just a baby. My father George Gascoigne de la Gascoigne has taken over the estate and my brother Freddie helps him with it.'

The smile was a positive beam now. It should have come as no surprise that the social standing of her family name would carry far more weight than any written recommendation, even from someone as eminent as Montague Montague.

'Now, let me ring for tea, then I will tell you all

about it.' She got to her feet and moved so slowly that Dee began to feel wicked for staying in her seat. Next time, she would know to offer to do this for Miss Marriott. If there was a next time. At last the woman came within arm's reach of a long embroidered strap that was hanging from the ceiling and which she gripped briefly and yanked downwards. Then with a deadly slow manoeuvre, she turned carefully and edged her way back to her seat.

She had barely sat down when the door opened.

'Ma'am?' the red-faced, red-eyed young woman said. She glanced at Dee but glanced away again immediately. It was the same young woman who had opened the door to Dee, stared at her, then blushed a vivid crimson, and with stammering and apologies, invited Dee to step inside whilst she went to speak with her mistress. Dee thought now that she looked as though she had been crying.

'Ah, Doris. This is Miss Dee, from Mr Montague's office in London, come down here to help us. And she obviously needs a cup of tea.'

'Ma'am,' said Doris again, and she bobbed a kind of half-curtsey and went out, darting anxious looks at Miss Marriott as she went.

'Doris,' Miss Marriott explained, 'has been with me a little over ten years. She is a kind of cook-housekeeper, though of course she has whatever help she needs.'

Dee nodded.

'Are you in a rush to hurry back to London? Did you come down on the train, or did you drive?'

'I came by train, but I'm staying in the village for a few days, so there's no rush.'

'Surely not at the public house? A young woman on her own?' Miss Marriott sounded on the verge of being scandalised, as if it was still the age of Victoria.

Dee hastened to set her mind at rest.

'Actually, I'm staying at the guesthouse.'

'Not the Didsbury's old place!' she exclaimed, every bit as horrified. 'Not at all the thing. You wouldn't know this, of course, but it's the poor daughter who runs the guesthouse. Her parents died years ago and left the place to her and her husband. Though the Lord alone knows where young Henry Padham took himself off to, leaving his wife to run the business all on her own. Well, you can't stay there. It's horrible. Or so I've heard. You shall bring your things back here after we've had tea, and stay as long as you need to.'

Dee thanked Miss Marriott warmly, grateful, though she felt unable to refuse in any case, the old woman was so emphatic. But it would be nice not to be under the beady eye of Mrs Padham. Not that Dee had any intentions of taking a man to her room, of course, but she had felt rather closely scrutinised. Clearly Mrs Padham had thought nothing of expressing her rather forceful opinions to everyone.

The tea came in: a full old-fashioned, afternoon tea of sandwiches and other savouries, little cakes and tempting sweet treats, and a big fat china teapot under a knitted cosy in cheerful stripes, along with the milk jug and sugar basin. Doris served them their drinks then left them to wait on themselves.

'I've just been to take a look around the churchyard,' Dee said.

Miss Marriott's expression immediately softened. 'Beautiful spot, isn't it? It makes my blood boil to think of three hundred council houses being built all over that loveliness. In any case, there are much better places where the houses could go.' She leaned forward. 'I know I sound like a dreadful snob. But it's not simply that I don't want three hundred working class families moving in just here, though I'd be a liar if I said I liked the idea of living cheek by jowl with a building site.

'But it's more than that. To begin with, there's the difficulty that three hundred more families will cause. To local traffic, for example. The road through the village is very narrow, and just at that point, extremely so. The bus can't get through to that part of the village, the dustcart certainly couldn't, there is no pavement, so pedestrians would be walking side-by-side with the traffic, which in the dark mornings and evenings of winter would be disastrous, especially where little ones are concerned. Oh, I know they could put up better street-lighting, but will they, that's the question. So I have concerns about the churchyard being touted as the best choice for the new houses. There is some farmland at the other end of the village that would be far more suitable in so many ways. Mr Everard is about to retire and has no one after him to inherit his farm. At the moment he rents out a field to campers.'

She sighed, then turned her attention to her tiny triangular smoked salmon and cream cheese sandwich.

The door opened and Doris came in looking a little worried.

'Yes, Doris?' Miss Marriott glanced up.

'I'm so sorry, ma'am, I forgot all about your sweeteners.' Doris slipped a small box onto the table close to Miss Marriott.

Miss Marriott nodded. 'Oh, goodness, so did I, dear. I've already put sugar in my tea. Never mind, this'll do for my second cup.'

Looking relieved, Doris left the room again. Miss Marriott shook two small white tablets into the dregs in her teacup, presumably so she didn't forget next time.

Coming back to what they had been saying before the interruption, Dee said, 'I understand there's a meeting tonight.'

'Oh yes,' Miss Marriott agreed, quickly swallowing the rest of her sandwich. 'I plan to attend. You could too, if you wished. You may find it useful.'

'Good idea,' Dee said. 'I met a Mr Barton in the churchyard. He told me about the meeting.'

'That would be Clive Barton. Yes, a very pleasant man. He is also passionately opposed to the development.' Miss Marriott refilled her cup. She offered the pot to Dee, who declined.

'Now then, Miss Dee Gascoigne. How is it that you are still single? What on earth are the men in London thinking?'

It took all Dee's skill to evade those and several other questions without giving offense. She didn't want to mention that she was still married. That was, after all, why she had reverted to her maiden name. People could still be very opposed to a woman leaving her husband, even a violent man like Martin Clarke. How many times had Dee heard the phrase, 'You've made your bed, now you must lie in it'? Or variations of the theme, implying certainly if not stating outright that it was a man's right to hit his wife on a regular basis: no doubt she had done something to deserve it, they seemed to say.

Miss Marriott was in earnest about Dee staying with her. As soon as they'd finished their tea, Dee returned to Mrs Padham's guesthouse. As Mrs Padham had declined to give her guest a front door key, Dee was obliged to ring the doorbell.

With some trepidation, she began to explain that she was moving out, having been invited to stay with Miss Marriott.

Stony-faced, Mrs Padham turned to walk away, flinging over her shoulder, 'Well, you needn't expect a refund, that's all. Leave your room key on the hall table when you go.'

It was a shame about having to pay, but otherwise Dee felt that the conversation had gone about as well as could have been expected. She hurried up to her room, repacked her belongings and only five minutes later, she was leaving the room key on the hall table as instructed and letting herself out of the front door with a deep sense of relief.

*

Chapter Three

'I expect you think I'm just a stupid old woman, making a fuss over the relics of people who are long past caring what happens to them.'

Along with a number of others, they were walking extremely slowly in the direction of the public house, The Bird In Hand. The pub sign, hanging out over the village street, depicted on one side two human hands cradling a dove, and on the other side, a buxom lady with a man's arm about her waist. The sign creaked and squeaked in the breeze. Dee hoped it wasn't about to fall on them.

'No, not at all, I just...' Dee began, but Miss Marriott, leaning on her walking stick with one hand, and gripping Dee's arm for support with her other as she shuffled along, continued.

'But it's not really just about that. I've told you my misgivings about the place they've chosen for the development. In any case, it's more the fact that they didn't tell us what they were doing. We only found out when an anonymous person wrote to the local newspaper.'

Before Dee could answer, Miss Marriott said, 'And here we are. After you, Dee dear.'

As she entered the bright warm hubbub of the pub, Dee reflected that she and Miss Marriott had very quickly moved from 'Miss Gascoigne' to 'Miss Dee', to simply 'Dee dear'. Miss Marriott herself was a dear old thing, but Dee didn't feel able to call her anything other than Miss Marriott.

Miss Marriott chivvied her towards some empty seats right at the front of the large room at the back of the pub. Dee would have preferred to sit at the back, so that she could observe everyone at the meeting. She estimated eighty or so chairs had been set out in rows and these were already half-filled, with plenty more people still arriving.

In the empty space right at the front, a couple of plain wooden tables had been pushed together, and four chairs stood waiting. Two people, clearly speakers who were about to be seated at the front, were already there, standing slightly apart from the audience and deep in a low-voiced conversation.

'That's the mayor, the Honourable Edwin Windward, on the right, with the builder chappie, Nicholas Raynes, and that one just arriving is a reporter from the North Essex Times, our local newspaper. I can't remember his name. It might be David something,' Miss Marriott explained.

Dee wished she could hear what they were saying. Their discussion seemed quite animated though it appeared amiable as far as she could tell. As soon as she'd thought that, the mayor threw back his head in a hearty laugh and clapped the reporter on the shoulder like good friends do. The mayor was easily distinguishable by his expensive-looking suit, and wore a heavy gold chain of office about his neck. Raynes, the builder was wearing a casual jacket and trousers, whereas the journalist wore old-looking, baggy trousers, fraying at the hem, and a jumper with leather elbow patches.

A woman now approached them. Like the mayor she was well-dressed for an important evening. She wore a smart dress with a neat jacket over the top and her hair and make-up were perfect. The men broke off their conversation, and as the mayor greeted her with a smile and a kiss on the cheek, the journalist took the opportunity to quickly slip away, and was soon lost amongst the crowd at the back of the room.

Closer to hand, Dee was startled out of her observations by a man suddenly saying, 'Ah, we meet again!'

Turning, she saw Clive Barton's smiling face and she responded with a friendly, 'Mr Barton, how nice to see you again. I'm here with Miss Marriott,' gesturing as she spoke.

He nodded, looked disappointed, and murmured, 'Excuse me, ladies.' He went off and she saw him settle himself in a seat at the back.

'He's too old for you,' Miss Marriott said in a stage-whisper, taking Dee by surprise. Why was everyone so interested in her love-life? Although in Mrs Padham's case, perhaps she had become so bitterly opposed to anyone having a love-life after she herself had been abandoned. Dee wondered vaguely why Mrs Padham's husband—Henry, was it—had left her. Perhaps she had nagged him the way she nagged her guests.

'My goodness, I should think so,' she said vehemently to Miss Marriott's remark. 'Not that I'm looking anyway.'

'Taken, are you?' Miss Marriott's eyes bored into her, on the alert for any kind of response. Dee thought she may as well admit it and get it over with.

'Sort of.'

'I see.' Miss Marriott's smile was triumphant.

It seemed likely, even certain, that there would be further questions later. But now, with the room packed and a number of people standing at the sides and at the back, the woman at the front stood neatly to attention at the table and rapped on the wooden surface with a teaspoon from the cup and saucer in front of her.

'*They* get tea, I notice,' Miss Marriott whispered resentfully. Dee simply nodded.

'Good evening, ladies and gentlemen. Welcome to this open meeting to discuss the proposal to move the graves from the existing burial site to a new position at the north end of the village. I am Cynthia Miles-Hudson, head of planning at North Essex council. On my right, is the Honourable...'

'There's nothing honourable about Fast Eddie Windward!' someone yelled from the back. 'He's as crooked as they come!'

Cynthia ignored that. '...the Honourable Edwin Windward, who is of course His Worship the Mayor. Also with us this evening, the Very Reverend Trevor Michaels, Bishop for this diocese, and beside him, Miss Angela Baker from the Hartwell Priory and District Local History Society, and finally Mr Nicholas Raynes, head of Raynes and Son, building contractors.'

There was a brief awkward fuss as they realised they were a chair short, and Cynthia remained standing whilst someone was turned out of their seat at the back of the room and that chair was carried forward by the barmaid.

'Without further ado, I'd like to ask Mr Raynes to begin by reading a statement from Raynes and Son. Mr Raynes...' Cynthia was the only one clapping, and she quickly gave up.

Mr Raynes was on his feet. He was a tall, red-faced, meaty sort of man, probably in his early forties, Dee thought, and looked like a builder through and through. You could see he would be perfectly at home halfway up a ladder with a load of bricks, or laying foundations in the mud, or driving a digger towards a grave. He spoke in a hasty mumble, and the hands that held the paper he was reading from shook badly. Not used to public speaking, then, Dee thought, and wondered where the building company's spokesperson was, and why they were not here in his place to appease the local population.

'Good evening, ladies and gentlemen. My name is Nicholas Raynes, I represent a company by the name of Raynes and Son. Raynes and Son are a firm of building contractors who have won the contract to build houses on the land where the church and churchyard currently stand. We are a local firm and offer employment to local people.'

It was dull in the extreme, and information that even Dee, though new to the village, could have easily guessed. The cheers and catcalls increased, punctuating his speech, but Mr Raynes kept his head down and ploughed on regardless.

'Of course, we at Raynes and Son understand that this proposal raises many concerns for the residents of the village, and I'd like if I may...'

'No, you may not!' a voice bellowed from the back. Dee was fairly sure it was the same voice she had heard several times already. Mr Raynes faltered, went even redder in the face, but dipped his head down once more to doggedly continue his speech.

'...I'd like if I may to tell you, and hopefully reassure you...'

This was greeted with more laughter and some earthy comments that caused the Very Reverend Michaels to leap up and, holding up a hand to quieten the crowd, to say,

'Now please, ladies and gentlemen, I implore you. Do let's keep this civil, and gentlemen, I insist that you moderate your language. There are, after all, ladies present.'

'I'm no lady!' a female voice called out.

Laughter broke out around her, and a male voice was heard to say, 'No, you're not, Janice. I can vouch for that.'

Trevor Michaels, looking almost tearful, sank back onto his seat, his hand covering his face. Cynthia got to her feet and bashed on the table with her teaspoon.

'Now look,' she said forcefully. 'These interruptions won't get you anywhere. If you want your concerns to be taken seriously, you need to listen carefully, and comment in an orderly and helpful manner at the end. Mr Raynes, please continue.'

He did so, explaining in excruciating detail the great care and respect his company would accord the remains when they were removed from the old churchyard to their new resting place, and after speaking for another five minutes virtually without interruption, he said a rushed 'Thank you' and at last resumed his seat.

Then it was time for the bishop to add, with merciful brevity, that the builders had the church's full confidence and trust. He explained, 'The church records will be used to ensure family groups are reinterred together, that the right grave-markers are placed with the right... er...' Here he floundered a little, trying to find a polite euphemism for *corpse*. 'Remains,' he clutched at the word with evident relief. 'And a new burial service will be held once the work is complete to bless the new graveyard.' Having said this, he sat down immediately.

Dee sighed and fidgeted. She wished she could have read a report of the meeting rather than having to sit through it on a hard wooden chair. But, she reminded herself, she was being paid the handsome salary of ten pounds plus expenses—Mrs Padham's establishment, for example, she reminded herself crossly—to sit there nicely and pay attention.

The mayor got to his feet, and once again Cynthia had to call for silence so that the man could speak.

Dee disliked him instinctively and immediately. He smiled the perfect smile, not too broad or too familiar, and yet not too cool and aloof, around the room, seemingly encompassing everyone present. It was a practised smile, a pretend smile, an actor's smile. He was a professional smiler. She distrusted him and was prepared to believe his every word a lie. He kept one hand in the pocket of his jacket, the other clutching the front left of it, and for some reason this convinced Dee that he was too self-satisfied.

'I stand before you all this evening, not as a mayor of your local council, but as a local boy who has grown up in the area, and as one of yourselves. I understand your worries about this whole affair.'

This brought him suspicious doubtful looks from the audience, but he smugly swept on with his speech. The essence was, the council were determined to get the new houses built as soon as possible, and were reluctant to permit anything—or anyone—to get in the way of their schedule.

'Ground will be broken on this coming Monday, 6th September, as you are all no doubt very much aware. If anyone would like to oversee the proceedings, in a peaceful, orderly manner, of course, then he or she will be most welcome. All that is needed is for that person to put their name forward to my office.

'As our respected bishop has already explained, diocesan officials will be on hand to act as guides, with plans that will assist and indeed enable the builders to recover and remove all the *incumbents* to their new home.' He beamed at his audience.

It was unfortunate that he expressed himself in those terms. Dee immediately felt the hostility increasing around her. His tone had been too glib, too casual. No one was yet ready to laugh at the idea of the remains of their grandmothers and great-grandmothers being dug up to make way for three hundred three-bedroom semi-detached houses.

All around the room, voices and fists were raised in protest.

Demanding that the noise die down, Cynthia now introduced Miss Angela Baker who got to her feet. At once the hubbub fell away, and the proverbial pin dropping at that moment could have been heard throughout the room.

'I share your concerns. I share your sense of outrage. To think that the generations who created this village, who fought and even died for their country, should be uprooted so brutally. Not with the due care and respect accorded by church officials, or even by archaeologists, but by bulldozers and men with picks and shovels! Then tumbled carelessly into a hole in some hastily purchased corner of a farm. No matter what Bishop Michaels may say, or His Honour the Mayor, it is an outrage, pure and simple!'

Almost everyone was on their feet shouting. Even the mayor and the bishop were protesting over Miss Baker's words, so clearly designed to provoke the citizens of Hartwell Priory. Beside Dee, Miss Marriott was shaking her head in disapproval but whether at the volatile scene, or the topic of discussion, it wasn't clear.

It seemed like an age before anyone could make themselves heard. Banging her teaspoon again, Cynthia Miles-Hudson insisted several times that she must have order or would call off the meeting.

But before anything else could be said, before Miss Baker could resume her speech, the door at the back of the room was thrown open with a crash and a man rushed in shouting, 'That beatnik lot are at it again! I tell you, they're doing it again, right now! They're having another séance in the churchyard. Come on!'

He turned and ran from the room, numerous men and women following on his heels. All around, people were on their feet, impatiently pushing their way to the back, eager to go and see what was happening. Miss Marriott grabbed Dee's arm.

'Well come along. I want to see it for myself.'

And before Dee could talk her out of it, Miss Marriott reached for her stick and carefully got to her feet, moving forward inch by inch to join the throng. Dee, too curious to stay behind, immediately took the old woman's arm to ensure she didn't get swept along or toppled over, and eventually they found themselves outside.

*

Chapter Four

It was a relief to leave the hot angry air of the pub's meeting room and get out into the cool air of the evening. Most of the villagers who had attended the meeting were well ahead of them due to Miss Marriott's slow pace.

It was only half past eight in the evening, but night was fast approaching. At the horizon the sky was still pale blue, but higher up in the atmosphere the blue velvet sky was growing deeper, darker, and already Dee could see a few scattered stars twinkling as silvery pinpricks. She would have loved to stand and gaze at the sky, to enjoy the hush as the night-time settled around her. A night for lovers, she thought, and dismissed the image of her 'cousin' Bill. There was no time for that sort of thing right now.

She couldn't be sure he would ever be truly hers. Men liked to play the field, didn't they? And he seemed to be committed to doing exactly that. Busty Barbara had given way to Leggy Pam, Giggly Susan, then Wistful Wendy, according to Bill's mother, her Aunt Dottie. The last thing Dee needed was a man who changed girlfriends as often as his socks. Yet he'd sworn to Dee that he loved her... That he would wait for her. Perhaps waiting didn't mean saving himself? She sighed. Why were things always so complicated?

Snapping Dee from these unhelpful thoughts, someone came running up and spoke to Miss Marriott.

'You'll never guess what!' this newcomer exclaimed, excitement bubbling over as she giggled.

'Well, out with it, Sylvia, what are you on about?' Before Sylvia had a chance to explain, Miss Marriott was turning to Dee and grumbling, 'I do hate it when people hem and haw, and hint and don't say exactly what they mean. Hurry up, Sylvia, we've got to get to the churchyard!'

'That's where they're doing a séance!' Sylvia burst out.

Miss Marriott huffed. 'We already know that, dear, that's why everyone is rushing in that direction. Surely you realised that? Now do come along.'

'It's them beatniks, them seekers. They're doing it again!'

'We know that too, dear,' Miss Marriott told her again, sounding exasperated by this new person. Dee glanced at Sylvia, a young woman in her early twenties, dressed in a housecoat over slacks and a blouse. Her hair was scraped back severely in a ponytail that hung over her left shoulder.

As they went along, Sylvia continued excitedly, 'They're holding hands in a circle and calling on the spirits to speak to them. Oh it's so exciting!' She broke off to look at Dee. 'Sorry, but who are you?'

Dee introduced herself. 'I'm Dee Gascoigne. I'm

staying at Miss Marriott's for a few days. I'm here to find out more about what's going on in the village.'

'Police? Or a reporter?'

'Neither, actually. Miss Marriott's legal adviser sent me. Shall we...?' Dee pointed after Miss Marriott who was already some distance in front of them now.

Sylvia nodded. 'Ooh yes, let's!' as if it was a treat.

They hurried after the old woman who was moving faster than Dee had so far seen her move, albeit aided by her walking stick. The other people from the meeting were also headed that way, though many of them were already inside the walled expanse of the churchyard.

By the time they reached the area where the séance was supposedly happening, Dee had already seen two people stumble over half-hidden gravestones in the dark and sprain their ankles, and one person had fallen headlong and now had a suspected concussion. Little knots of people offered assistance to the injured parties, but in general, the mood amongst the villagers had turned from mere curiosity to that of an angry mob. Dee's heart pounded as she gave into the urge to hurry along. She had serious misgivings. When she saw the mass of people crowding into the area and heard a number of angry shouts a short way ahead, she halted, taking Miss Marriott's arm.

'I think we should just get you home,' she said.

Sylvia on the other hand, was still trying to urge them forward more quickly, impatient with them for holding her back when she clearly wanted to run.

'Oh what rot!' Miss Marriott snapped. She rummaged in her coat pocket and held out a key. 'Here, take this. You can go back, if you're such a ninny.'

With an inward groan, Dee gave in. Thirty or forty

yards ahead, she could see a bonfire burning in a brazier, whilst around it figures in silhouette were standing in a circle, chanting softly, their hands joined.

Even in the darkening twilight, Dee could see that their colourful robes were of a light floating fabric that reached to the ground. There were, she thought, perhaps eight or ten of them, men and women, all dressed alike in these robes, some in white ones, two men in purple, and nearer to where she was now, an older woman and two men in saffron-coloured robes, then there was one person, already crouching down on the ground who had on an emerald robe.

They wore flowers and strings of beads about their necks, and in their hair, and they sang a song without words, one that Dee instinctively felt she knew somehow. They touched no one, called out to no one, but were gathered by their brazier, arms raised to rattle tambourines or to beat a rhythm on a tabor or to chime cymbals together.

A saffron-clad man with hair reaching almost to his waist began to speak, and his cohorts stepped back and bent to sit on the ground, cross-legged and silent.

'Again the unclaimed one calls out to you, heart to heart, spirit to spirit, and begs to be brought home, to be mourned and released, no longer to be cast adrift between this world and the next. They cry out to you for your pity. Do not turn away from their plea. We who seek implore you...'

But he got no further.

A couple of men at the head of the rabble of villagers rushed forward to break through the circle of seated chanters, grabbing some of them by their arms or legs and dragging them away from the group.

Someone, a man, kicked the fire brazier over, and predictably instead of going out, the flames caught at the tall grasses and set them alight. People began to yell, the flames spread, someone threw a punch and within seconds there was a brawl. The flowing white robe of a young woman caught alight. Galvanised into action, Dee rushed forward to throw the girl onto the ground, tearing off her own jacket to quickly smother the flames. Mercifully, the girl was unharmed; Dee shuddered to think what might have happened had her jacket not been to hand.

'Are you all right?' she asked the girl, who appeared somewhat dazed. She nodded.

'I-I think so... Thank you...'

Dee helped her to her feet. Most of the robe had been burnt away, and Dee's jacket was not much more than a sooty rag on the ground. The young woman hurried away, no doubt to rejoin her friends. Dee looked about her for Miss Marriott, worried yet again that the old woman was too frail to be out amongst this chaos.

There was no sign of Miss Marriott and Dee began to panic. The shouting, the billowing flames, and the orange-black smoke already hanging all about her made it near impossible to see what was going on. She became aware that she was breathing shallowly due to the smoke, her eyes stinging, her hands shaking. She had to fight down a sense of panic and force herself to take her time to look about her properly. She stood for several minutes in the midst of all this noise, looking about her.

There, she thought, there she was. She made her way to Miss Marriott's side. The old woman clutched at Dee with relief. Her bony fingers pinched at Dee's arm, icy through the fabric of Dee's blouse.

'Oh my dear, I thought I'd lost you. I tripped, and

then somehow, I lost my bearings in all this smoke. And I can't find my walking stick.' She was looking all around her at the ground, hoping to spot it. But there wasn't a hope of finding it. They needed to leave.

Dee put an arm around the old woman and tried to guide her away. 'Don't worry about that now, you can lean on me.'

The bishop and the woman from the local history group were standing together by the arch of yew and watching the scene with horror. The bishop attempted to call for peace but he was shouted down. Dee once again tried to persuade Miss Marriott to return home. Sylvia was nowhere to be seen; it seemed likely that by this time she was much farther ahead.

A scream rang out—and finally people began to realise the scale of the problem, at last backing away to the safety of the lane. The fire had taken a firm hold and was snatching with greedy licks at the dry grasses, weeds and fallen branches. With lightning speed, it was conquering the churchyard.

Behind them, at the village entrance, police officers began to appear, running forward, waving truncheons haphazardly, and Dee grabbed Miss Marriott firmly by the arm.

'We're leaving now!'

This time Miss Marriott permitted herself to be led away. Walking slowly but steadily past two policemen, Dee said, 'Good evening, officers,' and kept going, worried the policemen might attempt to delay them.

They reached the house safely, but as they paused at the front door for Miss Marriott to fish out her door key, Dee glanced back to see the sky above the churchyard stained a raging red and orange. The fire was out of control.

Bells jangled as two fire engines raced by, slamming on brakes as the road became too narrow and congested to negotiate at speed.

An hour later, someone pounded at the front door with none of the conventional politeness.

Miss Marriott had already gone to bed. Dee had been sitting in the drawing-room, to all appearances as though she was reading the local newspaper she had found on a side table, but in fact, she was thinking over the events of the evening.

On hearing the pounding at the front door, she leapt up. She reached the hall, just in time to see Doris coming sedately towards the door in a calm, unhurried manner.

There was a brief discussion then Dee, back in her seat, heard the front door close. Doris tapped on the drawing-room door and half-opened it, poking her head around.

'Will you see Sergeant Wright from North Essex Police? I did tell him it was rather late, and you may not be available.'

But Dee, curious, immediately nodded and said, 'Oh yes, do please let him come in.'

Sergeant Wright was inclined to be officious and quickly irritated Dee with his manner.

Without waiting for an invitation, he made for the sofa and seated himself in the corner of it, notebook out on his knee. He said, 'Right then, miss, I want your name, then you can explain to me how you came to be in the churchyard this evening, and what you did while you were there.'

Dee stared at him.

He continued, 'And where is Miss Marriott? She will need to give an account of her movements too.

Have her sent for.'

Fixing him with the stern eye she had previously used as a teacher of teenaged girls, Dee said firmly, 'I cannot possibly ask Miss Marriott to come down and speak with you. She is elderly and infirm, and has been in bed for some time. You'll have to wait to speak with her tomorrow, though I doubt there's much she can tell you.'

'That will be for me to decide, thank you very much. Now, have her called.'

'No.' Dee folded her hands neatly in her lap. 'I shall endeavour to answer your questions. You will come back and speak with Miss Marriott at a more reasonable time of day. Now, what is it you wish to know?'

'I'm a police officer in the prosecution of my duty, and if I say that I want to speak to a suspect, then I will do so, and no chit of a girl will tell me otherwise.'

He was getting very red in the face and perspiring. He was easily several years younger than Dee herself. She was not about to let him bully her.

Calmly, she said, 'What exactly is Miss Marriott suspected of?'

'Rioting,' he said. 'And causing affray, causing actual bodily harm, and...'

'What?' Dee couldn't keep the scorn from her voice. 'Oh, that is ridiculous. We barely got into the churchyard when the scuffle broke out between some of the men. One of the villagers kicked over the brazier and caused the fire to spread. I think he probably...'

'I don't want to know what you thought, missy. Just tell me about the brazier being knocked over.'

'I've already told you. A man from the village...'

'Who? You're doing him no good by protecting his identity.'

'I don't know who. I'm new to the village, and...'

'Ah, now we're getting somewhere. When did you get here, and who sent for you?' He licked the tip of his pencil, ready to start making notes.

Dee frowned. She felt harried, as he'd no doubt intended her to feel. His constant interruptions were obviously designed to keep her on the back foot. 'Well, this afternoon, but...'

'Oh really? My, my, my, how convenient.'

Dee frowned. 'What do you mean, convenient? You make it sound...'

'So you've been paid to come down here and cause trouble, have you? Who put you up to this? Who's paying you?'

'This is ridiculous,' Dee said, but she knew she was blushing guiltily. After all, she *had* been sent for, she *was* being paid, she reasoned, though obviously not to deliberately cause trouble. Bill Hardy always said that trouble was just the normal result of her nosiness.

'Someone said they saw a woman throwing something at the man who was the leader of the group carrying out the séance.'

'That's ridiculous,' she repeated. 'That doesn't mean it was *me*. Because I didn't. And what do you mean, 'was' the leader?

He gave her a tight-lipped, humourless smile. 'Was. Because someone tried to kill him this evening. Hit him over the head with a heavy object and left him to die in that churchyard like a dog. Now he's fighting for his life in hospital and they don't give much for his chances. So I ask you again, what did you do on arriving at the churchyard?'

'Michael Wright, how dare you come into my home at this time of night and harangue my guest in this manner! Your mother—God bless her—would have had a few choice words to say about that!'

Miss Marriott entered the room, looking every inch the Edwardian lady, dressed in her night-gown, dressing-gown and bedroom slippers, her long hair neatly plaited and curled up under a hairnet. She presented a charming, old-fashioned image. But she looked furious, and Dee could almost feel sorry for the young sergeant, twice Miss Marriott's size, as he began to stammer an apology, quickly sliding his notebook and pencil into his pocket and jumping up guiltily, ready to leave. Miss Marriott remained by the door, barring his way, her arms folded across her bosom.

'Oh no, young man. You will take a seat, and you will take my statement, seeing that you've barged your way in here. The chief constable—dear young Anthony, I was at school with his mother—will hear of your conduct.'

Neither Sergeant Wright nor Dee dared to contradict her. Dee wondered if, once he had gone, she would be in trouble for allowing him into the house. But Miss Marriott came to sit beside her, patting her arm reassuringly.

'Now then, Michael...'

'It's Sergeant Wright nowadays, ma'am.'

She pinned him with her eye. 'Now then, Michael,' she repeated firmly. 'You may take this down:

'We attended the public meeting concerning the churchyard removal along with practically the whole village. It concluded rather prematurely when someone—can't remember who, but it was a man—burst in to announce that a séance was being conducted in the churchyard. Almost everyone rushed out and headed that way. We went outside with everyone else and slowly began to make our way towards the churchyard. Just then, that foolish young woman Sylvia Guthrie, with whom I believe you are walking out, told us it was those beatnik people who were conducting the séance, which we already knew, but she urged us to come and see. Miss Gascoigne and myself continued in that direction. Well, sadly things got out of hand very quickly indeed. Mr Philpott, the younger one of course, not his father, shouted something obscene and kicked over the brazier, and there ensued a scuffle. As the fire began to spread, Miss Gascoigne managed to save the life of one of the people conducting the séance when her robes caught alight. Then deciding that it seemed foolish to remain there, we left at that point and came directly home.'

'...directly ...home,' Wright muttered, his tongue poking out of the corner of his mouth as he concentrated on scribbling everything down. That done, he looked up. 'And that's everything, is it? You didn't happen to see anyone throw any punches, or anything else of note?'

'We weren't looking,' Miss Marriott said firmly. 'The ground was uneven, the place was crowded, and we were concerned only with leaving as quickly as we could without breaking an ankle.'

'So you can't tell me anything about the attack on Mr Tristan Summers or,' he glanced down at his notebook, 'Miss Serafina Rainbow?'

Miss Marriott and Dee exchanged puzzled looks. 'Miss—who?' Miss Marriott queried.

Dee was shaking her head. 'I'm sorry, Sergeant, I don't know either of those people...' She stopped, then then leaning forward, she asked, 'Sorry, but is it possible she's given you a false name? That doesn't sound like a real name. It sounds like she's trying to get away with something.'

He snapped his notebook closed and stuffed it into

his pocket. 'That's her name all right. And his. You didn't see anyone attack either of them? What about Jimmy Philpott? Could he...?'

'We have already told you, Michael. We left practically the moment we arrived. We saw nothing after the brazier went over and the fire caught. Who are these people with the bizarre, and I may say *highly unlikely*, names?'

'Mr Summers was the leader of the Seekers of Light. That is what they call themselves, these people. All into that ghost thing, and table-turning and whatnot. Communing with the other side. And the Rainbow woman is—was I should say—one of his group.'

"Was'?' Dee felt a sudden rush of anxiety.

'Yes. A knock on the head, we think, and left in the long grass just as the fire was spreading. The fire brigade found her later. Beyond help, of course. Poor woman.'

Dee, horrified, simply stared at him, her hand going to her mouth. Miss Marriott, sounding unperturbed and perfectly matter of fact, said,

'And what about this Summers fellow?'

'Him? Yes, as I've already told Miss Gascoigne, someone hit him over the head too. Luckily one of my men found him and got him to hospital. I'm told only time will show whether he will survive. But they don't seem too optimistic. At the moment, it's impossible to say either way.'

'But why would anyone...? I thought we were all just going there out of curiosity. But as soon as some of the people from the village began to head that way, it was clear that things would quickly turn violent. They were already angry from the meeting,' Dee said.

'All credit to you, my dear, for trying to persuade me to go straight home from the meeting. But,' Miss

Marriott defiantly told Wright, 'I was curious. I wanted to know what was going on, and who was involved. Oh, it's as if the devil himself has come to our dear village.'

The old woman lapsed into silence, looking down at her hands, her expression carefully controlled in the old-fashioned manner from when ladies were taught from a young age to never give way in public. Dee wondered what she was really thinking, or if she had known either of these two unfortunate people personally.

At last, Sergeant Wright took his leave.

Dee offered to make cocoa, supposing that Miss Marriott would be keen to return to her bed. It was half past ten by now, and of course country people tended to keep early hours, she remembered.

'Make it for yourself, if you wish,' Miss Marriott said with a curl of her lip. 'I should infinitely prefer a brandy.'

Having said that, she tottered across to the drinks cabinet and poured herself a triple, which she drank in two large gulps.

'Well, goodnight my dear. I hope you sleep well after all this excitement.' Miss Marriott called for Doris to come and help her to bed.

*

Chapter Five

Dee went up to her room. She'd decided to have a hot bath, and then, once she was in her nightclothes, she would come back downstairs for a cup of cocoa to relax before bed. It was well after eleven by the time she made her way to the kitchen, and although she was exhausted, her brain still felt wide awake.

To her surprise, Doris was still seated at the kitchen table, with a cup of cocoa and the newspaper.

'Oh miss!' She jumped to her feet, slopping some of her drink on the tabletop, narrowly missing the newspaper. She dabbed up the mess with the sleeve of her cardigan.

She turned to Dee. 'Is there anything I can get you, miss?'

'I just fancied a cup of cocoa,' Dee said. 'But I don't want to disturb you, I'm very happy to get it myself.'

'No, no, miss. I'll get it for you. Just you take a seat. Or I can bring it to you in your bedroom, or in the drawing-room. Wherever you prefer, miss, just say.' She bustled about, heating milk in a pan, and spooning cocoa powder into a cup. 'Sugar, miss? It's a bit bitter without.'

'Just one, please.' Dee pulled out a chair at the kitchen table and sat down. She looked around the room. Then at Doris's cup beside the newspaper.

Doris brought the drink over and set it before Dee. 'How about a little something with it? Cherry cake? Or some rich tea biscuits, or how about a couple of garibaldis?'

There was no need to even think about it. Dee beamed at her. 'I would love a small slice of cherry cake, if I may. A *small* slice,' she repeated.

Doris laughed and brought her a huge slab of cake.

'That's very naughty,' Dee told her. 'But thank you. I hope you don't mind me interrupting your peace and quiet?'

'Not at all, miss,' Doris said. She tapped the newspaper. 'Now then, miss, tell me. What do you think about this idea of digging up everyone's dead relatives and moving them somewhere else?'

Dee thought for a second. 'Well it's hard to know how a person might feel. I don't think I would mind too much, if on the one hand I could be sure the move would be done carefully and with proper respect for the deceased. And on the other hand, if the new churchyard was fairly close by. But I don't have anyone in the churchyard here, so I really don't know how I would feel. What about you, Doris? Have you any relatives interred here at the village church?'

'Yes, miss. I have. My grandparents. My baby brother. Several aunts, uncles, a couple of cousins. Quite a bunch of them, really.'

Dee nodded. 'It must be harder to face when it's a close relative such as grandparents or a brother.'

Doris nodded. 'I must admit, it's only Davey, my

brother, that I feel upset about. The rest of them... Well, it's unfortunate and all that, but...' She exhaled, sending her hair fluttering up in the air before it gently lay itself back upon her forehead. 'I'm not so bothered about the others, but Davey... I suppose I still feel like I need to look after my brother, as he was so little when he passed, even though it was fifteen years ago now, but I'm not so worried about the others.

'And there's no denying that we do need more houses. We've had a lot of people coming down from Colchester, or even Ipswich, or out all the way from Chelmsford and further still, from Cambridge and even London. They buy up houses for their weekend breaks or summer getaways, and that means there aren't so many houses for the locals. And it drives up the prices so that even to rent a house locally is really expensive. Then people complain that everyone's moving away from the village. But what choice do we have? Oh, I know houses—especially these tiny modern boxes they put up—are not pretty to look at. But... Well, we've all got to live somewhere.'

Dee nodded. 'That's a very good point. But I imagine most people aren't able to see it that way.'

Doris shook her head. 'Feelings are running very high. Everyone's that upset and angry.'

'We saw that earlier. The situation was completely out of hand.' Dee held her cup to her chest, glad of the warmth. She wished she'd brought a thicker dressing-gown with her, this one might be pretty but it wasn't really warm enough. 'Do you know the people who were doing the séances?'

Doris was shaking her head again. But in frustration, not because she didn't know anything. 'Oh miss, those crazy people! They arrived about six weeks ago, as soon as the announcement about the churchyard was in the news. There's about a dozen of them camping at one of the farms just on the edge of the village. Everard's. He has a field he lets campers use, for a small fee you understand.'

'Of course,' said Dee, who hated camping.

'They are sort of odd beatnik types. Lots of beads and long colourful gowns. And headbands. The men have all got long hair. And some of the women have their hair cut really short. Honestly, in their get-up, it's hard to tell who are the men and who are the women!' Doris laughed.

Dee smiled. 'I see them all the time like that in London. It's something of a trend.'

'I bet you do, miss.'

'So have they given any trouble at all, these odd people?'

'Not exactly trouble. I mean, the leader, that Summers bloke, he held a sort of protest last month in the church itself. It was unlocked to allow the cleaners in, and for the warden and verger to collect a few belongings. I was there with Miss Marriott, and a few other people. That was the last time the Reverend Riley was there.'

'The vicar?'

'That's right, miss. Oh, miss, he's gorgeous. I reckon most of the women only went to Sunday service so's they could get a look at him. The Reverend Kenneth Riley. Tall, dark and handsome. And single, which is even better. But yes, now the church is closed he's been moved to Greater Hartwell, five miles away.'

'And what happened with the protesters?'

'Well.' Doris leaned forward, her eyes shining. She was thoroughly enjoying herself, Dee could see. 'Seeing that the church was unlocked and the door standing open, they just came straight in, and right at the front by the altar, they sat down in a group and refused to move. Of course, this brought in quite a crowd, as you can imagine, once word got out.'

'Of course.' Dee nodded, engrossed.

'The top man, this Summers chappie, he went into a sort of trance. They were all chanting and such, and poor old Kenneth Riley was trying to persuade them to leave—he wanted to lock up—and he was trying to stop Philpott and some of the other men from forcing them out bodily. This Summers, he says in a kind of sing-song voice, 'The unclaimed one says, let me be brought back into the fold.' Spooky, don't you think?'

Dee sat back, trying to make sense of that. 'Definitely. 'The unclaimed one'? What does that mean, I wonder.'

'No one knows. They never said anything straight out, so's you could understand what they were getting at. Anyway, so then the vicar makes them leave. He grabs that woman by the arm and hauls her to her feet, and says, 'Look, Sara, you've got to leave, before there's any trouble. I don't want you to get hurt.'

'Sara?' Dee asked. 'She must have been the one...'

'She was, miss. Well, that was what I thought he said at the time, but now I think perhaps he said, Sera with an E. Because the woman that died this evening, her name was Seraphim or something, Miss Marriott was telling me just now. Like the angels, isn't it? Cherubim and Seraphim?'

'Very true.' Dee's mind was racing, trying to fit the pieces of information together.

Doris drained her cup then got up to carry it to the sink to rinse it, leaving it upside down on the draining board. 'Now, miss. Don't forget your drink, it will be getting cold. Will you be wanting anything else?'

Dee shook her head. 'No, thank you.'

'And about breakfast. Miss Marriott always has her breakfast on a tray in her room. You could do the same if you wish?'

'I prefer to come down for breakfast, thank you.'

'And will you be wanting a nice cooked breakfast, or...?'

'Oh, good grief, no, thank you. All I usually have is tea and toast.'

'Very good, miss. In that case, I'll say goodnight.'

'Goodnight.'

Dee sat there for another half an hour, puzzling things over. It certainly sounded as though the vicar knew the poor woman who had died, or at least he knew her name. And was Doris correct, that she was definitely the same woman who had died, the one the policeman had told them about? Or had that been someone else? Possibly there was a Serafina and a Sara. And more importantly, what lay behind the odd words the man named Summers had spoken? Had they been mere nonsense or some kind of veiled message or warning? If so, whom was he addressing this evening, and a month ago, that day in the church? Or was it all just set-dressing, merely put on to grab attention? After all, what else could it have been?

She sighed and got up. She pushed her chair back neatly into place, rinsed her cup - after tipping away her barely touched, now cold, drink. Yawning, she put out the kitchen light and went up to her room.

From her window she could see there were still lights down by the church. Clearly the police or the firemen were still busy in the churchyard.

*

Chapter Six

It felt like only minutes later that Doris pushed open the curtains and declared the day to be, 'Yet another lovely one. Your breakfast will be ready in twenty minutes.'

Feeling oddly disoriented, Dee sat up in bed and looked about her. Her travel alarm clock showed the time was eight forty, which made her smile. If she had stayed at Mrs Padham's splendid establishment along the lane, she would have already missed her breakfast. Here, she thought with a blissful stretch of her toes, she was at liberty to wander downstairs when she felt like it, and her breakfast would appear as if by magic in Miss Marriott's rather creepy dining-room.

As she washed and dressed, she thought about the evening before, the evening which had ended with one person dead and another fighting for his life. She wondered if there was more news about Tristan Summers, fervently hoping that if there was, it would be to say that he was already recovering well and had named his attacker.

Coming down the stairs into the hall, Dee saw that Miss Marriott was on the point of going out.

'Good morning. I hadn't expected to see you so early, Miss Marriott. I thought Doris said you enjoyed a leisurely start in the mornings.'

'Oh, my dear! I hope you slept well? I barely slept at all. But there was no point in simply lying there, so I thought I'd get up and go out early. The fresh air might do me some good. I have a few errands to attend to, then perhaps I'll feel able to have a nap later. I do hope you'll be happy to amuse yourself this morning? I shall be back well before lunch.'

Miss Marriott gave a firm pull on the short veil on the front of her aged hat, and the thin stuff came down almost to her chin. With a nod of satisfaction at this, she then allowed Doris, hovering in the doorway of the drawing-room, to help her on with her coat. Finally, collecting a new walking stick from the stand, Miss Marriott was off, slowly but with determination, a wave over her shoulder for both of them. Doris closed the front door behind her, then with a smile at Dee, headed back to the kitchen.

In the dining-room, a place had been laid for her and almost immediately Doris carried in a tray loaded with toast and a pot of tea.

'Now, Miss Dee, are you sure that's all you want? It won't take no time at all to rustle you up a nice bit of bacon and some eggs?'

'Oh no, thank you. I don't want to put on any weight!'

'You girls these days,' Doris said with a severe shake of her head. 'Always fussing over your figures and half of you is gone away to nothing as it is. A man wants something to hold onto, you know.'

Dee laughed at that, and having celebrated her thirty-first birthday just a couple of months earlier, reflected it was nice to still be included in 'you girls', even if she guessed she was about five years older than Doris herself. 'Well, if I meet one of these men who like their women 'with something to hold on to', I shall immediately come back for my bacon.'

'You do that, miss.'

'By the way, I'll probably go out in a bit.'

'Thank you for letting me know, Miss Dee. To be honest, I'm rather worried about Miss Marriott, she's not herself this morning. I got the news from the milkman. That chap, that Mr Summers we talked about last night? He died, in the night, you know. Poor fellow. He was a bit odd, but all the same... Miss Marriott was upset when she heard it. She shook her head and said, 'Two deaths, two deaths, Doris, it's terribly wicked.' If I'd realised how it would upset her, I'd have told her a bit more gently. As it was, I practically blurted it out like it was exciting news.'

'Oh dear,' Dee said. 'But you weren't to know.' She too shook her head. 'It is terrible, Miss Marriott's right about that.'

After she had finished her breakfast, she took her papers from Monty and went into the bright sunny morning-room, and sat there, thinking about things and planning her day.

Who should she speak to first?

Standing in the narrow lane, Dee looked to the left and right, and saw no one. Considering it was a Saturday morning, the place seemed deserted.

She opted to turn to the left, humming a tune as she went, and hoping that someone in the village shop might be able to tell her where Clive Barton lived.

The shop had a stand of newspapers hanging up right inside the door, making the place appear crowded and dark due to the way it jutted out, forcing her to squeeze by carefully to avoid knocking all the papers down. Apart from the newspapers, there was a vast array of cigarettes and alcohol on the shelves behind the tiny counter, and another small shelf arrangement in the corner held packets of tea, sugar, and a few loaves of bread. It wasn't, in Dee's opinion a proper general store such as she would usually expect to find in a village. She couldn't see a single wellington boot, candle, or coal shovel.

She felt obliged to make a purchase, it was too awkward to just stand there in the middle of the shop. A small woman in a flowered overall watched her from behind the counter, unsmiling and rather forbidding. Dee grabbed a newspaper from the rack and with a bright smile, headed over to pay for it.

'Good morning!' She put as much cheer into her voice as she could as she reached into her bag for her purse.

'Good morning, miss. And a very nice morning it is. Or would be if not for those fearful goings-on last night in the churchyard.'

It was the perfect opener. Now the woman appeared relaxed and friendly after all, now they had exchanged a greeting.

Dee responded with, 'My goodness, wasn't it awful? I was glad to get Miss Marriott away before the worst happened.'

'With Miss Marriott, were you?' The woman's eyes brightened with interest. The mention of her hostess's name gave Dee a certain air of legitimacy that she realised could be useful.

'Yes, I'm her guest for a few days. We went to the meeting last night, then someone burst in, announcing that a séance was being held in the churchyard, and that was that.'

'Terrible,' the woman commented with a shake of her head, though whether it was the meeting or the interruption, or the séance that she was referring to, Dee couldn't tell.

Dee simply nodded. 'Yes it was.'

'All kinds of unholy goings-on, like as not. Not just a séance. Conjuring up the dead, I heard, and making 'em speak curses on the living. It's a good thing someone done for that chap that leads them.'

'He died in hospital during the night, I understand,' Dee said, dropping her voice and leaning closer. She placed the money for the newspaper in the woman's hand. The woman didn't check it was correct but threw it directly into the drawer under the counter then slammed the drawer shut. Dee folded the newspaper and squashed it into her bag.

'No more'n he deserved,' said the woman with a sniff. Before Dee had a chance to say anything more, the bell jangled and in came Clive Barton.

'Ah, good morning, Miss Gascoigne. Have you heard the dreadful news? Pack of Benson and Hedges, please Lesley.'

The woman behind the counter turned to get his cigarette pack off the shelf behind her.

Dee said, 'Oh yes, I've heard. In fact a policeman came to Miss Marriott's house last night to talk to us about what happened.'

'Lord yes, someone came to me too. Asking damfool questions. And now they say Scotland Yard has been called in.'

'They're at the pub already,' Lesley said from behind her counter. She handed Mr Barton his cigarettes and he counted the money into her palm.

Again she threw it into the drawer as if it was of no account.

Dee felt at once elated yet a sense of doom. She wondered who the Yard had dispatched to clear up the village's two awful sudden deaths. If it was who she thought it was, that could be awkward, to say the least. She must have made some kind of sound as Clive Barton now glanced at her with some concern.

'Do forgive me, Miss Gascoigne, I appear to have pushed in front of you. Were you in the middle of making a purchase?'

Dee smiled. 'Oh no, not at all. I've already paid for my newspaper. I was about to leave.'

'Then perhaps you'll join me for a pre-lunch drink?'

Too surprised to think of an excuse, she said, 'Thank you, I'd like that.'

This, Dee thought, was exactly what she wanted: the opportunity to pick his brains.

They wished Lesley a good morning, and as they turned to leave, Dee could see the woman's eyes were practically on stalks. Dee sighed to herself. No doubt it would be all over the village by teatime that she was 'carrying on' with Clive Barton.

Outside the shop, Dee said, 'Actually, if you don't mind, I'd rather like to take a look at the churchyard before we go to the pub. Oh, I know it seems rather morbid,' she added hastily on seeing him hesitate. 'But after talking to Sergeant Wright last night, I'd rather like to fix the place more clearly in my mind. I didn't get a proper impression of the scale... Well, I have my reasons,' she ended up, hoping he wouldn't ask what they were. Though he already knew why she was in the village anyway.

'Do you mind if I take a pass on that? What say we meet in the pub in half an hour? Will that give you enough time?'

She beamed at him, then wished she hadn't. He flushed a gentle pink and beamed back. She tried to sound brisk and impersonal as she made a show of adjusting her bag on her shoulder, and said,

'That would be perfect. I'll see you in a short while, Mr Barton.'

'Clive, please.' He winked at her and walked away, turning back to smile and wave.

Oh dear, she thought. It was no part of her plan to ensnare the heart of a widowed gentleman in his, what... late forties? Early fifties? Fifteen or twenty years her senior, anyway.

She turned towards the churchyard, immediately putting him out of her thoughts, at least for the present.

It was a scene of utter devastation. At least half of the churchyard was reduced to ash. The flowers, the bees were gone, and the now-denuded gravestones, both upright and tumbled, were exposed to the light, their tributes still illegible, blackened with soot. Here and there a tiny whorl of smoke still spiralled up into the air. And there on its side, butting up against a gravestone, lay the brazier, burned black inside and out, and empty except for a small amount of wet, pungent ash.

The sight of it brought a flash of memory to the fore of Dee's brain: the man coming from behind her right shoulder and in one vicious sweep, kicking the brazier with all his might onto its side and starting the whole desperate sequence of events.

A fellow named Philpott, Dee recalled Miss Marriott had said. Not the father, according to Miss Marriott, so a younger man, presumably the son, and likely to be anywhere between twenty and fifty. Dee sighed and huffed to herself. If only she'd arrived in the village a few days earlier, then she would have had a better chance of getting to know the residents, their faces, their names, and it might be easier to figure all this out. As it was, all she had was the odd flash, the odd picture in her mind, and a sea of unknown faces in the darkness, indistinguishable purely because they were all the faces of strangers.

Looking at the dismal scene now, it seemed too fantastic to think that two people had actually died. Two lives. Two human beings. Just... gone.

Dee hoped that somewhere, even if not here at St John the Apostle, someone might say a prayer for those two souls. They may have died as a result of malice, or they may have died purely due to Mr Philpott's reckless behaviour and the impulse of the crowd of villagers. Whatever the cause, two people had lost their lives, and that was something that couldn't be changed.

Her mood sombre, she walked on to find the wall where she had sat the previous afternoon. If only one could go back in time, she thought.

Sitting there in a sunny spot, she looked away from the scene of the fire to notice with deep joy that the other side of the churchyard was still flourishing and as Eden-like as ever. Soon the ashes would become the nourishing bed for more meadow flowers and grasses, the bees would return, and...

Or would they? Memory stirred again and she remembered the whole reason for the meeting, and for the anger of the residents. Probably then, in a year or two, this whole place would be buried beneath so many tons of bricks and concrete as the houses were built, and along with those, the paths and lanes that would give access to the three hundred new front doors and the three hundred new refuse bins.

If she stayed here any longer, Dee thought, she'd be storming the council's offices herself. But, at the same time, Doris was right too, people needed homes. She got to her feet, dusted off the back of her dress and began to head back to the lane and her promised drink with Clive Barton.

And at that moment, half-expected, yet still catching her off-guard, she caught sight of a familiar male figure approaching, and her heart leapt. She came towards him through the section of mercifully preserved buttercups and tall swaying grasses.

'You look about five,' he grumbled.

She stood on tiptoe to kiss his rough cheek. 'Hello, Inspector Grumpy. Are you here about the murders?'

'Yes, arrived a couple of hours ago, we're staying at the pub.'

'The Met are quick off the mark, getting you both down here so soon after the events.'

'Requested by the local chaps. What are you doing here?'

'I'm working, believe it or not. Look, sorry but I'm supposed to be meeting someone. Can we talk later? I'm staying at Miss Marriott's.'

Hearing her own word 'murders' echo around her mind, Dee's sombre mood retuned. Two people dead, she remembered, and silently she made a promise to them to find out just what had happened here last night.

Another man came forward, a wide smile on his face.

'Hello Nat,' she said shyly. 'You're looking well.'

The detective sergeant resisted the urge to hug her hello as he was on duty, but he shook her hand for almost a minute, clasping it tightly between both of his, and saying in his strong Trinidadian accent,

'My dear Miss Dee. It's very good to see you here. A little unexpected, perhaps, but very good all the same.'

She was on the point of speaking, when Bill Hardy said,

'Look here, are you involved in all this somehow, or what? It seems odd that you should just 'happen' to turn up on the spot like this. What are you up to?'

She took a step back, all too aware of Clive Barton waiting for her in the pub. It would take more than a moment to tell Bill and Nat everything.

'As I said, I've got to go, I'm meeting someone. But I'm here on a job for Monty. Shall I come and see you later? Or perhaps you could come to Miss Marriott's.'

'I'm not sharing any police information with you, so don't bother asking.' Bill warned her.

She rolled her eyes. 'I know, I know! You're turning into a parrot. You don't need to tell me that every time we meet.'

She turned on her heel to walk away, waving once she reached the road. She glanced back to see him still staring after her.

He had noted that her light cotton dress fluttered about her in the breeze. Her hair, backcombed for fullness, was gathered into two short beribboned ponytails that rested on her shoulders. Her nose was littered with new freckles. Sun-kisses, they used to say when he was a child. He would have liked to kiss her, even though he was on duty. But she was gone now, quite out of sight. Bill shut his mouth, and ignoring the ache in his heart, he turned to Nat Porter.

'Right, well... er...'

'We've seen all there is to see here, I think, sir. The fire clearly spread very fast, then was brought under control and extinguished by the fire brigade. It's lucky this whole area wasn't burnt too. It's very pretty just here.'

Hardy gave a curt nod. 'Yes, it is. Now then, let's go and see about some lunch, then we can decide what we want to do next. Perhaps it would be best to go together to interview witnesses.' He caught Nat's disappointed look. 'I'd value your insights. Let's see what we make of these people.'

'Of course, sir.'

They turned to leave the churchyard, Hardy hoping he would catch a glimpse of Dee somewhere along the lane. But she wasn't there.

Nat was elated. Since he had been assigned to the inspector, his working life had improved dramatically. Hardy listened to his ideas, trusted him with important aspects of an investigation, and discussed cases with him. He didn't just bark orders at Nat like previous senior officers.

One of the most exciting changes this new partnership had brought about was that occasionally they were required to work away from home. Their first job together had been a case down on the coast. Nat had never been to the coast before, having lived in central London since he was nine. He had been incredibly excited to see the sea—though it had been far too cold to go in, as he had discovered upon throwing aside his shoes and socks then rolling up his trouser legs for a paddle that had lasted all of fifteen seconds. They had stayed in a pub, all expenses paid—the closest thing he'd ever had to a holiday—and had eaten good home-cooked food with an appropriate amount of alcohol—certainly nothing the top bosses could complain about. To top it all off, they'd solved the case. With a little—all right, he conceded to himself—a *lot* of help from a certain young lady who was now, it seemed, a real detective.

Then, Nat had met the love of his life. At forty-four years of age, he had thought he'd missed his chance for romance, but fate—and a murder investigation—had brought him into contact with a lady named Violet Davies, and when she had come to London to work for Miss Gascoigne, he had taken the opportunity to get to know her better. And now, he felt proud as he thought of it, now she was wearing the modest engagement ring he had given her, and they were planning their future together. They had even talked about having a family, they were both still just about young enough. He shook his head as he thought again how wonderfully, how dramatically his life had changed in just six months.

'Something wrong?' Hardy asked, seeing the head shake.

'Oh no, sir. Although, I do hope we're not too late for lunch.'

'So do I. I'm ravenous.'

*

Chapter Seven

Dee hurried into the pub and found Clive waiting there as arranged. She slipped into the seat opposite him. 'I'm sorry, Mr Barton. I didn't mean to be so long. I ran into the police from Scotland Yard at the churchyard, and that held me up a bit.'

He began to get to his feet politely to greet her, then as she was already seated, he sat back down. Was it her imagination or was he surprised—and not in a good way—to hear about the police? He had chosen to sit in the corner at a small round table, the top of which was deeply scored and pitted from decades of drinkers banging down bottles, tankards or glasses. There was an excellent view of the door from here—and of the street through a small window beside him.

Dee took out her purse then dropped her bag onto the floor by her feet.

'Can I get you another?' She nodded at his almost empty glass.

That surprised him too. Women rarely bought him a drink, it seemed.

'Do call me Clive. And yes, thank you, that would be very nice.' He smiled. 'Just a half of Best this time, please.'

She grinned back and went to the bar, returning within a minute or two with his half-pint of bitter and her own glass of Babycham. She made a mental note to drink it slowly. It would never do to get tipsy when it was barely lunchtime. She resumed her seat, took a sip, then said,

'There was still a bit of smoke rising up here and there in the churchyard, I noticed. You don't think it will catch fire again, do you? Should I tell someone?'

He shook his head as he fastened wet lips to the edge of his glass in a way that made her feel uncomfortable. Not that she'd been romantically interested in him anyway, but after that, she was definitely not. She hated wet slippery lips. A shiver went down her spine. He set his glass down, already half empty.

'I shouldn't think so. I'm sure a fire brigade official will come by every so often to check all is well.'

'Oh, of course,' Dee said, feeling silly.

'What made you want to take a look? Something to do with your job?'

She'd forgotten she'd already told him she was here on behalf of a law firm. No point in fobbing him off with some made-up tale. He might even be able to help. She said,

'As I told you, I wanted to go there in the hopes that it would help me to remember last night more clearly, so I could tell the police. The local chap, Sergeant Wright, came to see us last night, and he rather pressed Miss Marriott and I for any details of what we may have witnessed. But it was all such a blur. I wasn't much help, I can't remember a thing, it all happened so quickly.'

'It certainly did.' His expression was grave. He drank a little more of his beer. Then, 'It's shocking when you see how rapidly a fire can take hold and spread. Really, it was lucky more people weren't hurt.'

'I'd already tried to persuade Miss Marriott to go home, but she was adamant she wanted to see what was going on. In the end, of course, she realised just how dangerous it was and came away.'

'Yes indeed. And I for one am grateful you managed to get the old battle-axe out of there. She is rather inclined to stick to her guns no matter what.'

'She certainly is.' Dee smiled at him. His eyes met hers and he smiled back at her very warmly. A bit too warmly, she thought, and again she feared he would feel she was encouraging him in a romantic way. To distance herself, she leaned back in her seat and fidgeted with her glass.

'Now the Scotland Yard men have arrived to take over the investigation, so they will probably want to talk to me again,' she commented.

'I suppose they are always called in for an unexplained death, let alone two. But you're a stranger in the village, so you can't possibly help them. I wouldn't worry about it.'

'Actually, I may be a stranger to Hartwell Priory, but I'm a cousin—more or less—to the police inspector, so he will definitely talk to me in one capacity or another.'

Clive said nothing to that, other than to raise his eyebrows in surprise and watch her closely over the rim of his glass as he took another drink. There was a new wariness in his eyes.

Dee thought she might as well begin her

investigation right where she was, with one of the only people she knew in the village. 'Do you know this bunch who did the séance in the churchyard? It's not their first, I understand?'

'No. Well, slightly, I suppose, just by sight. I've seen them about the village a couple of times. They've been here a few weeks, I think. I've never spoken to any of them, though.'

'I was wondering whether they genuinely believed in this 'beyond-the-grave' mumbo-jumbo, or if they were trying to find some way of making it pay.'

He leaned away, fiddling with something, perhaps a lighter, in his jacket pocket. A faint click came to her ears and she hoped he wasn't about to accidentally set himself on fire. When he withdrew his hand, he was holding a ballpoint pen. Dee almost giggled at her own foolishness. She forced herself to pay attention.

Without looking at her, he said, 'Oh the latter, I should think. Those sorts of people, they're always out for what they can get, aren't they?'

'I suppose so,' she agreed.

He looked at her now and she was right, his expression was definitely wary. But why?

'Well, what else could it be?' There was an underlying impatience in his tone. 'After all, there isn't anything in it, it's all just hokum, so what else could it be but an attempt to try to make some quick cash?'

'True.' She was thinking of something else to ask, when he gulped down the rest of his drink then leapt to his feet, holding out his hand to shake hers and saying,

'Well, this was delightful, Miss Gascoigne. But I'm afraid I must be off now. I'm expecting a visitor and don't want to keep them waiting. I hope you enjoy your stay in the village. Good afternoon.'

And he was gone before she could even reply. She sat staring after him. As he ducked his head to go out of the side door, she saw him glance back, a worried expression on his face, the earlier warmth completely gone. He didn't smile or wave but simply left.

Odd, she thought. Very odd indeed.

She still had half her drink and was in no hurry to leave—through the window she could see rain was beating down heavily on the lane. That was good, she thought. The rain would definitely put paid to any lingering sparks in the churchyard. The pub was now filling up with the lunchtime regulars, and a few people who were there to get something to eat.

She pulled out her notebook and pen and began to make a list of names of the people she thought perhaps she should speak to, the few people she had already come across or heard mentioned.

She put Clive Barton's name down first. She had spoken to him more than any other person in the village apart from Miss Marriott yet still knew almost nothing about him. It was unfortunate that his initial interest in her had now cooled since she had begun to ask her questions—and told him she was related to Scotland Yard. But why should either of those things set him on his guard? Yet on his guard he now most definitely was. If only she'd asked her questions sooner. She wondered if he would seek to avoid her from now on. She would try to catch him again, though, and put him at ease. He would be able to tell her the history of the village, and how the local history society were viewing this issue of the new housing development.

This thought led her to write down the name of his historical society colleague, Angela Baker next. She hadn't got very far into her speech at the meeting the previous evening before everyone had rushed outside and the meeting was effectively abandoned. What had she been planning to say? It was possible she might have more information than Clive, though about what, Dee didn't really have any firm idea.

She began to ask herself what she was in Hartwell Priory to achieve. Her main, original task had been to find out on Miss Marriott's behalf who Tristan, the leader of the beatnik group had referred to in the séance when he had talked about 'the unclaimed one'.

Dee closed her notebook and put it away. Perhaps, after all, the first people she should speak with were the remaining members of the Seekers of Light, as they called themselves. She wondered if they might be at their campsite in the field of the local farmer Miss Marriott and Doris had mentioned, a Mr Everard. But where was that, exactly? Leaving her drink behind, she went over to the bar.

'Yes, miss?' the barman enquired, wiping his hands on a towel. A row of glasses were drying upside down on the counter behind him.

They made it in plenty of time, gave their order at the bar and went to find a table far enough away from other patrons that they could discuss what they already knew about the case.

As they waited for their food, Hardy looked around. Across the room, on his left, he could see the back of a familiar-looking woman. It was Dee, of course. There was a man with her, plying her with alcohol, and leaning towards her, his eyes fixed on her, his hand resting on the table mere inches away from hers. Hardy was aware of a stab of acute jealousy. Who was the man, and just how well did Dee know him after only twenty-four hours in the village.

'Two shepherds pies with greens, and apple crumble with custard for afters. Thanks, gents.'

The food looked good and smelled even better. They began to tuck in. Hardy glanced up a moment later to see Dee was now sitting alone at her table, one elbow propping her chin, as she stared down at a notebook. She took a sip at something that looked like her usual tipple of Babycham. He wondered if the man with her had gone to the men's room. But he didn't reappear, and a few minutes later, Dee herself got up and left. Lost in thought, she didn't even notice Hardy and Porter were sitting a mere twenty feet away.

'Eat up, sir, or your pudding will be cold.'

'Hmm.' Hardy tried to pull his thoughts away from his cousin. This wouldn't do, he had to keep his mind on his work.

'I wonder exactly what it is she's doing here, Sir. Miss Gascoigne, I mean.'

Hardy suspected Porter of reading his mind. Had he seen her leave? Or was he referring to the unexpected meeting in the churchyard?

'Hopefully we'll find out later. Now then, I think next, we'll go to the local police station. We can talk to whoever came out to last night's incident and get their impressions. Then we'll get their official reports and go through those.'

'And we will know who to speak to,' Porter added. He pushed aside his empty plate and reached eagerly for his dessert bowl.

'Exactly.'

Dee was striding along the lane under the protection of an umbrella borrowed from the pub's lost property box.

At the end of the lane, the road divided into two. Part of it sloped up to the right to join the main road that led to the coast. The other part, barely more than a dirt track, led a short way downhill to a field.

Dee enjoyed the walk. The rain pattered like fingertips on the umbrella. Waving grasses, vibrant in the rain, lined the track on the higher ground that lined each side, and here she was sheltered from the breeze. There was a slight tang of soot on the air, but she ignored that, knowing the rain would wash away the smell in a day or two. She hummed a pop song to herself as she went along.

As she rounded the bend at the bottom of the hill she had to wait for a rather smart car—a jaguar, she thought—to go by before she continued. The field was on her left. Over the hedge she could make out the tops of various tents and a caravan or two further away.

The gate to the field was standing open and was blocked by a small battered-looking van, stationary but with the engine running. The doors at the back were wide open, and a couple of long-haired young men and a woman with extremely short hair were loading haversacks and rolled up sleeping bags inside.

Dee felt sure that these three were from the beatnik group who'd held the séances. And a sudden realisation of what was happening caused her to rush forward, calling out.

'Excuse me, excuse me please. Are you from the Seekers of Light?'

'Not anymore, love. We're leaving,' one of the men informed her. He didn't sound too friendly. Clearly the group wasn't into universal peace or love along with their meditating. Or had it all just been a scheme, after all?

Before she had time to ask anything further, he got into the driver's seat, the other man and woman jumped out of the back of the van, slammed the rear doors then ran to get into the front on the passenger's side beside another woman already sitting there, hiding her face with both hands as if Dee was about to whip out a camera and take photographs. With a grinding of gears, the van lurched forward and sped off along the track. Dee saw it turn to the left and onto the main road. Then they were gone.

She dithered for a moment. It seemed as though she'd missed her chance, and she was about to berate herself for being too slow, not up to the job, when the sound of voices caught her attention. She glanced across the narrow strip of grass to where two women were consoling each other with hugs, and a man, standing near them, had his hands on the hips of a long loose white garment that was being spattered by the rain

Dee hurried over. 'Excuse me,' she began again. 'Are you part of the Seekers of Light?'

They eyed her warily but nodded. A woman was wiping her eyes and blowing her nose. The other one, an arm across the first one's shoulders, said,

'Who are you? Press?'

Dee thought the woman sounded too tired and discouraged to be hostile. Dee quickly said, 'Oh no, nothing like that. But I did just wonder if I might have a quick word with you. Though I expect you're sick of questions.'

'We are a bit,' the woman agreed.

The weeping woman looked hard at Dee. Then she said, 'Hold on, aren't you the woman who helped me last night? You put the flames out with your jacket. I thought I'd had it, but then you... Thank you so much. It was terrifying. And if you hadn't come along just then...'

'I'm so glad I did,' Dee said. 'Are you all right? You didn't have to go to hospital, or—or anything? It was absolutely horrible. I was in a panic to do something useful.'

'I'm very grateful you did. Thanks to you, I'm completely unharmed. Thank you for all your help.'

'We might as well go and sit down out of this weather,' the man said with a glare up at the sky. He held out a hand to Dee. 'Bartholomew Lovecraft.'

Dee shook his hand, made no comment about what she assumed was a false name, but simply said, 'Dee Gascoigne.'

'Shall we?' He indicated the tent behind them. They all squeezed inside, crouching to get through the gap, and gathering up the hems of their robes to avoid tripping over them. There was nowhere to go other than to sit on some cushions on the groundsheet floor. With four adults in there, it was rather snug. Dee glanced around, not wanting to be too obviously nosy, in spite of her keenness to get a good look.

There were two pillows on top of two folded sleeping bags. There was a small kerosene lantern, not lit at the moment, and a couple of haversacks. Other than that and the cushions on which they were sitting, there was nothing else in there.

They looked at her in the odd twilight of the tent, the rain drumming on the canvas in a soothing manner. The two women introduced themselves.

'I'm Adelle, this is Janna. I'm Bartholomew's—um—girlfriend, and Janna is his sister.'

Clearly she was more than just his girlfriend, Dee thought, but probably she hadn't quite wanted to say 'mistress'. She thought they were living as man and wife even though they were unlikely to be actually married. One heard of such things, especially amongst more 'artistic' people. Her mother still called it 'living in sin', whilst many younger people just called it 'common law marriage' and didn't see there was a problem with that. Whatever they called it, Adelle and Bartholomew, surely only in their late teens or early twenties, were living as if they were a married couple.

'I thought I'd come and see how things were,' Dee said, and felt idiotic for putting it like that. It wasn't really any of her business, after all. 'Sorry, I meant... well... After what's happened, it must be just terrible. Are you all right? Or do you, you know, do you need anything, any help?'

That seemed to surprise them. She was surprised herself. She hadn't really known what she was going to say, but they seemed rather down on their luck. And at close quarters, she could see just how very young they were, and so thin and pale. It seemed only the two who had died had been older, but as for the rest of them, she doubted any of them was over twenty years of age.

It was Bartholomew who said, rather sarcastically, 'Well, we've got no money and no food. So there's that. I don't suppose that was what you meant, though, was it? You meant, do we want to tell you our story, so you can make a big splash with it in the newspapers.'

Dee shook her head. 'No not at all. I'm not from a newspaper. Nor am I a freelancer.'

'What are you then?' Adelle asked, trying to sound tough, aggressive, but instead she just sounded very young and frightened.

'I'm a private investigator. I've been sent down here to find out about the churchyard being moved, amongst other things. I got here yesterday afternoon. I was at the village meeting when someone came in shouting about a séance and then everyone rushed outside. I saw someone kick over the brazier—you know what happened after that.'

They certainly did. Adelle's eyes filled with tears. She rummaged in her sleeve for a handkerchief. 'I've never been so scared,' she said. 'One minute it was so peaceful and beautiful. I had my eyes closed and I was just lost in the 'seeking'. It's such a freeing experience, to just give yourself to the harmony, the prayer-song, to reach out with your spirit into the between-world. And then, the next minute, it was chaos, terrifying. People were shouting abuse, they were so angry, then the brazier went over and everyone was screaming, and Bartholomew was pulling me back from the fire, and it was spreading across the grass like—I don't know—it was like watching the tide coming in at the beach, waves of fire just eating up the grass so fast. And then on the other side of the flames I could see Janna was caught up in it, she had flames all up one side of her robe, and I couldn't get to her, and I thought... I thought...'

She burst into tears, sobbing on Bartholomew's shoulder. His arm came around her and he patted her shoulder, gently kissing her cheek and shushing her. A glance at Janna showed her sitting with her head bowed. A tear, like a tiny shining crystal, fell onto her knee.

Adelle tried to continue, her voice shaking. 'The smoke. The screaming. If Bartholomew hadn't pulled me back, if he hadn't...' She couldn't say anything more.

Janna said, in practically a whisper, 'After you'd saved me, I managed to skirt around the outside wall of the churchyard to make my way back to them. A couple of villagers came after me, throwing stones at me and yelling at me, saying I deserved to be burnt at the stake like the filthy witch I was. I had to run. It was... I felt as though I was trapped in a nightmare. I'm ashamed to say that at one point I even cried for my mother, and she died when I was ten.'

Bartholomew took her hand and held it fast, glancing at her and biting his lip, fighting to keep his own composure.

But after a moment, Janna was able to continue. 'Then I found Janna, but we couldn't find Barry or Tristan or Serafina, and Jake and Jon were already running away.'

'I was looking for you,' Bartholomew said. 'The smoke, I got completely lost at one point, and I kept tripping over. Then I saw Philpott again and had to make a run for it.'

'Jake and Jon?' Dee asked Janna.

'You saw them just now, getting into the van along with Brigitte, Jon's wife, and Joy her sister was with them too.'

'Ah yes.' Dee nodded. 'Are they coming back, do you know?'

'I shouldn't think so,' Adelle snuffled. 'It was only Tristan that kept us all together. That builder chap was just here, telling us to clear out if we know what's good for us, saying he had a few pals who would be happy to pay us a visit. Now Tristan's gone, there's nothing left., so we'll be leaving anyway, there's no reason to stay.'

'I'm so sorry,' Dee said. 'It's been a dreadful experience for you all. Are you all related to Tristan or...?'

'Oh no. He is—was, I mean—my tutor. We're all at university in Cambridge. Tristan taught a course on Belief Systems and Organised Religion which I was doing, as part of my overall bachelor's degree course in Philosophy. But Barry—er—Bartholomew is studying engineering, and Jake was doing applied mathematics. I don't know about Jon and Brigitte, but Brigitte's sister Joy was taking a course in medieval literature. At the end of the semester, Tristan told us about this cool idea he'd had—and we all wanted to be part of it. We just took off for the summer and ended up here. He had read about what was happening in the newspaper, and well, we knew the area quite well, so...' She shrugged her shoulders.

Bartholomew added, 'The cracks were already beginning to show though, before yesterday's séance. If this—this thing—hadn't happened, I think we'd have all been going our separate ways pretty soon anyhow.'

The other two nodded their agreement, but no one seemed to want to elaborate.

Janna said, 'Anyway... In a couple more weeks we'll be back at our desks like a bunch of little goody-two-shoes as if nothing had happened. Because no matter how much you want to change the world, you've still got to eat, right?'

Dee nodded sadly. 'Yes, I know what you mean.'

She thanked them for their time and said goodbye, leaving them a pound from her expenses to buy themselves something to eat.

It was only as she was standing at the front door to Miss Marriott's house, waiting for Doris to let her in, that she realised she'd forgotten to ask them if they'd seen who hit Tristan Summers or Serafina Rainbow, and she'd even forgotten to ask about the 'prophecy' Tristan had spoken at either of the séances.

She sighed. 'I'm no good at this, after all.'

*

Chapter Eight

'Miss Marriott's in the morning-room. Excuse me rushing away, miss, I've got something on the stove to see to.'

Doris left the door wide open and hurried off down the hall. Dee came in, closing the front door behind her and putting her 'lost' umbrella in the stand next to several umbrellas and walking sticks.

Miss Marriott was indeed in the morning-room, with a newspaper on her lap. She glanced up to smile at Dee. 'My dear! What did you do with yourself today?'

But before Dee could reply, she continued, 'Lunch will be ready in twenty minutes or so. I usually have a light meal at this time of day, and a proper full dinner later. I hope that suits you? I believe we are having soup and cheese.'

'Oh yes, thank you very much.' Dee hovered just inside the door of the morning-room, not quite sure what to do or say. Did Miss Marriott expect her to wait in her room, or what?

Miss Marriott was sitting in an upright chair by the window, the newspaper spread out, her lorgnette in her hand as she perused one of the middle pages. Almost absent-mindedly she remarked, 'Really, the drivel they print these days. 'My Typical Day', it says here, and it purports to be an excruciatingly detailed trip through the everyday life of some fellow called Sonny-Ray Smith. Though I must say he seems awfully dull yet at the same time full of self-importance. And apparently he's some sort of heartthrob. What do you say? Is he the stuff girlish dreams are made of these days?' She turned the page right round so that Dee could see a grainy picture of Sonny-Ray's face with his smarmy grin.

'My goodness,' Dee said, coming over to get a closer look at the picture. 'I met him not very long ago—and I agree with you, I definitely can't see his appeal.'

And she told Miss Marriott about Sonny-Ray and the bingo evening, which had ended with her being attacked in the cottage where she had been staying.

Miss Marriott attended very closely, asking for more details. In the end, it was just easier to go back to the beginning and tell the whole story of the events in Porthlea that Spring.

At the end of it, Miss Marriott nodded slowly. With a smile, she said, 'You really are good at this job, aren't you?'

Since her arrival in Hartwell Priory, Dee had begun to feel just the opposite, that she completely lacked the skills and instinct necessary, so Miss Marriott's praise, coupled with her attentive expression, provided a much-needed reassurance.

On the point of asking a question about Miss Marriott's own situation, Dee was forced to wait. At that moment, Doris poked her head around the door to tell them that lunch was ready if they were.

Dee excused herself to quickly wash her hands and tidy her hair. She switched her sturdy outdoor shoes for some slippers and was downstairs again in less than five minutes.

Miss Marriott was taking her seat in the dining-room which was distressingly decorated with deep red painted walls, heavy oak beams on the ceiling and a large quantity of the heads of dead animals on the walls. Their glassy eyes seemed to stare down reproachfully at the two women, doing nothing to enhance Dee's appetite.

They sat adjacent to one another at the nearest end of an unnecessarily long dining-table clearly from an era of large families and even larger numbers of guests.

'A relic of days gone by,' Miss Marriott said. 'When I was a child, we always had a houseful of guests, and a houseful of servants to run around after them. My parents loved to entertain. Mainly, I think, because they dreaded being alone with one another—they never got on. These days, one would simply demand a divorce, but it rarely happened years ago. In those days, if you got married, you tended to be stuck with one another unless you could afford an act of parliament.'

Doris came into the room to see if they had all they needed. Miss Marriott sent her away with a good-natured, 'Oh go and get your own lunch, Doris, dear. We are perfectly fine.'

They had asparagus soup, with a choice of cheese and crackers or tinned fruit and tinned cream and a pot of coffee to follow.

'What did you do with yourself this morning?' Miss Marriott asked.

Dee told her about going to see the remnants of the Seekers of Light people.

'I meant to ask them about their séances,' she added ruefully. 'But it completely slipped my mind. I'm afraid I'm just an amateur, after all.'

'Nonsense, dear. You're still getting your bearings. You've only been in the village for twenty-four hours. There must be so many questions buzzing around in your head, and so many people you need to speak to. I'm terribly grateful to you—and to dear Monty for sending you.'

'Were you there when they held the séance in the church?'

Miss Marriott nodded. She quickly finished the last of her tinned fruit, which was of course the cherry that everyone saved for last, eating it without any of the tinned cream that tasted mostly of the tin.

Tinned cream had been a favourite treat of the headmistress at the school where Dee had worked before the school board had got wind of the fact that Dee had left her husband and planned to divorce him when the three years was up. Miss Evans had attempted to champion Dee, but the board would have none of it, and she had been forced to leave her job. Dear Miss Evans, Dee thought with a sudden pang.

'Yes, dear. I was there with several others, we had to go in a few times to see to the removal of the hangings—you know, tapestries and pictures, the crucifix and some statuettes too. All the decorations of the church, in fact. The pews and the altar were about to be removed. A lot of the other things had already gone. My goodness, but it looked so bare and it was dreadfully echoey, if you know what I mean. Most of the items stored in the vestry had also been taken out. Though the vicar, dear Kenneth Riley, was still packing vestments, and candles and so forth, to take to his new parish a few miles away in Greater Hartwell. One would have thought a big place like that would have its own candles, but there we are.' This last comment was caustic. Clearly Miss Marriott was very bitter about the loss of the village church and its equipment and staff.

Dee said nothing, just nodded with understanding, and Miss Marriott continued:

'And then suddenly, there they all were, eight or ten of them. Or perhaps there was a full dozen of them, I can't quite...'

'Don't worry about it. I can find out,' Dee said, seeing that Miss Marriott was in danger of going into a kind of panicked spiral in her thoughts. 'So they just came in and started?'

'Yes. We heard them chanting and banging on the tambourines. They were all wearing those long flowing gowns, robes I suppose you'd call them. Very colourful. Even the men! And of course, like most young men these days, the fellows all had long hair, and they wore headbands and beads down to their waists and goodness knows what else. I thought they looked rather like fairies or angels, or something. You know, like in the children's story books. Oh, and one of the girls had some of the tiniest cymbals you've ever seen, just on the tips of her fingers, clinking and clanging. They were already singing before they entered the church, then they came up the aisle and as far as the altar, and all the followers sat down on the floor, and the leader fellow, Tristan, was it? He stood there to make his proclamation or whatever you call it.

'He stepped forward and said some things, that the spirits of the departed were in turmoil, that they felt abandoned and betrayed. The vicar came forward at this point and told them they had to leave, but one of the girls said that he no longer had any authority, that the spirits had turned away from him.

'In a way, it was quite exciting, rather like a theatrical production. The most exciting thing to happen in our village since Philpott senior let off an air-rifle in the saloon bar of the Bird in Hand. Sergeant Wright—who was just a constable back then—had to take him in. Of course he wasn't right in the head. Mr Philpott, I mean. I remember it was Henry Padham and Clive Barton who got the rifle away from him.'

Distracted by this fascinating aside, Dee couldn't help herself. 'Why did Mr Philpott fire an air-rifle in the pub?'

'Oh my dear, he'd just found out that Henry Padham was sleeping with his wife. With Mr Philpott senior's wife, I mean, the mother of our resident hothead, Young Jimmy. Mrs Philpott was quite a bit younger than Mr Philpott. She was seventeen when she married him, and he was about forty, which is an awfully big age gap. I don't know what her parents were thinking. Although of course, she *had* to get married, so I don't suppose they felt there was any choice in the matter. A single mother wouldn't be countenanced in the village in those days. But she and Philpott were never happy. The—whatever it was—attraction, I suppose—had already run its course by the time they got married.'

'Is she still in the village?' Dee asked.

'Oh no, dear. She went off just after this incident, years ago now. And hasn't been back. She must have been about thirty-eight or so then, so still a young woman.'

'Did she go off with Mr Padham?'

Miss Marriott stared at Dee, momentarily at a loss.

'D'you know, I'm not sure. I can't remember if... No, I don't think they left at the same time.' She shook her head. 'I'm sorry, dear, I can't be sure.'

Dee nodded. 'Of course. Never mind. So, coming back to the séance at the church...'

'Oh yes. It was quite good fun. Not that anyone else thought that, I'm sure. I'm afraid tempers rather flared as usual. Mr Philpott—the younger one, the son—he grabbed poor Tristan and hauled him bodily out of the church, and a couple of the other men pulled some of the girls out too. One of the beatnik fellows got very angry about the village men pulling the girls about so roughly, and tried to push the man—I can't remember who it was—and of course a scuffle ensued. Men get so hot under the collar, don't they? But in the church doorway, Tristan looked back and in a loud voice he shouted, 'But the unclaimed one must not be left behind. They demand to be acknowledged and released. Justice is mine saith the Lord. I shall repay.' Which of course infuriated the vicar even more.'

'Vengeance,' Dee said automatically, thinking over what Miss Marriott had said. 'It should be, vengeance is mine, I shall repay.'

Miss Marriott gave her a pleased look. 'Exactly, Dee dear! I'm so glad you've picked up on that.'

'Odd, isn't it? Them being so different in their approach and behaviour, yet quoting—or rather, misquoting—the Bible as part of their message?'

'Isn't it?' Miss Marriott pushed her chair back and rose carefully from her seat, reaching for her walking stick. 'Now then, dear, if you've finished?'

'Yes, I have, thank you.' Dee got up too and pushed her seat neatly back into place.

'I usually go up to my room for a—well, a nap really. I pretend I'm going to read or do some embroidery in my sitting-room, but really I'm just having a nap. Now I don't know what your plans are for this afternoon. If you're not otherwise engaged, I've invited a few people to afternoon tea. Does that suit you, dear? I thought you might be able to get something out of them.'

'That will be wonderful,' Dee said with a broad grin.

'Until four o'clock, then.' Miss Marriott slowly creaked her way to the door, then called, 'Doris, I'm ready to go up now.'

Doris ran from the kitchen to assist the old lady to slowly and carefully climb the stairs.

'Oh,' Dee said. 'I'm sorry. I didn't realise. I should have helped.' Once again she felt she had failed to repay Miss Marriott's kindness.

'Nonsense,' said the old woman over her shoulder. 'Doris is always my right-hand man, don't worry yourself about it. Toodle-oo.'

Smiling and shaking her head over this, Dee went back to the morning-room with its big French doors that gave a wonderful view of the garden, and she made herself comfortable in a well-placed armchair, mulling over what she had so far discovered and planning her next move.

On seeing her there a few minutes later, Doris suggested Dee might like to sit in the garden, now that the rain had cleared up and the sun was shining.

The large space was mainly lawn, with shrubs and trees in the borders on three sides, and a narrow strip of patio right outside the house. Some chairs and a table had been placed here, no doubt so that Miss Marriott and her friends could enjoy the sunshine and pleasant view of the garden.

'If you like, Miss Dee, we could take a couple of

these wicker chairs across to that bit of lawn under the birch trees. They don't give a lot of shade but it's a pleasant spot.'

If Dee was surprised at Doris's use of the word 'we', she said nothing, but readily agreed. She was delighted when, the chairs in situ, Doris said,

'Oh, I am so sorry, miss. I should have asked first. Is it all right if I join you? If you'd rather be alone, just say, it's quite all right. I always forget my place, but Miss Marriott never seems to mind too much what I do, so when we've got visitors...'

'I'd be glad of your company,' Dee grinned at her.

Doris said, with a cheeky grin back in reply, 'I expect you'll want to ask me questions about all the people in the village. Miss Marriott said you might.'

'In that case, I'm really going to make the most of this and pick your brains,' Dee told her, and kicking off her shoes, she stretched out in the wicker chair, leaning back with her eyes closed, and just soaking up the early autumn sunshine.

'We might not get too many more days like this. It'll soon be frosts and damp air.'

'Ooh, don't say that, miss. I hate the winters. Usually, Miss Marriott spends the winter in the Canary Islands, or she might go to the Caribbean or Spain or just anywhere. Anything, she says, to get away from a British winter.'

'Usually?'

'Between you and me, Miss Dee, I'm not sure she'll manage it this winter. She's been so much frailer than usual of late, and she's got so slow in her movements. I'd worry about her going off on her own, you know, in case she had a fall.'

'She goes alone? I'd have thought she'd have a companion, or that you might go with her.' Dee didn't like the sound of a woman of Miss Marriott's age and frailty going all that way unaccompanied.

'Sometimes she stays with some people she knows. They meet her at the other end, but she does all the travelling on her own. But she's got a weak heart, and then after the nasty fall she had at Easter... It shook her up. She's not really over it yet. The doctor told her she must be careful, and that she must be sure to use her stick for support. And not to try to do so much. But she gets that bored and fretful.'

'I can imagine she does,' Dee said. 'I think I'd be the same. Oh dear. Poor Miss Marriott. Well, I hope she'll find someone to go with her—then she can have her cake and eat it.'

'Speaking of cake, I must just go and check the oven.' Doris leapt up and hurried inside. In less than two minutes she was back, looking pleased. 'That's going to be a good one, though I say it myself.' She grinned at Dee again as she sat back down in her seat. 'Well, go on then, ask me something.'

'All right.' Dee thought for a moment. 'Are you seeing anyone?'

That took her by surprise. 'Ooh, cheeky! I thought you were going to ask me about the other people in the village, not myself! No, sadly. I was going with a young fellow who worked on Everard's farm last spring and summer. But he left about this time last year and so now I'm back to being an old maid again.' She gave Dee a sly look then added, 'What about yourself, miss? Are you seeing anyone?'

Dee pulled a face. 'I married a wrong 'un as they say. I left him a few months ago.'

'Going to divorce him?' Doris asked. 'You ought to, you know, to protect yourself. I know it takes a while, but I read about a woman whose old man died and left a load of debts he'd run up. And 'cos they'd never got divorced, she had to pay it all.'

'Goodness, how awful. Yes, I do intend to divorce him when I can. Though I know he'll be as difficult as he can be about it.'

'Men!' Doris said sagely.

'Exactly.' Then Dee said, 'Has Miss Marriott ever been engaged or been courted by anyone?'

Doris shook her head. 'There was apparently a young chap once when she was young, but he jilted her just before they got married and ran off with some other girl. She was in her early twenties, and he broke her heart, by all accounts, and she never recovered. Her mother even had to take her away for a while, said that travelling would help Miss Marriott to forget the chap. But when she came back, she seemed just as heart-broken, they say.'

'How sad. Poor Miss Marriott,' Dee said for a second time.

*

Chapter Nine

'You already know Clive, of course.' Miss Marriott said, drawing Clive Barton closer to Dee's side. They smiled awkwardly at one another and began to speak at the same time, Dee saying, 'Oh of course I do,' whilst Clive said,

'Yes indeed. Hello again, Miss Gascoigne.' His eyes glanced away from hers as he took a step back. No longer either a friend or admirer, clearly.

They were spared any further discomfort when Miss Marriott brought another, older woman forth.

'This is Miss Tilda Didsbury, she lives at the end of Church Lane.'

Dee put out a hand to Miss Didsbury, murmuring something conventional, aware of Clive wandering away.

Next there was a husband and wife to be introduced to: 'Mr Eric Merchant and his dear wife Vanessa. Mr Merchant used to be a newsreader for the BBC, you know.'

Dee did know. She could remember watching him on television on the early evening news, and before that he had read the news on the radio. He shook her hand rather too firmly, and staring her straight in the eye, as if he were looking down the lens of a camera, he announced,

'Last night, absolute carnage raged in the village.'

'Yes, indeed.' Dee tried to tear herself away from his gaze, feeling slightly disappointed he didn't say in his newsreader tone, *'In Hartwell Priory, Essex today, witnesses described the scene as...'*

He added, 'I hear you were there with Miss Marriott.'

Dee nodded, 'Yes, I was.'

'Shocking. Absolutely shocking.' He was shaking his head sorrowfully.

Dee managed to turn away slightly to smile at his wife, a small, very young, very pretty woman who appeared to be extremely bored already and was looking about her as if she was searching for one person in particular. Mr Merchant was immaculate in a brand new-looking if rather old-fashioned suit and tie, whereas his wife wore a very short dress, lots of make-up and beads, and up-to-the-minute high-heeled shoes. Dee judged Mr Merchant to be in his mid-sixties, and his wife couldn't have been much older than Dee herself. Interesting, she thought. He wasn't the kind of television personality one would expect to have the glamorous sex-appeal of, say, a film star or a pop singer.

In response to Mr Merchant's comment, Clive drew a little closer, and by degrees was drawn into conversation with Merchant, whilst Vanessa said to Dee,

'I do like your shoes. Are they from Harrington's?'

Dee, having forgotten for a moment which shoes

she had on, glanced down. 'Yes, they are actually.'

'I love shoes. I especially love Harrington's shoes. Don't you just the adore Harrington's? I think their styles are something else.'

'Oh, er, yes. Yes they are. Though they can be expensive.'

Vanessa shrugged, almost spilling her tea. 'Nothing worth having comes cheap.'

Seeing Eric Merchant glance briefly at his wife as she said this, Dee wondered for a moment if Vanessa included herself in that statement.

'Oh, I don't know,' Dee hedged, torn between the desire to point out all the wonderful things in the world that cost nothing, or next to nothing, and the desire to preserve a social politeness.

Clive hummed a tune softly under his breath and it took Dee a moment to place it. *Can't Buy Me Love*, last year's smash hit by The Beatles. She had to smother a laugh with her handkerchief, pretending to wipe her mouth.

'Oh do excuse me, a sip of tea went down the wrong way,' she explained, and glared at him.

Clive smirked back, her friend again. How mercurial he was, she thought.

Dee turned towards Eric Merchant who was pontificating once more.

'I'd string 'em all up,' he was saying to Clive. 'I have no time for this 'no capital punishment' nonsense that's always being put forward today. You want people to obey the law, put the fear of God into 'em!'

A couple of people nodded, and one man said, 'Hear, hear.' On the other hand, Vanessa rolled her eyes and said, 'God, politics is so boring.' then setting down her cup of tea, she glanced around. 'Is there any alcohol? Or is it just tea? I was hoping for champagne or a cocktail. Or even just a glass of sherry.'

'It's just tea,' Eric snapped. 'So damn well mind your manners.'

There was a frosty silence, though Dee wasn't sure whether it was fostered by local disapproval of him or of his wife. Vanessa looked like a sulky child now, folding her arms across her chest, which made her dress even shorter.

Into this awkward silence, Clive said, 'Steady on, Eric. I mean, those beatnik types are all someone's children at the end of the day. Just kids, most of them, and they're all out to promote peace and love, not violence. It was the villagers who brought the violence into it, and who set the churchyard on fire. And let's not forget that one of the women died, as well as the fellow who ran the group.'

'He was their university lecturer,' Dee chipped in, and noted they seemed surprised to hear that.

'Then he deserved all he got,' Eric said. 'Poisoning young minds, leading them astray.' She expected him to pronounce another headline, such as, *Shock as Cambridge lecturer leads students into disaster, more to follow after this break.*

'Did you meet any of them?' she asked.

'No, no. Wouldn't want to mingle with those sorts of people.'

'They are all kids from good families, wealthy backgrounds,' Clive said. He seemed determined to take their side, Dee thought. So much for knowing nothing about them.

'Some of them were even local,' Dee pointed out. That seemed to shock Clive.

'Oh, really?' He stared down at his cup. Dee sensed he was unhappy that she knew that, but why? Sure enough, a moment later, just as in the pub, he made an excuse to wander away to talk to someone else.

Dee managed to engage the elderly Miss Didsbury in conversation.

'I didn't go to the village meeting, of course,' she told Dee. 'I feared things might become heated. But I noticed that quite a few people were heading into the churchyard a while later, and I stood at my window watching them. My dining-room looks out onto the churchyard, as I'm sure Miss Marriott has told you. It was terribly shocking to see the flames rising high into the air and spreading. I was worried that the fire might spread as far as my garden, but in fact, the fire brigade arrived very promptly, and much of the churchyard was completely untouched.'

'My goodness, that was lucky,' Dee said, eyes wide, even though she knew this already.

'Yes indeed. And so when someone forced their way through my hedge, I didn't say anything to the police. They must have been fleeing from the blaze, no doubt in a total panic, as I myself would have done in their place, they wouldn't have meant to vandalise my property. So I said nothing.'

Dee nodded, her interest immediately captured. 'I'm sure you're right. How much damage did they cause?'

'Oh it was just one part of the hedge, really I'm making too much of a fuss about it. But it's always the small things that irritate one, isn't it? Someone had pushed through, and broken off a lot of tiny twigs, leaving a hole. I daresay in time it will grow back, but for now anyway, there's a hole.'

Dee nodded again. She felt a quiet sense of excitement brewing within her. This was useful, possibly vital information. 'And did you see who it was?'

Miss Didsbury shook her head. Her expression as

regretful. 'No. Although it was definitely a man. He was about Mr Barton's height, and probably as broad in the shoulder as Clive as well. And wearing a dark jacket and dark trousers.'

So not a floaty robe, Dee thought. Though it would be simple enough to pull off a robe and throw it aside. She assumed the beatnik group kept their everyday clothes on underneath.

'Perhaps it *was* Clive?' Dee suggested, more out of a sense of mischief than anything.

Miss Didsbury thought about that far more seriously than Dee had intended. 'Well,' she said after a long pause. 'I suppose it *could* have been Clive. But I'm sure if it had been him, he would have made a point of apologising for the damage. He's always such a gentleman.'

'Yes, I'm sure he would,' Dee agreed. To change the subject, she added, 'And do you have any ancestors buried in the churchyard here?'

Miss Didsbury became quite upset, drawing Dee away to a sofa, and fishing down between that and the armchair next to it, she pulled a dainty handkerchief out of the handbag she'd left there. She dabbed at her nose.

'Oh my dear, it's all so, so dreadful. Poor dear Mama, and Papa of course. And my Great Aunt Catherine. And Uncle Alfred and Uncle George. Really, it's such a dreadful, *dreadful* sacrilege. To uncover the remains of the dead! Oh, my dear!'

She was almost weeping now, and Dee wished she hadn't been so flippant. She tried to comfort the woman, saying, 'Please don't upset yourself, Miss Didsbury. I'm so sorry, I should never have...'

'Oh no,' Miss Didsbury gasped. Dee could see she was trying to calm herself. One or two of the other guests were glancing across and looking concerned.

Miss Didsbury herself was pink with embarrassment, her hands trembling as she patted her eyes with the hanky. 'No, I'm being silly. I'm all right really. And my mama brought me up better than this, I assure you. It's just, I do feel so strongly about it. I keep thinking of all the things that might go wrong. What if the mechanical digger crashes through my mother's coffin and, well, *damages* her? Breaks her leg or arm or something? Or what if they drop another person on top of my poor mother? Suppose they drop the remains of a *man* onto my mother? Suppose they became somehow *entangled* with one another?' And here she lowered her voice to a horrified whisper.

Dee suppressed the urge to giggle like a schoolgirl, realising that Miss Didsbury's concerns were real and borne out of a desire to protect and cherish the remains of her loved ones.

'They have promised to take the utmost care,' she reminded Miss Didsbury.

'I suppose so. Do you think I'm being silly?'

'Not at all. I think a lot of people will be feeling the same. But I do think you're worrying yourself unnecessarily. I'm certain these people know what they are doing and will be very, very careful to avoid any kind of difficulty or disrespect. So please don't allow yourself to dwell on things that are highly unlikely to happen.'

Miss Didsbury patted her arm. 'You're very kind. Will you be there on Monday when they 'break ground' as they call it?'

Dee was surprised. 'I hadn't thought about it.'

'I shall be there at half past ten, ready for their eleven o'clock start.'

'In that case, I shall be there too,' Dee promised.

'Them London coppers? Yes, love, they're in my back room. Got it set up like their own office at the Yard by now, I don't doubt. Just through that door and on your right. Says 'private functions'.'

Dee thanked the barman and went in the direction he had indicated. She saw the door with the 'private functions' sign on it, knocked once then turned the handle.

She saw before her two men, leaning back in their chairs, feet on the table, both in the middle of reading reports. Sergeant Porter had a cup halfway to his mouth, and on his lap, a plate bearing a large slice of chocolate cake.

'Hard at work, gentlemen?'

Nat grinned at her, and Bill, an inspector through and through, almost smiled then thought better of it, greeting her with his habitual frown.

'I thought we said after dinner?'

'No,' she said, immediately irritated by him. 'We said 'later'. Unfortunately, you failed to define exactly when 'later' was. So here I am.'

'Very well.' With an exasperated sigh, he took his feet off the table, removed the pile of folders from the chair beside him and bid her to sit herself down.

'So what have you found out?' she asked.

Nat said immediately, 'The chap was hit three or four times with force with a blunt object with a narrow smooth surface.'

'Oh, interesting,' Dee managed to get in before her cousin said,

'Sergeant! What have I told you before?'

Nat Porter managed to convey the impression of an apology but quickly shot a very unapologetic grin at Dee, whom he considered an ally.

To Dee, Bill Hardy said, 'And perhaps you can now explain how you managed to get to my crime scene before I did?'

She blew him a kiss, which only increased his irritation. Then she said, 'You'll never guess what! I work for Monty now. I'm an Associate of his firm.'

Bill frowned again. 'So you said earlier. But how can you be?'

She rummaged in her bag for the letter of introduction and her business cards and thrust them into his hand. As expected, he spent far longer than truly necessary scrutinising these items before returning them to her. All he said was,

'Seems a bit fishy to me. What are you actually doing here?'

'One of his clients wrote to ask him to look into things down here. He didn't want to come himself, he's far too busy. And also, he thought it might turn out to be a big waste of time. So he asked me to come down here on his behalf. He's paying me to investigate.'

'Investigate what exactly?'

Here her story came unstuck somewhat as she wasn't too sure herself why she was really here. The client's plea seemed rather thin. In lieu of a direct answer, she told him about the village meeting, and the events at the churchyard.

It was clear, she could tell, that they already had some idea of what had happened but didn't really see the depth of the problem. Dee ended up telling them everything she had so far been told by the people she had met, ending with Miss Didsbury's emotional outburst. It took rather a long time, and she found it disconcerting that Sergeant Porter wrote it all down in his neat shorthand. When she had finished, Bill and Nat just stared at her.

Bill said, 'It must be time for dinner by now. Will you join us?'

She'd been expecting a question or comment about the information she'd just given them. She hesitated for a moment. Then, 'I'm not sure I can. Miss Marriott is expecting me to join her for dinner. She has invited the vicar along, and possibly some other people. I think she thought I'd find it useful to speak with them.'

It seemed as though a light went out in his eyes. He looked away, reaching for his almost-empty teacup and draining the dregs. Once he'd set it down, he said, simply, 'Of course. Not to worry.'

'Why don't the two of you come after dinner? You could join us for coffee. I'm sure Miss Marriott wouldn't mind. In fact, I'm sure she'd find it quite interesting.'

He nodded, exchanged a glance with Nat, who also nodded, excitement on his face. He loved to see inside the large houses of the well-to-do.

'Lovely. I'll tell Miss Marriott and Doris that you'll be there at, what, about a quarter to nine, shall I?'

More nods and grunts. Still no real conversation or reaction from the wooden lump beside her who claimed he was madly in love with her and was supposed to be her future 'intended', as soon as her divorce came through. Not for the first time she wondered if she'd ever understand what went on inside his head.

She got to her feet. 'Right. I'll see you both later, then.' And she was halfway out of the door before he replied, with a bland, unenlightening, 'Yes.'

Idiot man, she grumbled to herself and went back to Miss Marriott's. As expected, Miss Marriott was perfectly happy to have the men come in for coffee after dinner.

Doris was right, the Reverend Kenneth 'Call me Ken'

Riley was indeed gorgeous. Dee put his age at about thirty-six. His hair was thick, wavy and dark with just the odd grey hair here and there to add character. Dee—and probably most women who met him—had to curb the urge to run her fingers through it. He was tall and well-built, looking sporty rather than clerically-bookish, had laughing ditchwater-bright brown eyes and a wide smile that revealed very white, very straight teeth. He was a very sexy man, she thought. His suit was a conservative one in keeping with his profession, and he wore a pristine white dog-collar on his plain grey shirt. He was witty, chatted about London shows, books, cinema and music, and was a thoroughly entertaining gentleman.

But Dee knew a little about these things, and she noticed the minute indicators that perhaps others might miss: the way he glanced several times at Clive Barton when he laughed at something his hostess had said. Clive was also an attractive man, and looked forty-four rather than the fiftyish he must truly be. Dee saw Riley watching Clive move when he got up from the table and went to close the curtain slightly to prevent the setting sun shining too brightly into his hostess's eyes. Riley's glances took in Clive's shoulders, his groin area, and his behind. As Clive squeezed behind Riley's chair to return to his own seat, she saw that Riley held his breath then swallowed hard, a sure sign of attraction.

So as she'd suspected, the Reverend Riley—like Dee's beloved younger brother Rob—was most definitely not 'a ladies' man'. And this was something that could be a real problem if his parishioners found out and complained to the bishop. As Dee knew from experience, most people were antagonistic towards men of his 'persuasion', and with intimate relationships between men still illegal, there would always be the worry of a threat to the security of his career.

Not that she could see how this might have any kind of impact or bearing upon the death of the two people in the churchyard the previous evening. It was more that it was another small fact to add to an accumulated number of small facts. This investigation, she decided, was becoming rather like a patchwork quilt. There were lots of little pieces, but it was hard to see how they fit together to form any kind of meaningful pattern.

Across the table from her were the Merchants who had come to tea that afternoon. Dee didn't particularly like either of them, and had felt a sinking feeling on seeing them arrive. Luckily, Clive was chatting with Vanessa Merchant, and Eric was exchanging stories with Miss Didsbury about collecting Chinese porcelain: it seemed they had a mutual passion for the stuff.

Riley now turned to reply to a question from Miss Marriott. Dee was left to smile awkwardly at her other neighbour at the table, Nicholas Raynes, the builder who had been such a bad speaker at the meeting. She made a comment about the wine they were drinking.

He smiled then mumbled a comment she couldn't catch. Then after a few seconds, he said, 'Forgive me for asking, but is it true you're a journalist?'

Dee was astonished. 'No. It's certainly not true. Why did you think that?'

He shook his head. 'I'm so sorry, didn't mean to offend you. Someone said it this afternoon.' He was silent for a short while before adding, 'Oh yes, it was Eric there.'

He nodded at Merchant who was laughing uproariously with Miss Didsbury. Dee was dubious that Chinese porcelain could be that amusing.

'It was when we met at the golf club at half past five this afternoon. We had to go along to a short meeting. To vote for a new club treasurer and chairman, and so forth. Mundane stuff. Bumped into him there, and he said, 'Watch yourself, won't you, at Marriott's tonight, as she's got a tame reporter there.'

He was watching her closely.

'I can't think why he would say that.' Dee felt quite angry about it. 'I'm certainly not involved in newspapers or reporting in any way, shape or form.'

He nodded. He seemed relieved. But then he leaned forward, pinned her with a cool gaze and in a low voice, said, his mouth lifting slightly at the top corner in a sneer, 'So what are you up to?'

She stared at him. She tried to think of what to say, instinctively knowing he'd be no happier to hear she was investigating events his company was involved with.

Before she could speak, he added, 'You're not a relation of the old girl's. As far as I know, she's never seen you before yesterday when you arrived in the village. And I saw you at the meeting last night, and you left with everyone else to go to the churchyard. Then I saw you again at Everard's field this morning. So again, what are you up to?'

She was saved from the need to reply by Miss Marriott rising from the table, with the words, 'Well, shall we go through to the drawing-room? We'll have our coffee in there, I think.'

'At least I'm not going about threatening people. Nice jag, by the way,' Dee said and got up from the table.

Raynes looked annoyed at her using this opportunity to avoid him by latching onto Miss Marriott to help her walk to the other room.

When the two policemen arrived a few minutes later, Dee was aware of a profound sense of relief. Raynes had been asking people questions about her and had taken it upon himself to question her right to be there. It was a problem that might not go away easily. She would need to avoid him until she had a plausible explanation that would allay his suspicions. After all, he could well prove to be the object of her enquiries.

*

Chapter Ten

Dee was not in the least surprised that the vicar immediately went to sit beside Sergeant Porter, welcoming him to the village with an eagerly outstretched hand and asking him if he preferred the countryside or London. Nor was it surprising that Vanessa Merchant took it upon herself to take the inspector by the arm as if she'd known him for years and pull him about the room, introducing him to everyone.

They halted in front of Dee. Vanessa said,

'And this is Dee Someone. I'm afraid I don't know your surname,' she said to Dee and before either Dee or Bill could supply it, she swept on with, 'Anyway, she's staying here with Miss Marriott, but she's not from the village, so she's of no interest.'

Bill looked annoyed by the comment, but Dee just shook her head slightly at him. It wasn't worth causing a scene over. He frowned but let it go. Vanessa, as oblivious to his response as she was to everything else unrelated to herself, was nevertheless enjoying the company of the attractive young man—she leaned extra close to him every time they moved past a chair or other obstacle, such as a coffee table or her husband. She gave Bill an excellent view down the front of her dress and giggled a great deal.

Dee wondered how Eric Merchant felt about this, but he was still deep in conversation with Miss Didsbury and didn't appear to notice. Perhaps he was used to it, Dee thought.

Clive Barton materialized at Dee's side, bearing a plate of chocolate-covered mints.

'These are very nice with the coffee,' he suggested, and took the seat beside Dee's.

'Thank you.' She took one, bit into it. He was right, it was delicious.

'Look, I'm sorry about running out on you at the pub. And I'd promised to buy you a drink, too, hadn't I, then it was you who bought me one. Will you give me another chance? I promise to behave this time.' His puppy-dog eyes pleaded for mercy, and she laughed, patting his arm.

'Oh, it's all right. Don't look at me like that, you're forgiven. Just tell me, why did you run off like that?'

He shrugged. 'I just—panicked—I suppose. I was afraid you were here to find out all my deepest, darkest secrets. But Miss Marriott has explained how you came to be here.'

Dee wasn't convinced, but she played along. A sip of coffee and another of those mints bought her some time. She was thinking furiously. Surely, she thought, *surely*, this meant that he did in fact have a deep dark secret. At least one. She immediately wanted to know what it was. But he spoke again,x

'And was it true what you said, that the policeman is your cousin? I presume you meant the one who is now playing Romeo to our resident Juliet? I mean, not the other one?'

'Inspector Hardy is my cousin. Sort of. Sergeant Porter is a dear family friend.'

He nodded. 'But the police being here is nothing to do with you? I mean, you didn't call them in?'

She laughed. 'I don't have that kind of power. Unfortunately. I'd love to be that important. But the sad truth is, I'm of no interest, as Vanessa Merchant has just told Bill.' She smiled at Clive. 'It was you who pointed out that Scotland Yard are almost always called in when there is an unexpected or suspicious death. But they have to be requested by local police authorities, not by civilians. They're here because two people died yesterday in the churchyard.'

'Of course, of course.' His look was the look and tone of a man who worried he'd said something stupid but wanted to keep his dignity.

Curiosity getting the better of her, Dee decided to be blunt. Making it sound gentle, playful, she said with a broad grin, 'Clive Barton, what are you up to?'

He looked a little startled, but his smile was boyish, genuine. 'I suppose this does all sound a bit cloak-and-dagger.'

'Just a bit.'

'The truth is... well in fact there are several truths here.'

'All right.' She leaned back in her chair, cradling her coffee cup in her lap, and fixed him with a look. He leaned back too, and in doing so, brought them closer together than they had been when sitting upright. Across the room, Inspector Hardy frowned the Hardy frown at her, whilst Vanessa Merchant hung off his arm, desperately trying to draw his attention to her young, firm bosom and her barely-concealed thighs.

'First of all,' Clive began in a low voice, 'My son and daughter are members of that group of dropouts who did the séances.'

Dee understood immediately. 'Of course! Bartholomew? Is that Barry? And Janna is your daughter Jane?'

'How did you...?' He looked taken aback then rather impressed. 'Well, yes, very good. That's exactly who they are. But if the locals here knew, they'd expect me to somehow intervene, to make them leave.'

Dee nodded. That made sense. 'But don't the locals recognise them?'

'No, the dropouts have been keeping a low profile most of the time, keeping away from the village. In any case, Barry now has a beard and long hair, and Jane has dyed her hair. Even Barry's girlfriend has changed her appearance quite a lot over the last two years since she left here. And she's not from this village, but one a few miles away.'

'You might be glad to know that some of them have left already. Though your children are still here, as I expect you already know. But I think they may leave soon. They told me they are on their uppers financially, and the deaths of Tristan and Serafina have obviously been an awful shock.'

She wondered whether to tell Clive that Janna's robe had caught fire and that the girl could have been seriously hurt. But what good would it do to upset or worry him about that now?

He nodded. 'I'll go and see them in the morning, give them a bit of cash. They're not bad kids, you know. I don't think they expected things to go so badly wrong.'

'They're planning to go back to university, at any

rate, so that's good news,' Dee told him. 'And Barry and Adelle seem very devoted, even if they are rather young.'

He nodded slowly, concentrating on his drink. When he'd finished it, he set the cup aside, but now, he had nothing to do with his hands. One hand slipped inside his jacket pocket and began fiddling with his keys or loose change in a loud, annoying manner. Dee resisted the urge to smack his hand away.

'And what is your other deepest, darkest secret?'

He looked at her, startled.

'How did you...?' Then he smiled and shook his head. 'You're good at this. No wonder they sent you down to investigate.'

'Well?' She didn't want him to get side-tracked. She smiled back at him, wanting to keep things amicable. But he was looking rather agitated. He leaned a tiny bit closer. His voice was barely above a whisper as he said,

'It's all going to come out anyway when they start moving the remains this week. So you may as well know.'

That sounded serious. Ominous, even. Dee was on the point of saying that he needn't tell her if he didn't want to. But then he said,

'After all this time... I can't believe I'm finally going to be rid of this—this albatross—this millstone round my neck.' He glanced about him as if making sure no one had heard. 'Do you want another coffee?'

'No!' Dee hissed at him. He seemed rather taken aback by that, so she added in a calmer tone, 'No, thank you. Just tell me whatever you were about to tell me. Then, if you want another coffee, by all means have one.'

He nodded. 'My wife left me. Years ago, this was. It

was, oh, a year or so later that I received notification that she'd died in Spain. So I had a grave set up for her. But she's not actually there.'

Dee was immensely puzzled. Had she understood him correctly? 'But she *is* dead?'

'Yes.'

'So...?' she shook her head. 'I'm sorry. I don't understand.'

He sighed. 'All right. Here's what happened. I'm not proud of what I did, but I was angry and upset, obviously, that she'd left me for another man. I told the children she'd gone to visit her sister in Cornwall because the sister wasn't well. Then I said she'd stayed there because her sister needed her help, then a bit later, I told them that she had died in an accident. So we had a funeral, and a burial. And the children still think to this day that she is in there, in her coffin, under that headstone.'

Dee nodded. 'I see. So far, I'm with you.' Her brow furrowed. She still didn't quite...

'But she's not. As I said, she left me and went off with another man. I never heard from her again. Never heard anything about her, until a priest from a church in Spain wrote to me, offering his condolences, and said he regretted to inform me that my wife had been killed in a road accident. That was in 1957.'

Wheels were turning in Dee's brain. Questions began to form, but she held back, waiting for him to continue.

'He said that she'd been interred there because of the hot weather and because the authorities were told she had no family. Well, that was understandable. But then this other man, her lover, began to feel guilty, so he told the priest the truth and that was how the priest came to write to me. But

I-I wanted to have a service for her, I wanted the children to be able to mourn her. And it seemed only right to commemorate her. So, I told everyone that I'd had her remains brought back from Cornwall to our local church here. I arranged a funeral, only, of course, I didn't. I paid an undertaker a large sum of money to lie for me. The vicar we had back then, I never told him the truth, he received the coffin, but of course he never looked inside, why would he? No one knew. So you see, when the digging starts...'

She did see. It would be discovered that there were no remains in Maureen Barton's grave, just an empty coffin. She stared at him. What on earth was he going to do? She wondered if he would go to prison when it all came out, or if a lenient, sympathetic judge might let him off with a slap on the wrist or a small fine. Was it even a crime? She just didn't know, and clearly neither did he.

She glanced at him to see he was staring into space, a worried look on his face.

'Well at least they are not likely to get to your wife's grave right away. The position of the grave gives you a day or two's grace.'

'Yes, bless you, that's true.' He half-smiled. 'Should I flee the country in the middle of the night, or stay and take my punishment like a man?'

'I think you should stay. It might be a good idea to talk to the police. Make a clean breast of it. And, if you like, I can speak to Monty—the barrister who employs me—and ask his advice.'

'Hmm. Let me think about it overnight, would you?' After a pause he added, 'My God, that's the first time I've ever spoken about this to anyone. I do actually feel lighter.'

Dee nodded. 'They say confession is good for the soul.'

'It's true, I can vouch for that. Ah, look, I'm being summoned. Hopefully I'll see you later. But if not, what about that drink? Tomorrow evening? Shall we say nine o'clock? That should give your hostess time to get dinner out of the way.'

'Nine o'clock is perfect,' Dee assured him, and without thinking, patted him on the knee. 'Now then, if Miss Marriott wants you, you'd better go.'

As soon as Clive had gone to sit with Miss Marriott, his place was taken by a bad-tempered policeman. Dee gave him a bright smile and received the usual frown in return. He said,

'He's far too old for you, you know. And a bit of a fast worker if you only got here yesterday.'

'He's just a friend,' Dee said.

'Humpf.'

'You got away from Vanessa unscathed, then? And with your honour intact?'

'Did you know her husband is that fellow who used to read the news? She's young enough to be his granddaughter.' They both glanced across the room. Vanessa had turned her charms on Nicholas Raynes, who was responding with more enthusiasm than Bill had done, and Eric, standing with Miss Didsbury, easily twenty feet away from his wife, was watching her with a gloomy frown as Miss Didsbury talked his ear off about her latest acquisition.

'Well, his daughter anyway. Yes, I met them this afternoon. How is the investigation going?'

'Well so far, I've found out nothing. No one knows anything. No one saw anything. The Merchants say they weren't even at the meeting and neither did they go to the churchyard. And the same goes for Miss Didsbury.' He sounded thoroughly fed up.

'Well, that's understandable,' said Dee. 'I mean, she's far too old to be mucking about stepping over gravestones in the dark. Did she tell you about her hedge?'

He shook his head, looking puzzled.

Dee quickly told him what Miss Didsbury had said about someone pushing their way through it from the churchyard last night. As soon as she mentioned Miss Didsbury's comment about the man appearing similar to Clive, Bill's eyes lit up. She sighed inwardly and hoped he wouldn't make too much out of it, the last thing she wanted was Clive on the wrong end of a personal vendetta.

'What about the vicar?' she said.

'I haven't spoken to him. I'm hoping Porter will get something out of him. Do you think the vicar is a bit—you know?' He grinned at her.

'Like Rob? Yes, I think he is. He made a beeline for the attractive sergeant and completely failed to be lured by Vanessa Merchant's heaving bosom.'

'Yes,' he agreed. 'She heaved it in my direction a few times.'

'She's not your type, anyway.'

'She's married, more to the point.'

'As am I.'

'Oh, Dee love, that's different, you know it is.' He briefly touched her hand then sat back, just as Clive had done earlier, leaning towards her, staring at her. 'So there's nothing going on between you and the old bloke?'

'He's not old,' she hissed at him. 'And no, I told you, we're just friends. We only met yesterday for goodness' sake! Are you going to be like this every time I talk to a man? Because if you are... I had enough of that with Martin, mostly directed at you, I might add.'

'I know. I'm sorry. It's just clear that he likes you. He was all over you.'

'Said the man who was monopolised by Vanessa Merchant's heaving bosom for the best part of an hour. What rot, Bill.'

'Oh, so what? A girl likes a little attention, a little conversation sometimes.'

'I think Vanessa probably gets more than enough attention.'

She wondered if she ought to tell him about Clive's wife. But before she could say anything, the Merchants and Nicholas Raynes got up to take their leave, followed by Miss Didsbury, and before Dee knew where she was, the two police officers were also saying goodnight and following everyone else out. Dee looked at her watch. It was almost eleven o'clock already.

As soon as the guests had all gone, Miss Marriott said goodnight. Doris came to take her upstairs to bed, and Dee, suddenly realising what a long and busy day it had been, decided that she was also very ready for bed. At least tomorrow would be Sunday and a day of rest. Or at least, she hoped it would be.

*

Chapter Eleven

The door opened a few inches, and a man peered through the gap. Hardy held up his warrant card.

'Inspector Hardy, London Metropolitan Police. Are you Nicholas Raynes?'

The man nodded, but with obvious reluctance. He glanced from Hardy to Porter then back again.

'We would like to ask you a few questions, sir, if you don't mind.'

'Perhaps we could come in, sir?' Porter added. Then smiled to set the man at ease.

'What's all this about?' Raynes didn't move.

'Just a few questions about recent events in Hartwell Priory, sir.' Hardy smiled too but Raynes still looked worried.

'I-I don't... I don't know anything. I wasn't even there. Look, you do know that it's a Sunday, don't you?' He tried to shut the door but Porter's large boot was there to stop that. Porter smiled again.

'Yes. Sorry sir, I'm afraid police officers often have

to work on a Sunday. Just a few questions, sir. It won't take long.'

Defiance replaced anxiety. With a lift of his chin, Raynes said, 'I'm not saying anything without my solicitor present.'

Hardy stepped forward, reaching into his pocket for some handcuffs. 'In that case, sir, I will have to place you under arrest for obstructing a police investigation. We'll take you to the police station to wait for your solicitor.'

Raynes looked from one to the other of them again, the defiance gone already.

'Just a few questions, sir,' Hardy said again, putting the handcuffs away.

'Oh all right. Come in.' Raynes turned away from the door and began to disappear along the hallway.

The policemen came in, shut the door and followed Raynes into a room on the left. It was a sitting-room, well-decorated, and neatly furnished in a spare, uncluttered style. And on one of the sofas sat a scantily clad woman holding a glass of wine. She sat up, alarmed to see two strange men entering the room.

'Nick, what is...?'

'It's all right, Cynthia. It's just the police with a couple of questions. Put your skirt on, there's a good girl.'

Hardy pretended to consult his notebook. 'Would that be Cynthia Miles-Hudson? Head of planning at the North Essex council?'

She glared at him. 'Oh, shut up.' She grabbed a pile of clothes, and, attempting to hold them in front of her to cover herself, she shoved past him. They heard the sound of her running up the stairs.

Hardy beamed at Raynes, and took a seat on the nearest sofa, remarking, 'What a charming home you have, Mr Raynes.'

Coming back to the pub a little later, the two policemen from London found themselves in great demand. They had been invited to Sunday lunch and cocktails by none other than the mayor himself, who'd added that he felt it was only right to 'throw open his private home' to entertain the officers who were working so hard for the benefit of the mayor's community, as a thank you and a welcome to the area.

He'd already been a remarkably difficult man to get an appointment with for an interview, and so neither Hardy nor Porter felt particularly in the mood for socialising with the man and watching him patting himself on the back.

'If I thought there would be even a small chance to get him to ourselves to ask a couple of questions, I might be tempted to accept,' Hardy grumbled.

'It'll never happen. He'll just keep giving us the run-around,' Porter said. 'He's much too important to be questioned by the likes of us.'

'True.'

There had also been an invitation from Miss Didsbury, which they viewed far more favourably. Bill in particular was rather keen to go, in the hopes of spending time with Dee, as Miss Didsbury's maid had mentioned that Miss Marriott would be there. And by extension, Bill reasoned, Dee might be there too.

Even Sergeant Wright, the officious local policeman had invited them to a roast dinner at his parents' home, adding with pride that no one made Yorkshire puddings like his mother did.

All these invitations, Hardy politely declined, pleading too much work to be done. Porter was disappointed but could hardly contradict his senior officer.

'So what will we do about, you know, lunch? And dinner?' Porter was anxious, not liking to be separated from food for too long. He'd had plenty of hungry years in his early life, he had no intention of going without now he was in his forties and had a good job. Though if the food could be acquired on expenses, so much the better.

'I've arranged a private lunch for us here at the pub,' Hardy said. 'We'll spend a couple of hours going over what we already know, then plan our next steps. Then, how about we take a drive over to Greater Hartwell this evening and get a decent dinner at the hotel there?'

Porter nodded gravely: the idea had possibilities. 'We could take along your cousin,' he suggested. He enjoyed Dee's company—she was less inclined to seriousness than Inspector Hardy, and so the evening wouldn't be all work. After all, it was Sunday.

'Good idea.' Hardy frowned as usual, as if something terrible had been suggested, but on the inside he was excited. He would see Dee after all, and they could enjoy a lighter evening—all work and no play etc etc, he reminded himself. 'I'll order us a couple of coffees now and we can get started on the statements again.'

'Of course, sir,' Porter sighed. He hoped when the coffee came there would be a slice of cake too. Usually there was. Mrs Guthrie had little to do with the running of the pub, but devoted her entire day to baking delicious treats, and creating some of the best pub meals Porter had ever known. His mouth was already watering in anticipation. He hoped it would be cherry cake. The cherries were always so...

'What was your feeling about Nicholas Raynes,

when we spoke to him earlier?' Hardy asked suddenly. Porter sighed again and pulled his attention away from cake and back to work.

Dee had a long lie-in on that Sunday morning. She felt guilty about being slothful, but then simply turned over and went back to sleep.

Coming downstairs at eleven o'clock, she was not especially surprised to find there was no one about. She assumed Doris spent Sunday with her family somewhere locally, and that Miss Marriott slept late, then perhaps had a cold buffet lunch, or something else that Doris had left her, ready to prepare without too much fuss or effort.

Dee went to the kitchen and made herself tea and toast, and while she waited for the bread to brown and the kettle to boil, she noticed that it was raining quite heavily again. When the toast was just right and the tea made, she went into the morning-room with it, settling in a well-upholstered armchair of butter-soft leather. With the cushions at her back, she gazed out at the tranquil rainy scene and concentrated on her breakfast.

It was almost twelve o'clock when Miss Marriott wandered in, leaning on her stick as usual, and greeted Dee with a smile.

'Good morning, my dear. If it is still morning? I hope you haven't felt too neglected?'

'Not at all, Miss Marriott. I only came down myself a short while ago. I've just had my breakfast: a cup of tea and some toast. Can I get you something?'

Miss Marriott lowered herself carefully into an adjacent chair. 'Oh no, my dear, that's quite all right. Doris brought me a cup of tea earlier, that's all I needed. I wondered, do you have any plans at all for today?'

'Not really.' Dee waited. Did Miss Marriott have a request?

'It's just that I always go to Tilda's on a Sunday for lunch. Miss Didsbury, you know. She always does Sunday lunch in style, of course, and she invited you to join us, but I wasn't sure if you might be busy with your very attractive cousin? It's entirely up to you if you'd like to join us or not. I did tell Tilda I wasn't sure that you'd be free.'

'Oh, er...'

'The thing is, my dear,' Miss Marriott swept on, 'Tilda's lunch isn't served until almost three o'clock, so really my visit takes up most of the afternoon. I'm rarely home before six o'clock, and as you've probably guessed, Doris doesn't come in on a Sunday. She'd be more than happy to leave me something, but after a big meal at Tilda's I never want anything other than a slice of cake and a glass of port for dinner.'

She said this final part very much as if it were a guilty confession.

Dee laughed. 'I completely understand. Really, there's no need to worry about me, I can look after myself.' She thought a moment. 'I hope Miss Didsbury won't be offended if I turn down her invitation?'

'I'm sure she won't be. I believe she invited your inspector and his sergeant, but they were unable to attend due to their workload, Sylvia said when she rang and earlier and spoke to Doris. I assume that means you and your young man will be dining tête à tête this evening?'

'I have no idea,' Dee commented frankly. 'I haven't heard from him, so...'

The telephone bell interrupted her. With a glance at Miss Marriott, who understandably showed no sign of getting out of her armchair, Dee hurried to answer it, sitting at the desk in the study to do so.

'Hartwell 21,' she said in her best telephone manner, reading the number off the dial.

'Dee? It's me,' he said, perfectly on cue. 'How about dinner tonight? Nat and I are at a loose end, so if you're not busy, you might as well come along.'

She wanted to tell him to go and boil his head, but that would leave her with either having to go to Miss Didsbury's or eating toast for dinner as well as for breakfast. She said, 'Since you've asked me so sweetly, I shall graciously accept your invitation.'

'Oh, Dee, sorry, I just...'

'Eight o'clock?'

'Perfect,' he said. 'I'll pick you up.'

'No need, I'll call at the pub.'

It was a race between them to each put the phone down on the other. Dee won. Though only just. Irritated but glad to have somewhere to eat that evening, she returned to the morning-room.

'Dinner plans?' Miss Marriott asked, eyebrows arched, a smile on her lips.

'Dinner plans.'

After Miss Marriott went out, Dee spent the afternoon wandering around the house. She had watched the television in the morning-room for a while, a favourite old film was on, Pride and Prejudice, with the elegant Laurence Olivier in the role of Mr. Darcy. As she watched the familiar scenes, almost able to quote the script by heart, it gave her a chance to mull over the events that had happened there in Hartwell Priory.

When she had been a teacher, up until a few short months ago in fact, her pupils had always told her that they did their homework to a background of pop music on their transistor radios. And now, Dee realised how much it helped to have something going on as a kind of theatrical backdrop to her thoughts.

She thought again about the day she had arrived, just two days ago, but seeming so much longer ago than that. How quickly she had got to know people, mainly thanks to Miss Marriott, of course. But people had necessarily to be viewed from outside, and you could only get to know them to the extent that they let you in. Some shut the door in your face, so to speak, whilst others were charming and friendly. Yet did you really know them any better, or was charm and friendliness just another kind of barrier? She thought about the way Clive Barton could be charming, but sometimes became reserved, even withdrawing completely if she said something that unsettled him. He was a man of secrets, that much was certain. But had she been told all of them? Or was there something else he was holding back? Had it been him forcing his way through Miss Didsbury's hedge, when he'd previously said he wasn't in the churchyard that evening.

Once the film had finished, she put off the television and went to look about the house. She got herself a glass of water from the kitchen. She'd had a late breakfast and so she skipped lunch completely.

She didn't want to pry, exactly. It would never do to abuse Miss Marriott's generous hospitality. But she was bored. Returning to the morning-room, she examined the pillars on either side of the large French doors. The pillars went from floor to ceiling, and stood easily four feet wide, with a depth of almost the same. The lower parts of the pillars were panelled with a dark wood that she thought was probably oak. It was the same dark wood that cropped up all over the house, a common building material in very old houses such as this.

Dee tapped and prodded. And in pretty much the same spot as the one at home, a panel slid aside perfectly soundlessly, revealing two shallow steps down onto a sandy-floored nook big enough for one or two people to hide. A priest-hole.

Feeling a little worried, but reminding herself she was alone in the house, Dee stepped through the gap and went down into the priest-hole, dipping her head as she went. She wasn't a tall woman, but historians always said people in the past were smaller.

It was dim in here, although there was a metal loop set into the wall to hold an old-fashioned flaming torch, she assumed. Though she felt concerned by that. Surely that would have burnt up the oxygen too quickly, even though the light would have been welcome. There was an absolute silence in here, the thick walls around and above efficiently cut off all outside sounds. She shivered and stepped out, irrationally relieved to be back in the relative brightness of the over-ornamented, darkly-panelled morning-room.

She closed the priest-hole and went across the hall to the drawing-room. At home, there was a fairly large space behind the chimney. But in Miss Marriott's home, all the panelling in here had been removed, and the walls decorated with fresh smart paint and panels of flowered wallpaper. If there was a priest-hole there too, Dee couldn't see any way to access it.

'Perhaps that's all to the good,' she thought aloud.

By the time Miss Marriott returned, much later than she'd anticipated at a quarter to seven, Dee was in the bath, preparing to go out for dinner. When she came downstairs at a quarter to eight, in her best frock, her hair freshly washed, dried and piled up on her head with a few curly tendrils hanging down, Miss Marriott was beside the wireless listening to a concerto and munching a crumpet, a large glass of port on the table beside her.

'Did you enjoy your lunch at Miss Didsbury's?' Dee asked.

'Oh it was all right. We talked a good deal about the old days, as us old women always do. And we drank rather a lot of sherry.' Miss Marriott beamed at Dee, and Dee noted the very flushed cheeks and the suggestion of a giggle.

'You should sleep well tonight, then.' She grinned back at the old woman.

'Yes, indeed. All ready for your evening out? If it's all right, I will give you a latch key, that way I can lock the door securely. Then if you're late coming in, that will be quite all right. Now let me see, where did I...?' As she got up, Miss Marriott wobbled slightly. Dee immediately ran to grab her by the arm.

'Ah, there it is,' Miss Marriott grabbed the key from a silver tray on the table just inside the door and she held it out to Dee, who took it.

'If you're sure?'

'Oh yes, dear. I shan't want to get out of bed to let you in, you know. And of course, dear Doris won't be here to let you in, so...'

Miss Marriott returned to her crumpet and her concerto, whilst Dee popped the key into her tiny silk evening bag, and calling goodnight over her shoulder, left the house.

'Is there going to be an inquest into the deaths of Tristan and Serafina, by the way?' Dee asked, her fork hallway to her mouth.

Nat groaned. 'Not shop talk already? At least wait

until we get to the coffee.'

She grinned at him. 'Sorry.'

Bill said, 'A joint one is scheduled for next Wednesday. I'm hoping to have it all wrapped up by then. We, I mean,' he added with an apologetic nod at Porter.

'*Me*, I think you mean. I'm fairly sure that on behalf of Montague Montague of London, legal services *I* will have this 'all wrapped up', as you say.' She smirked at him and got the predictable frown in reply.

'Tell me again how that came about,' Bill asked.

So Dee explained once more about the job offer from Monty, and the letter he'd received from Miss Marriott asking for help. And although she knew she'd already told him all this, she told him again about the meeting and the fire on Friday night, and what Doris and Miss Marriott had said about the previous séance in the church, and how angry and upset people had been then too.

By this time, they had finished their main course and were waiting with eager anticipation for their desserts. Once these had been brought to their table: a peach melba each for Bill and Nat, and a meringue and cream confection with a few late strawberries for Dee, work talk ended and they ate almost in silence, appreciating their food. Then finally, their coffee came, and they sat back, conversation inevitably returning to the events at Hartwell Priory, and its people.

'One person I still haven't spoken to properly,' Dee said, 'Is the owner of the building firm that is doing all the work. Nicholas Raynes. He spoke—briefly—at the meeting in the pub on the night of the churchyard fire. Then I saw him—or rather, I saw his car—at the field where the beatniks are camping. One of the seekers told me he had been there to tell them to leave. 'Or else', he'd said. Later I met him at Miss Marriott's when she invited everyone for afternoon tea, and he mentioned seeing me at the field. But I didn't really get anything out of him, he was too suspicious of me and hostile, demanding to know what I was up to. I didn't like him.'

Bill stretched his long legs out, then his arms up above his head, easing his cramped muscles before giving a loud, long-lasting yawn.

'Ugh, sorry, sorry. I didn't sleep too well last night in that bed at the pub—it's a bit lumpy. Nicholas Raynes. Yes. We spoke to him this morning, didn't we, Nat? A bit too full of himself. I had to threaten to arrest him just to get him to answer a few questions.'

'That's right,' Nat said. 'He really didn't want us there—but he had a reason, as we quickly discovered.'

'When we finally got invited in, it was to find a half-naked woman drinking wine in his sitting-room.' Bill said, unusually forthcoming.

Dee's eyes were on stalks. 'My goodness, who was she?'

'Cynthia Miles-Hudson,' Nat said before Bill could give him the go-ahead to reveal her identity.

Dee sat back, her brow furrowed as she thought this over. 'So Raynes is carrying on with the woman in charge of planning. Hmm. I wonder if he's using her to get the contract for the building work, or if she's using the building contract to get him? It must be him using her for the contract, surely, I don't see anyone actually wanting him.'

When they took her back to Miss Marriott's a little later, Bill asked Nat to take the car back to the pub car park, and he walked Dee up to the front door.

Feeling a little awkward, she tried to make a joke out of it. 'You didn't need to walk me back, I don't think I'll get murdered right on the doorstep.'

'People do,' he said. Then as if he realised he'd just made things a bit too grim, he put an arm around her. 'I'm glad you're here, but I do worry about you.'

She kissed his cheek. 'I know. Well, thank you for dinner and for walking me to the door.'

'I might see you tomorrow when they break ground, it should be interesting. I wonder how much of a protest there will be as work begins. Sergeant Wright said he's asked for extra men to be on hand in case things turn violent.'

She nodded, a sense of dread in the pit of her stomach.

'Right. Well, goodnight.' He didn't try to kiss her, which was disappointing, but cupping her cheek for a second or two, he smiled, then turned to walk away, waving a hand above his head without bothering to turn around.

Dee unlocked the door and went inside. 'Stupid man,' she told herself crossly. He could at least have kissed her goodnight.

*

Chapter Twelve

A deep, dreamless sleep gave way to an abrupt awakening at half past seven, and a sense of anxiety accompanied by a headache. It took Dee several seconds to remember where she was and the fact that it was Monday morning, and that her anxiety related to the fact that today was the day of the official ground-breaking for the new development.

What she wouldn't give to bury her head back under the covers and pretend everything was all right. Or to be away somewhere else. On holiday perhaps, travelling for pleasure, enjoying new scenes, meeting new people, just having fun. She could picture it now, herself on a deckchair eating an ice-cream, the sun beating down, waves lapping at the shore a little way off. She might even have the chance to read her book, still languishing untouched on the table by her bed. What if being an investigator, after all, was not what she wanted from life, not her calling?

With a heavy heart, she swung her legs over the side of the bed, pulled on her dressing-gown and pattered across the hall to the bathroom that she had completely to herself, as Miss Marriott had her own bathroom next to her bedroom at the other end of the corridor.

When Dee returned to her room, Doris was waiting for her.

'I wasn't sure about bringing you a cup of tea, miss, as I thought you might be going out early with Miss Marriott?'

'Yes, that's right. Though I hope we'll have time for some breakfast before we go?'

'I'll do your toast now, if you like. I've just given Miss Marriott her tray in bed as usual. Then once I've done your breakfast, I can come back up and help Miss Marriott to get dressed.'

Doris looked agitated, not at all her usual calm self.

Dee said, 'I'm sorry to give you so much extra work. I can get my own toast and tea, you know.'

Doris looked uncertain but tempted.

'Go on,' Dee said. 'Miss Marriott probably needs you.'

'I've got to go down for more hot water, so I'll put the kettle on and light the grill so it's nice and hot to make your toast, then if you don't mind doing the rest, that will be a huge help.' Doris was already moving towards the stairs.

'Fab, Doris, thanks. I'll be down in two ticks.'

Now Dee had to hurry herself, afraid she would keep Miss Marriott waiting. Over a plain blouse with floaty sleeves she threw on a practical pinafore dress with big patch pockets, then opted for her sturdier shoes in case she had to do a lot of walking. She heaved her bits and pieces out of her smart patent leather handbag and into a bag that resembled a brightly striped knitted sack. She would do her make-up very quickly after breakfast when she came up to brush her teeth.

She hurried down the stairs and reached the kitchen just in time to lift the kettle off the gas as it began to whistle. She made herself a cup of tea, and placed two slices of bread under the grill to toast. As she did these things, she was jigging and humming along to a tune on the radio—one of her favourite songs, released the previous year and still very popular. Her mood was lifting. Perhaps everything would be all right. And if not, well, the police would be there to keep an eye on things.

'No handsome face can ever take the place of my guy. My guy-yyyy.' It was a good thing no one else was around to hear her caterwauling, she thought.

The mundane tasks calmed her anxiety and her headache. And speaking of *My Guy*, she thought, Bill—and Nat too, of course—would be there when the diggers pulled up the first bit of greenery in the churchyard later that morning.

She was impatient now to get outside. There could be a chance to have a last look around the churchyard before work started at eleven. She ate her toast over the sink, student-style, rinsing away the crumbs, and only drank half of her tea. Doris, presumably still helping Miss Marriott, hadn't yet reappeared.

Dee tidied the kitchen, then ran upstairs again to clean her teeth and put on her make-up. She gave her hair a last quick brush then caught it back from her face with a stretchy band of vivid red, deciding that would have to do, and hurried downstairs again.

Doris was in the kitchen now.

'Did you have your breakfast, miss?'

'Yes, I did. I hope I didn't leave any mess?'

'Quite the opposite, miss. No one would ever know you'd been in here. Miss Marriott isn't quite ready, she didn't have a very good night, I'm afraid. She said if you wanted to go on ahead, to do that, and I'll bring her along later. She said to tell you she'd only be about twenty minutes or so. But that really means at least twice as long. She's still eating her breakfast, then she wanted to have a look at the newspaper, so you can see she'll be a while yet.'

'That's all right,' Dee said, keen to be off. 'In that case, I'll see her later. There's no rush.'

Outside the house, the lane was deserted. Dee was surprised at that. She wondered if there would be more people at the churchyard itself, waiting for things to get started. Going past the pub, she couldn't help glancing at the door, hoping to see Bill, still disappointed he hadn't taken more time to say goodnight to her last night. But the door was firmly shut; no one was there.

With the cheerful tune of Mary Wells's *My Guy* still in her head, Dee strode along the lane through the village, and in two minutes, she was at the churchyard.

It was far too early for the workmen, she thought, no doubt they wouldn't arrive until just before the eleven o'clock start. But she could see that Clive Barton was already there, deep in conversation with Angela Baker, the woman from the historical society who had been at the village meeting.

As Dee approached them, she called out, 'I expected that far more people would be here early, ready for when things get going.'

'Everyone will be here later, I think that's certain. If we can't stop the builders, we can at least slow them down. Make their lives a misery.' Angela Baker was clearly furious about the situation.

'Did you come to the churchyard the other evening? When the meeting ended?' Dee asked her.

Mrs Baker hesitated then glanced away. She snapped, 'No, of course not. Why would I have done that?'

'Everyone else did,' Dee said with a shrug and a disarming smile. 'So did you wait in the hall to see if anyone came back to the meeting? Or did you...'

'Why are you questioning me? What business is it of yours? We've nothing to say to the likes of you, so leave us alone.' She linked her arm through Clive's and turned her back on Dee, spinning Clive around.

Dee said sweetly, 'Clive, dear, what time did you say we'd go for that drink?'

He looked embarrassed, and Angela Baker was clearly livid. Dee felt sorry for him, and wished—too late as always—that she'd kept her mouth shut.

'Oh, er...' He looked panicked now.

'It's all right,' she said gently, and walked away. She turned into the churchyard, thinking she might as well have a last look before the digging began and ruined everything.

She saw the stooping form of a woman by a headstone that leaned at a precarious angle. This was one of the few graves that was not overgrown. A neat, six-foot long rectangle was marked out in front of the grave with smooth white pebbles, and inside that perimeter, early heathers bloomed in cheery mauves and pinks.

A headscarf had obscured the side of her face, but sensing Dee approaching, the woman had turned and Dee now saw her. The woman was Mrs Padham from the guesthouse.

There was a moment when Dee wished she'd turned away sooner and gone in a different direction.

And another moment when Mrs Padham also seemed to hesitate over whether or not to ignore her.

'Good morning, Miss Gascoigne,' she said after a moment, her tone neutral.

'Good morning, Mrs Padham.' Dee halted, not sure if they were going to converse or not. Mrs Padham nodded at the gravestone.

'My parents. Been gone a few years now. They were very good to me. Even if the guesthouse is a millstone round my neck, at least it's mine, thanks to them.'

'You've kept the grave up beautifully,' Dee remarked. 'I think it's about the only one where you can read the inscription.'

She read it now. It said, simply:

Sacred to the memory of
William Didsbury
1883 – 1943
And of his wife
Mary Didsbury nee Raynes 1886 – 1941

'Is Miss Didsbury a relative of yours?' Dee asked in surprise on seeing William's surname.

'She's my aunt,' Mrs Padham said with a sniff. 'We don't speak.'

Dee suspected Mrs Padham was a woman who was easily offended, whereas her impression of Miss Didsbury was that she was a nice old thing, apart from her attitudes to others and her love of gossiping with Eric Merchant about porcelain, or as Miss Didsbury preferred to call it, *chinoiserie*. Dee spared a moment to wonder, irrelevantly, whether Miss Didsbury called Japanese artworks *japonica* too. Coming back to Mrs Padham, Dee reminded herself that family relationships were often a closed book to those outside of the family. Andin a village everyone seemed to be connected to everyone else. Clearly there was a connection to the Raynes family too.

Dee replied, 'Oh, I'm sorry to hear that.' It was hard to think of anything else to add. Mrs Padham almost smiled at her.

'Just one of those things. She doesn't like me working for a living. Apparently, it's demeaning. Of course, as I've said to her before, if she'd helped me when I asked, I wouldn't need to work all hours and scrimp and save, and...' She broke off, took a deep breath, then said, 'Sorry. I got a bit carried away. I always do when I think about Aunt Tilda.'

She glanced sideways at Dee. 'Did you come here for the ground-breaking?'

Dee nodded. 'Yes, but I was expecting to find a lot of people here ready for the start at eleven.'

'Ready to throw themselves in front of the diggers? Hopefully no one will do that. They might say it, but they will never do it.' She waved a hand around her. 'And you can see the state of the place. It's not as if any of them really care about their dead relations.'

'I think it's beautiful,' Dee said, gazing about her.

'They're just weeds. They should have been pulled up ages ago before they really took hold. They attract courting couples,' she added sourly.

Dee couldn't help laughing. 'Yes, I imagine they do.'

Another assessing look from Mrs Padham, then, 'So you're staying with Lola, I understand?'

'Yes.'

'It's a wonder you didn't go straight there first instead of coming to me.'

'I'm sorry about that,' Dee said. 'I hadn't realised that Miss Marriott would invite me to stay with her. It was very generous of her. I didn't feel I could say no. I'm sorry if I inconvenienced you.'

'Oh it's all right. I-I'm sorry I charged you when you hadn't even stayed. I'll put the money through the door tomorrow.'

Dee shook her head. 'Keep half, it's not from my own pocket, and after all, you prepared the room and will have had to clean it and prepare it again for the next person, so that was extra work for you.'

'Well, thank you, that's very kind. So you're working for Lola then, not a relation or a friend?'

Dee looked at Mrs Padham. 'That's very well worked out. You should be a detective.'

'Like you, you mean?'

Again Dee was surprised. Almost without realising it, they were moving towards the lane.

'What is it you're doing here, if you don't mind me asking?'

'D'you know, I'm beginning to wonder about that myself. At first, it was just... this...' She waved her arm to encompass the church, with the blackened and sooty part of the churchyard on one side, the green eden on the other. 'Now I'm not so sure.'

'I think my husband was murdered,' Mrs Padham said suddenly.

Dee stopped dead and looked at her. 'I heard he had gone away.'

Mrs Padham shook her head. 'I don't think he did. Oh, I know everyone else finds it easy to believe he tired of me, tired of trying to make the guesthouse pay, and the rest of it. But...'

She looked beaten, exhausted. Dee wanted to hug her. If they had known one another better, perhaps she would have.

'But you don't believe he would have left?' Dee gently finished for her.

Mrs Padham shook her head and looked away. 'He

was lazy, and he liked to spend money. Far too much money. And he hated that we'd come down in the world. But he would never have left me to cope with it all on my own. Never. He loved me in his own funny way. Oh, he wasn't very good at being faithful, but he always came back to me. That's how I know he's dead. He would have come back long ago if he was able.'

'When did you last see him?'

'Nine years ago last January. He'd had his meal and gone out to the pub, I didn't think he'd go because of the snow and it was jolly cold, but he didn't want to miss his darts game. He put his big rubber boots on and kissed me on the cheek and went out. That was the last I saw of him. I asked Pete at the pub the next day, and he said Henry never went there that night. But he never came back home either.'

'Did he take any clothes? Money?'

'Only what he was wearing. And he had less than a pound in his pocket. I know that, because he'd asked me for more, but I didn't have it to spare, and I'd told him that what he had already would be plenty for a drink or two. He had quite a few choice words to say to me about that, but I didn't have the money, so he couldn't take it from me no matter how much he ranted and raved at me.'

'I'm very sorry,' Dee said.

'Do you agree with me, then? You think he might be dead? Is that what usually happens in these sorts of cases? The police—well that Micky Wright, who's a useless waste of space, if you ask me—he just shook his head and said, 'Sorry, Bet, but Henry's left you. That's all there is to it, he's done a runner, with that Maureen Barton.''

'I'm so sorry,' Dee said again, unable to think of

anything more useful to say. 'If you like, I'll tell the Scotland Yard men about it.'

Mrs Padham nodded. 'Thanks. They might be able to find out something, even after all this time. I hear you're his cousin, that chief inspector.'

'He's just an inspector, but yes, I am. He's a good man, he'll help you if he can. In fact they're both good men.'

There was an awkward pause, the point where the conversation had come to a natural end, and neither knew quite what to say or do.

Dee was caught completely off-guard when Mrs Padham put out a hand to just briefly touch her arm, and said,

'I'm sorry we got off on the wrong foot when you came to the guesthouse on Friday. The truth is, I hate that place. And I hate the kind of people who usually come there—workmen, travelling salesmen—they're rude, they get drunk, they bring girls back there. I always worry people will think I'm running a disorderly house. And it's all just so exhausting.'

'I understand, don't worry about it. And if there's anything I can do, don't hesitate to ask.' Not that she knew exactly what she was offering to help with.

Mrs Padham nodded quite seriously, as if that offer might come in useful someday. Then she said,

'Oh my God, look, they're here already!'

And looking in the direction Mrs Padham indicated, Dee could see that men had got into two bulldozers and were about to back them down off the delivery truck, and as soon as they started the engines up, the lane was filled with the deafening noise of them, whilst just outside the gate into the churchyard, a vanload of workmen had arrived and were already unloading equipment—picks and shovels and sledgehammers—all too obviously about to make a start. Beyond them, Nicholas Raynes, in a smart suit and shiny shoes, was just getting out of his sleek blue Jaguar Mk II and coming over to speak to a man who was no doubt a supervisor.

'They're very early,' Dee said, checking her watch. 'It's not even nine o'clock.'

Mrs Padham nodded. 'Aren't they just. That'll be Nick Raynes's idea. He's a distant cousin of mine, and a slippery fellow. You can't trust him an inch. No doubt he thought they'd get started early before anyone was here to make a fuss.'

'Is that legal?'

Mrs Padham shrugged. 'Probably not, but what can anyone do about it afterwards? They can't put it all back, can they?'

Too true, Dee thought.

Even as they watched, with their hearts in their mouths, a bulldozer came slowly but inexorably forward and pushed over the sweetly carved wooden lych-gate, the wood groaning and squeaking as it fell onto its side in a splintered heap. The other bulldozer closed in to take down part of the wall, and the workmen came behind armed with their picks and shovels to clear the debris, like so many ants swarming in set on destruction.

Dee felt a sickening sense of it being all too late to call to a halt. Events had been set in train. Nothing could stand in their way. Perhaps it had always been too late, even before she had arrived on Friday afternoon.

*

Chapter Thirteen

Beside her, Mrs Padham clutched her cardigan around her as if she was cold, her face blanched.

A few other villagers were drifting about in the lane now. Sergeant Wright arrived with two constables by his side, as if they were expecting trouble. Dee didn't think the three of them would be much use, though at the moment everything was still peaceful, if you didn't count the noise.

For the next two hours, Dee and twenty or so villagers—including Clive Barton, Angela Baker, Miss Didsbury, the Merchants, and Doris and Sylvia standing together, arm-in-arm, Doris with a hankie to her eyes—watched the men and the bulldozers as their relentless progress disposed of wall, lych-gate and then, the equipment moved into the churchyard itself to gasps from the watching crowd. The supervisor made a good show of checking the list on his clipboard, and marking off each gravestone that was lifted and removed. But Dee knew it was mere theatrics, they really didn't care a jot.

The bishop had visited briefly just after half past ten, but had gone again, leaving the two officials and the Reverend Riley to oversee everything two hours after work had started. But they did nothing, standing silently in the lane, watching the workmen. At Riley's side was Cynthia Miles-Hudson from the council. A reporter and a cameraman were there from the local newspaper to record the proceedings, meandering back and forth and getting under everyone's feet and chafing tempers already at boiling point.

The mayor also made a fleeting visit, seemed reassured that there was no big protest going on, no villagers actually lying in the path of the bulldozers, and after smiling, waving and glad-handing Nicholas Raynes and Cynthia, he got back into his shiny black Rolls-Royce, waving to no one, and was driven away, able to say he had 'done his bit'.

Dee was restless and chilled now that the sun had disappeared behind the heavy clouds amassing overhead. It looked as though rain might bring everything to a halt, driving away spectators and workmen alike. Dee was thinking fondly of Miss Marriott's morning-room and the possibilities of a cup of tea or coffee, and wondering where Miss Marriott herself was, seeing that Doris was there with Sylvia.

Mrs Padham, beside Dee all this time, suddenly said, 'I think I'll go indoors. I need to sit down, this standing up is doing my bad back no good at all.'

Dee nodded, not sure what to say. The pub wouldn't be open just yet or she'd invite Mrs Padham to go with her for a drink in there.

Mrs Padham said, diffidently, 'If you like, you could come in and have a cup of tea. Oh, there'd be no charge. Not as a guest, I don't mean. As a friend.'

Dee smiled. 'I'd love to. Thank you.'

They went through the door marked 'private' into the part of the guesthouse that was Mrs Padham's own home. The dark corridor led into a bright room, a kitchen, shabby but comfortable, and with a view of a small vegetable patch and a few pots of petunias that were coming to the end of their flowering season.

Mrs Padham immediately filled the kettle and set it on the stove to boil, then got out cups and saucers, mismatched but of a fine old quality. She motioned Dee to a chair at the table. Dee sank down in relief, heaving her bag off her shoulder and dumping it on the floor.

There were a few photos on a picture rail that ran all around the room just two feet below the level of the ceiling. Without getting up and going over to stare at each one, Dee couldn't make out the subjects.

'Do you have any children, Mrs Padham?'

'Two,' she said, bringing the milk and sugar over to set down in the centre of the table. 'Well, you know my Doris, don't you. And then there's my son Peter, though he's up at the docks at Harwich. He only visits every few weeks. But they're good kids.'

Dee was astonished. 'Doris who works for Miss Marriott? She's your daughter?' She didn't know quite why she was so taken aback. She wracked her brains to try to remember if she'd said anything critical or unflattering about Mrs Padham in Doris's hearing. She hoped not. She said, 'Doris is a lovely girl. We've had several conversations. She's so good with Miss Marriott.'

Mrs Padham came over with the teapot and took the seat opposite Dee. She smiled, immediately looking twenty years younger, and now Dee could see the resemblance between mother and daughter.

'Oh yes, Doris is a good girl. And a hard worker. She thinks the world of Miss Marriott.'

'It's mutual, I can tell. Miss Marriott thinks the world of Doris too.'

They were quiet for a moment. A clock on the shelf above the stove ticked loudly. It was the image of a clock in the kitchen of her parents' house, there when she was a child, and she remembered Mrs Greeley the family's beloved cook always complaining about the racket it made. 'Fit to wake the dead', she'd always said, which had made Dee and her 'twin' brother Freddie laugh. History, thought Dee. It's not about ancient kings and far-off wars or treaties. It's about your childhood home and the people who lived there, who shared your life.

'Have you lived here all your life?' she asked.

'Since I was married. My father signed it over to me and Henry. I used to live in the house next door to my Aunt Tilda. Miss Didsbury,' she reminded Dee who nodded. 'That was my parents' house, and that was where I was born, and my two younger brothers. When my parents died, the house was sold and the money split between my brothers. I didn't get a share because my father said I wouldn't need it as I had a husband to take care of me. I was very angry about that.'

'That was dreadfully unfair,' Dee agreed. 'And your brothers didn't share it with you?'

Mrs Padham shook her head. 'One of them may have, but the older of the two, Raymond, he talked Victor out of it. Said they had to respect our father's wishes.'

'What rot!' Dee was indignant, then realised what she had said. 'Oh I'm sorry, it's not up to me to criticise them.'

Mrs Padham shrugged. 'Well, whatever the right or wrong of it was, they both moved away. They invested the money, bought nice houses, made a packet and have comfortable lives, thank you very much. And I never see them. Just a card at Christmas for the last ten years.'

'That's very sad.'

Mrs Padham got up to get more hot water for the teapot. When she came back, she said, 'So what did you think about this morning's carry-on?'

Dee accepted the change of topic. 'I was surprised that it all went so smoothly. I don't quite know what I was expecting, but I certainly thought it might get out of hand like things did in the churchyard on Friday night. But it was surprisingly calm, though horribly efficient.'

'They moved fast, didn't they?' Mrs Padham agreed, heaping sugar into her tea and stirring it vigorously. She took a quick slurp. 'Doris told me she was going to try to keep Miss Marriott away. She's not well enough to get caught up in all that, not at her age.'

'Very true. The mayor didn't stay long, did he? Nor that woman from the historical society.'

'Just so long as they could be seen smiling and nodding. I thought someone from the newspapers would be there.'

'Oh, they were, along with a photographer. I think they were talking to people outside the pub.'

'I missed that. I wonder if the weather will hold off. We've had such an awful lot of rain lately.' Mrs Padham said, and Dee felt that this was her way of winding down the conversation.

After a few more minutes of talking about the weather, Dee thanked her for the tea and said goodbye.

Doris was still watching the work from the far end of the lane. She had a headscarf tied under her chin, and again Dee could see the resemblance to her mother.

Greeting Dee with a smile, Doris said, 'Miss Marriott sent me out to keep an eye on things. It all happened so quick, and no one did anything to challenge them. No protests, nothing. Jimmy Philpott threw some cow dung at the workers but no one got hurt. Sergeant Wright nabbed a couple of fellows who were about to get a bit mouthy with each other. Apart from that, it's been very quiet.'

'Yes, that's surprising, isn't it, after all the outrage and protests? By the way, I've just been having a cup of tea with your mother.'

'Really?' Doris seemed quite astonished. 'That was good of you, thank you, miss. She could do with some company.'

'Doesn't she get much company?'

'Not really.' Doris gave Dee a knowing grin. 'As you've probably noticed, she can be a bit prickly.'

'Well, we had a nice chat.'

'Them London police came looking for you about half an hour ago. I wasn't sure where to tell them to look for you, though I thought you must be around here somewhere. That handsome one, he just grumbled, 'She's usually right there in the middle of any trouble'. But Pete Guthrie came out to tell them they had a call and they had to go off somewhere so they said they'd try to catch you for lunch at the pub. About one-ish, I think they said.'

'Oh.' Dee looked at her watch. It was only just after twelve o'clock. She wasn't sure what to do next.

'Did Mum tell you about Clive Barton?'

Puzzled, Dee shook her head. 'No? What about

him? She didn't mention him.'

'Him and her had a bit of a thing a few years back. That's why my dad left.' Doris looked embarrassed.

Interesting, Dee thought, and mentally filed that away for later. 'Have you ever heard from your father since he left? A letter? A phone call?'

She shook her head. Her voice croaked as she replied. 'Well, I wouldn't, would I? He's dead. I just know he is.' She excused herself, tears in her eyes, and turned to walk back to Miss Marriott's house.

More and more people were gathering to watch what was going on, but soon their curiosity would be thwarted. It became apparent that the metal framework the builders were assembling along the edge of the churchyard were part of a six-foot tall temporary fence. A truck carrying a huge pile of wooden planks inched its way along the lane, the horn warning everyone to get out of its way.

Dee walked over to a workman who was nearby. 'Excuse me,' she said.

The man looked her up and down, leering at her bust. 'I'll do anything, love, even a 'ladies' excuse me'.'

Dee smiled sweetly, even though he was the last man she'd fancy a dance with. 'I just wondered why you were putting up a fence to screen the churchyard off?'

He winked at her. 'Let's just say, the nice people of Hartwell Priory don't want to see arm bones and leg bones poking out of the stuff our diggers turn up, nor skulls rolling along the ground neither. Well, it stands to reason, don't it, darlin'? Some of them bodies have been in the ground two, three hundred years. Don't matter how good your coffin is, if it's wood, it ain't going to last that long.'

She saw exactly what he meant. She nodded. 'Of

course.'

'Now then,' he said. 'How about I buy you a drink later in that pub along there. You know, we could get to know each other better.' He was still staring at her breasts.

She frowned at him now. 'No thank you.' She turned to walk away, and he shook his head in disgust, yelling after her,

'Stuck up cow!'

'Was he talking to you like that?' It was Clive Barton.

Of course it was, she thought, his timing was absolutely bloody perfect, and inwardly, if not outwardly she rolled her eyes. Naturally he was outraged on her behalf, but the last thing she wanted was for him to tackle the workman, intent on defending her honour.

'It's all right, Clive. Don't worry about it, just ignore him.' She almost put her hand on his chest to calm him down, but just in time, thought better of it. There must be something in the water, she thought. All the men here were so volatile.

Remembering what Doris had just told her, she wondered if there was a tactful way to find out if it was true. Tact, however, was not one of her strongest qualities. She was more of a 'take-the-bull-by-the-horns' kind of girl.

'Look here, Clive,' she said, lowering her voice and turning away from the knot of residents standing nearby, 'I know it's none of my business, but...' She almost chickened out, but then remembering Monty and his offer of ten pounds a week, she took a deep breath and said in something of a rush, 'Is it true you were once involved with Bet Padham?'

He was taken utterly by surprise. He stared at her, and she felt she could almost see the cogs turning as he tried to decide whether to quickly concoct a story, or whether it was easier to simply 'come clean', to use a common phrase from Dee's favourite television police drama.

'Yes.'

Dee was glad he'd decided to own up. She waited to see if there was more.

He took her by the arm and steered her away. His head was close to hers as he said in a low voice, 'I'm not sure who told you...'

'Doris.'

'Ah.' He nodded. 'Well, yes it's true. But it was over several years ago, I can assure you of that. She was going through a difficult time, as was I, and we—er—turned to one another for—er—comfort, you might say.'

Dee nodded. 'Of course. Thanks for being so open about it. I do know it's really none of my business. But I would have just kept wondering about it.' Too late, she realised this sounded as though she liked him and was already thinking of him as more than just a friend, or a casual acquaintance.

'Not at all, not at all.'

They'd gone some way along the road. He halted abruptly. 'Look, it's just after half past, so the pub's open now. How about that drink?'

'Super.' Best to get it over with, she decided, and hopefully there'd be a chance to—gently—tell him she wasn't interested in him in that way.

She found a table whilst he went to the bar. There were two men already waiting, so it was a few minutes before he returned with the drinks: a pint of bitter for himself and Dee's usual choice of a Babycham.

She thanked him and took a sip. The bubbles bounced and fizzed and felt zingy on her tongue.

Clive was staring at her. The tension was growing. She broke the tension with the only topic she could think of.

'They're putting up a high fence around the churchyard. That fellow I was just talking to said that it was so that local people wouldn't see the remains of their ancestors as most of the caskets would have rotted away, and it wasn't something most people would have expected.'

'Oh dear. Interesting. Well, of course it's obvious when you think about it, but as you say, it would be upsetting for anyone who was watching.' He drank a little beer. The yeasty waft of it assaulted Dee's nose. She leaned back slightly to escape the smell.

Clive continued, 'I must say, Angela—Mrs Baker—and I weren't too impressed with the gung-ho manner they've gone about things. I mean, literally just bulldozing everything in their path, exactly as we'd always feared, but completely contrary to what they had promised.'

Dee nodded. 'It all happened incredibly quickly. That sweet lych-gate, just flattened and broken to pieces within seconds.'

'They'd dug up six gravestones before the diocese officials arrived two hours early, clearly knowing from previous experience what to expect. The remains may be distributed amongst six new graves, but there will only be the haziest of ideas whose remains are whose.'

'But they promised everyone...'

He nodded, his expression grim. 'I know. And it's all because the work began hours earlier than it should have. Angela is filing a complaint. She says they obviously planned to do things this way from the very start, just to show their might, so to speak.'

'Do you know whose family the graves belonged

to?'

'Not really.' He shrugged. 'The gravestones were so badly worn, and not particularly well cared for, covered with weeds and moss. I know one of them was a relative of Miss Didsbury's, and one was the grave of a young child, it's the first one—or rather it *was* the first one you'd see when you came in at the gate. David William Padham, aged three years and two months. Tragic.'

'Mrs Padham's child?' Dee hazarded. 'Doris mentioned a young brother named Davey.'

He nodded. 'Yes, it was his grave, poor little chap.'

As she took this in, sorrow wrapped itself like a cloak around her shoulders. Her arms prickled with goosebumps, causing her to shiver. Another sip of her cold drink chilled her even more.

'How awful,' she said, in practically a whisper. 'So it must have been a Didsbury plot. Mrs Padham told me she was a Didsbury by birth.'

'Yes. Most of the villagers are related to one another in some way. Not me, I'm afraid, I'm a blow-in. An arrival from outside the area.'

'Are you still working?' Dee asked. 'Or what did you do before you came here?'

'Not working anymore, no. I was in the army. Never excelled at anything especially, never progressed beyond the rank of warrant officer. But I did my twenty-two years' full service and retired at the age of forty. That was when we came here, twelve years ago.' He blushed then, as if he'd realised he'd just told her how old he was and had injured any hope that she might mistake him for a few years younger.

'So your wife wasn't a local girl?'

'Lord no, she was a Londoner through and through. We met at a dance on the base where I was stationed. Her father was in the army too.' He took a rapid swig of his beer then had to suppress a belch. 'Sorry. Went down the wrong way. I do apologise.'

'It's all right.' She made herself smile at him, trying to ignore the yeasty smell again.

'So. What about you? How did you come to be working as a private detective? An odd choice of profession.'

Her mind heard the unspoken words, '...for a woman'.

'It's a new job,' she said. 'I used to teach but I lost my job, and then I realised I didn't fancy teaching anymore. A few months ago, I got tangled up in something down on the Sussex coast, and it seemed as though I might have a flair for it. A friend of the family has a legal practice in London and he offered me work. Solicitors, barristers and so on, they use investigators regularly.'

He nodded in understanding. She knew exactly what he would ask next. He asked it now.

'And no—er—entanglements—of a romantic sort?'

She had to be honest. She hoped he wouldn't be angry. Or hurt. 'Actually yes.'

His face fell. Here goes, she thought. I've got to tell him now.

'I left my husband at the end of last year. He was violent. That was how I came to lose my job—the board of governors were horrified at the idea of a woman in their employment deserting her husband with a view to divorce. But well, I've got a kind of—I suppose you'd say an understanding—with my sort-of cousin. We will have to wait three years, of course, before I can be divorced, but then we can be married.'

She felt a quiver inside. A sudden doubt. *Would* they be married? Did Bill love her enough for that?

Did she, would she, feel ready to be married again? Oh, she couldn't think about that now, she needed to be alone to think about that in private.

Was she imagining that Clive's tone was cooler, that his expression was less confiding, less friendly? He leaned back in his seat, hiding behind his beer-glass, and with a smile that didn't reach his eyes, he said, 'How does one have a 'sort-of' cousin?'

'I was adopted into the family. So we were raised as cousins but there's no actual blood connection.'

'Ah.' He nodded, then fell silent. He was fiddling with the hem of the curtain again. In a moment he'll make an excuse and leave, she thought, resigned to the fact that he was only friendly whilst he thought there was a chance of a romance between them.

'Sorry if you thought...' It was a pointless thing to say but she couldn't help herself.

He shook his head, seemed to shake his whole being. And finally smiled a proper, warm smile. 'It's all right. I'll admit I was hopeful. But... Well, he's a lucky fellow.'

She smiled back, relieved. 'Thank you.' Another sip of Babycham, this time not seeming quite so chilly. 'Coming back to what's going on in the churchyard, have they already dug the new graves to move the bodies into? I thought it was all still under discussion?'

'Well, it is supposed to be. But it's clear they've got tired of waiting for the process to go through, and rather pre-empted the decision.'

'Surely it can be halted if there's a protest from the villagers? What was the point of the meeting the other evening if they'd already planned to just bulldoze the place and—what? Heap up the bones and hope no one seemed to mind?' She pressed her lips together, frowning angrily. 'It's a disgrace.'

'Yes it is. I suspect an under-the-table deal has been done between the council and the builder, that Raynes chap. But to come back to your question, some work has begun on a site, but whether it's ready for the remains to be reinterred, I'm not sure. I can take you there if you like, it's only a ten-minute walk from here.'

She nodded. 'Lovely.'

They drank up and left. He held open the door for her and gave her a big grin, seeming to have recovered from his sense of disappointment. As they walked along the lane, Clive said,

'So is this the same sort-of cousin who is in the village at the moment, looking into the deaths in the churchyard on Friday night?'

It was the perfect moment to ask her that question as the very man was just getting out of a car a few yards ahead of them.

Dee nodded, 'Yes. He's a detective inspector with the London Metropolitan Police, you know, Scotland Yard. You met him at Miss Marriott's on Saturday. And here he is again now.'

Clive shot her a look of what she took for alarm, but quickly schooled his features.

Bill turned to face her as they drew near. He came forward to kiss her on the cheek, a proprietorial hand on her waist for a second. 'Hello Dee. How're things in the churchyard?'

'It's a horrid mess, Bill. They just came in two hours early and started bulldozing away. It was awful.' She took a step back from him. 'Bill, this is Clive Barton. He's a resident of the village and a member of the local history society. He's about to show me where the new graveyard is situated. Clive, this is Detective Inspector Bill Hardy.'

The two men exchanged what she could only

describe to herself as 'measuring' looks as they shook hands and although outwardly polite and friendly, she could tell they had taken an instant dislike to one another.

'Mind if I tag along?' Bill asked, and of course, she *did* mind, and so did Clive, she was certain. They made neutral, nondescript sounds, and he gave a quick instruction to his driver and fell in step with them.

'Where's Nat?' Dee asked. 'Detective Sergeant Nahum Porter,' she told Clive, who gave a resentful nod. 'He's Bill's right-hand man and a good friend of ours. He was at Miss Marriott's too.'

'That the black fellow?' Clive asked, immediately going down in her estimation for the dismissive way he said it.

'Yes,' Dee said. 'He's of Trinidadian descent.'

'An excellent fellow, I'm very lucky to have him. Excellent people skills, decades of experience,' Bill added, narrowing his eyes as he looked at Clive.

Clive nodded. 'It takes all sorts, I suppose.'

They fell into an irritable silence for the rest of the way. When they reached the end of the lane, instead of going down the hill to Everard's farm, they crossed the main road and walked a little way along on the grass verge. Dee noticed trails of mud down the middle of the road. Clearly the diggers had been along here already.

'Here we are,' Clive said. On their right was a hedge. In the middle of the hedge was a stile to step up and over. They did so now, both men preceding Dee then both turning to hold up a hand to help her to jump down on the other side. Inwardly Dee sighed again. She hoped this wasn't going to turn into some kind of competition. She held out a hand to each of them and jumped down.

'And here we are,' Clive said again.

In front of them was a large green field. At the far end, away to their left, a long section of the hedge near the road had been removed to allow access by the vehicles. No graves had been dug as yet, but a large area of the top grassy layer had been removed and the grass stacked up. And beside it on a tarpaulin, was another heap, brown and greyish white from here.

'What on earth...?' Dee said and began to run across the field to see it.

When she got there, the impact of what she saw made her gasp, her hands coming to her face. Tears threatened. There, on the outspread tarpaulin, lay a heap of dirt containing a selection of bones. A tiny skull lay by itself where it had rolled to the far corner of the first tarpaulin.

'Oh!' she said, distress hitting her suddenly. For even though these were not the remains of her own family, she could imagine Doris and Bet being devastated by the sight. 'How could they do such a thing?'

*

Chapter Fourteen

She half-expected Bill to cancel their lunch together but eventually he arrived, twenty minutes late and before he even sat down, he was apologising that he couldn't stay long. By now Dee had had the chance to compose herself after seeing the casual heap of discarded remains. But her sense of outrage and sorrow on behalf of the descendants persisted.

'What's happening?'

'I left that Barton chap there to wait for the local police. I'm concerned that local residents will hear about the bones. So I ran all the way here to telephone from the pub's back room. Er—shall we order? I can't be long.'

'You need to eat,' she said. 'And it's not as though there's been another murder.'

He shrugged. 'I know. But two murders already and now this. And the stupid thing is, I don't even know if it's actually illegal or merely—you know—an immoral, despicable thing to do. I'm waiting for advice from on high. I'm having the cod and chips, by the way. And a coffee. What do you want?'

'Oh I'll have the same.' She knew he didn't mean to sound so brusque, his mind was elsewhere. It wasn't exactly a romantic dinner for two anyway, just a quick lunch. 'I'll go and order it, you relax for a moment.'

'Certainly not. I can put mine on expenses.' He was out of his seat, about to head over to the bar.

She gave him a cheeky grin. 'So can I!'

But he went over to the bar to give their order, his male ego too outraged at the idea of her paying for him. He was back almost immediately. He smiled his warm smile that lit up his eyes and smoothed away the grumpy line between his brows. He was a real dish, she thought, and not for the first time.

'Sorry to be so irritable. And not that it makes any difference, but I think Monty made an excellent choice in giving you this job.'

She was taken completely by surprise. 'Thank you.'

It did her good to know he thought that. Reflecting it was always nice to know your loved ones appreciated your talents, she beamed at him. Their eyes met, he reached for her hand, lifted it to his lips and kissed it, quickly, discreetly.

'As I said last night, I'm so glad you're here. Just—do be careful, won't you, love? There's a killer on the loose. Don't lose sight of that in the middle of this other thing.'

'I won't. And you be careful too. That warrant card doesn't make you invincible, you know.'

He nodded. 'I really want to talk to you about everything. I'm assuming you've been interrogating suspects and picking up clues. You probably have all the answers I've been looking for. I meant to ask you more last night, but I just... didn't. Though when I'm going to have the time to actually sit down and talk it over with you, God knows.'

'What happened to 'stay out of my case'?' She smiled at him as she said it, teasing.

He grunted. 'I suppose I'm becoming resigned to the situation.' He glanced across to where the barman was lifting the flap to come over with their food. 'I'm not happy about it—you know how much I worry about you. But even I can see that you're good at this kind of thing. As you know, I'm not good with people, whereas you are. I'm selfishly hoping that your investigation can help mine. They do seem inextricably linked.'

The barman put their plates down in front of them, brought over salt and pepper and vinegar, and said he'd be back momentarily with their coffees. When he left, Dee replied, saying,

'As I've said before, when Monty first told me about it, he said he'd had a letter from a client asking him to find out who that beatnik bunch were referring to in their séances when they said something about the new one not being left behind. But to me, that seems so vague, and... I just don't buy it, as they say on *The Man From U.N.C.L.E.*'

He grinned. 'You watch that?'

She shrugged. 'Of course. It's got David McCallum in it. You know I've a weakness for blond men.' She glanced at his dark hair and eyes, managing to appear unimpressed.

That comment brought out his grumpy side again, but she just laughed at him, nudging his knee with her own. The barman came over with their coffees on a tray, a milk jug and a bowl of sugar lumps. He departed with the empty tray, scattering loose sugar crystals all over the floor. That would become very sticky later, Dee thought, irrelevantly. She immediately reached for a sugar cube. Not that she took sugar in her coffee. She dipped it in the coffee and then popped it into her mouth, crunching it delightedly. Inspector Grumpy shook his head and reluctantly smiled.

'You're such a child. Now. About this case you're on...?'

'Oh yes. Well, like I told you, all I know is the client who wrote to Monty was Miss Marriott. But when I got here, she actually didn't seem as perturbed as the letter seemed to suggest, and she was a bit surprised I was there.' She shook her head. 'I don't know.' She ate one chip, then another, staring into space as she thought it over. 'I'd almost think Monty made up the whole thing just as an excuse to give me ten pounds. Except that, now, with these murders, everything suddenly seems far less silly and far more sinister. But perhaps just writing the letter was enough to calm Miss Marriott's fears? And she did insist on going to both the meeting and the churchyard that evening.' She squeezed her lemon quarter over the fish, then swamped her remaining chips with vinegar.

Bill was doing the same. She looked at him closely again.

'Nice suit,' she said. 'Another new one?'

He looked down at it as if to say, what, this old thing. Then said, 'Yes. Mother told me to replace the fawn one. She said she hates me in brown, and that one of the cuffs was fraying. So...'

'Aunt Dottie is right. You look awful in brown. Even light brown. Whereas in that grey, Inspector, you look good enough to eat.'

She spoke lightly, without thinking, but his gaze arrested her and she felt a frisson of tension. She made a show of rolling her eyes, and said waspishly,

'Not everything's about sex.'

'Then it damn well should be.' But he glanced away, reaching out to steal one of her chips—the biggest—and shoving it into his mouth whole, laughing out loud at her look of outrage.

'That's police brutality! Or—or something.'

They ate in a companionable silence for the next few minutes. As always, she had to resist the urge to just gaze at him. Get a hold of yourself, woman, she thought. He ate as if he had a taxi waiting outside, and she remembered he'd said he couldn't be too long.

'Will you do me a favour?' he asked a little while later. He pushed his now-empty plate aside and stole another chip from her plate.

'Depends what it is.' She narrowed her eyes, automatically wary.

'Ask Miss Marriott exactly why she wrote to Monty to ask for help. Find out what she thought he'd be able to do. I'm just—intrigued.'

'All right,' she agreed. 'But now I want you to tell me something—I want to know exactly what Tristan Summers said at his séances. There have been two or three of them, and I'm really interested in why he did it. Not just him, the whole group of them. I've spoken to a couple of them and they said that he was just their college tutor, that they had thought it would be a fun way to spend the summer.' She shook her head, puzzling over it afresh. Unable to finish her food, she set her plate to one side, putting her coffee cup in front of her. Bill obligingly polished off her last four or five chips, swiping them with his fingers rather than the knife and fork he'd been given.

'Why does it bother you so much?'

She shook her head. 'I don't really know. All I know is, either he planned it as a joke, or as some kind of a con, or as some kind of political or philosophical protest, or he genuinely believed what he said.'

'I don't see how it could be used to make any money, so the idea of a con is out,' Bill said, munching chips as he pondered this.

'That's why I don't really believe it was a con. Or even a protest of some kind. I could almost see it as a kind of a joke or cruel trick, but even then...' She heaved a great sigh. 'It's so frustrating. I just keep coming back to this over and over again. He was a philosophy lecturer, and his specialty was belief systems and religion. So I wonder if he might have believed that what he said was true. Some of the girls seemed to really believe in it. Therefore, it follows that we need to know exactly what he said, who he said it to, and why.'

She slumped in her seat, thinking hard. His hand came over hers.

'We'll get there. I'll see what I can find out. Not sure how much I'll be able to tell you, of course, but I'll see.'

He was on his feet, ready to leave. She looked up at him, once more thinking how gorgeous he was. Their eyes locked again, but he smiled and the tension fizzled out, leaving just a warm affection.

'Right. I've got to go and see the mayor and the local chief superintendent. And I've got to find my sergeant. I left him to tackle Raynes, the builder chap, again on the terms of his contract and so forth. Oh, and I need to make sure that the local police are keeping the hordes at bay and have relieved your boyfriend of his post.'

'He's not my boyfriend,' Dee grumbled, arms folded.

He bent to kiss her cheek. 'He'd better not be.'

As he was about to leave, Dee commented, 'I don't know if you already know this, or even if it matters, but two of the people in the beatnik group are Clive's children.'

He looked surprised. 'Really?'

'Yes. They go by Bartholomew and Janna, but really they are just plain old Barry and Jane.'

He nodded. 'Interesting. I'll bear it in mind. Right, behave yourself. I'll try to come to the house later this evening. It might be quite late. Is that going to be all right with your Miss Marriott, do you think?'

She nodded. 'I'm sure she won't mind. Bye for now.'

She blew him a kiss and watched him smirk at her then turn and walk away.

'I take it you're paying then, miss?'

It was the barman. With the bill for their food.

'I thought he paid when he ordered?'

'No miss, I said I'd bring the bill over when you'd finished eating as I had to give your order to the kitchen and I had someone else waiting for drinks.'

'Hmm. I suppose he just forgot, he was in a bit of a hurry.' She sighed. 'Yes, I suppose I am paying, then.'

Bill Hardy was almost at the main road when he remembered he hadn't paid for the food. He could have kicked himself. He stood there for a minute debating whether or not to go back.

Dee would probably not have the wherewithal to pay even though it wasn't a huge expense, but he knew things had been difficult lately. Surely the barman would put it on the tab for the room, wouldn't he? And although she had said something about having an expense account, he didn't know if she was just joking, or...

'Hello Inspector. I've just been relieved by your

men.'

It was Clive Barton, sauntering towards him, his hands in his trouser pockets, cool, calm and collected. Hardy thrust aside his sudden rush of jealous anger. He really must control himself, he thought. And he smiled a pleasant, if rather wooden, professional smile.

'Mr Barton. I'm glad they finally got there. Thank you for your help.'

Barton had now reached him, and they stood there. Barton jingled his loose change.

Hardy said, 'Though I should just add, that they're all locals, not my chaps at all. I can't take any credit.'

'Of course. Just an expression, I didn't mean anything by it,' Barton said irritably. Which of course put Hardy on the wrong foot for being overly pedantic. And made him more irritable too.

'Actually I'd like to ask you a couple more questions, if I may,' he said now.

'Fire away.' Barton seemed in no particular rush to leave, although his eyes narrowed and his easy smile came nowhere near reaching them.

'Here? Or at your home later?'

'Here's fine.'

Hardy was annoyed with himself for giving Barton the option. Now, if he needed to make any notes, he'd have to do it standing up. And really all he could think of to ask at that moment was a rather Old-Testament-style, *what are your intentions towards Miss Gascoigne*? And if Dee got to hear of it, she'd be furious with him. He really needed to get a grip on his emotions.

'Hmm.' Then inspiration came. 'Yes. I understand that two of the beatnik group who carried out the—er—rather impromptu séances are actually your children.'

Barton seemed annoyed by that, but he said smoothly, 'Yes, that's right. It's not a secret. One of the appeals of this venture was the opportunity to be in the area where they grew up.'

That felt like a point to Barton, Hardy thought. He nodded and tried to look as though he was thinking. 'Did they speak to you about the night Tristan Summers and Serafina Rainbow were killed?'

'Only in passing. We agreed it had been a dreadful tragedy.'

'I see. And did you yourself witness the attacks on Summers or the woman?'

'No. I'm afraid I was on the other side of the churchyard, in a discussion with Mrs Angela Baker, the chairwoman of the historical society I'm a member of. She had been a speaker at the meeting in the pub that evening.'

'The meeting that broke up when someone burst in and announced the séance in the churchyard?'

'Yes.'

'Was the séance planned in advance, do you know? Was it general knowledge?'

Barton shrugged. 'You'd have to ask the kids. But I hadn't heard anything about it, certainly. Not that they'd necessarily confide in me. They'd done one a few weeks earlier actually there in the church, which I wasn't too pleased about. But I'm not sure there would have been any planning, as such.'

Hardy nodded. He was silent, thinking.

Barton said, 'I think they've all left now, anyway. Not mine, but the others. The—er—beatniks as you called them. I think they've gone.'

Hardy was startled. 'Surely they were told not to leave the village until the case was resolved?'

Again Barton shrugged. 'I really couldn't say.'

Hardy nodded. 'Of course not. Well, thank you for

your time. And for guarding the field over there until reinforcements arrived.'

'Think nothing of it, inspector. Oh, and by the way, the local chief superintendent and the assistant chief constable arrived, along with the mayor and someone from the bishop's office. They all arrived about half an hour ago, I suppose it was, in their cars. I think they're anxious to speak with you.'

He smirked as he said it, and Hardy with a final thank you, took off almost at a run, arriving breathlessly a few minutes' later.

They were all gathered there, in their nice shiny brand-new wellington boots, surveying the scene whilst several surly workmen stood shuffling their feet and growing increasingly impatient beside their discarded tools. Three uniformed police constables stood in front of them, and Hardy wondered how long it would be before there was a full-scale tussle.

He pulled out his warrant card as he approached, stating, 'Good afternoon. I'm Detective Inspector Hardy of Scotland Yard.'

The chief superintendent introduced himself—he and Hardy had only spoken on the phone—then he introduced the assistant chief constable of the county's police force, the mayor, and two senior officials from the town council, along with the bishop who had, he said, 'dropped everything' as soon as he'd heard. Nicholas Raynes hovered behind them, clearly not sure of his exact role, and looking like a man who would rather be anywhere else than here.

'Well, well, this is something of a disaster, isn't it, Hardy?'

Bill nodded. 'I'm afraid things don't seem to be going to plan, sir.'

'And where have you been? Having a leisurely lunch with your girlfriend? That's not what I expected to hear when I arrived under circumstances such as these.'

Barton had tattled, then. Again Bill felt wrong-footed.

'I had a very quick lunch, yes. Sir,' he added hastily. 'And the woman is not my girlfriend. She is staying in the village and had some information for me.'

The chief super looked politely sceptical. 'What information was that?'

'It related to the group who carried out the séances in the village, two members of which were murdered.'

'And?' The chief super conveyed in that one simple word his irritation at having his own lunch cut short to stand here in the mud listening to a man he deemed far too young to have been promoted to the rank of inspector.

'Well, she told me that two of the group are the children of Mr Clive Barton whom you will have seen here when you arrived just now.'

The ACC now said, 'I don't see what help that is. Is that all you've come up with so far?'

Bill tried not to let them see him floundering. 'And an elderly resident of the village, a Miss Marriott, wrote to her lawyer in London to ask for help in finding something out from this beatnik lot.

'Find out what?'

'I was on my way to speak to the lady when I heard what had happened here.'

'Hmm.' The ACC and the chief super both glared at Hardy, before exchanging a look. Then the ACC said,

'Now look here, Hardy. I know it may seem a little—unusual—to see the remains of a couple of disinterred bodies from the churchyard handled in this way. Even, as it might appear to the layman's eye, simply dumped in a heap. But there was an unfortunate accident with one of the mechanical diggers, as the supervisor has just explained to me. You would have heard this for yourself if you'd been here instead of at the pub. So that's how this-er—unfortunate—er—this happened. There's no real harm done, and we've been assured that measures have been taken to ensure all is well. Now, we really must just let these good gentlemen get on with their work. The sooner we get out of their way, the sooner those remains can be moved to their proper place.'

'But there's nowhere for the remains to be put at the moment, sir. And no diocesan officials were on hand to offer guidance because the workmen started two hours before the agreed time.'

'Well, what's done is done. You need to concentrate on finding out who killed those two dropouts and let everyone else get on with their jobs too,' the chief super told him.

'But sir, if local residents get to hear about this, I'm concerned there will be another protest. People will be outraged at the way their deceased relatives have been treated.'

The ACC and the chief super exchanged another look, and the ACC nodded at the mayor who was about to step forward. The mayor stayed put.

'Now then, get on with your work, laddie,' the ACC growled. 'Or I'll be speaking to your superiors. I don't know what you're allowed to get away with in London. But here in Essex, we don't allow police college graduates with practically no experience to talk back to seasoned senior police ranks. Is that understood?'

'Yes sir.' He held in his frustration, keeping his expression bland.

'Now get back to finding out who killed those

dropouts the other evening. Probably one of their own group, I shouldn't wonder. Doubtless they are all on some drug or another.'

'Sir.'

They didn't budge. It was Hardy who had to turn—inwardly seething—and walk back to the village.

*

Chapter Fifteen

As soon as he reached the edge of the village, Hardy found himself confronted by a group of half a dozen or so men who were clearly heading towards the new burial site at full pelt. There was no doubt in his mind that they were furiously angry, and in no mood for reasonable conversation. But he had to try. He grabbed the arm of the last man, pulling him to a halt and saying,

'I'm Detective Inspector Hardy from Scotland Yard. I must urge you all to rethink your actions.' The group paused to look back at him. 'All of you,' he went on, 'it won't do you any good at all to...'

But he got no further. The man he had grabbed swung out of his grip, then turned back to shove Hardy onto the ground. Before he could get up, two more had come back and kicked him in the stomach and side before they all rushed off. It was over almost as soon as it had begun, and Hardy fell back against the road, doubled up in agony, and as he looked back to where the rabble had come from, he saw Clive Barton glance back at him then hurry inside, as keen as ever to get away from anything that looked like trouble. He rolled onto his knees, reeling in pain, his head swimming.

Two women hurried over to help him up. One tried to persuade him he needed to go into her house and lie down on the sofa whilst she sent for the doctor. It was probably wise advice but he declined as politely as he could manage and hobbled to the pub, clutching his side as he went, hardly daring to breathe due to the pain.

'We're closing in fifteen... Oh sorry, sir, it's you. Your other half is at the usual table.' The barman had his hands full with dirty glasses so nodded in the direction of the table.

Hardy felt a momentary sense of elation fizzle away as he realised it was Nat Porter, not Dee, sitting there, halfway through a late lunch. Porter was already on his feet as Hardy limped over and slowly, carefully, lowered himself into a seat.

'What happened?'

Hardy told him. As soon as he heard about the attack, Porter was on his feet again, running to the bar and shouting to the barman to call a doctor. Then he helped Hardy up the stairs to his room. It seemed to take forever; every slight jolt was unbearable.

'Your lunch...' Hardy pointed out.

Porter shrugged. 'I've had most of it.'

There was a knock at the door.

'Good lord, that was quick. Here's your patient, Doctor.' Porter stepped aside to allow the doctor to enter—a young man for once rather than the usual grizzled doctor approaching his retirement.

'I was already on my way, Mrs Padham phoned me a few minutes ago.'

They helped Hardy off with his jacket, tie and shirt. The doctor poked and prodded with cold fingers, then told Hardy he could get dressed again.

'I'm fairly sure there's nothing broken. Though I'd like to see you when the swelling goes down just to be sure. In fact I've half a mind to send you for an X-ray now...'

'I haven't got time for that, doctor. Can you give me some painkillers? This hurts like a bugger.'

'Did you see who did it?' the doctor asked, handing him a bottle of pills from his leather bag. 'Take one every four hours today and tomorrow, but no more than eight in a twenty-four-hour period.'

Hardy nodded. Then said, 'Sorry, I don't know who they were. Men from the village, that's all I know.'

Porter helped him to get his arms into the sleeves of his shirt and jacket then helped him with the buttons.

'Good thing I'm here, sir.'

Hardy nodded then let out a groan of pain as he tottered onto his feet to tuck his shirt into his trousers. 'Ugh. Yes, you'll make some lucky chap a fine wife someday.' He groaned in pain as he lowered himself onto the bed, gathering up his tie and simply stuffing it in his pocket.

Porter laughed. 'Bloody cheek.'

The doctor said goodbye and left them to it. Porter went for a glass of water so Hardy could take one of his painkillers. When he'd taken it, he lay back against the pillows and closed his eyes, hoping it wouldn't be too long before the pill started to take effect. He was already wishing he'd let the doctor drive him to the hospital just six miles away. He began to tell Porter all about the new burial site and what he, Dee and Barton had seen there, then about going back after lunch and seeing all the local dignitaries there. Porter was suitably disgusted. Hardy went on to say,

'The two women who helped me, I'm fairly sure one was Doris, the maid at Miss Marriott's where Dee is staying. Would you go along and just ask her if she saw the men who attacked me and get their names and addresses? I think I'll just stay here for a bit. I don't feel as though I could move, much less interview witnesses. And I'm pretty sure it was Clive Barton who told the men what was going on at the new site. He was in the village too, watching them attack me.'

'If the local men go up there while the ACC and chief super, among others, are still there, well sir, we'll have missed a good old-fashioned punch-up, I reckon.'

Hardy sighed. 'I can't seem to work out what's going on, Nat. I just...' He shook his head and immediately winced.

Porter said, 'I'll go and find out what Doris saw, if anything.'

'If it *was* Doris.'

'If it was Doris,' Porter agreed. 'And I'll get the barman to bring you up a good strong cup of coffee. I'm thinking you're going to need it.'

'Thanks.'

Porter was only away for twenty minutes. He found Hardy sitting on the side of the bed, looking no better than when he'd left.

'Perhaps you have got a broken rib or two, after all?' Porter suggested.

Hardy was in too much pain to shrug his shoulders, so he simply said, 'What did you find out?'

'Well, sir,' Porter said, perching on the edge of the bed. Hardy gritted his teeth as the additional weight caused the mattress to dip. 'It was Doris you saw—and she was with her mother, a Mrs Padham who also lives in the village. Mrs Padham runs a guesthouse and had come out to get some milk from the shop, and Doris was also going to the shop on an errand for Miss Marriott. They met one another outside and stood chatting for a few minutes. Anyway, they both say they definitely saw three men standing over you. She said they didn't see which one it was that pushed to you to the ground, so they aren't witnesses to that. But they both saw one Jimmy Philpott and a Paddy Jones kick you when you were down. The third man was William Whittaker. Then they saw the three men, with several others, heading off up towards the main road. I asked both ladies—Mrs Padham was at Miss Marriott's for a cup of tea in the kitchen with her daughter—if they saw Clive Barton talking to the men. They said no, they didn't actually see him speak to them, but Mrs Padham said she glanced back and saw Mr Philpott give a thumbs-up to Mr Barton and Mr Barton waved back.'

'That's something, I...'

There was a sudden pounding on the door. Porter opened it. Sergeant Wright was there, looking either very agitated or excited, Hardy couldn't tell which.

'Can you come? Tempers have all boiled over at the new graveyard. I need any extra men I can get.'

'He can't help,' Porter said, getting to his feet and nodding at Hardy. 'He's already been attacked. But I'll go with you.' Porter immediately grabbed his jacket and put on his hat.

'Porter!'

'Sir?'

'Be careful.'

'I will, sir.'

Hardy nodded. 'All right. Come back and get me in two hours, will you.'

'Two hours?' Porter couldn't help sounding dubious.

Wright was fidgeting, raring to go. 'Come on.'

'Yes, two hours. I want to speak to those idiots myself,' Hardy called out as they turned to leave.

The door closed behind them, and Hardy leaned back against the pillows, and as he settled himself, the pain caused some choice words to relieve his frustration as he tried to get comfortable.

Doris bustled in with the afternoon tea—just for Miss Marriott and Dee today, no guests had been invited.

'You'll never guess what!' she announced as she took everything off the huge tray she'd carried in and set it out neatly on the drawing-room coffee table.

'What?' Miss Marriott smiled at her. 'You seem very excited, whatever it is.'

Doris looked shamefaced. 'Oh I didn't mean to sound so excited, ma'am, it's terrible really. Someone told everyone in the pub that the remains dug up from the churchyard had been chucked in a heap in the new graveyard field. No new graves were ready, so there's just a heap of bones and skulls and such all rolling about.'

'We already knew that,' Miss Marriott told her. 'Miss Dee was one of the first to find that out.'

Dee had told Miss Marriott about the heap of bones, but she hadn't said a word about the tiny skull she'd seen, not wanting to upset either Miss Marriott or more particularly, Doris by making her think it might be her brother's. To Dee, it seemed entirely possible that it was little Davey's.

'But did you know that a bunch of blokes from the pub decided they'd go up there and find out what's going on? And when that handsome policeman—the fellow from London—tried to stop them, they knocked him to the ground and kicked him. The inspector, I mean. That other fellow came here just now to talk to me and Mum, as we were right there when it happened and ran to help him, the one who got hurt, I mean. The sergeant's rather dishy too. A bit older, but there's something about him.'

Dee thought she was going to be sick. She ran from the room to the nearest W.C. in the back hall. She wasn't actually sick but she stood there for several minutes, clutching the cold edge of the basin and willing herself not to faint. The rushing in her ears, and the lurching sensation in her stomach calmed. Oh, but Bill...

'Are you all right, miss?' Doris knocked on the door. 'I'm so sorry I just blurted it out like that. I didn't think. Miss Marriott just told me who he is. I'm so...'

Dee opened the door. 'It's all right, don't worry.'

'...sorry. Oh miss, you went that white, I thought you were going to faint.'

'So did I.' Now tears threatened. Dee stemmed a couple that escaped.

'Let me help you, miss.' Doris insisted on supporting Dee back to the drawing-room like an invalid. Miss Marriott was no longer there. But before Dee could ask, Doris said, 'She's gone to telephone. There now, you sit yourself down.' Doris fussed over her the way she fussed over Miss Marriott, and Dee felt like a fraud. A silly, hysterical fraud.

'Right, now, here's a nice cup of tea for you. I've put a spoon of sugar in for the shock. Just you get that into you.'

'Doris!' Miss Marriott called.

Dee's heart seemed to sink, pounding, into the pit of her stomach. Was Miss Marriott just calling Doris for the normal help she gave, or did she have terrible news she needed help breaking to Dee?

Her hand trembled, and the cup tipped slightly, slopping tea all over the front of her dress. She fumbled for a napkin to blot it with, and the simple act of doing that helped to steady her nerves. She set the napkin aside, had two gulps of the remaining tea then sat to await Miss Marriott's painfully slow approach.

Before she was even in the room, the old lady was speaking.

'Dee, dear, he's all right. I've just spoken to Peter Guthrie the publican. He says the doctor has seen your young man and given him some painkillers and he's resting. The doctor doesn't think there's anything broken, though he is very badly bruised.'

By this time, Doris was supporting the old woman to lower herself onto the sofa. Dee, greatly relieved, though keen to see him for herself, thanked her profusely.

'Perhaps pop along to see him when you've had your tea. If you're anything like me, you'll need to see him for yourself to be satisfied he's all right.'

'I will, thank you.' With a deep sigh, she sank back against the sofa cushions and closed her eyes. She used the phrase that seemed to come in useful so often lately:

'Bloody men.'

Doris and Miss Marriott both laughed.

'He's in room three, miss,' the publican told her.

She thanked him and hurried up the stairs. The door was right opposite her as she came up the first flight. It wasn't locked. She tapped softly and went straight in.

He was asleep. Rather, she hoped he was asleep. He looked terrible, his usually good and clear complexion a rather terrifying kind of concrete-greyish-green. She sat on the edge of the bed and took his hand.

'Bill?' she whispered.

He opened one eye then the other, and stared at her, his focus hazy, his grin lopsided when it came.

'Deedee, my darling!' He spoke as if they hadn't seen each other for years.

'I've just heard what happened. I...'

'Kiss me.'

She stared at him. 'What?'

'Kiss me. Please. I just really need you to kiss me.'

'I don't want to hurt you.'

He shook his head then groaned at the pain that travelled through his body.

She leaned forward and tentatively kissed his cheek, but he turned his head and intercepted her lips, locking his mouth on hers. The kiss became passionate, lengthy, their first ever such kiss. When she drew away, they stared at one another for a few seconds, both breathing heavily.

'Just what the doctor ordered,' he laughed. 'I feel better already.'

'Oh shush,' she said getting up. 'You always turn everything into a joke.'

He grabbed her hand then had to fall back onto the bed with a yelp of pain.

'I'm sorry. Please sit down again.'

She did, and took his hand in both of hers. 'Where's Nat?'

'He's gone with Wright up to the new burial site. As expected, the locals are revolting. Hopefully they'll do me a favour and deck the local chief super and the ACC before Wright, Nat and a few local constables lay them out with their truncheons.'

'Why?'

He told her about his meeting at the burial site with the local top brass, and the instructions he'd been given, not to mention the manner in which they had been given, and from which his pride was still smarting. However, he didn't tell her that he thought her precious Clive Barton had been the one to pass on the information to the men in the village. But it cheered him greatly to see how angry and indignant she was on his own behalf.

'I should be working,' he said, attempting to sit up straight. 'I don't think these painkillers are doing anything apart from making me drowsy.'

She grabbed the bottle from the bedside table and read the instructions.

'There's nothing here to say you can't have some good old-fashioned aspirin with them.'

'Just not a good old-fashioned Old Fashioned,' he said with a smirk. 'Some alcohol might have helped.'

She took his hand again. 'Do you know the identity of the men who did this?'

'Yes. Nat got the information from Doris.'

'Ah yes, she mentioned Nat speaking to her. She seems quite taken with him.'

Bill rolled his eyes, the only part of him he could move without being shot through with pain. 'He has that effect on women.'

'So do you, you know you do. I'm sure you the only reason you solve any crimes is because women can't wait to tell you everything they know.'

'What about my clever mind and my unerring instincts?'

She shrugged them away and laughed.

He rolled his eyes again. 'Another kiss? I've been

very brave, you know.'

'No,' she said. 'Not if you're going to get all worked up again.'

'What I really want is a lot more than that, so I think a mere kiss is a huge compromise on my part.'

She smiled, and leaned in to kiss his cheek, making sure she leaned back again quickly to avoid a repeat of his earlier trick.

'You've got to wait.'

He groaned. 'I suppose, on the bright side, it's now only two and a half years.'

'Exactly.' She got up. 'Right, is there anything you need? Apart from the obvious,' she warned him on seeing his expression.

He shook his head. 'No, I'm fine. I'm going to have a quick nap and then hopefully wake up ready for action. See you later, I hope?'

She said he would, and at the door just before leaving, she turned back to blow him a kiss.

*

Chapter Sixteen

Miss Marriott was still having tea when Dee arrived back. Doris was dispatched for a fresh pot of tea, pausing as she went to say over her shoulder,

'It's no bother, not in the least, the kettle's already boiling.' She was back again almost immediately, depositing the teapot close to Dee's right hand then returning to the kitchen.

'I feel such a fraud,' Dee said, as she had earlier, accepting the large slice of cake that Miss Marriott cut for her. 'You've been so kind. It's not as if it was me who was hurt.'

'But it was someone you care about. In any case, my dear, it does us all good to be a little spoiled now and again. And how is your beloved? Or shouldn't I say such things?'

'You shouldn't really,' Dee said with a smile. 'After all I am still married. And who knows what might happen over the next two and a half years? But actually, Miss Marriott, I've been meaning to ask... I wondered if you'd mind me asking you a few questions. For starters, why did you ask Monty to come down here? What was it you really thought he could do?'

Miss Marriott set aside her cup and surveyed Dee with what seemed like a sorrowful air. She was shaking her head. Dee was afraid she'd offended her generous hostess.

'Oh my dear. I'd hoped you would let that drop. Or that you might have worked it out for yourself by now.'

Dee stared at her. 'I don't...'

'I can't answer your question, Dee dear.'

Dee still didn't understand.

'It wasn't me who wrote to Monty. It was Doris.'

Dee managed to shut her mouth; she realised she was sitting there with it open as she tried to fathom Miss Marriott's meaning. 'I still...'

'When you knocked on the door on Friday, it was something of a shock, I must admit. You see, I knew nothing about the letter until that moment. And Doris, bless the child, after she'd sent the letter—and that was a good two weeks ago—she had second thoughts. She wondered if she ought to write again—still posing as me, of course—and say that everything was all right, and that Monty shouldn't trouble himself. But, as she told me when you arrived, when there was no reply, and no one telephoned or arrived at the house, she convinced herself that the letter had got lost in the post and so there was no need to write another. Silly child. I doubt you noticed when you arrived just how upset she was. She'd just had to confess everything to me, and then she was terrified I'd dismiss her. As if I'd do any such thing.'

Dee nodded slowly. She did remember noting that Doris looked upset. Now it made sense, she thought.

'I'm rather surprised Monty didn't realise it wasn't your handwriting.'

'Doris writes all my letters for me. Usually I dictate them, of course. But you see I can't hold a pen properly because of my arthritis. And she has done letters to Monty for me before, so if he even noticed the handwriting at all, which I doubt, it's no different to that of my previous correspondence.'

Nodding, Dee leaned back, mulling this over. 'So then was it you or was it Doris, who was worried about the séances, and what Tristan Summers meant by the things he said?'

'It was Doris.' Miss Marriott offered Dee the plate of small cakes. The plate shook violently, being too heavy for her to hold. Dee quickly chose a lemon tart and then took the plate from Miss Marriott and set it down before there was an accident.

'Was she worried about her baby brother being dug up?'

'No. I mean, that is a concern, naturally. But not the main one. No, it's a bit worse than that. You remember I told you that Henry Padham left a few years back? Doris's father?'

'Mrs Padham told me she thinks he's dead,' Dee said, licking lemon curd from her fingertip. 'And Doris...'

'Yes, Doris believes that too. And because she knows that Clive Barton had a bit of a fling with Bet Padham, well, I think Doris honestly believes that Henry is in Maureen Barton's grave.'

Dee thought about this. She could see that she'd need to pop into the kitchen in a few minutes and have another chat with Doris.

'Did Henry Padham disappear at the time that Maureen Barton died?'

'Yes. That's why people always said they ran away

together. It had been known for some time that they were 'seeing' each other, as I believe the saying goes.'

'So Doris thinks that Clive killed Henry? Is that how it is?'

Miss Marriott shrugged. It seemed that the conversation was over when she gingerly got to her feet and edged towards the door. She hovered by the door, looking back to Dee.

'Who knows? It was a long time ago now. I think poor Doris should try to put it out of her head. As one gets older one realises that there are some things one just can't get to the bottom of. Now then, I'm going to lie down for a bit before dinner. I'm glad your young man is not seriously hurt, Dee dear. I hope it won't prevent him from wining and dining you. I know that he is busy, and is here to work, but I presume he is at least allowed to eat, isn't he?'

Dee grinned at her. 'Most definitely he is.'

'In fact, I would be delighted if they could join us for dinner tomorrow evening, if they are available. Perhaps you could ask them.'

'Thank you, I shall. I'm sure they will be only too pleased to come.'

Miss Marriott smiled and nodded then left. Dee heard Doris in the hall, gently scolding her. She'd left the kitchen door open so that Miss Marriott could wave to her when she was ready to go upstairs.

'You're supposed to wait for me, not start off up them stairs all on your own, honestly ma'am! The doctor would go mad if he knew what you was up to,' Doris was saying.

They were like mother and daughter, Dee thought. That was an interesting idea.

Suppose Miss Marriott had an affair with a man that resulted in a pregnancy. All those years ago, the early years of the war, it was not the done thing for a single woman to have a baby. Dee's own birth was testament to that. It still wasn't the done thing, if it came to that. Perhaps Miss Marriott had gone away secretly and had her baby, then placed the newborn child with a local family—the Padhams—so that she could watch her daughter grow up, even if the child never knew who she was.

It was an intriguing, even compelling notion. But Dee immediately had to dismiss it. If you had money, and status, there were other choices available. Doris could have been passed off as the child of a cousin who had died giving birth. Or she could have been the child of a family friend who had died in an accident or an air-raid. Or she could just as easily have been an orphan taken in when she needed a home, an adopted child. There could have been any number of ways around the situation.

And besides, it now occurred to Dee, Miss Marriott would have been in her early fifties when Doris was born. Not impossible, but not very likely either. She dismissed the whole idea as implausible.

She yawned and stretched. Time to get on with something useful. She pushed aside the pleasing fantasy and began to carry all the tea things through to the kitchen. She had time to pop into the study to make a quick telephone call to the pub, asking for a message to be delivered to the policemen about dinner the following evening.

By the time Doris came downstairs and caught her tidying the kitchen, the dirty cups and plates had all been washed. All Doris needed to do was to pack away the leftover cakes.

'That's very naughty of you, miss,' Doris tsked.

Dee just laughed. 'I'll tell you what's very naughty. Writing to poor Mr Montague and pretending to be Miss Marriott, that's what.'

Doris looked horrified. 'She never went and told you!'

Dee laughed again. 'Yes, I'm afraid she did. Don't worry about it, though. I shan't tell on you. But can I ask you a couple of questions?'

'Of course, miss. Come and sit down.'

Seated at the table in the centre of the room, they looked at one another for an awkward moment, then Dee said,

'Why did you write to Monty? What did you think he could do to help you?'

Doris was twisting her handkerchief this way and that, screwing it up into a ball then smoothing it out on her knee, quite without being aware of what she was doing as she tried to decide how to answer those questions.

After a while, hesitantly and in rather a muddled way, she began to explain herself.

'The thing is, miss, as I told you, a few years back my mum and Mr Barton had a bit of a fling. I was about fifteen or sixteen then. Not very old, but old enough to have an idea about people carrying on. I used to come home from school, and he'd be there. It was always when my dad was at work. Dad was an accountant at a big firm in Greater Hartwell. Mum said to me I wasn't to say anything about it to Dad, she said he wouldn't understand and he'd get upset. So then, of course, I knew. I don't think she realised that I'd cottoned on. But she was so happy with Uncle Clive, and my dad was a terrible man, so I was happy for her. I thought, hoped, that both of us would go and live with Uncle Clive in his house, and that we'd leave the guesthouse forever. I hate the place. It's dark, it's dingy. All the floorboards creak. The whole place wants decorating—there's never been the money to get it decorated nicely, it's still just the same as when we moved into it when I was a little kid. The plumbing was done on the cheap and it doesn't work like it should. And the whole place always smells of cabbage. Even if there hasn't been any cabbage. I hate it there. And I know my mum does, too.

She crossed to the sink and got herself a glass of water, drank it down in two or three gulps then came back again to sit at the table.

'I wanted to go to college, to train as a hairdresser, but my dad said I had to get out to work, that he was tired of keeping me, that I had to earn my own living and stop sponging off him. We rowed. Sort of. You couldn't row with my dad, not really. He'd just sneer and snarl and then lash out with his fist when he lost his temper.

'Then Miss Marriott told me she wanted someone here, and that I could sleep in. It seemed perfect. At first I thought I'd stay here until I'd saved up some money, then I'd leave them all behind, run away and work my way up until I had my own salon. But in the end, I just stayed here. After a while I didn't even mind, Miss Marriott is such a sweetheart and so good to me. I know she pays more than most others would pay for the same job, and she never minds if I pop down the road to watch a bit of telly with my mum if the guesthouse is empty, which is most of the time. And Miss Marriott lets me take leftovers home too, as things are pretty tight for my mum.'

Dee nodded. She understood the worry of making ends meet. 'Go on,' she said. 'You're doing really well.'

Doris flashed Dee a smile, but she was still fiddling with her handkerchief in her lap. 'One night, my dad didn't come home from the pub. My mum moaned to me about it the next day. 'Gone off with his fancy woman,' she said, 'and leaving me to do all the work here as usual.' Well miss, I'd never heard her say that about him having a fancy woman before. That was new. I didn't know if she was just guessing or if she knew for sure. I asked her who it was, and she just looked daggers at me and said, 'Well, who do you think?' Like I should know. The only one I could think of was Maureen Barton. And then I thought it was a bit much for Mum to be upset when he was only doing the same as her. Anyway, I didn't say anything. But that night too, he didn't come home. And the next day, his work phoned to ask if he was ill, and when did Mum think he'd be back. I don't know what she told them, but later she went and banged on Uncle Clive's door, and he was there giving Barry and Jane their tea, and saying that Maureen had gone, that she'd left him. So Mum said it was obvious that Dad had gone too, gone with Maureen Barton.'

'But you didn't think so? Deep down, you didn't believe it?' Dee prompted her gently.

Doris shook her head, frowning at the memory. 'No. Right from the outset I knew he was dead. I don't know how I knew, I just did. I mean, there were the signs: I read my horoscope and it said something about needing courage to overcome a personal tragedy. Then too, I saw the three magpies.'

Dee's brow furrowed. 'Isn't that supposed to mean a baby girl? 'One for sorrow, two for joy, three for a girl and four for a boy'?'

Doris shook her head. 'That's the modern version. There's an older version, I learned it from Miss Marriott. Uncle Clive's not the only one locally that's interested in history.'

Dee nodded, practically holding her breath.

'Well it goes like this,' Doris said. 'One for sorrow,

two for joy, three for a funeral, four for birth, five for heaven, six for hell and seven for the devil, his own self.'

Dee felt foolish, gullible, just for listening to this superstitious old nonsense, but the goosebumps on her arms were real enough, as was the chill at her neck. Trying to sound calm, she said,

'How interesting. I've never heard that saying before. It's a bit pagan-sounding, isn't it?'

Doris smiled. 'Yes miss, it is a bit. But that wasn't all. I bought some flowers into the house. Lilies. Old Mrs Mason—she's long gone, God rest her—she used to do the flowers for the church, and she had some lilies. White ones and yellow ones, ever so pretty. I thought they were, anyway, and when she gave me a couple of spare ones she had left over, I couldn't believe my luck. I know it doesn't sound much, but I'd never been given nice flowers before. Still haven't, if it comes to it.' She made a tsking sound and rolled her eyes and laughed. 'Anyway, I was so excited. Of course, I took them home to my mum, and she was so angry. I didn't understand why. But in church, lilies stand for what's pure and good, or so Mrs Mason said. But in a house, that's a different matter. My mum took one look at them, grabbed them off me and threw them out the window, and she yelled at me, 'Don't ever bring lilies into the house again!' I was so upset, I just burst into tears. I ran back here to Miss Marriott's. When I told her what had happened, she said, 'Oh my dear,' the way she always does, 'Surely you know that lilies mean a death is coming to the house? They are bad luck, except to the dead, of course. Nothing can touch them. A wreath of lilies is the perfect tribute to the deceased,' Miss Marriott said.'

Dee nodded. 'I suppose I've heard that said about

lilies, but... I'm afraid I don't really see...'

Doris looked down at her hands. 'I just knew that he was dead. The magpies and the lilies and the horoscope, they all told me. But I didn't really mind—I wasn't upset. I just wondered which one of them had done it. And then nothing happened for a few years. Well, apart from Mr Barton's wife being sent back home dead from somewhere abroad. I don't remember where.'

'Somewhere in Spain, he said,' Dee obligingly told her.

'Was it? Oh.' Doris nodded, only vaguely interested. 'I remember being a bit worried Dad would come back for the funeral. But he didn't, so that seemed to just confirm what I thought. Anyway, the years went by, and I thought they'd got away with it, whichever one of them it was. I think perhaps it was both of them. Or Uncle Clive did it but Mum helped or at least knew about it. Either way, I thought it was all going to be all right, then this thing about moving the churchyard happened... The new one, the Seekers said. No one's been buried in that churchyard since Mrs Barton, so... either it was her they were talking about, or it was someone no one knows about, someone who shouldn't be there. Like my dad. I even thought maybe Mrs Barton had died of guilt or a broken heart if it was her that somehow killed Dad. Well, I don't know, I was just trying to find something, anything that made sense. I'm so scared they will find an extra body in Mrs Barton's grave when they dig her up. Or—you know—a grave where there's not meant to be one. Can they tell who someone is if all they've got is bones?'

Dee shook her head. 'They can tell if it's a male or a female, and they can even tell roughly how old the person was and how tall.'

'But it will just be bones? If it's been nine years or so since the person died?'

'Probably. It depends on how they were buried. What, if anything, they were wrapped in, and whether they'd been embalmed. And the type of soil. All sorts of factors can have an effect, but usually, after that amount of time, yes, it's very likely it will just be bones. But short of a plastic or metal nameplate or jewellery or some special keepsake a relative could recognise, they won't be able to be certain whose remains they are.'

Doris absorbed this information for a moment. Then added, 'Well, that's something at least.' She sighed. 'Those dropout people. When they said what they did, I thought that means every single body that comes up, the authorities are going to check and double check who it is.'

'I would have expected them to do that anyway,' Dee said. 'That was what they promised to do. I mean, knowing how much the dead mean to those of their family still living. You'd expect a lot more care and yet they didn't do any of what they'd promised, did they?'

Doris shook her head. 'Shame on them for not having proper respect. Everyone is so shocked at what was discovered this morning up in the other field. But hopefully now it means if my dad is there, no one will ever know. You won't tell, will you miss? Please promise me you won't.'

'I can't promise you that, Doris. But I'll only tell if I'm asked, or if an innocent person might be arrested.'

'That's good enough for me,' Doris said.

When Porter returned two hours after leaving, looking none the worse for his exploits apart from a button missing from his jacket, he found Hardy sitting on the side of his bed cursing viciously.

'You know, sir, I'm not sure you shouldn't be in the hospital.' He said it gently, but kept well back. Hardy was cranky at the best of times. Now, instead of the response Porter had expected, he got nothing more than a withering glare—a half-strength one at that. The boss was definitely not right.

'I'm just bruised, sergeant. I'm not an invalid. But if you could hand me my jacket and tie, I'd be grateful.'

It took him almost five minutes to get down the stairs and out to the car. By which time he was bathed in a cold sweat. Once in the passenger seat, he began to relax. He asked,

'Did you manage to get them all?'

'Yes sir, we did. By the time Wright and I and his men got to the new graveyard, there was a full-on shoving match going on, and the chief super was trying to calm everyone down. The ACC, the bishop and the mayor had all taken refuge in their cars. There was a villager with a bloody nose and a builder with only one sleeve to his shirt. Not too bad, considering.'

'No indeed.'

'I told the chief super what had happened to you. I have to say he didn't seem very concerned.'

'Hmm,' grunted Hardy. Just sitting there was putting a strain on his bruised ribs. It actually hurts more since taking the painkillers, he thought, and he made the decision to flush the rest of the pills down the toilet.

'There is just one thing, sir,' Porter said.

'Which is?'

'I need to take you to the local photographer to take some photographs of your injuries, sir. They don't have their own police photographer here at the moment.'

Hardy sighed. 'That's just perfect.'

'Sorry, sir.'

'Not your fault. Shall we get going? The sooner this is all over, the better.'

'Sir.'

'The photos will be ready for collection tomorrow,' the photographer said as Porter helped Hardy get his shirt and tie back on for what seemed like the tenth time that afternoon. 'You can have them in a range of sizes, or...'

He caught Hardy's eye. He quickly added, 'Or just the standard size.'

'Standard is fine, thank you. I'll send a constable over for them tomorrow.'

'There's just the small matter of payment,' the photographer added, his expression anxious. In a confidential tone he added, 'They're not good payers, our local plod.'

Hardy fished his wallet out of his jacket pocket and settled up there and then. Another little thing to add to his expenses. 'I'd like a receipt, please.'

'Certainly, sir.'

They made their way across the street to the police station, Hardy holding his breath as much as possible, and walking slowly and with great care.

'I feel like an old man.'

'You'll feel better in a day or two, sir,' Porter soothed. 'And I'll get you a nice cup of tea once we get you settled at a desk. They've given us an office on the ground floor, not too far from the holding cells where our new best friends are.'

'Can't wait to chat with them,' Hardy said.

Eventually he found himself face to face with the

first of his attackers, who was sullenly seated beside a legal representative courtesy of Her Majesty.

'You got no right to drag me in here! I know my rights!' the man began. Then taking a proper look at Hardy, he subsided.

Hardy sat, wincing as he did so, nodded a greeting to the solicitor and said,

'So, Mr Philpott. Let's begin with you telling me why you and your friends attacked me when I attempted to dissuade you from heading to the new graveyard site?'

Jimmy Philpott opened his mouth to speak but his solicitor put a warning hand on his arm, and, clearing his throat, said to Hardy:

'You cannot possibly know what Mr Philpott's intentions were when he and his friends met you in the lane. It is pure supposition on your part that they were headed for the gravesite.'

'But that is where they went,' Hardy responded, a slight frown creasing the space between his eyebrows.

'Yeah, but that's only 'cause...' Philpott began, and again, subsided upon a look from his solicitor.

'No doubt Mr Philpott and his friends merely wondered to what you had been referring and went to take a look for themselves, out of sheer curiosity. It is, after all, the village where they all live. Anything that happens there might affect any one of them.'

'That's right. We was all wondering to what he was referring to,' Philpott said with a smirk, sitting back in his seat and folding his arms. 'Any one of us could of been affected.'

'We'll have to charge you with a breach of the peace,' Wright butted in, to Hardy's frustration.

The solicitor, with a slight smile, said, 'Mr Philpott deeply regrets that he bumped into Inspector Hardy and that in the course of helping the inspector to rise to his feet, he accidentally bumped the inspector in the chest or stomach area. It's well known that the inspector had been lunching in the public house a little earlier. Perhaps he was somewhat unsteady on his feet after that lunch?'

'I had coffee with my lunch, nothing more,' Hardy insisted.

'Yeah,' said Philpott, still smiling. 'It was all just a naccident. A misunderstanding. He was probably plastered.'

'I most definitely...'

'That's all right then,' Wright said now, with a nod and a smile at Hardy then the solicitor. He stood to his feet. To Philpott he said, 'You can go now, just remember to watch yourself in future, you don't own the place, you know.'

Philpott and his solicitor strolled from the room, whilst Hardy, fuming, sat there glaring at Wright.

'You're just going to let them off?'

Wright sighed. 'From upstairs. Got to keep the villagers on our side during these difficult times. I've been told they're all to get a telling off and to be told to behave themselves.'

Hardy got up and left the room before he said something he shouldn't.

*

Chapter Seventeen

Early that evening, as a golden sun hung just above the horizon painting everything orange, red and shades of gold, Dee returned to the churchyard.

The two bulldozers loomed still and silent. The work had been halted, Doris had told her, having heard it from her mother. The mayor himself had stepped in to demand everything cease until the day's events had been gone into with the help of a magistrate and the chief constable.

But in Dee's view, the damage was done. Two people had died, an officer of the law had been attacked, and the remains of some villagers' ancestors lay in a disrespected heap in a field, whilst here in the village, the churchyard wall had been shoved aside, the lych-gate smashed and now, great raw gouges scarred the ground. A previously upright headstone had toppled forwards into a deep rut left by one of the vehicles, shattering across the middle. Dee did not think of herself as a particularly sentimental or superstitious person, but even to her, this seemed like an ill omen.

A bench, previously hidden by weeds, had been uncovered by the work. She sat there now and looked about her. The birds had gone. There was no buzz of bees. Even the sun seemed to have grown cold. The rosy autumn had changed into a precipitate winter. She shivered. She would not stay long. She longed for London again, for the comforting noise and bustle and familiar faces.

'Hello there,' a woman called, and Dee glanced up. It was Janna, or Jane, from the séance group, standing some distance away. Barry/Bartholomew and Adelle were with her.

Dee waved and they came over.

'You look so sad,' Janna said. 'Is everything all right?'

Dee gave herself a mental shake. 'Oh, it's just this place. I first arrived on Friday, and I came in here, and it was so beautiful, a real paradise on earth. Now look at it. And then there's the fire. And two people dead, deliberately killed. The police inspector knocked down and kicked. And now, the terrible way the builders are just scooping up everything—*and everyone*—and just dumping them in a heap, and...'

Suddenly she was weeping, yet astonished at herself, embarrassed and wondering where that had come from, whilst Adelle swept her into a motherly hug. The other two looked on, appearing genuinely concerned. Almost immediately Dee pulled herself together, feeling like every kind of fool, and rummaged in her bag for her handkerchief.

'I'm so sorry. I can't think what came over me. I was perfectly all right a minute ago.'

'You're right, though. It was such a special place. And now look.' Janna waved a hand. 'It's ruined.'

'Paradise lost,' said Bartholomew. 'Not especially original I know, but from the heart nevertheless.'

He sounded a little like his father, Dee thought, when Clive was at his best. She sniffed and smiled, wiping her eyes and blowing her nose. 'Have you been out somewhere?'

'We've just been to see my father,' Janna said. 'We're planning to leave soon, so we went to say goodbye. We probably won't be back until Christmas.'

'Have the police said you can go?' Dee asked, remembering Bill's surprise and dismay when she'd said she thought the seekers had already left. He'd be glad to know the three of them were still here, at least.

Bartholomew snorted. 'No. But if they want us, they can come and get us. We're not staying here anymore, just the three of us.'

'Fair enough.' Dee pondered, then said, 'I know you're probably sick to death of going over all this, but... Do you think Tristan Summers really believed the things he said about the new one saying don't let me be forgotten. Or words to that effect, I think it was? Did he really believe it came from the spirit world?'

They looked at one another. It was the look of a shared guilt. Complicity.

'What is it you know?' Dee urged them. 'Tell me. Please.'

Janna shrugged. 'I suppose there's no point in going on with this now. Tristan was paid ten pounds to say that. Both times. But to be honest, I think he just loved the mystery of it, the idea that messages could come from the other side. He loved all that. He longed to believe in it so much that I'm pretty sure he would have done it for nothing. Though twenty pounds is a decent sum of money, he was really pleased about that.'

'And you all knew?'

Bartholomew shook his head. 'Not the whole time, not right away. We were a bit surprised when he told us, I'll admit, but we'd been... Well, smoking, so none of us exactly had both feet on planet earth. If you know what I mean.'

Dee knew. Not from personal experience, but from what other people had told her. She nodded, aware of a vague sense of disappointment. We all long to believe, don't we, she thought.

Janna said, 'I just feel so ashamed.'

Dee looked at her. 'Of Tristan, do you mean? Taking money for the prophecy?'

Janna shook her head emphatically. 'No, no of myself. For being so—naïve, I suppose—so gullible. I can't believe I fell into his trap.'

'I'm not sure I understand what you mean,' Dee said, but gently, as she could see how troubled Janna was.

'It wasn't the local church, or the churchgoers he was focussing his research on. It was *us*. I see that now. *We* were his guinea pigs, his foolish, credulous, blind followers. We swallowed the whole act.' Her eyes filled with tears.

'He conned you, like a used car salesman. That's to his shame, not yours. It was very wrong of him to take advantage of you.' Dee waited a beat then asked, 'And who was it, do you know? Who paid Tristan?'

The three of them shook their heads.

'All we know is, it wasn't our father. Tristan assured us of that. But he didn't want us to know who it was—said he'd promised to keep it to himself,' Bartholomew told her.

'It seems odd—I mean, awful, yes. But odd too that

he should have been killed that night. Do you know if he had fallen out with anyone locally? Anyone he had argued with, or upset, or angered?' Dee asked.

'Just the whole village,' Bartholomew said with another shrug. He was fidgeting now, bored and ready to leave. She wouldn't get much more out of them.

'No one wanted us here,' Janna agreed. 'Even my dad wasn't too enthused. He thinks I should be at home taking care of the house, and Barry should be getting a job.'

'I have got a job,' he protested. To Dee he added, 'I've got a promise of a job with Rolls Royce next summer, working on their new engines. I've just got to finish my degree first. It's good money, and a secure job.'

'Is that in Derbyshire?' Dee asked. When he nodded, she said, 'One side of my family comes from there, I think you'll like it. Well, good luck, all of you. Take care of yourselves.'

'And you. If it helps, I think you're doing a good job yourself. You'll find out what you need to know,' Adelle said, and awkwardly but sincerely, gave Dee another hug.

'Is that a prophecy?' Dee asked, laughing. Adelle didn't smile but went rather pink. 'Thank you,' Dee added. 'I'll admit, I have been feeling rather discouraged. I really want to solve this—er—case.'

They left. Dee stayed for a while, but the sun had gone, and all the world seemed darkened and cold. She went back over the conversation. The bit about Tristan having been paid—that had disappointed her, but she wasn't surprised. Quite the opposite, it was just as she'd suspected all along, and it explained why he had carried out the séances.

Bartholomew and Janna had said they didn't know

the identity of the person who had paid Tristan, but Adelle, sitting beside Dee at that moment, had carefully kept quiet. Did Adelle know something she wasn't sharing? But they had gone, she was too late. She could have kicked herself for not asking enough questions. A stiff breeze rustled through the trees all around, and she shivered again. She had better go, she decided. She wanted to go back to Miss Marriott's to change for dinner. And she needed to do her hair—that alone would take her an age, now that it had grown quite long.

This thought reminded her of Doris saying of the seekers that all the men had long hair, and looked like women, and two or three of the women had very short hair. Bartholomew or Barry's hair was past his shoulders, smooth, and very dark, and his beard too, was a dark brown. Tristan's had been the same, and the other men had also worn their hair very much longer than conventional. The women had short hair except for Serafina who had long dark hair heavily threaded with grey that came almost to her waist. She had been a tall woman. As tall as Tristan. What was it Doris had said, it's hard to tell which are the men and which are the women?

Was it possible?

If seen from the back...?

She wondered if Tristan and Serafina had been wearing the same coloured robes that night. Tristan had been in a saffron-coloured robe, and she remembered vaguely there had been one or two others in the same colour. She must remember to ask Bill...

Dee got to her feet, turning back to the house, still absorbed in her thoughts. Had Serafina been killed before or after Tristan? By the time Dee reached Miss Marriott's, she was convinced that Serafina's death had been a mistake.

It was a fascinating idea.

'Where's Nat?' Dee asked as she sat down opposite Bill, who politely rose to his feet to greet her.

'Going to ring Violet, from what he said, then he's planning on having a long bath and getting an early night.'

'Is he just being tactful and sweet and giving us some privacy?'

'Probably. Though he is certainly going to ring Vi. I think the phrase was something along the lines of, 'She'll have my guts for garters if I don't.'

Dee laughed. 'They make a lovely couple. I can't wait for them to get married. She told me she's never been so happy. 'I never thought it would happen to me' is what she said. It made me all weepy and silly.'

'I'm glad too. She's had a hard life. They both have.'

They turned their attention to the soup, a hearty chicken and mushroom one served with freshly baked crusty rolls. They had agreed no shop talk until the meal was over.

'I must ring Rob tomorrow. If I ring him at Monty's, I can tell them both everything at the same time. I imagine Monty will expect a progress report.'

'I'm sorry about leaving you with the bill for lunch. I'll pay you back, of course. Have you enough money to stay down here?' Hardy's voice lowered, he didn't want anyone to overhear him ask, didn't want her to be embarrassed.

She smiled at him. It was sweet of him to think about practical matters. 'Yes, I'm fine for money, thank you. And you don't need to repay me, I'm a modern girl.'

He nodded, reluctantly accepting that. She

couldn't seem to think of anything to say, but the silence was comfortable, and she enjoyed her food, and just being with him. It was very relaxing.

Once the food was over, however, and they were sitting over cups of coffee, inevitably the conversation turned back to recent events. When he'd met her, he'd winced as he sat down, and she noticed he moved very carefully, and as little as possible.

'Are you still in pain?'

He smiled an ironic, bitter smile. 'Oh yes. The painkillers from the doctor are not the slightest bit of use.'

She bent to delve into her bag. 'Here. Try these,' she said. 'These' proved to be common-or-garden aspirin. 'They will be every bit as good as whatever the doctor gave you.'

'Thanks.' He took a couple with his coffee.

'So did you snooze all afternoon, or...?'

He scowled at her but smiled. 'I'll have you know I was hard at work going through all the witness statements local police have gathered.'

'Interesting.' She wondered if he had them with him, and if he'd let her take a look. Unlikely, she thought, remembering his grumpy, 'Stay out of my investigation' from the last time she'd intruded on his professional territory, though admittedly he seemed to have softened a little of late.

He leaned forward, and very briefly covered her hand with his. 'I was very proud when I read one particular statement.'

She shook her head, unable to think what he was referring to.

'Your quick thinking saved that poor girl that night. When her robe caught alight. I'm so proud of you, that was clever and brave.'

'Anyone would have done the same. I couldn't have just walked past her.' She felt ridiculous for blushing, pleased that he was impressed.

'All the same.' He could see she was embarrassed and changed the subject. 'Right then, madam investigator, what have you got to tell me?'

'Well, that's charming. Why do I have to give up all my secrets, and you coppers keep all yours to yourselves?'

'I might give you a couple of hints,' he teased. 'It all depends on the quality of the 'goods'.'

She leaned forward to speak quietly. He couldn't lean forward, so he got closer by turning sideways in his seat and resting the arm of his injured side on the back of his chair.

'I had another chat with the remaining séance group. They were just coming out of Clive Barton's and saw me in the churchyard. They are going back to university as soon as they can, so if you want to keep them here, you'll need to nip over there pretty smartish in the morning.'

He wrinkled his nose. 'I'm not sure we need them. We know where they'll be if we do.'

'That's what they said. Though I suppose there's always a chance it was one of them—or one of the others who've already gone—who killed Tristan Summers.'

He glared at her. 'Don't make me doubt myself now.'

'Do you think they killed him?'

He shook his head. 'No. I think someone from the village did it.'

She nodded. 'Yes, I agree. I asked them if Tristan really believed in his 'prophecy' and they finally admitted that he was paid by someone to say it. On both occasions.'

'What!'

'Exactly. It was obvious he had a reason for saying what he did. Though none of them know who it was that paid him—so they say—or, just as importantly, *why* they paid him to say it. Oh, but they also said that he told them it wasn't Clive Barton. Apparently Tristan wanted to set their minds at rest about that.'

'Interesting, but I have no idea where this leaves us, or if it's even important.'

'Well I think that Janna, who is Jane, thinks the same as Doris: that Henry Padham is dead. And Janna thinks he's buried in Maureen Barton's grave. No one has heard from Henry for years, and it was thought that they ran away together. Doris also thinks he was secretly buried in Maureen's grave, as does Bet.' She outlined for him what she had heard about Henry Padham, Bet Padham, and the Bartons.

He ran his finger along the edge of his coffee cup as he thought this over. A thin white line, an old scar, marked the back of his hand. Dee remembered the day he got that injury messing about with barbed wire on the edge of a field near her childhood home. She remembered she'd tied her handkerchief around his hand to stop the blood going everywhere. He had been about eight years old which meant that she had been about ten. She smiled at him, suddenly grateful for all the years of shared history they had.

'I wonder if that's enough for me to get Mrs Barton's grave opened.'

'They'll open it soon, anyway,' Dee pointed out.

'I don't know. With work being brought to a standstill by this afternoon's events, it could be weeks, even months before it starts up again. If ever.'

Dee shook her head, seeing again in her mind's eye the child's skull. 'Why couldn't they have done everything with the respect and dignity they promised?'

He reached out and took her hand and squeezed it gently. 'In the end, they'll have to, or lose the contract.'

She nodded. 'I hope so. Do you think you could get permission to open the grave? Who can give you that, the local inspector, or is it more complicated than that?'

'It will have to be approved by a magistrate. In any case, the local inspector had a heart attack last week and is still in hospital. I've either got Sergeant Wright to deal with, or the chief super, who is not my greatest supporter at the moment.'

'Bill,' she said abruptly. His head came up, anticipating something he wouldn't be happy about. 'There is something I think you ought to know. I was hoping I wouldn't have to tell you, but I think I shall have to.'

'I knew it,' he murmured. 'Well? What have you done now?' But there was a twinkle in his eye.

She told him everything Clive had told her about his wife, that she had left him, died and been buried abroad, and that he had bribed the undertaker to carry out a fake funeral for her.

Hardy was every bit as astonished as she'd expected. 'So she's not even in the grave?'

'No.' Dee bit her lip, waiting to see what he would say, or do. The last thing she wanted was for him to tear round to Clive Barton's and start shouting questions at him, but she knew she had no control over what Bill did in his role as a detective inspector. She blurted out, 'He won't go to prison, will he?'

'He'll probably get away with a fine,' he said. 'Other than that...' He shrugged. 'I mean it was a few years ago now. It depends on the court and how the judge views the matter although I'm inclined to think they would be lenient. But it does mean I'm even keener to find out what or who is underneath Maureen Barton's headstone.'

Dee bit her lip, pondering. 'Hang on. If she's not there, and we already know she isn't, but Henry Padham is... How and when was his body put there? I mean, he had been missing for a while, the same length of time as Maureen, and it was quite a while—a year or so—before Clive was informed about Maureen. So has Henry been there all that time, and if so, why did no one notice his body when the grave was dug for the empty coffin to go in, or was his body kept somewhere else until that time, or...?'

But before they could discuss this, Porter appeared in the doorway. 'I hope I'm not interrupting, sir, I wondered if you would be interested in a liqueur? Get you off to sleep nicely, sir. And you, miss.'

Dee laughed. 'I don't think I'll have one, but you two go ahead. I'm going to go back to Miss Marriott's shortly.'

The two men discussed drink options and Porter went to give their order. Dee waited until he came back before she said goodnight.

'I'll walk you back,' Hardy immediately said.

She shook her head and motioned for him to stay in his seat. 'Don't be silly, you've just got your drink, besides, you're the walking wounded. Anyway, there's no need, it's only along the lane a hundred yards or so.'

'I'll go with her, sir, I'll just be two ticks.'

As they walked along the lane, Dee apologised for dragging him away but he reassured her that it was no trouble, adding,

'And in case we forget, someone around here has killed two people, so there was no way I was going to let you walk back alone. And here we are at your lodgings, miss.'

He knocked on the door, and as soon as Doris answered, with a lift of his hat he bid them both goodnight and returned to the pub.

Miss Marriott was already in bed. Yawning suddenly, Dee said goodnight to Doris, and began to make her way up the stairs, mulling over the evening. Porter's words came back to her:

Someone around here has killed two people.

It was possible he was wrong, of course. It now seemed to Dee entirely possible that someone 'around here' had killed not two but three people. Dee was convinced that if and when Maureen Barton's grave was opened, it would be found to be occupied by the remains of one person only. But that person would not be Maureen Barton. What was troubling her was how that body had come to be in that particular grave.

*

Chapter Eighteen

Her thoughts kept her awake half the night. Rather like the drum of the new washing machine in her parents' scullery, her own ideas, or snippets of conversation, random images and questions churned round and round in her mind, leaving her restless and in need of a solution to events in the village.

What if Serafina had been killed by mistake, in the belief that she was Tristan Summers? She was as tall as he was, and if seen from the back, in the saffron robe—assuming of course that she was wearing the same coloured robe as Tristan, she would need to check that—in the alarm and haste of that night. And with all the smoke, yes, Dee thought, she could see how easily such a catastrophic mistake had come to be made. She had a dim memory of several people in the deep yellow robes that night, the man who came forward to speak, but others too, a man, she thought, and definitely a woman too. Had that been Serafina? Dee remembered now, or perhaps it was just hindsight suggesting the idea to her, but she thought she had noticed that the woman in yellow was older than the other women, and long-haired.

Who had paid Tristan to say what he did? And why? What had they hoped to achieve with this so-called prophecy? Who was it the prophecy referred to? Who was the new one that mustn't be overlooked? Was it an actual person, or merely a mischief-making lie? Was the person who had killed Tristan and Serafina the same person who had paid Tristan to say what he had? Or was the killer someone whom the 'prophecy' had touched, made to feel unsettled and threatened?

Sitting up and reaching for the glass of water on the bedside table, she tried to work out who could possibly gain from the killings.

Or had the killings, after all, just been opportunistic—some angry man from the village lashing out because everything seemed to conspire at that moment to present him with the perfect opportunity? She thought of the terrifying way they had pushed Bill to the ground and kicked him. She shuddered to think how easily he could have been very seriously hurt, if not killed. The mob mentality, she thought. When a crowd gets out of control, each one's anger pushes his cohorts to greater and greater lengths to react and do whatever their instincts told them to do, all reason lost. It was petrifying. Did their womenfolk—or indeed the calmer, more reasonable of the men--look at them in horror or disgust, fearing to trust them or to be near them? And if so, how could a village like that survive? Perhaps by taking away the church and its burial ground, that was a way to remove the heart—the damaged, raging heart—of the village, diluting the population with the addition of three hundred new families. Then perhaps, these volatile men would no longer see themselves as the 'protectors' of the village.

Dee didn't know any more if she was in favour of the new scheme or not. In any case, her opinion didn't count. She wasn't a local and had no influence on either side of the battle.

Her clock's luminous hands showed the time was 2.47. She lay down, punching her pillows into plumpness, and turned to lie on her other side.

Was Henry Padham dead? The thought sprang into her mind to hold back sleep once more. His wife thought he was. His daughter thought he was. It was no exaggeration to say in fact that both women hoped rather than thought he was dead. But did either of them have definite knowledge?

And what about Clive Barton? He had been seeing Bet Padham secretly, and it was believed that his wife had been seeing Henry Padham. Not that it was much of a secret, Dee reflected, everyone seemed to know all about it. Which one of the two women did Clive really love? Or did he not care for either? Did he feel jealous and resentful of Henry's affair with Maureen, or relieved that it freed him of his own guilt over his relationship with Bet? How far would he have been willing to go back then, to secure his own happiness. And, Dee reminded herself, let's not forget he's an ex-military man, fully conversant in the various ways of disposing of an unwanted person. Or two. The newspapers were full of tales of family, friends and neighbours shaking their heads over a convicted killer and saying, 'He seemed like such a nice man'.

Dee's eyelids were heavy now and drooping. In the night-time silence she picked up the tiny sound of her eyelashes brushing the pillowcase beneath her head as her eyes drifted closed. Tiny sounds. A cat meowing along the long. An owl hooting in a tree somewhere.

In her mind she saw the owl spread its wings wide and drop from its high branch into the air, gliding over the church, over the churchyard, over the torn and broken ground with its graves. Over the ash where the bodies of Tristan and Serafina had lain.

I'm asleep at last, she told herself, as the owl continued its flight, silent, serene, across the village rooftops.

But what if Tristan was killed first?

She sat bolt upright, sleep a thousand miles away, as she felt her mental kaleidoscope shift, changing the pattern completely.

Did it make a difference?

Yes, she realised. Because thus far she had been assuming that Serafina was either killed first, mistaken for Tristan. Or killed second because she had witnessed his murder.

But suppose it was the other way round—and *she* had been the target. If she could be mistaken for Tristan, surely, *surely* the reverse could also be true? A tall woman, with long hair, in the same robes as Tristan... Again, Dee pictured that night in the churchyard. In the darkness, with all the excitement and uproar, amongst the smoke and the flames, suppose he had been killed instead of her. Or he may have seen her murder and been killed to protect the killer's identity.

Was that possible?

She lay back against the pillows yet again, her brain puzzling over this.

Had they been looking at this whole thing back to front? How could she find out? Even if she could find out, what did it actually mean? Who would have a motive to kill the woman? No one had even really mentioned her. One or two had talked a little of Tristan Summers, but Serafina Rainbow? She was still a closed book.

Then Dee remembered the former vicar of Hartwell Priory—the Reverend Kenneth Riley who, Doris had said, called Serafina 'Sara' in the church that day, as if he knew her.

Dee's mind was now made-up. As soon as possible, she would go and speak to the Reverend Riley in Greater Hartwell.

At last her thoughts became quiet. She fell asleep. The owl called from its branch but no one heard, certainly not Dee Gascoigne.

On Tuesday morning, Dee waited for the bus to take her to Greater Hartwell, the bigger town some five miles away. The only two others who were waiting were a teenage girl Dee hadn't seen before, and an elderly woman with a wicker basket on her arm, and strong opinions about the events of the recent days.

'If my Jack was still with us, he'd have been in the middle of all them protests. If you ask me,' which Dee hadn't, 'they all want stringing up for what they done. Throwing all our passed over ones on a rubbish heap like that. Proper wicked it is, and the police and the mayor right there letting them do it. Well, I never did. And if you want my opinion,' which Dee didn't, 'it's a blooming disgrace.' Nevertheless, Dee could completely understand the woman's point of view. It really was a blooming disgrace.

At last the bus rumbled into view, and Dee, the last to arrive at the bus-stop, therefore the last to get on, climbed the steps and presented her shilling to the driver who handed her back a pale green paper ticket, fourpence ha'penny change, and gave her a broad wink. She grinned at him and hurried to get into a seat before the bus lurched forward, jolting everyone on board.

There was something restful in a jerky, noisy way about being on a bus. She didn't need to worry about the sharp bends, tight turns or about other traffic. She gazed out of the window, the scenery gliding by as she focussed on her thoughts.

It had been next to impossible to haul herself out of bed that morning. She'd been too tired to eat any breakfast, and had only drunk half of her tea. As Doris had been on the point of leaving to return to the kitchen, Dee had asked her how far it was to Greater Hartwell. She had been thrilled to hear that a bus went every hour, on the hour, and so she immediately planned to catch the nine o'clock bus.

Doris was obviously bursting with curiosity but Dee didn't know how much to tell her, so said quite vaguely she had an errand to carry out for her cousin the inspector.

It occurred to her now that if she'd asked Bill or Nat—especially Nat as Bill could be so sniffy about sharing information—about Serafina, he might have been able to tell her quite a lot and no doubt save her the bus trip. Oh well, too late now. For a few minutes she sat back enjoying the view. The bus stopped several times to let on passengers; it was getting quite full.

'Greater Hartwell!' the driver called out at last, and several people scrambled to their feet, clinging for dear life onto the upright poles or the backs of seats as they waited in the aisle for the bus to come to a stop. Which it did somewhat abruptly, throwing everyone forward then back as the brakes came on with the familiar lack of gentleness of all country buses everywhere.

She climbed down from the bus, and crossed over the road to look up the times on the departure board of the return bus stop. Then she was at leisure to look about her at the busy market town. It was a shame it wasn't market day, she thought, but things would have been far more hectic and it was quite busy enough already, thank you very much. From where she was beside the market square, she could already see the spire of the church, so headed in that direction.

She found the Reverend almost immediately, near the front of the church, kneeling, his head bowed forward onto his folded hands that rested on the altar rail. She assumed that he was praying, though she was too far off to be sure.

Intending to wait for him to finish, she took a seat right at the back of the church and hoped that her presence wouldn't disturb him. She also, admittedly selfishly, hoped his prayer was not going to be of the all-day sort. Perhaps he came into the church at nine o'clock in the morning and prayed for the whole day until six? She had only the vaguest idea of what a vicar actually did each day.

After ten minutes or so her eyelids were becoming heavy. And not just her eyelids—her whole being felt weighed down with fatigue after the disturbed night she'd had. But she spotted the Reverend Riley getting to his feet, making the sign of the cross and turning to head towards the back of the church. As he caught sight of her, he smiled and gave a wave of acknowledgment. Drawing closer, he was still beaming at her, she could see. That boded well. He called,

'Ah, Miss Gascoigne! Very nice to see you this morning. Are you sightseeing in our humble town, or did you want to see me?'

She got up, waiting for him to reach her. He paused to gather up a pair of errant hymn books, placing them on a shelf with all the others as he drew close to her. He shook her hand heartily, still grinning.

Dee said, 'How are you?'

'Very well, and yourself?'

'Yes, I'm quite well thanks. A bit tired. I didn't sleep very well last night. I was thinking too much, probably.'

'About these awful events in Hartwell Priory? It's just heart-breaking, isn't it? Such wickedness. I was just praying about it. It's all so horrible, prayer seems like the only solution. To leave everything in the hands of the Lord.'

Up close now, she noticed he looked pale and tired, as if the events had affected him deeply. He looked down as if only just realising he was still holding her hand in both of his. He released it immediately, and said, 'Is that what you wanted to see me about? Do you need prayer for your anxiety?'

'Actually, I wanted to ask you a couple of questions. Get a bit of background on the village, that sort of thing. I thought that as an adoptee of the village, you might have some useful insights.' She smiled again, not wanting to sound as though she wanted to really interrogate him.

He looked a little alarmed but laughed it off with a protest. 'Oh, I'm glad to help, of course. I'm just not sure I'll be any use to you.'

They'd turned to walk to the door, and now he motioned for her to precede him, then turned to lock the door with an impressively large black key hanging from his belt.

'Won't lose this in a hurry!' he quipped, and she smiled again, doing her part.

'Definitely not!'

But he didn't appear too keen to go with her. Was he uneasy because he was afraid that she was there to flirt with him? An attractive, single man, he probably had women falling over themselves to flirt with him, or to talk to him, bake him cakes and pies, just to somehow get his attention. Did he think that was her true aim in coming there? She wondered how to tell him that she knew she wasn't his type. At least that might set his mind at rest.

'I'm so sorry to trouble you like this. I realise you must be busy. It shouldn't take long,' she started, hoping this might relieve him a little.

He was still all smiles, no matter how he really felt. She decided he looked troubled, anxious. The smile was a half-strength one at best, and his darkly-circled eyes were wary. Perhaps it was the upheaval in his old village that was upsetting him.

He shook his head now. 'Oh, it's a fairly quiet morning. This afternoon and evening are quite busy. Meetings, you know, and a wedding rehearsal.' He stood looking about him as if debating something. 'Do you fancy a coffee or a cup of tea, perhaps? There's a tearoom down that street over there. It's not exactly all the rage, but it's quiet and pleasant. They do a very nice sticky bun and one of those frothy coffees for a good price. I like to pop in there from time to time.'

'That sounds lovely,' she said, and realised that she was now ready for her breakfast. A sweet, spicy sticky bun with dried fruit inside and icing on the top would be the perfect thing to perk up her weary brain.

'Morning, vicar. Your usual?' asked the plump woman behind the counter with a wide smile. Clearly his 'from time to time' was something of an understatement.

'Oh yes please, Mrs Mason.'

The woman was already putting a sticky bun onto a plate for him with some rather unwieldly-looking metal tongs. 'We haven't seen you for a few days, Reverend. I hope you haven't been poorly?'

The simple enquiry caught him off guard, and he blushed furiously as he said, 'Oh just a slight chill, nothing serious.'

'I'm very glad to hear it. And for the young lady?'

'The same, please,' Dee told her, leaning forward with a smile.

They sat at a table by the window. Almost immediately the woman behind the counter, Mrs Mason as Riley had called her, brought over their sticky buns, sliced in half and generously buttered, then came back with their very modern, frothy coffees in large cups that would never do in Dee's mother's drawing-room. They thanked her and she withdrew. For a couple of minutes Dee's crucial business was on hold as they attended to the matter of sugar for the coffees, and Dee took the first bite of her bun.

The sugary, spicy goodness was an immediate comfort. Dee identified cinnamon but wasn't certain about the other spices she could taste; she wasn't a baker or renowned in any way for her ability in the kitchen. Other than the washing up of crockery and pans, of course. She left the cooking to Violet or to Rob if it was Violet's day off. Even though Dee was happy for Violet, now that she would be leaving to get married, it would mean they would be without any help at the flat, something she and Rob would need to tackle at some point.

'Delicious,' she pronounced, and saw that Mrs Mason had heard and nodded, pleased.

'Aren't they?' Riley took a big gulp of his coffee.

'Now then, what was it you wanted to ask me?' He leaned back, warily watching her, arms folded across his chest as some kind of defence mechanism. Dee noticed there were white sugar crystals on the sleeve of his black cassock.

'Right. Yes, how long were you at Hartwell Priory?' It was an easy one to begin with.

'Just over three years. It was my first post as the incumbent. Before that, I'd had a couple of posts where I was in a part-time or an assisting role, so I was quite excited, as you can probably imagine, to have my own parish.'

'And now you're here?'

'Yes. Though I must say, just between you and I, I miss the old place terribly. It was much nicer. The people here are very nice, of course, but perhaps the church here isn't quite as central to town life as the village church was—or could have been.'

'So you'd have preferred to stay?'

'Given the choice? Oh yes, Hartwell Priory felt like home. And I was convinced—but it was probably just arrogance on my part—that I could increase attendance at the church. Still, here we are. Though numbers here are no better than in Hartwell Priory, and I'd even be inclined to say slightly fewer, relative to the size of the population.'

'So you never met Henry Padham?'

He stared at her then looked again, puzzled. Whatever he'd expected her to ask next, this wasn't it.

'H-Henry...? Er, no. That was well before my time. I've heard of him, of course. But I never met or knew the man. Sorry, but if it's him you want to know about, I doubt I'll be much help.'

'It's all right,' she said. 'I just wondered, that was all.' She ate more of her bun, trying to pace herself.

Even though her stomach felt hollow, she managed to resist the urge to cram her food in her mouth all in one go. 'Actually what I really wanted to ask you about is the Seekers of Light people. Did you know them well?'

He was already shaking his head. She had the feeling he was going to do that no matter what she asked. She waited, just in case he did add something.

After a while, he said, 'I knew them slightly, I suppose. Like most of the villagers. They'd come to the church a couple of times. They held a kind of séance, as they called it, first in the churchyard, then they came right into the church itself the last time I was there to finish packing up some of the items. I must say I highly disapproved of them doing so. It's not at all the sort of thing the church can condone, as you probably realise. Some would even say it's dangerous.'

'And what did you make of them? Did you believe them to be sincere, if perhaps somewhat misguided?'

'One or two of the young women, yes, I think they definitely believed in what they were doing. The others—no, I just think they wanted a bit of fun. And to cause a bit of mischief, and if at all possible to make a bit of money.'

'What about Tristan Summers, their leader?'

'What about him?'

'Did you know him? Did you ever talk to him?'

Again he was shaking his head while she was still speaking.

'No.' He looked away, then seemed to make up his mind on some point he'd been considering. He turned to face her. 'Look, you might as well know, Miss Gascoigne, as I'm sure someone will probably tell you at some point, I had a bit of an argument with the chap. That last week I was there, in fact. I'd got annoyed over what they were doing. As I say, a couple of the young girls in the group really believed in it, and I felt that Summers was manipulating them, fooling them with his so-called otherworldly pronouncements. I had a sense of moral—not to mention spiritual—outrage. They were innocents, and genuinely believed he was a prophet. They drank it in, all his mumbo-jumbo. Oh I'm perfectly aware that most people these days will say I do the same, of course.'

'But you felt he was a cynic, a conman?'

'Definitely.'

She nodded, biting her lip as she mulled this over. 'Interesting. I've begun to think the same.' She saw his expression soften as he heard this, and he relaxed. She continued, 'What would you say if I told you that some of the group have told me that Summers was actually paid to make those prophecies about a newly buried person not wanting to be left behind?'

He was clearly surprised, rocking back in his chair. 'My goodness! They've actually told you this?'

She nodded.

He seemed to be struggling to find the words. When at last he spoke, his outrage was to the fore. 'This is... this is appalling! I'm utterly... I shall complain to the university where he works...' He halted mid-sentence as he remembered all over again. He sighed, his chin dropping almost to his chest. 'For a moment there... I'd forgotten. Well, clearly he paid a very high price for his deception. I—I feel terrible for my anger. The poor fellow. What he did was a dreadful, cynical act, but he didn't deserve to die for it.'

Dee waited for a count of three. She let him pick up his coffee, then said in a soft voice, 'Nor did Serafina

Rainbow.'

He dropped his cup. A very unholy curse escaped his lips as the hot coffee splashed all over the front of his cassock, rapidly soaking through to his trousers underneath. He glanced up, shame-faced.

'I'm so sorry. I shouldn't have said that. I'm most awfully sorry you had to hear that.'

She laughed. 'And they say 'in vino veritas'. It should be in coffee veritas, apparently.'

He smiled, pink-faced with embarrassment. Mrs Mason was coming over with a towel for him to dab at the wet patch but nothing was going to fix the mess apart from a good soak in hot, soapy water.

Next Mrs Mason brought him over a replacement coffee. These kind interruptions frustrated Dee who had wanted to strike while the iron was hot, as she termed it to herself. But she saw now that she should have expected this to happen. Well, she'd seen that he was rattled, at least.

He fussed with the sugar again and she knew he was trying to delay any further questions. But he ran out of things to do, and finally had to look up and meet her eyes. Instinctively she knew that he was going to tell her what she wanted to know.

'You obviously think that I knew her.'

She nodded. 'I know you did.' Then she waited again for him to decide what he was prepared to say.

He drank half of his new coffee down in a great gulp that must have scalded his throat. To Dee's dismay, Mrs Mason returned yet again, this time with a white overall. She held it out to him. She shook her head and tutted.

'That's not going to fit you, is it?'

He beamed at her, his saviour, and Dee knew their interview was over.

'I'll carry it in front of me, folded over my arm.

You're a life-saver, Mrs Mason.' He was on his feet, preparing to leave. He kissed her cheek, making her blush and giggle. He turned back to Dee. With a broad though insincere smile that didn't touch his eyes, he said,

'I'm terribly sorry, but I have to get back now. It was very nice to see you again, Miss Gascoigne.'

'But you haven't answered my question,' she protested.

He shrugged. 'I know you think I knew her, but actually I didn't know Sara at all. Now, I'm so sorry, but I really must dash. Good day to you.'

And he was gone. She watched him as he walked off rapidly in the direction of the church, the white overall in front of him to disguise the coffee spill.

Sara.

He'd be livid with himself over that slip when he realised later, she thought. Short of pinning him down, Dee didn't see what she could have done to make him stay. She was furious with herself that she had failed to get the answer to her most vital question.

'Should have asked him that one first,' she grumbled to herself.

'All right, dear?'

Dee smiled at the friendly Mrs Mason. It wasn't her fault she'd given him the opportunity to escape. 'Yes, yes, perfectly all right, thank you.'

'I'll just pop the bill there, shall I? There's no rush to pay. I must say, it's very modern of you to be the one who pays. And of him of course. A lot of men don't like a woman to pay for them, even these days. And him being in the clergy, well, they take longer to get used to new ideas, don't they?' She placed the slip of paper on the edge of the table, weighted down by the sugar basin.

Dee stared at it. 'Bloody men!' she grumbled below her breath, hardly able to believe it had happened again. Why did she keep getting stuck with the bill? Her expenses were going to be huge at this rate. She wondered if there was an upper limit to Monty's generosity.

'It's nice to see him out with a pretty girl, mind you. I was beginning to wonder if he was one of them queer ones. You know, all la-di-da.'

'Does he come in here often?'

'Once or twice a week. He's always here on a Friday mid-morning. Comes in with a young fellow he says is his cousin, but I don't know. Still, he brought you in today, didn't he? So he must be normal.'

'Oh, it wasn't a personal meeting,' Dee said. 'We only met up so I could ask him a few questions. I'm a private investigator.'

Mrs Mason stared. 'You never are! Oh my gawd! Just you wait till I tell my old man. He'll be proper excited.' She thought for a minute. Then, 'What's he done?'

'I wish I knew,' Dee said. 'But he's hiding something.'

'Oh, I say!'

Dee got to her feet, rummaged in her purse, and placed the money on top of the bill. 'And has he ever come in here with a woman? A tall woman with long dark hair, with quite a bit of grey, and who wore lots of beads?'

The woman shook her head. 'Sorry ducks, you're the only woman I've ever seen him with.'

'Thanks anyway.' Dee said.

*

Chapter Nineteen

By the time Dee arrived back once more in Hartwell Priory, it was more or less lunchtime. And something was going on: a large crowd—for a village of this size—was gathered along the new fence at the perimeter of the church. Dee hurried over to find out what was happening.

Porter was standing there amongst the onlookers. He turned to greet her.

'Afternoon, miss.'

'Hello sergeant,' she said, remembering to remain formal as they were near other people, and he was on duty. 'What's going on? I thought work had been stopped?'

He led her slightly apart from the crowd, keeping his good strong baritone quieter than usual. 'And so it has.' He tapped the side of his nose. 'This is strictly hush-hush—or would be if word hadn't somehow got out and brought the whole world and his wife over here to watch. We got the approval this morning to open up Maureen Barton's grave. To see just how many corpses there are in there, if any.'

Dee spared a thought for Clive Barton who must be in a terrible state of nerves by now. She scanned the crowd but couldn't see him.

'I presume Clive Barton knows about this?'

'Oh yes. He tried to stop it, in fact, but the magistrate was very much on our side, for once. Mr Barton is at the police station now, just for an informal chat at our request, to help us to understand what happened to his wife.'

'And what about Bill? Where's he?'

'He's at the police station in Greater Hartwell talking to Mr Barton. The inspector wanted me to stay here, said I was his eyes and ears in the village.'

Dee smiled. The two men had become firm friends, despite the age gap of fifteen years between them. She looked again at the people milling about, all trying to get a better view of what was going on.

'Everyone seems fairly calm for once, if rather nosy,' she observed.

'As you say, it makes a nice change.' He folded his arms, eyes fixed on the heads of the workers he could make out above the privacy screen. 'You know, Dee, I've never before known a case like this where it's all—I don't know, like loose threads—nothing leads nowhere. It just feels like blind alleyways in every direction, nothing solid to really get your teeth into.'

'Hmm. I know what you mean. I wonder how long this will take. Do you think you'll know by the end of the day?'

'I should hope so. If it takes more than another hour, I'll not be at all happy. It's not like they've got to dig up the whole place to find a body—they know where it is, or at least, where it should be, I suppose.'

Even as he finished speaking, two men edged

around the screen and ducked under the rope put in place to hold everyone back. They came towards the crowd, and a hush fell over everyone. They were all waiting, expectant.

'Sergeant Porter? Is Sergeant Porter here?' one of the men called, scanning the people for a response.

Even as Porter held up his hand, calling out, 'Yes, here!' and drawing Dee along with him, he began to move forward.

A voice from further along called out: 'Mike Smith, North Essex Times. Would you mind telling us what you are looking for, gentlemen? Sergeant Porter, are you acting on information received? Is this the new one who didn't want to be forgotten? Are you looking for the body of a murder victim?'

It was the same man as before, Dee saw immediately. Not David something as Miss Marriott had said, but Mike Smith.

No one answered the man who was left shifting from foot to foot, impatient and annoyed. The crowd parted to allow Porter and Dee to reach the two men, who then ushered them into the churchyard, with a slightly surprised glance at Dee in her short skirt and not at all workmanlike heels, and across to the spot where they had been digging.

The headstone now lay on its face on a tarpaulin to one side of the grave. And beside it, where just days earlier there had been an overgrowth of weeds and grasses, and the lichen Clive had said he was planning to remove, there was a raw-edged, gaping hole, more than six feet deep by Dee's calculation and about three feet wide. The soil was in three large mounds on the opposite side to the headstone.

One of the men pulled off his hat to mop his brow with a large handkerchief. He was shaking his head. 'I can't explain it, Sergeant. There's just nothing there. I mean, it could be that the headstone wasn't put in the right place, I suppose, although that's pretty unlikely. But this soil has all been dug out before, for the lady's funeral, it wasn't the compacted earth of an undisturbed site. So there should be remains. You can see the remains there of the coffin...' He nodded behind him to where splintered lumps of wood lay on another tarpaulin. 'But there was nothing in it.'

There were also four rusted mud-caked coffin handles, obviously not the finest quality if they were rusted so badly, Dee thought. But then how much would Clive have invested if he knew that the coffin was always going to be empty? Not a lot, she'd wager. Something that looked like an oblong rotted cushion lay beside the wood and the handles. The inner padding of the coffin.

The man was still explaining to Porter. 'There's nothing, no sign... And these graves are all fairly close together here, there's no room to put a headstone in the wrong place. And anyway, like I said, vicars and sextons know their job, they wouldn't make a mistake of that sort. There's nothing here.'

Porter glanced at Dee to see if she caught the significance of all this. She nodded solemnly at him. He turned to thank the man before leaving.

As he and Dee returned to the lane, the crowd once again parting to let them by, everyone casting questioning looks at them. The reporter called out to them several times, growing increasingly frustrated.

Porter said, 'I've got to go and tell the boss. You want to come too?'

'Oh yes. I don't want to miss that.' Her eyes shone at him. This should be good.

They fell in step with one another, heading quickly along the lane to the pub and to the unmarked police car that was parked behind it.

They were both mostly silent on the way to the police station. Porter was clearly mulling over the news and its effect on the case, whilst Dee, deep in contemplation, was staring out of the window at the countryside, the same countryside she'd seen on the way to the town earlier, and on the way back. Now, viewing it for the third time in one day, it seemed quite familiar.

Who was Serafina Rainbow?

Dee just couldn't shake the idea that this was significant. If she could discover who Serafina really was, then she was convinced she'd have the solution to both murders.

It wasn't about Tristan Summers, she felt certain of that. It never had been.

They parked the car in a side-street opposite the police station. Above the tops of the buildings, Dee could see the church spire, and wondered if it would be too much to ask Porter to come with her to find and talk with the Reverend Riley again. But she had no concrete evidence for her suspicions—less than a suspicion, more like a wild guess—and didn't want to waste police time or test Porter's legendary patience.

The police station was housed in an attractive early Victorian building, all big square windows and high ceilings. Even the reception area was a room of quiet elegance, if you discounted the long, battered-looking counter atop the high desk, the posters reminding people to make sure they locked their doors and windows properly, or the uncomfortable wooden chairs that had never even seen a drawing-room, and the incessant ringing of at least two telephones.

She followed Porter through the gap in the

reception desk, carefully setting the flap down again behind them, then they went along a corridor to a small office at the back of the building. There they found a morose detective inspector. Hardy was staring at a wall, a pencil sticking out of the side of his mouth, cigar-like, as he puzzled something over.

Porter knocked softly on the door. 'Got someone here to see you, sir,' he said, then stepped back to allow Dee to enter first.

'Ah, a spy in our midst!' Hardy grinned at her. He started to get up, but the pain in his side stopped him. He drew a sharp intake of air and promptly leaned back again. 'Sorry, I'm afraid...'

'Those ribs are broken,' Dee snapped at him, suddenly irritated with him. 'And you need to stop messing about and get to hospital. I'm sure Nat will take you.'

Porter, caught by surprise, nevertheless quickly agreed, darting a worried look at his boss then back at Dee. 'You really think...?'

'I do,' she said firmly. 'It's no good pretending you're just a bit bruised, you know.'

'The doctor said it would be a day or two before...'

'You've got one or more likely two broken ribs, Bill.' She paused, then added in a gentler tone, 'Look, I know you hate hospitals. But we'll go with you. It won't take long.'

'All right, well, perhaps a little later, I'll...'

'Make sure you do.' She perched on a chair across from him, her arms folded, and she glared at him. Then to Porter she added, 'And you make sure he goes, or I'll be after both of you.'

He nodded. Then possibly, because he felt a change of subject would be a good thing, he said, 'Guess what, sir? I've just come from the churchyard. The forensics people have done their investigation.

No remains at all of any kind in Maureen Barton's grave.'

'None?' Hardy stared at him. He let out a long low whistle of surprise. 'Good God. I think we were both expecting to find two sets of remains. But to find none at all... Damn.'

'What did Barton have to say?'

'Nothing. He refused to speak until his solicitor can be here. The man is in London and not expected back until around six o'clock. Barton says he's happy to wait until then, so he's been put in an office along the corridor. Couldn't put him in a holding cell, as he's here voluntarily and besides, we've nothing to charge him with.'

The three of them sat in silence.

Dee began to think about her problem. 'What have you found out about Serafina Rainbow?'

Porter and Hardy stared at her, puzzled.

'Next to nothing. Why? What have you found out?'

'Nothing, Bill, that's just the problem. I can't seem to find out anything from the people I've spoken to. Where does she come from? Is that her real name? I'm assuming it's not. Have her people been informed?'

'Well, no, I mean, we don't know who she is, so...' He lifted his hand, then let it drop back onto his knee. 'That's why we'll have to ask for an adjournment at the inquest, to give us more time to find out those things.'

'I'd forgotten all about the inquest,' Dee said. 'When is it?'

'Next Monday. It should have been yesterday, but someone was off sick, one of the court officials, so it's been put back a week. Not that we've got much information anyway.'

'After all,' Porter said, 'those people hadn't been in

the village very long—just a few weeks. So it's not such a surprise that no one knows anything about her.'

'All we know is she wasn't a student from the university some of the others came from. I mean, she was older, anyway, so she wasn't likely to be a student. We thought perhaps she was a member of staff, but so far, we've found nothing. There's no birth record for that name at Somerset House.'

'I see.' Dee said. She got to her feet. To Hardy she said, 'Come on, you, let's get you to the hospital. You've got until at least six o'clock before Clive will talk to you, you may as well sort yourself out.'

'We need to have something to eat, too,' Porter said.

'Gosh yes,' Dee replied. 'All I've had since I got up this morning is a sticky bun.'

Porter had to help Hardy to get into the car, then having received directions from the duty desk sergeant, they set off, Dee in the back, enjoying the luxurious leather seat of the old Wolseley police car.

It was almost two hours before they returned to the police station.

There were a number of patients already waiting, but as a police officer he was allowed to take precedence, unfairly in Dee's opinion, although it saved them a lot of time. The inspector was hurried through to a consultant, examined then sent for some X-rays due to two suspected fractured ribs. The X-ray department was upstairs. Hardy was put into a wheelchair and taken up in the lift.

The X-rays taken, he then had to go back to the consultant who promised to telephone in a few days when the results were known. Next Hardy was sent to be bandaged up by a nurse, and finally he was given a prescription for the hospital pharmacy to obtain stronger painkillers. At every stage, there was a fifteen- or twenty-minute wait and the inspector grew more irritated by how long everything was taking. But at last they helped him into the car to return to the police station.

'I think we've missed our lunch,' Porter remarked sorrowfully. 'And knowing our luck, if Barton's solicitor isn't arriving until after six, we'll miss our dinner too.'

Dee glanced sideways at him, saw his sad expression and laughed. 'Let's get you some food. Look, there's a chip shop over there.'

He pulled the car over, and she jumped out, returning ten minutes later with three portions of cod and chips.

'You'll have to feed him,' Porter said, jerking his head to indicate Hardy snoring softly in the back seat under the influence of the new painkillers.

'Nonsense,' she said. 'He can do it for himself. Hopefully it'll do him good to get some hot food inside him.'

She gave him a gentle shake. At first he was reluctant to wake, but as soon as he realised she had some food for him, he was dragging himself into an upright position, swearing viciously, but ready to eat.

Dee left them at the police station, and took the bus back to the village. Again, she had been tempted to try to find Riley and question him further, but she decided against it, opting instead to give him some time.

The bus journey was more tedious and less of a pleasure this time around, but when she finally reached Miss Marriott's, she was delighted to find that she was just in time for afternoon tea.

'Good afternoon, Montague Montague of London,

legal services,' came the familiar voice, just as she'd hoped.

'Rob! It's me! I was hoping to catch you. Look, do you think you could come up here? I really need your help.'

'It's possible. I'll have to go and ask. Just a tick.'

For once the line was amazingly clear. She heard him lay down the receiver, push back his chair and walk from the room. She pictured her elegant baby brother knocking on Monty's office door, imagined Monty calling to him to come in. Then there would be a brief exchange, and because Monty was an old softie, he would say yes, Rob could leave after lunch and stay until Tuesday on full expenses.

She heard him coming back, heard the creak of his chair again as he sat back down, and the fumble as he picked up the receiver.

'Dee? I can come down tomorrow. But I'll need to get home on Saturday so that I can come into the office on Sunday to prepare some papers Monty needs for court on Monday. How's that?'

It wasn't quite what she wanted, but it was something, and very good of old Monty. She said it was perfect, adding, 'That's wonderful, thanks, Rob. And say thank you to dear Monty for me! I think I can wangle you a room here. Miss Marriott will adore you.'

'Why do you want me? Not that I'm sorry to get away for a few days.'

'I need someone to talk to about things here. I'm getting nowhere and horribly afraid that I'm not going to be any use to Monty at all. And I might need to dangle you in front of an attractive clergyman as a kind of inducement.'

'My goodness, you know I'm taken, don't you? No, seriously, that's all right. I was worried you needed me to act as your bodyguard, or to do something manly and dangerous.'

Dee's response was a laugh. He said, 'I suppose you want me to drive there?'

'Good idea. I could do with my car. So much easier to get around. Will Kelvin be coming too?'

Kelvin was her brother's 'special friend' as her mother termed it, Rob's boyfriend, the man he shared his life with. The two of them were madly in love, and planned and hoped to have their own home together in the near future, with both of them saving hard for that day. Would the day come when they could actually stand up in front of their families and friends and take their marriage vows together like any other couple in love? Dee hoped so, she wanted them to be happy, but for now, intimate relationships between people of the same sex were still illegal, in spite of the campaigning that had gone on for years.

'Sadly not. He's had to go to Gleneagles or somewhere. His new boss, that American fellow I told you about, he's a keen sportsman. I think it's going to be a proper huntin', shootin', fishin' week.'

'Then it's a good thing your big sister is on hand to provide entertainment.'

She spent a few more minutes telling him how to get there, then said goodbye. It had been good to hear his voice, and she felt buoyed by the prospect of seeing him and talking everything over with him. He would help her get to the bottom of all this.

Dee went to find Miss Marriott, and found her sitting by the window in the morning-room, reading a book. When Dee asked her about Rob, Miss Marriott's forehead furrowed as she said,

'Tomorrow? That's Wednesday, isn't it? Oh of course, my dear! It will be lovely to have him here for a few days.'

At least Miss Marriott had reacted as predicted. Dee thanked her profusely.

'Just pop and let Doris know, would you. She'll need to air the room and get it ready.'

*

Chapter Twenty

Later, Dee went to the churchyard again, as she seemed to do so often. No one was there, the forensic people and the villagers alike having left. A few spades and picks had been abandoned near the entrance to the churchyard which was open. The wooden fence around the place already looked ready to fall down, though whether due to people pulling at it and trying to bring it down deliberately, she didn't know. The bulldozers had been left parked there too, still, silent, almost a part of the statuary. If they stayed there another hundred years, would people from the future think the bulldozers—by then rusted and creeper-covered—were part of some ancient sacred ritual? Would they make effigies of bulldozers to place in the churches of the twenty-second century? It was an intriguing thought. How much of what we see and learn of the past stems from context or as a result of misunderstanding, she wondered.

She sat on the wall. On this untouched side of the

churchyard, to her intense relief she saw that it was business as usual for the bees and butterflies. Birds chattered and sang in the trees nearby and in the private gardens behind her. She turned, facing out of the churchyard rather than into it. Above the tall hedges, between the trees, she could make out the upper windows and the roofs of two or three houses. There was a thin patch, damaged, almost a hole in the hedge just twenty feet away. This must be Miss Didsbury's property, she realised.

She swung herself down off the wall, brushed the crumbs of mortar from her skirt, and careful to avoid potholes and ditches, she went over for a closer look.

It was possible to push aside some of the thinner branches that covered the gap to create a person-sized hole in the hedge. She peeked through to see a manicured lawn, neat flower beds, and to the right, at the end of a path far away from the house, there was a potting shed.

The soil under the hedge was damp and sticky: mud, essentially. And there were footprints. Several, but they overlaid one another, so that it was impossible to make out any clear individual print. She sighed. It couldn't have been that easy, could it?

She went back to the churchyard, walked out the front onto the lane, then round the bend into the next lane. At the end, there was Miss Didsbury's house, beside two others. All three were very grand and of a similar style. Dee thought they could be Georgian, or perhaps earlier. Certainly none of them was as grand, or as old as Miss Marriott's house.

She knocked on Miss Didsbury's door, hoping it was not Miss Didsbury's custom to rest before dinner as it was Miss Marriott's, once again the afternoon had rather got away from her and now evening was fast approaching. At least it was still light outside: in a few more weeks it would be dark by five o'clock, then by mid-November it would be dark at four, such a depressing thought.

Almost immediately the door was opened by Sylvia. Dee hadn't seen her since the night she had gone into the churchyard to see the séance with Miss Marriott, Sylvia urging them on impatiently.

'Oh, miss! Do come in. I'll let Madam know you're here.' Sylvia stepped aside and they came into the hallway, with its chess-board tiles of black and white, and wide airy feel. So different from the dark, closed space of Miss Marriott's much older home.

Sylvia directed Dee to a side room, with rather the atmosphere of a waiting-room at a doctor's surgery, just a carpeted room with several chairs, and a view of the blank end wall of the house next door.

'My goodness, you stupid girl,' Miss Didsbury was saying angrily a moment later. 'What on earth were you thinking?'

The voice was coming closer. Dee was fearful of being summarily shown out of the house.

But Miss Didsbury came in, her hands outstretched in welcome. 'My dear Miss Gascoigne, I'm so sorry that dratted girl threw you in here instead of bringing you into the drawing-room. I don't know what's wrong with her. She just never gets things right somehow.'

Dee's hands were gripped by Miss Didsbury's cold bony ones, her apology for calling at an awkward hour waved aside, and she was pulled into the drawing-room and practically bodily placed in a large squashy armchair covered with a bright floral fabric that hurt the eyes. Even the furnishings were a long way from Miss Marriott's sober and formal leather-covered or faded chintz sofas. Miss Didsbury's beloved Chinese porcelain dominated the display cases and shelves about the room.

'Sylvia!' Miss Didsbury bellowed, apparently not having a bell like the one Miss Marriott used to summon Doris.

Sylvia, looking frightened, arrived at a run.

'Tea!' Miss Didsbury commanded. Sylvia bobbed a kind of curtsey and ran off again. 'She's an idiot, that girl. I don't know why I put up with her. But then it's so difficult to find staff out here.' Miss Didsbury sighed heavily and took a seat opposite Dee. 'But you haven't come here to listen to my servant troubles, I'm sure. How are you, dear, and how is your investigation going? Sylvia has heard all about it from Doris, you know. I must say, I'm intrigued. A lady detective. How terribly modern.'

The tea arrived and Sylvia, with an anxious smile, departed once again at speed. Miss Didsbury served Dee with a cup of tea.

'China, of course, and with a slice of lemon. I don't take milk. I was brought up to see lemon as the correct way to take one's tea. Father was a diplomat in Hong Kong when it became a British outpost of the Empire. And before that, in fact.'

The conversation became general: where did Dee live, what did Dee do with her time when she wasn't being a private investigator, and who did Dee know socially. It quickly became clear that Miss Didsbury was the worst kind of snob and not at all the sweet little old lady she'd at first appeared. She had hardly a good word to say about anyone in the village. Even Miss Marriott, her closest friend, was dismissed with a shake of the head and the comment,

'She is of course, the only other person of real rank in the village, but sadly far too intimate with the workforce,' By which Dee assumed Miss Didsbury meant Doris—Miss Didsbury's own relation. 'Though

Lola's house is admittedly very fine and the oldest one still standing here in the village. The hall and drawing-room are part of the original house, dating back to the 1370s, don't you know.'

From curiosity, and perhaps a sense of mischief, Dee told Miss Didsbury that she'd enjoyed a cup of tea with Mrs Padham, adding, 'I believe Doris and she are relations of yours? Is Mrs Padham your niece, or your cousin, or...?'

With a curl of the lip, Miss Didsbury said, 'Mrs Padham is my niece. But we rarely speak. That side of the family are sadly sunk in the ranks, having married into Trade. I have nothing to do with her or her offspring.'

'What a shame,' Dee commented boldly. 'Life can be so lonely at times. I don't know where I'd be without my family.'

'*Your* family didn't marry into Trade.'

Dee was not prepared to allow that. 'Oh, of course we did. We all do. We've got people who own and run businesses in our family. And people who work for other people and not for themselves. I used to be a teacher. But we're lucky enough to have those in the professions too. My grandfather is in the legal profession, as well as in finance. And my uncle and cousin are in the police. Another of my brothers is in investment banking, and the third will shortly qualify as a barrister. Where would any of the old families be without some new blood? Or love?'

'Love?' Miss Didsbury sniffed. 'Well,' she said, as if that explained so much.

There was rather a long silence. Then, an idea came to Dee and she said,

'So the Padhams aren't a county family?'

Miss Didsbury sipped her tea and set it aside. She rearranged her shawl about her shoulders and sat back.

'They were—still are in fact—rather middling. I believe there is a judge, and another is an accountant, as was Elizabeth's own husband, of course, though we don't speak of him. Some of them have money, but no breeding. And in Henry and Elizabeth's case, they had neither. And as for Doris...' She shook her head, frowning. 'Such a working-class name. And she's had no education. She speaks like any other maid or servant and buys her clothing from a *chain store.*'

Ignoring all this, Dee asked, 'So was the guesthouse a Padham property, or from the Didsbury side?'

'It was purchased from the Marriott estate by Elizabeth's father, my brother William, then left to her in his will. It's a good thing, in a way, I suppose, that she has it to provide her with a modest income. Henry Padham was no use to her in that respect. A common waster. No one has seen him for almost a decade. You've probably heard that he ran off,' She pronounced it orff, 'And abandoned his family like a scoundrel. The house was originally the manse—the home of the rector of the church, when that was in the Marriotts' hands, more than a century ago. But when the diocese took over the church, they built that dreary bungalow on the other side of the church when Lola Marriott sold the manse to William Didsbury. Lola needed money rather badly back then for estate repairs or some such thing, oh, I'm talking about fifty years ago.'

'Death duties, I suppose,' Dee said, thinking this was a very clever way to find out more.

'Possibly,' came Miss Didsbury's unsatisfactory answer. 'And so the guesthouse, as you call it, or the old manse as I prefer to remember it, came from the

Marriott family into the Didsbury family.' She sat up straight and reached for her cup, took one sip, then another, and set it back down again. 'What Elizabeth was doing when she decided to take that on instead of just selling it, I can't imagine.'

Dee assumed that by *Elizabeth*, Miss Didsbury meant Bet Padham. No doubt the name Bet was too working-class. Dee said gently, 'Mrs Padham finds it a struggle to keep things going. It must be terribly hard work. And she says that the clients aren't always the most considerate or gentrified of people.'

'I suppose she wanted you to ask me for help? Or money?' Miss Didsbury demanded.

'No, not at all. But it's clear from everything she says, and just looking around the place that she really needs help. Or perhaps she just needs a push to convince her to sell the place and move into her own bungalow.'

'Well, you seem to have plenty of opinions.' Miss Didsbury regarded her with close attention, her eyes bright and probing. Hawk's eyes, Dee thought. 'On a mission, are you? Here to make me help my family. Hmm, I see.'

'I'm sorry to poke my nose in where it's not wanted,' Dee said. 'And no, that's not why I'm here. But as you said, it is your family we're talking about.'

'Hmm.'

As far as Dee could tell, Miss Didsbury didn't seem seriously offended. But there was another long silence. Then, thinking she'd better leave, Dee said, 'I wonder if I could just have a look at that hole in your hedge? You told me about it the other day.'

'Do you need me to come with you?'

'Not at all. I just need your permission to go and take a look.'

'Of course, you may. Sylvia!' Dee practically leapt

out of her skin as Miss Didsbury startled her once again by shouting for the girl. Sylvia arrived very promptly, as she had before.

'Madam?'

'Take Miss Gascoigne into the garden, will you, she wishes to view the hedge.'

With a puzzled look, Sylvia nodded and bobbed, but was no more able to question Miss Didsbury's instructions that she would cut off her own hand.

Dee got up. 'Thank you so much for the tea, Miss Didsbury.'

'Do come again, my child. It was most refreshing to speak with you.'

The imperious Miss Didsbury didn't get up. She was taking another sip of her tea. Then on the point of following Sylvia out of the room, Dee suddenly thought of something else.

'Did you say you thought the person who came through the hedge looked rather like Clive Barton?'

'It was him, I'm certain of it now.'

Dee nodded. 'Thank you, Miss Didsbury.'

And now she hurried after Sylvia.

Once they were safely outside and unlikely to be overheard, Dee said,

'My goodness, how on earth do you stand it here?'

Sylvia shrugged. 'There's not much choice.'

'You could get the bus into Greater Hartwell and get a job in a shop. You could work five or six days a week, have all your evenings free, and get better pay too.'

Sylvia rolled her eyes. 'Oh don't tempt me. The way she yells at me sometimes, you wouldn't credit it. Even in the pub, no one yells at me like that, and they're blokes, and drunk too, as often as not.'

'The pub?'

'My dad's Pete Guthrie, the pub landlord. I just wanted to get away from the blokes staring at me or pinching my bum. And the smell of beer. *And*, Dad always made me clean the lavs. The smell and mess in there—you wouldn't believe it.'

Dee wrinkled her nose. 'Ugh. I can well imagine it.'

Sylvia looked at her. 'Did you really want to look around the garden, miss? Was it the flowers you wanted to see? I'm afraid most of the summer ones have started to go over by now.'

'No, it was the hedge at the end of the garden. Where Mr Barton came through on the night of the churchyard fire. At least, Miss Didsbury seems to believe it was him.'

Sylvia, lips pressed firmly together, nodded and turned to follow the path a hundred feet or so to the end of the garden. She waved a hand to indicate the hedge, but stayed put, silently watching and waiting for Dee to step forward and carry out her inspection. With a curious glance at Sylvia, Dee did so.

Here too the ground was a muddle of shoe and boot prints, indistinguishable from one another. The hole in the hedge was still just a hole in the hedge. Dee was frustrated by the lack of glaring clues. Being detective was a lot harder than she'd anticipated.

She looked closely at the ends of the broken and bent twigs. In many places, the bent parts showed green under the outer layer. Fresh, then. But some were brown, dry, brittle.

'Is this gap new, do you know? I thought Miss Didsbury said it was created on the night of the fire, but to me, it looks as though someone's come through here quite a few times.'

Sylvia shrugged but said nothing. Dee looked at her again. Beyond Sylvia was the garden shed. Dee stepped around Sylvia to go over for a closer look.

'It's just a shed, miss.'

But Dee noted the nervous edge to Sylvia's voice. Dee took hold of the door handle and pulled. The door opened easily, and she looked inside.

On one side, there was a bench stacked with pots and gardening tools—a trowel, a small hand fork, a couple of watering cans and some wooden plant labels. On the other side, deckchairs had been folded back against the wall, along with wooden-framed sun loungers and a couple of rattan lawn sofas, one stacked on top of the other. The cushions from all these were piled in two heaps on the floor in front to make a shallow padded platform.

Sylvia was impatient to get Dee away.

Dee said softly, 'Who is it you've been meeting in here? Sergeant Wright?'

Wide-eyed with surprise, Sylvia shook her head automatically.

'Clive Barton, then?' Dee hazarded.

Sylvia's scornful expression gave the answer to that even before she said, 'What? Yuck. He's old enough to be my dad!'

'Who then? You can tell me, Sylvia. I promise Miss Didsbury won't hear about it.'

Sylvia hesitated. She's wondering whether to trust me, Dee thought. She went outside, and Sylvia followed, shutting the door behind them, relief making her shoulders drop and her features relax.

Something shone in the crack of the path. Dee bent to pick it up. It was a bead. And she spotted another one, then another, easily a dozen or so small round beads in bright red and green glass.

'Not Clive, then. But his son?' Dee suggested.

Sylvia flushed bright pink. She folded her arms across her chest.

'Did you see him that night?'

Sylvia nodded. 'I saw him in the churchyard. When the fighting started, and then the fire, he grabbed me by the arm and we ran back here. At first it was just to get away from what was happening, but then, well, you know...'

'One thing led to another?'

'Exactly, miss. It usually did with Barry. I've known him for years, and I've always liked him. And then his father came through the hedge and caught us. Luckily things hadn't gone too far... Mr Barton grabbed him, that's when the beads broke.'

'I'm surprised he didn't take the beads off,' Dee said dryly. 'What did Mr Barton say? Why was he following Barry?'

'He was upset about the séance. Angry really. And he'd been trying to talk to Barry for several days. He thought the group were trying to con someone out of money. And of course, when he saw Barry with me, he was even more angry because Barry is already engaged to...'

'Adelle? She's also one of that group.'

'Adelle!' Sylvia said in scorn. 'Ada Tripp, that's who she is. Oh she puts on the accent, acts real posh, but her dad's just a gardener for some well-off people in Greater Hartwell. Anyway, Barry's only with her because he got her in the family way, and he had to promise to marry her. But now she's lost the baby, he wants to come back to me.'

Dee doubted that would happen. He and Adelle seemed quite devoted. No doubt he'd just wanted a final fling. 'Miss Marriott said you were seeing Michael Wright.'

Sylvia sighed. 'We just have a drink together sometimes or go to the pictures. I haven't even let him kiss me. I don't like him that way, he's too bossy. And he's a terrible dancer.'

Dee nodded, thinking it over. ‘Barry told me he's got a job lined up at Rolls Royce, over in the Midlands. It sounds like a good opportunity for a career. But it means he’ll be moving away.’

Sylvia nodded, looking down at her hands. ‘I know. I’m hoping he’ll take me with him. I can’t wait to get out of this dead-end place.’

‘So that night, after you'd seen Miss Marriott and I going into the churchyard, you came back here to be with Barry. On your way here, did you see anyone attack Tristan and Serafina?’

Sylvia shook her head. ‘As soon as that brazier went over, I just wanted to get out. I was scared, I wasn't paying attention to anything else. And in case you're thinking it, Barry could never do such a thing, neither. He made sure I got out of there once everything started up. He's a good man at heart, though him and his dad never did get on.’

‘Why was that?’

Sylvia shrugged. ‘I suppose it was the usual father-son stuff. Barry didn't like being treated like a kid, told what to do all the time, told where he could go, who he could see. And he was close to his mum, so when she went, I think he blamed Clive for that, for driving her away.’

‘People have said to me that she went away with Henry Padham.’

Sylvia shook her head. ‘I don't think she did. Oh, I know everyone said they were carrying on, but I don't think they were really. She just enjoyed getting a bit of fuss, a good-looking man flirting with her a bit. I heard her telling my mum he made her feel young and pretty again. Not that I really understood that then, I was only twelve or thirteen. But now, I feel a bit sad for her. I can understand it better now.’

‘So you think she just left on her own?’ Dee asked.

‘That she didn't go with Henry, that she only wanted to get away from Clive?’

Sylvia shook her head again. ‘I don't think she went, full stop.’

‘Then what happened?’

‘Clive Barton killed her. I'm sure of it.’

*

Chapter Twenty-one

Everything seemed to come back to the—not *exactly* a love triangle, she thought—but certainly a tangle of relationships between the Bartons and the Padhams, with each side seemingly suspecting the other.

Dee wanted to speak to Clive again, but wondered if he would be willing to speak to her now that he had met Bill.

It was worth a try, she decided, and went along to knock on his door. She waited. And waited. Then knocked again. Still no reply. As she walked away, she glanced back and spotted a movement upstairs. Someone had been at the window looking out—or watching her—but there was no time to see who it was before they stepped back into the shadows of the room and out of sight.

She looked at her watch and saw it was just turning seven o'clock. She had half an hour before dinner at Miss Marriott's. Purely on the off-chance, she went into the pub, and there was Clive, sitting in a gloomy corner, half-hidden behind a newspaper, his usual glass of bitter beside him. As she approached, she was wondering, who, then, is in his house?

He didn't see her until she sat down in the empty seat across from him, taking him by surprise.

'Do you have a cleaner?'

'Good evening to you too. Yes, as a matter of fact I have. Sylvia cleans for me twice a week, Mondays and Fridays, from ten till twelve, if that's all right with you.' His tone was sarcastic, but Dee smiled at him, and he grinned back.

'I'm so sorry. I was just voicing my thoughts and didn't think how it might sound to say them out loud.' So, there was no cleaner in his house just now. In any case, no cleaner would still be at work at this time of day. Then who? The answer seemed pretty clear.

'All forgiven. Can I get you a drink?'

'Thank you. Just a fizzy orange please.'

'Sure?' He was on his feet, holding his glass he was obviously planning to have refilled.

'Sure.' She smiled again. She grabbed his newspaper whilst he was gone. He had been looking at the announcements. Immediately she saw why:

***Barton**, Barry and **Tripp**, Ada Adelle are delighted to announce their engagement. The marriage will take place in the New Year.*

Oh dear, Dee thought. Poor Sylvia. Her hopes of a reunion with Barry were to be dashed for a second time. And no mention of a father and mother being 'delighted to announce' as was conventional in these types of announcements. Dee's eyes drifted down the page and saw another item.

***Summers**, Tristan. Suddenly on Friday 3rd September. All our thoughts and prayers are with* *you, sweetheart. There will be a memorial service on Wednesday 8th September at St Martin's chapel, Cambridge at 7.30 pm. We will be saying our goodbyes at Saint Peter's church, Cambridge, on Monday 13th September at 3pm. Family and close friends only at this difficult time, thank you.*

'Which one caught your eye?' Clive was back, setting down their drinks then taking his seat.

'Both of them actually. Congratulations on your son's engagement. I expect you're thrilled.'

'Well yes, of course. Not that I knew anything about this, so as you can imagine, it's a bit of a surprise. Still, young love, here's to it.' And he raised his glass up before taking a drink.

Dee did the same with hers, observing him as she did so. He didn't seem terribly pleased, but then she supposed, weddings and so forth always seemed to be something women enjoyed far more than their menfolk.

'Do you know her very well?'

'Ada, do you mean? Or Adelle as she now calls herself. No, not really. I've met her a couple of times. She's one of those earnest sorts. Takes everything so seriously. Oh, I suppose she's pleasant enough. Barry obviously thinks so.'

'Are they staying with you long?'

He halted on the point of taking another sip, his glass a few inches away from his mouth, and shot her a surprised look. 'I don't know why I'm surprised you worked that out, Madam Detective.'

'I must admit it was partly a guess. I knocked on your door just now. No one answered but someone was by the window upstairs.'

Nodding, he said, 'Ah, so by a process of elimination you arrived at the truth. I'm here, so it couldn't have been me, and Sylvia doesn't clean for me on Tuesdays...'

'In any case, I've just been speaking with Sylvia at Miss Didsbury's,' Dee told him, and smiled, hoping to set him at ease.

He inclined his head. 'Therefore, it had to be... Well, what if I had a secret lover, that would have put a spanner in the works of your deductions.'

'True!' Dee laughed.

Clive laughed too. He was being very pleasant, very charming, but she was convinced that beneath the charm, anger was brewing. She still wasn't completely sure of him. What were his true feelings? She knew he was expecting, possibly even hoping, that she would come back to his comment with a question of her own: 'And have you?' But she didn't want to oblige him by asking, yet on the other hand she also didn't want to make him clam up and retreat from her by being too prissy.

In the end she gave in and said, 'And have you?' And she was annoyed with herself when she saw the glint of satisfaction in his eyes. These ridiculous mind games, she thought. But then he looked away, turning his attention to his drink.

'Alas, no. I had hoped... But I suppose at my age it's too much to expect.'

'Not at all,' she said, then could have kicked herself for needing to make him feel better. She added, 'You just need to find someone who's unattached.'

He smirked. 'Ouch. But, yes, probably true. I don't much care for your choice, though, if I'm brutally honest.'

'I assume your solicitor arrived in time to let you come back home?'

'Of course. Once I'd told your chap about how Maureen's grave came to be empty, he let me go. He said he will take advice, but he doubts that there will be any further charges. He said we may never know for sure the date and place of Maureen's passing. I couldn't remember the name of the priest who wrote to me, only that it was wintertime, so more or less a year after she left and I don't have the letter anymore. Your chap said the police would try to find out, but that I shouldn't hold my breath. Actually, I reluctantly admit that the inspector seems like a decent bloke.'

Dee nodded, just glad that whole episode appeared to be over. 'He is.'

He tapped the newspaper. 'Did you see the bit about Summers, too?'

'Yes. Obviously put in by a loved one. I hadn't even thought that he might have a wife somewhere waiting for him to come home. The poor woman.'

'Lord, yes, not the kind of thing you expect when your husband goes off on the camping trip with a few students. Bit odd, though, don't you think?'

'What is?'

'Well, for him to go off for a month or so, without his wife. Makes you wonder what was going on there.'

It had never even occurred to Dee until now, but thinking about it, she could see what Clive meant. Presumably if Tristan Summers hadn't died, he and his cronies would in all likelihood still be camping in Everard's field, pestering people with their séances.

She wondered yet again about the reasoning behind the group's visit—and if they'd planned to stay until the winter came, or just until university resumed, or for how long.

'Penny for them,' Clive said.

She shook her head. 'Oh, I was just daydreaming.'

'I'm quite a good listener if you need someone to talk to.'

'I know it's stupid of me, but I just can't shake off this question about why they were here—or still are here, in the case of some of them.'

'My children?'

'Yes.'

'Look, why don't you come back with me? Speak to them yourself. Or if you like, I can send them to Miss Marriott's to talk to you there.'

Dee wrinkled her nose. 'I wouldn't want them to feel as though they are being summoned. I'm not like the police, in any case, I don't have the power to demand someone gives me the answers.'

'Then come back with me. I'll make us all a cup of tea, we can all sit down like friends, and just have a chat.'

Dee looked at her watch. She should just about have time before dinner. 'All right, I will. Thank you.' She smiled at him.

He finished his drink then said, 'If you'll just excuse me a moment.'

'Of course.'

He was quite a while in the gents. She almost began to think he'd made his escape through the window, but then he came smiling back across to her, relaxed and as charming as ever, offering her his arm as they left.

It was a pleasant walk along the lane. As they drew parallel with the churchyard, he said, 'I wonder if the work will resume any time soon?'

'I suppose they'll be compelled to create the new graveyard first before they move any more remains. Pity about the lych-gate.'

'They could have kept that—it would have made an attractive entryway to the new housing estate from the village.'

'True.'

They reached Clive's cottage, and Dee let go of his arm to allow him to open the front door and hang up his jacket. He took her jacket from her, and turned to call over his shoulder, 'Barry, Jane, I'm back. I've brought a guest with me.'

No one appeared.

Dee saw beyond him the shiny black telephone on the side-table by the coat-stand. A suspicion began to form in her mind.

'I think...' she said, then decided to keep quiet.

'Yes?' he said. 'Let's go into the kitchen and get comfortable. I'll put the kettle on. I can't think where the kids have got to.'

Dee beamed at him. Two could be deceitful. 'I'm so sorry, Clive. But I've just realised I promised I'd get back to Miss Marriott's for dinner, and time's rather getting on. Do excuse me, won't you?'

He was still stammering a response and staring after her as she grabbed her jacket and rushed out of the door, turning back to give him a friendly wave once she reached the gate.

First stop the pub, she told herself. She went straight up to the bar. 'Excuse me. Mr Guthrie, isn't it?'

'Just Pete, love, usually.'

'Pete, I wonder, did Mr Barton ask to use your phone just now?'

Pete nodded. 'Yes, rang through to his son.'

'You didn't happen to hear what he said, did you?'

'He just told him to get out, that he was bringing back a detective. 'And she's bloody nosy', he said to Barry. Excuse the language, miss.'

She dismissed that with a motion of her hand. 'That's very helpful, thank you.'

'Are you the detective?'

She laughed. 'Yes I am. And he's right, I *am* bloody

nosy!'

'Then I hope you will find out what's going on around here.'

'Me too.'

She was deep in thought as she hurried back to Miss Marriott's. So she had been right. For some odd reason, Clive had rung ahead to tell Barry and Jane to leave, then pretended to take Dee back to his house to talk to them, and feigned surprise that they weren't there.

What *was* going on in Hartwell Priory? And how was Clive Barton involved in it?

There had been no time to have a wash or get changed, but at least she wasn't very late.

Dee and Miss Marriott dined quietly together beneath the glassy stares of the stuffed animal heads, and chatted about art, the theatre, anything but the recent events in the village. And after dinner, Bill and Nat arrived, apologising but clearly hoping they could wangle a coffee.

Miss Marriott was predictably generous and seemed delighted to have the two men there. Somehow, the conversation turned to music, and by nine o'clock, Nat was seated at the piano in the corner of the drawing-room, playing old romantic tunes for his hostess, who sat beside him on the piano stool, turning the page of the sheet music every so often, and begging him for a new piece whenever he came to the end of the previous one. Several times she turned to smile benevolently at Dee and Bill, sitting close together on adjacent corners of the two sofas; presumably Miss Marriott thought she was giving them a chance to spend time together by keeping the sergeant busy.

'I haven't had this much fun in years!' the old lady

said, and Nat grinned at her, perfectly happy to entertain her and leave the other two to talk, no doubt about the case.

The music was lovely, and Dee wondered why she had never known about this skill of Nat's. She must ask him later where he had learned to play so well. She sipped her coffee and leaned back, perfectly relaxed.

She told Bill the story of Miss Didsbury's hedge, and what Sylvia had told her about Clive catching her and Barry in their 'meeting place'.

'It's interesting,' he commented.

She nodded. 'Yes, though I'm not sure it's useful, as such, although Clive has been acting rather oddly.' She went on to tell him about that evening, and the way he had pretended to take her back to his house for a chat with Janna, Barry and his girlfriend Adelle.

Bill made a mental note of all this. But he sighed. 'I don't know if it means anything though. It could just be a normal family desire to protect one another. It's hard to see if it helps to provide any of them with a full alibi for the events on Friday night. It still gives any or all of them time to attack Tristan Summers and Serafina Rainbow, if they wanted to. You could say it makes it seem as if Barry Barton really does have something to hide, just because his father's working so hard to keep Barry out of things.'

'Probably he's just protecting Barry from Adelle's anger if she finds out what he's been getting up to with Sylvia.'

Bill nodded, a grin breaking through his usual dour expression. 'Young idiot.'

'By the way, Rob's coming up tomorrow, and staying until Saturday.'

He grinned again, pleased for her. 'So you'll have your customary assistant with you. Everyone needs a

Dr Watson.'

'I think I'm the Dr Watson, he's the Holmes.'

He glanced over to the piano and saw that neither Nat nor Miss Marriott was looking this way, then he leaned forward to quickly kiss her lips. 'Don't do yourself down, love. You're definitely the Holmes.'

Later as she was getting ready for bed, she realised with irritation that once again, he had not given away anything about the case from the police side of things. She shook her head. She would have to get better at prising information out of him.

It was almost lunchtime on Wednesday when Dee spotted the car pulling up outside. She ran to the hall to open the front door, and as her brother unfolded himself from the car and stretched, she took him by surprise as she ran to hug him.

'Steady on, Deedee, I've got a crick in my neck from sitting still for so long,' he grumbled, but kissed her cheek and grinned at her, laughing down from his height of six feet to her modest five feet three inches. 'Here, take my jacket, will you, and I'll grab my bag from the back seat.'

A minute later, rather like a new subject coming to pay homage at the queen's feet, Rob came forward to do an odd kind of shallow bow and then kissed the back of the delighted old lady's hand.

Miss Marriott very formally said, 'How do you do?' But her smile was wide and warm, almost cheeky, Dee noted. The old woman was certainly enjoying having her young visitors.

Doris hung up his jacket and went into the kitchen to put the kettle on to boil, whilst Dee carried Rob's small suitcase upstairs—what on earth did he have in there, she wondered, a few socks and pants and shirts couldn't possibly weigh so much—Rob himself sat in the armchair beside Miss Marriott and began the long process of answering all her questions with either the whole truth or a partial version of it.

By the time they all sat down to lunch, Miss Marriott was laughing at his jokes and very much enjoying herself. Dee felt more relaxed than she had since arriving at Hartwell Priory. She couldn't wait to tell him everything. Her spirits soared.

When Miss Marriott retired to her room after lunch, Dee and Rob were free to do as they wished.

First, Dee wanted to show him the churchyard. During lunch, Miss Marriott had alluded to 'our sad events here', and asked Rob if he was also involved in the investigation with Dee. He noticed Dee's tiny shake of the head and frown, and said with his usual disarming smile,

'Oh well, you know, not really. It's more the chance to get away from London for a few days and see my big sis.'

Dee doubted Miss Marriott believed a word of it, but at least the conversation took a lighter turn.

They sat on the wall and Dee told him all about that awful night. He listened in silence, his eyes looking at the scene right there in front of them and picturing with his inner eye the night of the fire. He thought it sounded like the sort of thing their mother would be better off not knowing about. He could only thank God that Dee herself had not been hurt.

His silence seemed to fill the air, Dee thought, and drifting to a halt, she realised the birds no longer sang, the bees had gone again. Goosebumps stood out on her arms and she hugged herself, wishing she'd worn a cardigan over her so-short dress, or even some slacks instead of the dress. After a few more seconds, she said, in practically a whisper,

'Oh Rob, it was horrifying. So frightening. The

mob-like violence. It was meaningless and completely beyond all control. Anything could have happened.'

'Sounds like it did,' he said, putting his arm across her shoulders. He produced a paper bag of liquorice allsorts from his pocket. 'Have a sweetie, the sugar will perk you up a bit.'

She selected a pink round with a liquorice core and popped it into her mouth. Around the sweet she said, 'Yes, isn't it terrible to think that two people died that night? Tempers were running high. The villagers were outraged over the cavalier way the work was going ahead in spite of their protests. There's so much ill will on both sides.'

He shook his head. 'Shocking.' He got to his feet and pulled her up behind him, placing her hand in the crook of his arm and they began to meander the churchyard.

They stopped at Maureen Barton's headstone, lying on its side beside the gaping grave itself. She wondered if it would ever be filled in again or the stone replaced. Logically that seemed unlikely. She told Rob all about Clive, what she knew about him and his wife's 'death', and about Janna and Bartholomew. And about how shifty Clive had been the last day or two.

After almost half an hour they finally moved on, and as they went, something snapped like a twig beneath Rob's foot. He kept going, unconcerned, but Dee glanced back at the 'twig'. It was blackened from the fire, and brittle, yet it seemed too smooth for a twig. She bent to retrieve it and held it up to look at.

'A walking stick?' Rob wrinkled his nose. 'Dropped that night, do you think?'

'Yes, I do. And I know whose it is. I recognize the knob on the end. It's Miss Marriott's. She was very upset over losing it in all the confusion, but I couldn't let her stay and look for it. Luckily, though, Doris found her another one at home.'

'And it's definitely hers? I mean, they do all look pretty much the same.'

'Oh yes, it's hers. That bit in the middle is—or rather was—a little etched gold cap inset into the wood. See? That's some kind of bird. You can't really make it out with the fire damage. I suppose there's no point in taking it back to her now it's in two bits.'

'Like you said, she's using a new one.'

'Yes.' Dee threw the two pieces aside. She looked about her, leading him a few yards ahead. 'So this is about where the fire started. The Seekers of Light as they called themselves were about here, by the brazier. There it is, look, almost unrecognisable.'

Rob glanced in the direction she indicated and saw it there on the sooty ground, just a jumble of twisted metal now.

'Ahoy there!' came a familiar voice.

They turned to see Bill and Nat coming towards them grinning broadly. Dee was relieved to see Bill was holding himself more naturally, moving more easily. Clearly his ribs were beginning to knit.

'Ahoy there'?' Rob queried with a smirk. 'Do we say that on land now?'

Nat was laughing. The three men all shook hands, as Bill simply shrugged and said,

'It just came out. I couldn't think of anything else. I presume you're here to intrude on my case?'

'Of course. And more than that, I'll lay you ten to one that we'll solve it first.'

'Only ten to one?' Bill quirked a dark eyebrow. 'Sounds like you're not too confident. I think the cops will have you beaten easily enough.'

Ignoring this challenge, Rob just laughed and said,

'By the way, Nat, Violet sends her love and told me to tell you to keep out of trouble.'

Nat laughed his big loud laugh that seemed to come from the depths of his barrel-like chest. Shaking his head, he said, 'Ah my lovely Violet. She worries about me.'

A little later that afternoon, Dee and Rob drove to Greater Hartwell and slipped into a pew at the back of the church as Kenneth Riley took his place at the end of a long table. There was a meeting of the Save Hartwell Priory Church Group who ironically had been meeting, Dee had discovered from a conversation with Miss Marriott the day before, every two weeks in the church at Greater Hartwell for almost six months now. He got up to greet the first few attendees, shaking hands and patting backs as they exchanged pleasantries.

Dee began to wonder if she should have tried to speak with the other people at the meeting, but she didn't recognise any of them, and anyhow, she had no authority to interrupt a meeting to ask questions.

She observed, from her place behind the pillar, that almost immediately Ken noticed Rob sitting there in his smart, flattering suit, his hair neatly combed instead of standing up on end like it usually did when he'd run his fingers through it in frustration or deep thought.

Ken Riley's gaze returned again and again to Rob, and Dee began to feel that it was wrong of them to distract him so badly from his job, taking advantage of her suspicions regarding his private life. She knew that he couldn't see her properly due to the pillar, indeed she had chosen to sit there for that very reason. But it meant that he was not on his guard until the meeting ended forty-five minutes later, and everyone had taken their leave apart from Rob and Dee. They stayed in their places and waited for him to approach them, as they knew he surely would.

He busied himself for a few minutes with collecting teacups and taking these through to the vestry, before coming back down the aisle towards them. He appeared partly resigned and partly irritated, already guessing that this was some kind of trap, and yet he was unable to resist his curiosity. Rob was, it seemed, a truly irresistible bait.

Riley sat in the pew in front of them, turning to lean his elbow on the back of the seat, and saying to Dee, whilst glancing several times at Rob, 'I've nothing more to say to you. Nothing. Just leave me alone. Please. I don't know why you've come here again, bothering me like this.'

Dee gave up her pretence of politeness and rolled her eyes. 'For goodness' sake, you must have known there were still things I needed to ask you.'

He huffed at her, the faintest of flushes stealing up his neck towards his chin, an excellent indication that he was ruffled. 'You're not the police, you know. I don't have to tell you anything. You can't make me.'

Rob spoke then, his voice soft, calm. 'That's true of course. But you can tell us things you can't tell the police, things that you just guess, suspect, or feelings you have, or ideas, and it won't be official. You won't need to make a legal statement.'

Riley nodded then shook his head as if waking up. 'I'm sorry, but who are you, exactly?'

Dee said, 'He's my brother, and he's a barrister. You can tell him anything, it won't go any further.'

With a cheeky grin, Rob said, 'And I believe we share some beliefs in common too. I know what it's like to have to keep your own secrets as well as those of others.'

Red-faced, Riley looked down at his hand, worrying at the cuticle of a fingernail with that of his thumb. Dee would have waited, giving him a few minutes to decide what he wanted to do, to quieten his conscience, or perhaps to consult it. But much to her frustration, Rob spoken again:

'Think of it this way. People—in your congregation, or perhaps people you meet in the wider world—no doubt tell you things. Oh, it may not be told to you under the seal of the confessional in the precise sense, but they would feel the benefit of unburdening themselves to you. Now obviously, what they tell you is private, and just as confidential as anything spoken in a confession. But the problem we have is this—two people have been horribly, brutally killed. And if there is even one thing that you can tell us about either of those people, it might be enough to see justice done in this life, as well as the next.'

'Sara, you mean?' A tear rolled down Riley's cheek and Dee saw now that he really was wrestling with his conscience. She should have respected that more, she realised. She waited, glad now that Rob had spoken. It had been a good idea to bring him along, not just as a lure, that had been unfair, but he was good with people, so gentle, so understanding. She felt rather in awe of him now. He was no longer just her cute little brother with a cheeky grin and a pretty face, he was now an advocate for justice.

Rob held out a neatly pressed handkerchief to the Reverend who took it with a brief embarrassed nod, his face even redder than before. He wiped his eyes and nose, and nodded again. Dee held her breath. He was going to tell them everything, she just knew it.

'I-I found her that night, you know. Or perhaps you don't. The fire... It was much too close to her, and I saw that she was just lying there, not moving. I pulled her away. And I could see that her legs were burned, really very badly burned. But I thought she might still... I thought at first it was the fire that had—hurt—her. I tried to revive her, but as I moved her, I saw the wound on her head, the blood, and her eyes were just—just staring. And so I—I realised I was... I was too late.' He wiped his eyes again with the handkerchief, his hand shaking.

Dee felt for the poor man; she too could not shake off the horror of that night, the noise, the confusion.

After a moment, he continued, 'Sara—Serafina as she called herself—came to see me, oh it must have been a couple of months ago now, almost as soon as it all started. She joined the Seekers of Light group, as you are no doubt aware. They had only just arrived in the village. But she didn't quite fit in. She was older than most of them. She was several years older than Tristan, the leader, but they'd met, got to know one another over the course of a couple of days, and er, well, become lovers, and so it seemed natural, almost, that she became part of the group.

'I think she believed in what they were doing—at least, in part. But part of her 'journey', if you want to call it that, was far more personal. She told me she had left the village of Hartwell Priory some years ago after living there for most of her life, but she had felt drawn back to revisit her old life. She asked me to pray for her, to receive strength. We met several times to talk and pray. I got to know her quite well, she was such a nice lady, but sadly unable to turn her back on the past.'

Dee and Rob exchanged looks of excitement. Dee's heart was pounding, it seemed to fill her ears, she hoped they couldn't hear it too. She folded her hands in her lap and fixed her full attention on Riley, determined to appear calm, professional. A thought came to her. Perhaps should she be making notes? She just didn't know. In any case, she thought, he's already started, and getting out a notebook now might give him a chance to change his mind and clam right up. So she kept as still and quiet as she could.

'She said Tristan was doing some kind of study into religion and fanaticism, and when he heard about the church closing down and the graves being moved it was the perfect opportunity to get a bit of handy research done on the cheap. But as I say, she had already come to the village for an entirely different reason, on a personal pilgrimage, of sorts. When she met with Tristan and heard about the Seeker's plans, she saw an opportunity to use the Seekers and their séances to force someone to admit to a crime.'

Dee nodded to herself. This was exactly what she had suspected about the motivation behind Tristan's so-called prophecy.

Riley seemed to have come to the end of what he had to say. Rob said,

'Did she tell you what that crime was? Or who had committed it?'

Riley shook his head. 'I'm sorry, no. She said very little more than that. She told me she'd once witnessed something terrible, and that was what made her feel she had to run away from the village. Years ago, she'd said, though she wouldn't be more specific than that. She said she had no proof, that the police wouldn't have listened to her and so she had no choice but to run. I'm not sure Tristan believed her, but he helped her. My instinct was that he just thought she was trying to provide herself with a reason to stay in the group. But in any case, he was more than willing to make the most of the chance to make mischief, or a name for himself, I suppose, and so their scheme was born.' He lifted his hands then dropped them again into his lap in a gesture of helplessness. 'I'm sorry I can't tell you more. That's all she told me. Honestly. As I say, I was mostly focussed on getting her to look to the future, to leave her sorrows over the past behind her. It grieves me that she wasn't able to do that. As I said, she was a nice lady. I shall miss her.'

*

Chapter Twenty-two

'Shall we take a drive to the university?' Dee asked as they came out of the church, leaving a relieved Ken Riley to get on with the rest of his afternoon. 'I know you've already spent a lot of time on the road today. Could you bear a bit more?'

'Isn't it in Cambridge?' Rob wrinkled his nose. 'Is that even allowed? I don't want to get surrounded by chaps with pitchforks and torches, running us out of town for being Oxford alumni.'

'Idiot!' Dee punched his arm. 'It seems too good an opportunity to miss whilst you're here. Or rather, while my car is here.'

'What do you want to do there?'

She shrugged. 'Try to talk to people who knew Tristan? Students or colleagues?'

He went round to unlock the car door and got in, leaning across to open hers for her. Dee hopped into the passenger seat, wondering why she was still letting her brother drive her car. Rob threw a map at her.

'Try to figure out the best way to go while I turn us around.'

Dee began to unfold the map, trying not to obscure Rob's view of the road. Why did they make these things so impossibly huge? She quickly turned the map up the right way before he could make a comment on women and maps.

They planned to stop for an early evening meal at some cafe before braving the university itself. Dee thought she knew where to find Tristan's particular college.

But no cafe appeared to be open. Dee looked at her watch. And feeling like an utter fool, Dee turned to Rob. 'It's almost six! I hadn't realised it was so late. And, it's Wednesday, half-day closing! Nowhere will be open.'

'Don't fret, we can easily go to a pub, we're bound to find one that does food. Or failing that, a hotel. If we go Dutch, I think we can afford a hotel.'

'Yes, but...' Another thought struck her. She closed her eyes in frustration. 'Oh, how could I have been so stupid! No admin offices will be open at the college at this time of day, either. The staff will have all gone home. And we've come all this way!'

She stood there in the street, feeling about an inch tall and calling herself all sorts of names. They'd spent just over two hours on the road since leaving Riley in his church, and all for nothing.

'Over there!' Rob was pointing.

It was a small restaurant. And outside, a welcome sight, a sign stating: "Lunches, dinners served here: no need to book".

That was something at least. They headed that way. Inside the dining-room there was a hubbub of conversation, and it looked at first glance as if all the tables were taken. But luckily the head waiter spotted one at the back, right near the doors to the kitchen. Not the best spot, but they couldn't afford to be fussy, and he led them over, leaving them with some menus to look at.

Almost immediately a waitress came to take their order. The first problem dealt with didn't make the other issue any easier though. There was no getting round it—they had come here for nothing. And the last thing Dee felt like doing was coming back another day. Even with roast beef and Yorkshire pudding inside her and an appetising-looking cherry pie and custard, she felt like an utter failure. How could she have made such a stupid mistake? She didn't know whether to scream with frustration or bang her head on the very solid wooden table in front of her.

Her voice was as low as her confidence as she said to her brother, 'I don't know what to do now. I suppose we may as well drive straight back to Hartwell Priory.'

'Hmm.'

She didn't know if his near silence was due to him being annoyed with her or he was just preoccupied with his food. She gnawed her lip, worrying.

He wiped his mouth on his napkin and leaned back with a satisfied smile. 'That was delicious.'

She nodded; her thoughts ran in circles over their problem.

'Finished, miss?'

Dee was started by a waiter placing a tentative hand on the edge of the plate.

'Oh, er, yes, thanks. Delicious.' Dee turned her startled expression into a smile. 'Thank you.'

The waiter cleared the table then brought over the bill at Rob's request. Both of them chipped in their share of the money then went outside where they stood looking about them.

'The college is that way,' Dee said, pointing at a sign.

They drifted along the lane, still somewhat aimlessly. Outside the gate to the college, there was a cluster of students who had clearly not gone home for the long summer break, either that, or they had returned early.

Dee approached them, saying, 'Hi there. I was wondering, do any of you know Professor Tristan Summers?'

A couple of young men shook their heads and wandered away. But two girls, about twenty years of age, nodded.

'Poor Tristan!' one of them said. 'Have you heard? He's been *killed*!'

'Actually killed, like, *dead*.' Her companion confirmed, nodding her head earnestly.

The first girl wiped away a tear. 'He was such a sweetheart!' Her voice turned into a wail towards the end. This could be useful, Dee thought, and felt lucky to have found someone who knew him.

The other girl added, 'And even though he was quite old, he was so dreamy.'

'Was he your tutor?' Dee asked gently.

Both girls shook their heads. Dee felt her optimism deflating. But then, the second one said,

'Oh, but he was such a character. Everyone knew him. He was always into all sorts of pranks, you know? Nothing like a stuffy old professor. He was fun. He was like one of us. Not that the other staff approved, of course. Rumour has it that he was always getting warned by the Dean.'

'I see,' Dee nodded. 'And did you know if he had a—um—lady friend?'

'No, I mean, we all knew he was married. His wife never came to any college functions, though she came to the Spring fair and, you know, family events, nothing too posh, no evening banquets or that sort of thing. I think they lived out at Fen Ditton. She was a bit of an old frump, I mean, compared to him anyway, he always seemed so 'with it'. They've got ten-year-old twin girls. He doted on them, often talked about them.'

'Remember, she came to that prize-giving event in May? She was much too old for him,' girl number one commented, then as if she thought she'd been too harsh, she hastily added, 'But she was very nice too, and they seemed happy, I suppose. But she was quieter than him, didn't have much to say.'

'He did all the talking!' her friend said with a giggle.

'Oh he loved the sound of his own voice!' the other agreed.

Dee couldn't think of anything else to ask them, so she thanked them with a smile, ignoring their avid looks at her baby brother who was, in any case, staring at a group of four young men. He went over to them. Dee watched him talking with them for a few minutes, and just as she was wondering if she should join them, he said something she couldn't catch and came back to her.

'Was that business or pleasure?' She smirked at him.

'Haha, very funny, sis. It seems they didn't know him all that well either, so I didn't really get anything other than the fact that Tristan was known for his stunts and schemes, and that he'd been warned about the fact that his behaviour could bring the college's reputation into disrepute. He seemed quite proud, even boastful, of the fact that everyone knew him as a bad boy and that he wanted to 'shake up' the stuffy, elitist establishment.'

'So he would definitely enjoy thinking up something controversial like the Seekers of Light and causing trouble in a village, partly for his research, but I suspect mainly for the sheer fun of it,' Dee said slowly, reflecting on it. 'But that doesn't mean he deserved to die.'

'No indeed.' Rob nodded back at the group of young men. 'They said if we are keen to find out more about Summers, it might be worth going to the memorial at the little chapel along the lane. Half past seven, it starts.'

Dee consulted her watch. 'In about twenty minutes, then.'

'Shall we try to find a few more people who knew him, or...?'

Dee looked about her. 'There's hardly anyone around. No, let's take a stroll along to this chapel and see if there are any early arrivals.'

There were plenty of floral tributes by the altar in the quaint little chapel. A quick look at the cards attached to the flowers indicated that, as they already knew, he had been very popular. The memorial was solely for Tristan Summers, of course, as Kenneth Riley had told them Serafina only met Tristan after he arrived in the village. Dee wondered if anyone was holding a memorial for Serafina somewhere. If not, that would be a dreadful shame.

By a quarter past seven, people had begun to arrive. There were a few older people Dee took to be college staff, but most of the attendees were young woman. She left Rob to wander amongst them, smiling his way along in the hopes he could winkle out some new information. Dee herself stood there looking about her and wondering what to do.

A man in a well lived-in tweed jacket came over. He smiled at her, a very charming smile, and said, 'Haven't seen you around the college before. Did you know Tristan Summers well?'

Dee treated him to her most encouraging smile and replied, hoping he wouldn't see through the lie. 'No, as a matter of fact, it was the other person who died in the fire, Serafina, that I knew slightly. We—er—we shared the same hairdresser.'

'Cool,' he said, the least hip fellow she had ever heard use the new slang. 'Don't know anything about her. Though no doubt she was delightful.'

Dee smiled again. 'She was. She and Tristan were a couple, you know.'

'It's a good thing the college didn't know that, they had enough problems dealing with his teaching methods and his rather casual approach to his timetable.'

'Was he the sort of man who had a lot of girlfriends on the side?' Dee asked. 'I rather got the impression he might be a married man?'

'He was married, yes. Certainly a few of us in the faculty knew his propensity for womanising. So long as he kept things quiet, the college was prepared to turn a blind eye. All though of late... To be honest, his private life wasn't the worst thing about Summers.'

Dee raised an eyebrow. 'Oh?'

He leaned a little too close. 'Yes, well, to be honest...'

That was the second time he'd said that, she noted, and wondered how reliable anything he told her would be.

'...he was a bit of a swine. Oh he pretended it was all in the name of research, but he really was a cynical, manipulative so-and-so.'

'You didn't like him, Professor...?'

'Simon Sayers. School of Sociology.' He sighed. 'Did I like him? If I'm honest, not really, no. Sorry. As I said, he was rather too full of himself for my liking, and one felt that it was a only matter of time before the college lost patience.' He looked at her. She smiled.

'As I say, he wasn't a friend of mine,' Dee replied. 'I was—concerned—about Serafina. It's interesting you used the word 'manipulative'. That's how I've come to view him too. And...'

A man in clerical garb took up his position in front of the altar, and a silence fell on the assembled crowd. A few last-minute stragglers quickly filled the pews at the back. Dee slipped into the nearest space, followed by Simon Sayers who sat a little too close to her, his wool-covered thigh pressing against hers.

'We are gathered here together on this fine autumn evening to commemorate the life of Professor Tristan Summers so brutally taken from us many years before his time. Please stand for the hymn, *To Thou Oh Lord I Cry*.'

The congregation stood. For the next hour they sang and prayed and listened to words of comfort before finally being set free once again into the last golden drops of evening sunshine.

'Oh, there you are.' Rob came over to Dee and they joined the throng of mourners leaving the chapel, Dee thinking it was rather too similar to that night when she and Miss Marriott had left the room at the pub to go in search of the Seekers of Light and their impromptu séance in the churchyard.

But outside it was still a mellow early twilight instead of dark night. And the crowds thinned and moved away peacefully, gentle laughter and the sound of conversation on the air, their footsteps echoing in a comforting way in the narrow lane.

Simon Sayers was right on her heel, not willing to leave her quite yet. 'Erm—I was wondering... What about a drink?'

She smiled back politely. 'Oh I'm sorry, I'm afraid I can't. I need to get off—we've a long drive ahead of us. Thanks anyway.'

He nodded, not pushing it, which made her like him a little more. 'Of course. Well, have a safe drive back. Bye.'

*

Chapter Twenty-three

As she came down the stairs the next morning, Dee was already planning the day, thinking about who she and Rob could speak to first. She was also hoping she would have a chance to spend some time with Bill. Lunch at the pub, perhaps, or failing that, tea or dinner, anything, she didn't much care, she just wanted to see him. And she was sure there was more he could tell her, if she could only find a way to weasel the information out of him.

Her main goals of speaking to Kenneth Riley again and going to Cambridge university to try to get information about Tristan Summers having been achieved, sort of, she had been wracking her brains about what to do next. Rob would be going back to London the day after tomorrow, and she wanted to make the most of having him there to discuss things with. After almost a week in the village, she wanted to leave and go home, but she couldn't do that until she'd found out who was behind the murders.

She turned the bend in the stairs and below her in the entrance hall, she could see Doris and Miss Marriott standing there by the open front door, leaning out to watch something that was happening just out of sight. Rob was there too, just behind them in the doorway to the morning-room. He glanced up to see her there.

'What's happening?' Dee asked.

'Not sure, but there's an ambulance just down the street. It arrived several minutes ago in a great flurry of noise.'

'My goodness!' Dee hurried the last few stairs and came over to them. 'Do you know what's happened?'

'I'm terribly worried, Dee, dear,' Miss Marriott said, turning, all a-twitter, one hand tangling in her pearls, the other still clutching Doris's arm for support. 'It might be something serious. What if someone we know has been taken ill?'

'Don't worry, I'll go and find out,' Dee said, patting Miss Marriott's arm. The poor old dear, as Dee termed her to herself, looked greatly relieved.

'If you're sure you don't mind, dear...'

Dee already had on her outdoor shoes, in expectation of going somewhere with Rob as soon as they'd had breakfast. She didn't bother with a jacket, it wasn't cold this morning and just rushed out into the lane. Glancing back, she saw Miss Marriott still there, watching, and Doris trying to persuade her to go in and sit down. Rob squeezed past the two women and ran to catch Dee up.

Now they were closer, Dee felt as though a cold hand clutched at her heart. Her brain began to make sense of what her eyes were showing her: the ambulance, its light still flashing, the siren off now, the people waiting outside the door of the house. The woman was weeping softly, and the man who comforted her was Barry Barton, and even as realisation struck and Dee began to come forward, the stretcher was wheeled outside: a form on the stretcher, coming out feet first under the blanket. But then she saw the head was not covered, so it was not too late... The grip on her heart eased as she came to the conclusion he was not seriously injured.

'What happened?' she asked for the umpteenth time in the last five minutes. Then she remembered it was not really any of her business, but already Barry was looking at her, his face a pale unrevealing mask.

Adelle was weeping on his shoulder, and beyond them was Janna, or Jane, white-faced, with her hands to her mouth, trying to hold back the shock.

'What is it?' Rob asked, then corrected himself. 'I mean who, who is it? Someone you know?'

'It's Clive Barton.'

There was nothing else to do but simply stand there. The ambulance was about to leave, the driver got into his seat and off it sped, the bell jangling everyone's nerves.

Along the lane, people looked out of their doors and windows. Pete Guthrie and a fair-haired woman Dee assumed was his wife, had come out of the pub—it was too early for opening time, they'd obviously heard the noise and come out like everyone else to see what was going on. Mrs Padham was at the door of the guesthouse, half-hidden, but even so, Dee could see the woman's hand gripped the edge of the door, the other one braced against the wall, steadying her. As the ambulance left, Bet saw the three youngsters standing by the door, saw their anxious looks and Adelle's tears. Bet began to stumble forward. You couldn't call it walking, she staggered as if drunk then fell on her knees in the lane.

Dee ran to her, but the woman was in a faint now,

on the ground, senseless. Rob pelted over, pulling off his jacket to lay over Bet, and as Dee looked about for someone else to help, a fine misty rain began to fall.

After a minute of hand-patting and coaxing, Bet, embarrassed and shocked, came out of her faint and was strong enough to stand, supported by Dee and Barry, one on either side of her. They took her back to the guesthouse and into the kitchen where Dee helped her into a chair and Rob, efficient as always in his slightly fussy manner, made a cup of hot sweet tea for her.

Barry hovered in the doorway, ready to leave as soon as it seemed appropriate, but Dee shot him a look, and demanded, 'What happened to Clive? Is he all right?'

He looked surly, like a teenager caught smoking behind the cycle sheds at school. Dee wanted to shake him. In a sulky low voice, he said,

'I don't want to talk about it.'

Confused, she said, 'What? What do you mean? How did your father get hurt? And how badly hurt is he?'

'He hit his head. Got a concussion, that's all. A day or two in hospital, he should be right as rain. That's what the ambulance chap said.'

Dee stared back at him. 'What happened?' she repeated.

He shrugged in that nothing-to-do-with-me manner that she found so infuriating. 'We fell out over something. It's none of your business.'

'Well at least tell Bet, so she can stop worrying.'

'Like I said, he's going to be all right, and it's nothing to do with anyone but me and my dad.' He turned on his heel and left.

Dee and Rob exchanged a look. Bet said, her voice a little unsteady,

'He always was a volatile lad, that one. It wouldn't be the first time he'd swung a fist at someone. He and Clive have always locked horns, Barry was more of a mother's boy.'

Dee seemed to remember hearing something like that before. Was it anything to do with the police digging up Maureen's grave, she wondered. And finding nothing, more importantly. Perhaps word had got out, it usually did.

'So much for being a Seeker of Light,' Rob said.

They stayed with Bet a little longer, then, sure that she was more or less recovered, they returned to Miss Marriott's and broke the news. Doris immediately gave a yelp of alarm, and with a nod from Miss Marriott, she threw aside her apron and raced along the lane to her mother.

A couple of hours later, Doris reported that Clive was sitting up in bed in the hospital and was having a ham sandwich.

'So Mum's a lot happier too,' she added. 'We got the bus over there to see him. Just to set Mum's mind at rest. They've said he'll probably come back home tomorrow.'

Rob said to Dee when they were alone, 'Looks like Bet and Clive are back to being Bet and Clive.'

Dee nodded, glad for Bet's sake that it was so, and hoping that this time things would work out between them. Although she felt a slight qualm. She still remembered how Clive had fooled her by phoning the house before taking her there, supposedly to see Barry, Jane and Adelle.

Miss Marriott had received a last-minute invitation to lunch at the Merchants', which included both her guests, with a bald-faced lie of an apology, stating that they had accidentally been overlooked when all the invitations had been sent out earlier in the week, and that this error had only just been discovered. If it was up to Dee, she would have turned it down. But as she reminded Rob privately, this was work, not pleasure, and her personal feelings had to be set aside.

It wasn't worth worrying about, he said. They'd get the chance to ask a few questions which could be useful.

It came as no surprise to Dee that Vanessa Merchant latched onto Rob immediately, and didn't seem to notice that her womanly charms held no appeal for him. Clad in another low-cut, very short dress, she took hold of his arm and pulled him about the room, introducing him to everyone as 'our top barrister-friend from London'.

Dee stayed with Miss Marriott, enduring several tedious conversations with people she didn't know about other people she didn't know who had died more than twenty years earlier or moved away from the village to live a life in greener grassier lands than Hartwell Priory. Dee chafed under the social constraints that prevented her from sitting everyone down and demanding that they answered her questions. It would be so much easier, she thought, if she wielded absolute power.

The mayor was amongst the honoured guests—no doubt a celebrated former BBC newsreader fitted perfectly into the mayor's social circle. But almost as if he had been forewarned, his honour Edwin Windward seemed to instinctively avoid both Dee and her brother.

Lunch was a formal affair. The guests—around twenty people in all—were seated on either side of a long table in what Dee termed 'boy-girl fashion': each lady was flanked on either side by a gentleman.

Couples were separated. And so Dee found herself between Merchant at the head of the table, and a man of about forty whose name she didn't quite catch. To her dismay, she found that this stranger was completely monopolised by Vanessa Merchant and her heaving bosom, and so with great reluctance, Dee turned to smile at her host.

'It's delightful to meet you again, Miss...er...' began Merchant in a vague yet pompous manner. He smiled at her, quite a charming smile, she had to admit. Perhaps this wouldn't be so bad, after all. 'Are you still staying with Miss Marriott? I wasn't sure if you had already left.'

'Yes, I am, and my brother has come to join us for a few days. We're very grateful for your invitation.'

'Not at all, not at all,' he blustered and seemed embarrassed, which she found a little surprising. Why after all should he care what she thought or if she was offended? 'Are you family, then or distant relatives?'

'Neither. Miss Marriott kindly invited us to stay with her. We've come here from London at her invitation to look into the recent events in the village.' Not quite true, but it served, she thought.

He was looking pensive. 'Reporter, aren't you?' And before she could deny it, he went on: 'Started out that way myself many moons ago. Not an easy life. Even harder for a woman, one hears. Need a big story to get you your start. Could be something in our little local drama.' He patted her arm in what she chose to view as a fatherly gesture. 'Just take care of yourself. Of course, women have equality, but you're just a little bit of a thing, any average-sized chap could overpower you. Hate to see you get hurt.'

It was hard to know the best way to respond to this. On the face of it, it could even be viewed as a threat, but she didn't think he meant it that way. Perhaps after all, he was better with words when they were given him to speak by someone else's pen.

'Thank you. But I'm being very careful.'

'Of course, of course. Never had a daughter, but I can imagine what it would be like. Worrying.' and here his eyes dwelt briefly on Vanessa, his wife, laughing uproariously with the men on either side of her. 'Anything I can do to help, just ask,' Merchant added.

She bit her lip. Did she dare? Telling herself that at worst it could lead to a frosty silence, she said in a rush, 'What do you know about the building contract for the new houses in the village? I believe you, the mayor and Raynes are all at the same golf club.'

He didn't seem especially surprised that she'd asked. He drank a little wine, seemed to be seriously considering her question, then gave a slight shrug. 'I don't actually *know* anything. But my suspicion? Under the table contracts were awarded by local council officials in exchange for romantic favours and other benefits. Never discussed within my hearing, not outright anyhow. Alluded to, hinted at, possibly. But nothing I could quote, so to speak.'

It sounded—as always—a little like a news bulletin, but his expression was still grave, his eyes fixed on Dee, watching for her reaction. She believed he was sincere.

She nodded. 'I've heard that suggested.'

'No proof, obviously.'

'No.'

'Not the kind of story that lasts, in any case. There's always a new tragedy to take over, and contracts, mishandling of public funds, boring stuff, all too common.'

Dee nodded again. 'Sadly,' she agreed. Then

remembering what Doris had said, she added, 'Although, everyone needs a home.'

'Very true. My parents still live in their council house in Bromley where I grew up. Staunch labour voters. Wouldn't move unless forced out. But being so close to London, house prices are rising beyond the means of the ordinary person. As you say, houses are needed for all. A roof over one's head is hardly a luxury.'

To her surprise, Dee found she was beginning to like the man. She followed his troubled gaze as he pondered his wife again. He finished off his wine and reached for a top-up.

'No fool like an old fool, as the saying goes. Daughter of one of my mentors at the BBC. Got me to my position five years ago. But she leads me a merry dance, I can tell you.'

'Then perhaps it's time to put the boot on the other foot,' she told him, feeling able to speak boldly. 'There are plenty of attractive ladies in their forties and fifties who would be a much better match for you. You're retired now, so it doesn't matter how Vanessa's father feels about you.'

He gave her a crooked smile. 'That's an interesting suggestion. I suppose you're not putting yourself forward as a candidate?'

She grinned at him. 'Sorry, I'm taken.'

He sighed theatrically and nodded. 'Of course you are, my dear. And far too young for me. See, I can learn my lesson, after all. Got any idea who killed those two in the churchyard?'

Relieved at the change of subject, she could only say, 'I've got a few ideas, but that's not enough.'

'I heard there was an attack on the London policeman that came down here?'

She nodded. 'Yes, on Monday. He wasn't badly

hurt, but it was bad enough.'

'The name Jimmy Philpott was mentioned at the golf club yesterday. Always been a bad lot. Went right off the rails after his mother left home. Latchkey child, neglected. Left too much to his own devices. Studies show that children like that tend to fall prey to criminal activities and associations.'

Dee thought this over. 'I believe he was interviewed by the police,' she said cautiously. 'But I don't think he had anything to do with the deaths. Not directly anyway. Though I've been told that it was him who kicked over the brazier that caused the fire.'

'And therefore morally, he is to blame.' Eric Merchant shook his head. 'Dreadful business. Those beatniks were troublemakers, but, well, no one expects to pay quite such a high price for tomfoolery. Did you know two of them are Clive Barton's youngsters?'

'Yes. He told me that.'

'Another couple of kids who struggled to cope without a mother.'

Dee considered this for a few seconds. 'There are a number of absent mothers and fathers in the village.'

'That'll be at the back of this whole thing, you mark my words. Oh, a good cup of coffee, the perfect ending to any meal,' he added, seemingly out of the blue, and Dee reflected that he now sounded like an advertisement. Perhaps he'd been offered a contract on Independent Television, selling beverages. And he'd probably make an absolute fortune, she guessed.

Most startling though, was the fact that the meal was over and she hadn't even noticed her food.

*

Chapter Twenty-four

As soon as they returned to Miss Marriott's, their hostess went upstairs for her customary nap, assisted by Doris. Dee and Rob went into the morning-room, comfortable and with that lovely view of the garden, and compared notes.

Dee reported everything that Eric Merchant had said, adding, 'I'm warming to him now. He seemed far more 'human' today. Even if he does speak in headlines. And he's very unhappy about his marriage.'

'Well, next time, I'll sit by him and look intelligent, and you can do the rounds with Vanessa. I have a bruise the size of a fist on my right buttock thanks to that woman. I even said, in my campest voice, 'Do you know any nice boys around here?' D'you know what she said?'

Dee laughed. 'No, what?'

"Only you, sweetie!' Even then she didn't take the hint. I won't be able to sit down for a week! I shall report you to Monty for leading me into dangerous territory.'

'But did you find out anything useful?'

Her shook his head. 'Nope. Nothing.'

'Oh well, never mind...'

There was a tap at the door and Doris peeked in.

'Excuse me, Miss Dee, Mister Rob, there's Janna and Adelle here to see you if you are 'in'?'

Dee and Rob exchanged a look. 'We are definitely 'in',' Dee told her.

'I'll bring them through.'

'Would you like a cup of tea?' Dee asked the two women who remained standing just inside the morning-room door. She knew Doris wouldn't mind at all, and it might break the ice a little. They looked like two people who wanted to leave, she thought. How else could she put them at their ease and improve her chances of them telling her something?

But Janna shook her head. Adelle was hesitating, Dee saw, and suspected she would have accepted the offer if Janna had been willing too.

'We can't stay, we're leaving in a few minutes to go back to uni.' Janna's voice was low, as if she had no energy left for anything. 'We just wanted to say goodbye and thank you for all the help.'

'I was glad to be able to help,' Dee assured her. 'Are you sure everything is all right? Is there anything you need?'

Adelle shook her head now. 'We're off back to uni. Barry has already gone. After the way he lashed out at his dad... Well, the engagement's off. I told Barry, I'm not marrying a man who loses control and lashes out like that. I need a man who can be trusted to keep his temper.'

'Don't we all,' Dee commented fervently. 'Well,

we're very sorry to hear that things have come to an end. But probably best now than...'

'When I've got a couple of little ones to worry about too? Definitely. That's what my family said. Not that Barry saw it that way. But, my mind is made up.'

'And why did Barry hit Clive, do you know?' Rob asked.

'We were there when it happened. I mean, I can understand Barry being upset, we both were,' Janna said. 'But you know, that doesn't excuse...'

'Clive had just told us about Maureen. That she isn't really buried in the churchyard here. That she wasn't killed in a car accident in Cornwall. He told us everything. Barry just blew up, couldn't believe Clive had lied to him and Janna all these years.'

'We went to our mum's funeral,' Janna said. 'It was one of the worst days of my life. Dad put us through that and never seemed to think anything of it. And it was all a lie. I mean, we even chose the words to put on her gravestone.'

'I think he just didn't know what to do for the best,' Dee said gently. 'He wanted to try to protect you from being hurt.'

'I know. I know that really,' Janna replied. 'But it hurts like hell now, and it's still going to take a while to get used to the idea.'

'Of course.'

'But thank you for everything, you've been very kind. I hope you get to the bottom of all this.'

'I hope so too,' Dee said. They hugged one another and the two women left.

'At least we know now what that was all about. Just as we suspected, wasn't it?' Rob said, flopping into a chair.

'This case is going nowhere,' Dee said. 'I'm going to be back in London before long, and with nothing useful to show to Monty. I feel terrible. I'm a fraud. Why did I think that because I got lucky in Porthlea and was able to work out what had happened, that I would be able to do that again? I don't have any proper training. I'm not an investigator. I'm just an unemployed teacher with time on her hands and an empty bank account.' With a frustrated groan, she threw herself back in her seat, arms folded, glaring up at the ceiling to avoid breaking down in tears.

What annoyed her even more was that her brother began to laugh. She wondered how many years in prison she would get if she throttled him here in front of everyone.

'Here' was a pub in Greater Hartwell. They had run out of ideas of things to do this Friday, and with Rob returning to London the following day, Dee felt under pressure to find something for them to do to while away the time. He got up and went to the bar to get another round of drinks, returning with them and still grinning broadly at her.

She continued to glare at him, not willing to let him laugh her into a better mood. She could always plead insanity, she reminded herself. And Monty might defend her, giving her a discount because of his close friendship with the family.

'Good afternoon, Miss Gascoigne.'

She looked up to see Sergeant Wright looming over her. Either he'd read her murderous thoughts, or was just being pleasant.

'Good afternoon, sergeant. How are you?'

'Do you mind if I join you?' and he took a seat, setting his own pint down on the table.

'Er... Please do,' she said, seeing that he already had.

'I wanted to say, sorry about the way I interrogated you on the night of the churchyard fire. I know I was a bit—hostile. I didn't know then that you were a private investigator or that you had the trust of Scotland Yard.'

Dee wasn't sure she'd call Bill's professional attitude to her meddling, 'trust' exactly, but she smiled and thanked the sergeant. 'And how is the case coming on?' she asked.

Sergeant Wright cast a doubtful look in the direction of Rob.

'Oh, he's all right,' Dee said. 'He's my brother and he is a barrister, or soon will be, with the firm I work for.'

Wright's brow cleared and he nodded, satisfied. 'In that case, miss, I'd say the case is coming along slowly and I'm not sure that it's as good as we'd like.'

She nodded sympathetically. 'I know. Mine's the same. We were just saying that very thing, weren't we?'

Rob smirked at her. 'Something along those lines, yes.' He turned to the sergeant. 'What's your instinct about this case, sergeant? If you had to point the finger at someone, who would be your culprit?'

Sergeant Wright wriggled in his seat, an expression of delight on his face. He was enjoying this, she could see.

'Well now you're asking! To my mind, it stands between one of two people: either it was Mr Barton, or it was Jimmy Philpott. By all accounts, Jimmy Philpott was proper off his rocker that night. He'd been drinking, according to his mates, and he was really angry about the churchyard being dug up. And look at the way he attacked that London copper. Could have been very nasty. Philpott's always been a hothead at the best of times, as you might have heard.'

Dee nodded. 'Yes, we have heard that.' And she could perfectly see why Wright suspected him.

'So there's him, and he'd be favourite, in my view. But all the same, I keep coming back to Mr Barton.'

'Clive Barton?' Dee asked, just to be sure they were talking about the same man.

'Yes, miss.'

'And why do you think he may be involved, if you don't mind me asking?'

Wright leaned closer, dropping his voice to a confidential pitch. 'You know he only pretended his wife was dead? When they dug up her grave, there wasn't no one in it.'

Dee was disappointed. This was nothing new.

Rob said, 'Yes but we know how that came about.'

'Ah but do we?' Wright tapped the side of his nose. 'Think about it. He's got no proof he ever had a letter from that priest. Interpol's already been back on to the London coppers this morning to say they can't find no evidence of her ever going to Spain, let alone being buried there. In fact, we can't find that she or Henry Padham ever even had a passport, let alone used it to travel to Europe. It's all just too convenient.'

'If you're saying Maureen Barton was killed by her husband, then why? And what did he do with the body, sergeant?'

'That's the thing, sir, we don't know for sure. As to the why, well her and Padham were carrying on, so Barton would have been angry about that. Felt humiliated, you mark my words. But it seems clear from the hints them dropouts gave that she was buried somewhere in the graveyard secretly. 'The new one', they said. You mark my words, there's a secret grave in the churchyard that no one official knows about. And I'm in half a mind to arrest Clive now for the murder of his wife, and of them two dropouts. Except I've been told to leave it to them Scotland Yard boys.'

Dee was lost in thought, only half-attending to all this. She was almost convinced by Wright's argument. She had suspected Clive had secrets. And it seemed highly unlikely that Maureen Barton was still alive after these nine long years. A thought came to her.

'Was there ever a newspaper appeal for Maureen Barton or Henry Padham?'

'Asking them to get in touch, to assure relatives that they were all right? For Padham, yes, I believe so. But to my knowledge not for Maureen Barton. Not until Scotland Yard put one out the day before yesterday, in the Times, I think, and the Daily Sketch. Not that she'd be likely to read the Times, but most people read the Sketch, don't they?'

'I suppose it's too soon to expect a response.'

'Oh no, miss, no, we've had more responses than we can handle. About four hundred so far. We've got a team wading through them all. None of them look promising, mind you, but there's always a lot of nutters that like to push themselves forward into a police case.'

'Of course.' Dee reached for her Babycham and took a dainty sip. Over the rim of her glass, she could see Rob was deep in thought.

A young woman came into the pub at that point, and the sergeant hastily got to his feet. 'Well, it was nice seeing you. And once again, miss...'

'Oh don't worry about it, sergeant.'

That evening was a dull one. Dee and Rob joined Miss Marriott for dinner, and after dinner, Rob entertained them with silly songs at the piano. Miss Marriott loved it. Doubtless she had been brought up on such things when she was a girl. But Dee would have preferred to put on the television and relax in front of some detective drama or comedy show.

She felt fed-up. Her brother was going back to London in the morning. She wished with all her might she could go with him. They were no closer to solving the case, she had been here a week and all she had was information, but no clue what to do with it. If anything she had too much information.

And she hadn't seen Bill. She had spoken to him briefly on the phone. He sounded as fed-up as she was and said that he and Nat had been invited to dine with the chief superintendent of the local force, and that it had been impossible to decline, but he was not looking forward to it.

'We'll have to mind our Ps and Qs,' he'd said. 'And it's already looking as though I won't get a favourable report sent back to Arsey Asquith as it is.'

Asquith was Bill's own chief super at the Met. It was safe to say, they were not firm friends.

Dee paused her thoughts to briefly clap Rob's latest offering. Miss Marriott said goodnight, and Rob thanked her warmly for her generous hospitality. He kissed the delighted old woman's hand and she went off on Doris's arm with a big smile on her face.

Rob and Dee lingered in the drawing-room.

'I wish we'd been able to solve this whilst I was still here,' he said, with a sorrowful shake of the head. 'But oh well, I know you'll get to the bottom of the whole thing.'

'I'm glad one of us has some confidence.'

'Come on, Dee, this isn't like you. You're not a giver-upper.'

'I am a bit. If I could only get some of this to make sense.'

'Well what do we know?'

'Two people died that evening in the churchyard a week ago.'

'Who had the motive to kill them?'

'We don't really know. It depends on why they were killed. If it was sheer brutality and rage, then it could have been any of the villagers who were there that night, including Jimmy Philpott.'

'Or Clive Barton,' Rob added.

'Or Clive Barton. I don't even remember if he was there that night. I saw him in the meeting, but after that...'

'What about Bet Padham? Was she there that night?'

Dee stared at him in astonishment. 'I don't know. I've never even considered Bet as a suspect.'

'Well there you go then.' He kissed her cheek. 'Night-night, Sis.'

'Night.'

He paused in the doorway to glance back. 'By the way, I've left a little gift for you on your bed.' He winked at her then left.

She sat there for some time after he'd gone up to bed, thinking things over. When she went up to her room at last, she found a packet of liquorice allsorts placed on her pillow.

*

Chapter Twenty-five

It was now Saturday morning. Rob had gone back to London, leaving Dee feeling somewhat at a loose end. She'd had a morning coffee with Miss Marriott who was expecting guests for lunch, none of whom Dee felt like spending time with, even though, she realised afterwards, she could possibly have learned a little more. To make matters worse, Rob had taken her car again, leaving her stranded. She'd forgotten he would need it. Her half-formed thought of going to see Kenneth Riley for a third time was abandoned. She couldn't bear the thought of taking the bus again, and anyway, she had nothing pressing she wanted to ask him.

So just before twelve o'clock, she went to the pub, hoping rather against hope to find Bill, or Nat too, though especially Bill, but of course they were out, presumably kicking down doors and dragging suspects into the police station for interrogation. She grinned to herself at the mental image of this unlikely scenario. More likely they were drinking tea in the station house just along the lane, courtesy of Sergeant Wright. She doubted Bill had ever kicked down a door in his life, he'd be too afraid of crumpling one of his smart suits or losing a cufflink.

She stayed in the pub, ordering a pot of tea and a packet of crisps from Pete Guthrie who was as always wiping glasses behind the bar. Somehow her order got added onto the policemen's account, purely by accident of course, and it would serve Bill right for lumping her with paying for their lunch the other day.

She chose a quiet corner and was about to take her seat when a woman's voice arrested her.

'Drinking alone, like me. It's a bad habit to get into.'

Looking over, Dee saw it was the woman from the historical society. Her first name was Angela, Dee recalled, but what on earth was her surname? Dee wracked her brains whilst smiling in a vaguely friendly way.

'Can I join you?' Angela What-was-her-name said, already up out of her seat and coming over to Dee's table with what looked like a double scotch and soda in her hand. She was sitting down by the time Dee was saying,

'That would be lovely, Miss...'

'Oh, there's no need to be stuffy. Just call me Angela,' said Angela, and took a swig of her scotch.

'Lovely,' Dee said again, and settled into her own seat, feeling a bit of a party-pooper with her tea and crisps. 'I'm Dee.'

'I'm glad to catch you as a matter of fact. You see, there's something I feel I ought to tell you. It's about Clive...'

Dee was immediately all ears. She leaned her chin

on her elbows on the table and gave Angela Thingy her full attention.

'Go on.'

'Look, I'm sorry I was so snarky with you the other day. But I've heard from a couple of people that you're a private investigator looking into the deaths of those two beatnik-types. I thought at first you were just there to make trouble or to get your name in the paper.'

'Tristan Summers and Serafina Rainbow,' Dee reminded her. Angela waved their identities away as irrelevant.

'Yes, them.'

'What was it you wanted to tell me?'

Well, it's about that night those two were killed. You were there at the meeting before that all happened, weren't you? I think I remember seeing you there with the old girl?'

'Yes, I'm staying with Miss Marriott. It was she who told me about the meeting and took me along to it, and then to the churchyard afterwards.'

'Exactly. Well, I went along too, though I was one of the last to arrive, as I was at the front of the hall, and I couldn't get away from the mayor and that Raynes fellow.'

More like she'd seen an opportunity to collar them both, Dee thought, but simply nodded. She was on the point of asking a question when she saw Angela Thingy's gaze move upwards. Someone was coming up behind Dee. She glanced over her shoulder, and immediately saw her cousin and Nat standing there. She huffed, rolling her eyes. Just when she had a chance of asking some questions.

'Now what do you want?' she demanded, turning in her seat to face them, and forgetting that five minutes ago she had been hoping to find them.

Receiving the Hardy frown with more than the usual intensity, she was then ignored completely as Bill, holding up his warrant card, said tersely to Angela Thingy, 'Miss Baker? I'm from Scotland Yard. I have some questions I'd like to put to you, if it's a convenient moment.'

Oh of course. Angela *Baker*, Dee thought.

To Dee, Bill said, 'We won't detain you, Miss Gascoigne. We just need a few minutes of Miss Baker's time.'

'She's not going anywhere!' Angela Baker told him in a not entirely friendly manner. 'You can talk to me in front of her or come back another time.'

Bill sighed and pulled out the chair next to Dee to sit down. Nat sat beside Angela, and immediately got out his trusty notebook, trying not to stick his elbows out too far into Miss Baker's ribs. He found a clean page, his pencil hovering over the paper, and looked up expectantly.

Dee exchanged a grin with Nat who had to look away to avoid laughing. Unaware of this, Bill frowned and said,

'Miss Baker, can you please tell me what you remember of the night of the—er—unrest in the churchyard?'

She was looking at him with a slight sneer, Dee saw. Clearly Miss Baker had no love for the police. And it was soon clear why.

'Why should I answer your questions? It's a free country, not a police state, the last time I looked.'

The Hardy frown made another appearance. Dee knew that usually it was just his concentrating face, but sometimes, as now, it was a clear sign of disapproval that made him look far older than his twenty-nine years.

'Because I'm asking everyone about that evening in

the hopes of finding the person who brutally murdered two people. And because if you've nothing to hide, you'll tell me what you remember of that night.'

'So you can twist my words, add a few extra bits of your own, then send someone to the gallows based solely on my evidence?' Hostility dripped from her tone.

'We don't do that anymore,' he said, then hastily corrected himself before she could pick apart his words. 'We don't hang people anymore. And the last time you gave evidence to the police, it helped them to secure a conviction against two men who had committed a heinous crime. As had you, need I remind you. Arson is regarded as a very serious crime.'

'It still didn't sit well with my conscience,' she said, but in a softer tone. 'I knew those men for years.' She was looking down at her hands now, all her hostility gone, leaving sorrow in its place.

'I'm sorry you felt it was your fault they hanged. At sixteen, you were not much more than a child really,' he said gently. 'It's easy for youngsters to get in with the wrong crowd. But you got out of it before you did anything—er—irrevocable.'

She nodded. Her lip trembled slightly. On an impulse, Dee reached across the table to take Angela's hand in hers. There was a short silence at the table, though further away, by the bar, a man threw back his head and guffawed, and closer to hand, someone dropped a glass on the floor, the sound making Angela jump, but jerking her back to the moment.

In a low voice, she said, 'I was just saying to Miss Gascoigne, I came out of the meeting a little behind the rest of the crowd. I was delayed because the mayor told me he was going to go home, he said no one would bother coming back to the meeting, so there was no point hanging about. Nicholas Raynes agreed with him and began to leave with Mrs Miles-Hudson. You know, Cynthia. I said perhaps they should wait and see, but they were having none of it. So I left them and followed on the tail end of the crowd going out into the lane. When I got to the churchyard, I saw the flames and the smoke, and I turned and went back to my car. I didn't want to go on, it was obviously pointless, people were coming out again, running, shouting. Only a fool would have kept going.'

'I see. Thank you for that,' Hardy said. They all glanced at Nat who was writing what she'd said down in a rapid and efficient-looking shorthand.

Hardy turned his attention back to Angela, giving her that disconcertingly close look that Dee knew people often found uncomfortable. 'And did you see anyone in that brief moment or two that you were near the churchyard?'

Angela was already shaking her head. 'No. Sorry. It was dark by then, and with all that smoke...'

He waited a few seconds but she clearly had nothing more to add.

'Of course. Well, thank you.' Hardy nodded to Porter, who closed his notebook with a snap and to Dee's astonishment, the two men got up and left, both with a brief smile and nod for the two women.

'He's a bit officious, isn't he?' Angela said to Dee then drank her scotch and soda down in one gulp. 'I hate the Fuzz. Half of them are corrupt, you know.'

Dee didn't know whether sticking up for Bill and Nat at this point might ruin her chances of getting information by putting her on the side of the Fuzz. Not that there appeared to be much information to get, but unlike certain policemen from Scotland Yard, Dee wasn't ready to give up right away.

'It was awful that night, wasn't it? I was there with Miss Marriott. I tried to persuade her not to go, but she was determined to find out what was happening.'

Angela was nodding. 'Yes, awful. I was shocked, I have to say. It obviously all happened incredibly quickly. I saw Miss Marriott there, hurrying through the smoke to get away. But I didn't see you there, not just then. Again, the smoke, I suppose. Like I said, it made everything impossible. I bumped into Clive. He told me to leave, saying that he was going back to see if he could do anything to help. He went back into the smoke. I thought he was terribly brave. At the time, you know. I—well, I rather like Clive, though I don't think he feels the same. But I'd be lying if I didn't admit he has a ruthless side. His army training, of course. Though actually that's what attracts me to him.'

Dee nibbled a crisp and reflected on that. Angela had effectively just told Bill and Nat that she saw nothing and nobody. But clearly that wasn't the case at all.

'Did you know that Clive was in hospital with a concussion? He should be home today or tomorrow.'

Angela nodded. 'Yes. I heard. It was a disagreement with his son, apparently.' She sighed. 'They are a pair those two, always locking horns. I'll pop in and see him tomorrow or the next day, make sure he's all right.'

'You didn't mention to the inspector about seeing Clive that night in the churchyard.'

'Nor did I mention seeing you.' A sly note crept into Angela's voice, as if she had done Dee some kind of favour.

'He already knows I was there. I told him that. And

he knows Miss Marriott was with me.'

'She wasn't with you the whole time, though, was she? You had the opportunity to bump off the two victims. As a matter of fact, I did see you with one of that group.'

Dee felt wrong-footed somehow. Was Angela accusing her of something?

'I was helping her,' Dee said. 'It was Clive's daughter actually. Janna as she calls herself now. Her robe caught alight.'

'Of course. Clive said you'd say that.' She got up. 'Well, that was pleasant. See you around.'

Dee was left sitting there alone now. She stared into space as she went over and over Angela's comments, trying to work out what she'd meant by them.

He turned up at the front door at a quarter past seven that evening.

'Can you manage dinner? I know it's rather last minute.'

It was worse than 'last minute': Doris was already setting the table and about to start bringing the food in. Dee ran to ask Miss Marriott if she minded and received an indulgent smile.

'Go dear, by all means. Have a lovely evening.'

'Oh, thank you.' On an impulse, she kissed Miss Marriott's cheek and looking back, saw the old lady had become pink-cheeked and wreathed in smiles.

Dee took the stairs two at a time to fling on a better dress and swipe some lipstick across her lips. She raked her fingers through her hair and decided that would have to do.

They drove into Greater Hartwell again. There was not a lot of choice, so it had to be the hotel.

'I'm afraid there will be a twenty minute wait for a

table,' the maitre d' told them. It didn't matter, they ordered some drinks and found a quiet table in the bar.

'How is the investigation going?' she asked him.

Bill shrugged and exhaled loudly. 'It's... you know...'

'Is it always like this? I know I'm new to this, and you'd probably say it's because I'm an amateur, but I just don't feel as though I'm getting anywhere. I have a lot of little bits and pieces, but they don't seem to amount to anything much.'

He smiled. 'I know the feeling.' He set his glass down, and something seemed to occur to him. He leaned, 'By the way, you might...'

'Your table is ready now sir, madam, if you'd like to come this way?' The maitre d' was already turning away to go back into the restaurant.

It took a couple of minutes for him to settle them with menus and to leave them alone once again.

'What were you saying before? I might what?'

'Oh I can't remember now. Probably nothing.'

She glared at him and he laughed.

'Sorry, only teasing. I was going to say, you might be interested to know that we spoke with Mrs Summers this morning,' Bill said.

Dee stared at him. She didn't know what part of this was the most interesting: the fact that they'd spoke to Tristan's widow or that Bill was actually mentioning it to her. Could he really be sharing information with her? It was almost a miracle!

'Of course, if you're not interested...' he said, and grinned.

She laughed. 'Oh I most definitely am. I was just wondering if it was my birthday, or Christmas, or something, that I should be receiving this astonishingly generous gift.'

'I'm glad you appreciate it. Not a word to anyone, obviously.'

'Obviously.' She leaned a little closer to him, ready to hear a secret.

'Actually, it's not really as exciting as you might hope. She admitted they lived largely separate lives, that she knew he had other women, and that he rarely came home except to visit their daughters.'

'But they were not separated as such?'

He shook his head. 'No, it suited them, and he didn't want to upset the college board any more than he already had done with his antics by adding the scandal of a divorce.'

Dee raised her brows. 'Well I think I can understand that,' she commented with feeling.

Bill continued, 'As I say, it suited them. There was no animosity, she said, they got on well as friends. But she hadn't approved of what she thought of as his less-than-professional conduct on certain occasions. And she more or less admitted that she also had a—shall we say, 'special friend'—who visits every weekend, an 'uncle' to her daughters.'

The waiter came to take their order. Then Bill was umming and ahhing over the wine list, trying to decide what to have with their food, and while this was going on, Dee mulled over what he'd just told her, smiling and nodding vaguely when he asked her what she thought about his eventual choice. She was a little disappointed his conversation with Mrs Summers wasn't more revealing, though it did go a long way to confirming what Dee had come to believe about Tristan Summers.

After the waiter had taken the order and left, she said, 'I suppose I owe you something in return for that news about Mrs Summers.'

He wisely resisted the urge to turn that into a

smutty joke. If he didn't watch himself, he'd end up on the shelf, an old maid, he realised and kept his mouth shut, merely adopting an interested look.

'After you left, Angela Baker told me a couple of small things.' Dee went on to tell him, adding, 'It's a bit much she's trying to make it sound as though I was up to something that night. And then she added that bit about Clive to give weight to her comment, as if he also thinks I'm up to something.'

'Perhaps he does think that?' Bill suggested. 'If he's well enough to see people, you could perhaps visit and ask him. Or I could?'

'I think he's gone off me a bit.' And she told him about Clive phoning his son from the pub to clear out of the house. Then she added the bit about Miss Didsbury's hedge.

It was a good thing their food arrived. She was in danger of going over the whole case again, and tying herself in knots with it. It was a relief to talk about normal things. They talked about family matters, and how their siblings were getting on with their studies: Bill's brother JJ was a year younger than Rob but studying the same discipline. They had plans to go into partnership together once they had both qualified.

Over coffee, he asked her if she had been to the cinema lately, and she had to admit she hadn't.

'Not since *Help!*'

He nodded. 'Oh yes, I saw that too. Great music.'

'I expect you went with Busty Barbara.' She couldn't help the caustic tone. He wasn't angry or defensive, he just nodded and said,

'Probably.' Not at all concerned, he drank some coffee. 'Would you like to go and see that one based on the Agatha Christie novel? I know you're a fan of mysteries. I think it's called *The Alphabet Murders*?'

She was on the point of accepting, when he added, 'We could take Jenny and Rob, Harry and JJ, even Freddie if we can persuade him to come to London, make an evening of it for all the cousins.'

'Lovely.' Disappointed, she fell quiet, playing with her teaspoon, stirring the dregs of her coffee.

'Do you want another?' he offered.

She smiled and shook her head. 'No, thanks, one was enough. I'd better head back soon.'

'Oh,' he said suddenly. 'There was another thing I had to tell you. We went to see that Cynthia Miles-Hudson woman from the council. She insists that her relationship with Nicholas Raynes began *after* the awarding of the building contract for the three hundred new houses in the village, and that his being awarded the contract was a unanimous decision of the council and that he did not gain any favouritism because of anything that was going on between the two of them. Sadly, the mayor said the same, though he suggested that he thought the relationship was, I quote, 'not ideal', but stated the vote was open and above board and without prejudice.'

Dee sighed. 'Oh well, I suppose they were always going to say that.'

'True. In any case, it's hard to see how any of that could have a bearing on the deaths of Tristan Summers and Serafina Rainbow that night.'

He drove them back to the pub, parking in the car park there, then walked her back to Miss Marriott's house. The night was chilly but dry. They strolled along in a companionable silence, hand in hand, and at the door, he kissed her once, on the lips, but quickly and gently, before turning to go back to the pub, waving when he got along the lane a little.

*

Chapter Twenty-six

When Dee woke the next morning, her second Sunday in the village, she was in a more determined frame of mind. True, she didn't have the answers to solve her case. But if she didn't solve it, then it wouldn't get solved and she would have let everyone down, not least of all Doris and of course, dear Monty. Therefore, she told herself sternly, she would have to sit and mull things over and put all those little snippets together into a meaningful picture. She didn't agree with Miss Marriott that you couldn't uncover the past, perhaps there were occasionally things you couldn't find out, but Dee's case was not going to be one of those, she was determined about that.

Miss Marriott was occupied upstairs with Doris and a large quantity of discarded clothing and household linens that required sorting then putting away until the spring or sending to various charities. Miss Marriott seemed out of sorts, with little to say and none of her usual conversation. Dee worried she had outstayed her welcome.

At lunchtime, she strolled along the lane to the pub, hoping to catch Bill, but was immediately told by Pete Guthrie that both the policemen had gone out some time earlier.

'Just as well, and all,' a man at the bar remarked, swilling down the last half glass of his beer.

'Shut up, Jimmy. You've done enough damage. You're lucky I still let you in here after the trouble you've caused just lately. One foot out of line, and you'll be barred for life.'

The man glared at Pete but wisely kept quiet.

That must be Jimmy Philpott, Dee thought, and as she wandered back to Miss Marriott's she thought about the things she had heard about him. A troublemaker since his mother left. And hadn't Miss Marriott said something about a rifle incident in the pub once upon a time? Then kicking over the brazier which caused the fire that Friday evening.

Dee arrived back at the house to find Miss Marriott was taking her nap and Doris, fastening her jacket, was on her way to go with her mother to see Clive.

'Give him my best wishes,' Dee said.

'I will, Miss Dee. I think he will be coming home this afternoon. Oh and speaking of this afternoon, Miss Marriott is going to tea at Miss Didsbury's. She said she knows you probably won't want to go, but if you should change your mind, that will be all right too. You'll be most welcome, she said.'

Doris left, and Dee sat in her usual chair in the morning-room, and half dozing, half awake, watching the antics of a blackbird, and thinking about her investigation. In no time at all she was deeply asleep.

She woke suddenly, and stretched, stiff and

chilled. She had been dreaming about the fire in the churchyard, but instead of being there, she was looking down over the edge of the heavens, as if the churchyard were in a fishbowl, she was so high above it all, and the figures were like ants beneath her. She saw Jimmy set aside his rifle by the gate of the churchyard and go in to kick over the brazier. Though in reality of course, she had seen almost nothing that night.

Her first thought, as she went upstairs to change her dress, was, 'No, you idiot, it was the older Mr Philpott who took the rifle into the pub, not the younger.'

But what difference did that make anyhow?

As Miss Didsbury's invitation to tea specifically included Dee, it seemed easier to give in than to try to wriggle out of it. In any case, she was at a loss what to do with her afternoon. She and Miss Marriott sat on the sofa opposite Miss Didsbury, and each of them sat with a smile fixed on her face. Dee could see the clock on the mantelpiece above the fire, and it seemed to her that time was passing incredibly slowly.

Miss Didsbury was keen to talk about the mayor and his wife, both of whom, it transpired, she knew well.

'I don't know if you are aware of this, Lola, but tomorrow is the charming Mrs Windward's fiftieth birthday party and his honour our mayor has thoughtfully invited me. I was at school with her mother, you know. Do you know her at all?'

'Not at all, Tilda. But if you recall, I was at Colchester Ladies' College, not at Manningtree Grammar School for Girls. In any case, rather you than me at Fast Eddie's tomorrow, I don't care for the man.'

Miss Didsbury didn't seem concerned that Miss Marriott disliked the fellow. Changing the subject, she turned to Dee. 'How is your investigation going? Did you ever solve the mystery of the hole in my hedge? I expect your brother helped you with that, didn't he? Does he always help you with all your cases? So useful to have a man to guide you.' Her tone was ironic; it seemed she had no confidence in Dee's ability.

Dee smiled politely and making up a partial lie on the spot, said, 'Oh yes, that was easy enough. I dealt with that before Rob arrived. Of course, it's useful to have someone to discuss points of law with, Rob is training to be a barrister, as you probably know, but he doesn't do any investigating as such. In any case, I couldn't take him away from his work, and I don't like people to interfere in mine. But you were right, it was Clive Barton that night. He told me he had seen Sylvia go through. You mustn't blame her—she couldn't reach the lane to go back the usual way due to the fire, and of course she was in a terrible panic, desperate to reach safety. Clive, of course, just wanted to be sure she was all right, but he was also unable to use the conventional entrance because of the fire.'

As soon as she said this, her confidence perked up. It came to her that it was true—she *could* rely on herself, and that she would have to do so, because she couldn't expect Monty to let Rob to simply drop everything and run to her side. She didn't even want her brother to do that, anyway, he had his own career to pursue. He hadn't helped her in her teaching job, and neither would he need to help her with her investigating job. She sat up in her seat a little straighter, proud at this.

'Naturally. Now it all makes sense.' Miss Didsbury turned to Miss Marriott, 'He really is an attentive neighbour. So interested in everyone's welfare.'

'Yes, indeed,' Miss Marriott murmured. She gave Dee a complicit grin. 'Does our dear mayor still live in that rambling old place on the other side of Greater Hartwell?'

'Yes. He always says he wouldn't leave it for the world. He was born there, you know, as was his father.'

'Not a truly old house,' Miss Marriott commented to Dee. 'But nice enough.'

'We can't all live in historic mansions such as yours, my dear,' Miss Didsbury replied. 'Do you remember, Lola, how we used to dare one another to go into the old passage at your house. We used to love to frighten one another half to death in those days, as children do. You, and me, and my brother William and my sister, Susanna, and your two brothers too. They were quite a few years older, weren't they, and merciless in their teasing.' To Dee, Miss Didsbury said, 'Lola was the youngest, and I'm afraid we were rather cruel to her, as children often are.'

'The younger of my brothers was four years older than I, which seemed like quite a lot in those days, and my older brother was another three years his senior, and they've both been dead for many years now,' Miss Marriott explained for Dee's benefit. She half-smiled, then said, 'Don't let's talk about the old days again. It's far too depressing. We are getting old, Tilda. I can't bear to think of it.'

'Not getting. Got. We are *already* old, my dear. Better to face it.' Miss Didsbury stared into space. 'It's odd isn't it, how children are always fascinated by the dark places, the places no one dares to enter.'

She laughed as she said it. 'And telling one another ghost stories. Do you remember that? I remember you wet yourself once when we jumped out at you in the dark. We were all hiding in your father's study...'

'...Calling to me in strange ghostly voices. It took me a while to work out where the sound was coming from. And then the little door creaked slowly open. But you all still gave me a dreadful fright.' Lola Marriott smiled ruefully. 'I must have only been eight or nine years old. So I suppose it's hardly surprising that I wet myself. And you all laughed. I believe I spent the rest of the afternoon hiding in the nursery and refusing to come down until you had gone home.'

Dee smiled politely as she listened to them reminisce. She had enjoyed Murder in the Dark and Hide-and-Seek as a child with three brothers and her cousins to play with. But they'd never scared one another quite to that extent.

'Oh, do let's talk about something else,' Miss Marriott said yet again, but with greater impatience.

From nowhere, a question presented itself to Dee and she asked it now. 'What was the name of Mr Philpott's wife. The one who ran away, who was so much younger than him.'

Miss Marriott stared at her, looking worried, shaking her head. 'Sorry, dear, I'm afraid, I can't remember.'

'It was Sara, I believe,' Miss Didsbury chipped in, to Dee's satisfaction. 'Really Lola, your memory these days!' And before Miss Marriott could protest or say anything else, she swept on, 'Did you know my maid Sylvia is walking out with that young policeman?'

'Michael Wright. Yes, of course. Everyone knows that. Have they named the day yet?'

'I think they are still waiting to talk to the vicar at

Greater Hartwell about it. But Michael has given her a ring, at least.'

'Just as well,' Miss Marriott said tartly. 'From what I hear, *she's* already given him everything, so it's high time he gave her something in return.'

Dee was interested to hear that, after what Sylvia had told her just a few days earlier. Of course, it was possible that Sylvia hadn't been entirely honest with Dee, though she had seemed genuinely uninterested in Sergeant Wright. But perhaps, Sylvia had seen the engagement announcement in the newspaper, or seen the way Barry and Ada were together, apparently so supportive of one another, so devoted, and had given up hope of ensnaring Barry's heart. Would it make any difference to Sylvia, Dee wondered, once word got around that the engagement was off after Barry had thrown a punch at his father?

There was a sudden commotion just outside in the hall, a sound of crashing china and a yelp of pain. Dee and Miss Marriott both sprang to their feet. Miss Marriott, slightly ahead of Dee, was on her knees by Sylvia's side in seconds.

'My dear, are you all right?' Miss Marriott asked the dazed girl. Then glancing up, said to Tilda Disbury, 'We must call for the doctor, Tilda. She's given her head rather a nasty whack on the door frame, she may well have a concussion.'

Sylvia herself began to get up, in spite of Miss Marriott's protests. But Sylvia insisted, 'No, it's all right, Miss Marriott, I'm absolutely fine, honestly. I really don't need a doctor. It was just a bit of a shock. I'll just sit in the chair for a moment and pull myself together. Honestly, Miss Marriott, I'm perfectly all right. It probably looks a lot worse than it really is. I was just taken by surprise, that's all. I walked into the door frame, somehow, I was so busy steadying the tea pot, it was spilling... I bumped my head. It was just a bit of a shock, that's all.'

Gradually they settled down again. Dee helped Miss Marriott to return to her seat, and as the two older ladies returned to their conversation, Dee, much to Miss Didsbury's chagrin, helped to clear up the mess in the hall, and a few minutes later, Sylvia returned with a new tray of tea, still insisting she was quite all right and had no need of a doctor, even though she sported a magnificent purple bruise on her forehead. Luckily there was no swelling or broken skin.

Once or twice, Dee glanced across to the square of polished floor just inside the door, puzzling over something she'd seen but not able to quite pinpoint what it was.

On the way back from Miss Didsbury's, Dee was thinking hard. They went along very slowly, Miss Marriott leaning heavily on Dee's arm as they went along the lane. As they came into the house, Dee looked about the dark hallway. It really was such an old house, ancient and full of secrets. She already knew of one priest-hole, but she thought it likely there were more. Just as there were at Ville Gascoigne, Dee's childhood home in Hertfordshire. She surmised the two houses were built at around the same time, a time of terrible religious upheaval and uncertainty.

She said to Miss Marriott, 'Was it you who told me the village is named after the priory that was previously on the site of the church?'

'No, dear, I don't think so. Who told you that? It wasn't me, I'm certain.'

'Oh someone. Perhaps it was Clive.'

'He rather likes you, you know. I think I'll have a sherry before I go for my nap. What about you, dear?'

'No thank you.' Dee said. 'Clive? Oh he can be charming, but he's not my type. In any case, as you know, I'm taken.'

'Of course.' Miss Marriott went into the drawing-room, directly across to where the sherry bottle, along with a few others, stood on a tray on top of a cabinet. Dee saw that she moved quickly and without any unsteadiness. Yes, she told herself, that's what I noticed at Miss Didsbury's. Miss Marriott poured herself a drink, bending easily to take a glass from the cabinet, and easing off the stopper. Turning, she saw Dee watching her, and immediately allowed her shoulders to slump slightly as she made her way to a chair, walking slowly, clutching at the furniture with her free hand.

'What made you ask about Philpott's young wife?'

Dee settled into a chair near Miss Marriott, and glancing up, saw the old woman's eyes were watching her. The hand that held the sherry was steady, but the other was clenched tightly, white-knuckled against the leather arm of the chair.

'Oh just sheer curiosity,' Dee said, keeping her tone light. 'It came to me that I didn't know her name. You know, I've heard so much about Maureen Barton running off with Henry Padham, yet I believe it was you who said that it was Mr Philpott's wife, not Clive's wife Maureen, who was carrying on with Henry. Hence the rifle incident in the pub that you told me about. And so that made me wonder. Did Henry really go off with Maureen? And if so, why? And then again, what happened to Sara?'

Miss Marriott lifted the glass to her lips and now, Dee saw, her hand was shaking. She set the glass down rather awkwardly on the table beside her, and reached down to pick up her handbag. She took out her pillbox, and swallowed two little white pills with her drink, then taking out her lorgnette, and carefully placing it on her lap, she snapped the handbag closed and lay it on the table. 'Just my heart medicine dear. I should have taken them after lunch, as Tilda said, my memory is failing me rather.' She shook her head slightly and went on, 'Henry and Sara? I really couldn't say, dear. And now if you don't mind, I think I'll...'

'Bet told me that he always came back. She said he loved her in his own way, and no matter what he got up to, he always came back to her.'

'Women don't always know... What she told you was probably just wishful thinking. What she's told herself over the years to get over the fact that he left her.'

'True,' Dee conceded. 'But Bet seems like a realist to me.'

'Well, I really wouldn't know about that, now you must excuse me...' Miss Marriott was on her feet, making a show of hanging onto the back of the chair for support. Her lorgnette fell to the floor, although she held on tightly to the strap of her handbag. She looked about her. 'Now, where did I put my walking stick?' she demanded, her tone querulous.

'You left it at Miss Didsbury's.' Dee said, bending to retrieve the lorgnette. 'It was lying on the carpet beside the chair. Not that you really need it, do you?'

Miss Marriott turned to look at her.

Dee said, 'Everyone seemed to think that Henry's body would be found in Maureen's grave, their assumption being that he never left, that he was killed and his body put into her grave. But of course, there was no grave until about a year and a half after they supposedly left. The date on Maureen's headstone was 1957. If he had been buried afterwards, then that still leaves the problem of where he had been all that time. Someone would have noticed if the grave had been reopened, in any case. There would have been fresh earth. And besides, the experts said the other day that there were no remains at all in the grave. So if he couldn't have been buried there, where was he? Where is he now?'

'Gone away,' Miss Marriott said, turning towards the door. 'He-he left.'

'Bet doesn't believe that. And neither do I. If he had gone away, some trace of him would have been found. You can't go abroad without a passport. You can't get a job in this country without a national insurance number. He's never registered with a doctor.'

'Well, perhaps he was smuggled into another country illegally.'

'And lived in constant fear of being caught? On a low-income job? Why bother?' Dee said. 'He already had a job here. He could just go a few miles along the road and get a job and a new house in some other town.'

'Perhaps he didn't think. Perhaps he simply acted on the spur of the moment.'

'There was time for him to calm down and think rationally. Which brings us back to this: Bet said he always came home in the end.'

'Obviously not, or...'

'He's dead. He has to be, it's the only thing that makes sense.'

'They would have found his body in the grave if that were so.' Miss Marriott's tone was almost sarcastic. She was standing perfectly upright, with a good tight hold on the doorhandle.

'He was never buried in Maureen's grave. He wasn't buried at all.' Then Dee asked her, 'Which room was your father's study when you were a child? The one with the secret passage where your brothers and friends hid to scare you?'

Miss Marriott's shoulders slumped again. She was quite pink in the face, it made her look soft, flustered. She seemed to be thinking over Dee's questions carefully.

Dee waited, watching her, understanding the dilemma.

Miss Marriott hesitated for a moment, then said softly, 'The same one I still use today. It's hardly changed in all these years.'

'I've been in there for the telephone, of course, but not had a really good look.'

Miss Marriott slowly crossed the dark-panelled hall to open a door and switch on the light. Dee stepped inside and looked about her, seeing the room now as if for the first time.

'It has hardly changed,' Miss Marriott said again. 'Even the wallpaper is the one chosen by my mother. Father was away on business and he had asked her to attend to it. I think she enjoyed taking care of that, even though it wasn't a room she particularly used. She preferred the morning-room, even in the evenings. As in fact do I.'

Dee thought she could see why. In spite of the gaily striped wallpaper—a pale yellow background with red and green stripes—it was dark in here, the trees too closely planted outside, the position of the house contriving to block out the sun. She noted all the bookshelves properly now, having barely noticed them before. There were wooden panels on either side of the fireplace on the wall that adjoined the hallway. The panels looked very old and of a dark wood like those in other parts of the house. Not so different to Ville Gascoigne, her father's ancestral home. Dee stared at the panels, thoughts whirling in her head.

Miss Marriott was watching her closely. 'I think perhaps a stiff drink would be in order. Or would you prefer a cup of tea?'

Dee didn't reply. She wondered if she dared do it. What if she was wrong?

She glanced back at Miss Marriott, frozen there in the doorway, wittering on about drinks, but her eyes were watchful, wary, her hands wringing one another in front of her.

Dee pressed some of the corners of the panels. When nothing happened, she felt a sudden wave of relief that she couldn't explain. But immediately she realised that relief was a lie, because as she glanced back at Miss Marriott again, she knew from the elderly woman's tense frame that her instinct had been correct.

'Miss Marriott?' she asked gently. 'How do you open the doorway?'

No doubt Miss Marriott would witter on a bit more and pretend not to know what she meant, and then Dee would have to insist, which would be awkward in someone else's home. But no, Miss Marriott just said, a little sorrowfully now:

'That shelf with no books, just on your left there. Lift this end of it.'

Dee looked and saw one shelf held only a few small ornaments. She went across, and gently, slowly, so as not to dislodge the ornaments—a small porcelain bell, a tiny music box in gold, a comical porcelain pig in trousers and waistcoat and with a monocle—she put her fingers underneath and when she had lifted it perhaps three inches, there was a soft click, and the panelled section to her right gently popped out about half an inch. She let go of the shelf and it stayed in the raised position. She went over, putting out her hand to pull the 'door' towards her until that whole lower section of the wall stood wide open at a right angle to the bookshelf. Inside was a cavernous black hole, and a chilly stale wind seemed to issue forth into the room, rustling the silk curtains like an unseen hand.

Miss Marriott started forward a step or two and then she stopped still again. Her hands were finally still. She gripped the back of a chair, breathing hard as though she had run a mile.

Dee felt sad for her. All these years. How the knowledge of it must have weighed on Miss Marriott's shoulders. But Dee had to ask, just to be absolutely sure.

'I suppose that is where Henry Padham is?'

Miss Marriott, coming around to sink down onto the chair, just nodded and began to weep softly.

*

Chapter Twenty-seven

Taking a deep breath—she wasn't fond of dark enclosed places—Dee ducked her head and at the same time, stepped over the lower wooden rim of the framework that normally supported the bookshelf.

She took stock, letting her eyes grow accustomed to the shadows. She saw that on her right, level with her head, there was a shelf and upon it, a modern electric torch. She grabbed it, relieved, and clicked the beam on. A glance back over her shoulder showed Miss Marriott still in her place, still weeping, hardly seeming aware of what Dee was doing. I only hope she doesn't shut the door on me, Dee thought. A shiver went through her, and a slight wave of nausea, but she pushed them aside. She had to do this.

She took a step forward, and another, shining the yellow beam before her, lighting the dirt path under her feet. The tunnel she was in seemed to go on for a short way, then there was a blank wall. Though as soon as she reached it, she saw it wasn't a blank wall at all but a corner, and the tunnel continued for several more yards. And there, propped up in the corner of another turn in the passageway, was a slumped bundle of rotting clothes, the suggestion of a shape amongst them, a shape like a person, and on top, bare bones partially clothed with straw-like hair and some browned leathery skin. On the ground, a hand stretched out, some fingers had flesh, one was just a bone glistening in the torchlight. Men's boots lay at an odd angle where the life had gone from the leg and foot muscles.

Here then, was Henry Padham, nine years missing, believed absconded with his lover. And by his side, Dee saw now, that odd, hunched bundle beyond him, with the bright green patent shoes poking out, still bright, still fresh, the bow on the front still neat, the perfect mid-fifties style from fashionable stores. Maureen Barton, lying side by side with her supposed lover these nine cold years, and not laid peacefully to rest in some hallowed corner of sun-drenched Spain after all. The unclaimed one.

Dee had seen enough. More than enough.

She had to put a call through to the pub, to Bill or Nat. She hoped they would be back there by now; she didn't want to delay things too much. With shaking hands, she closed the panel once more. 'Shall we move into the drawing-room?' she suggested. 'It will be more comfortable there. And you can tell me all about it.'

Dabbing at her eyes with an old-fashioned lace-edged handkerchief, Miss Marriott nodded, and getting to her feet, she allowed Dee to lead her slowly into the other room and to sit her down in the corner of one of the sofas.

'Could I just have a glass of water, do you think?'

'Of course.' Dee hurried to the kitchen, returning with a glass of water. Miss Marriott was just closing her handbag again. She smiled at Dee and took the glass.

Then, returning to the study, Dee put through her call. The policemen were there, she was told. Nevertheless, she held her breath. A moment later, she was almost giddy with relief to hear Nat's voice coming down the line to her. Before he had time to say anything other than 'Hello?', she was saying,

'It's Dee. You both need to come to Miss Marriott's immediately. She has something to tell you. It's urgent.' And without waiting for his reply, she hung up the phone and hurried to the drawing-room once more.

She sat opposite Miss Marriott in an armchair.

'Now then,' Dee said, trying to keep her tone gentle, as if she was speaking to a small child. 'Why don't you tell me what happened right from the beginning?'

Miss Marriott sighed and lay aside the handbag. Dee was a little surprised that there was no bluster, no denial, no desperately clutching at an alibi. Wasn't that what one was usually faced with when interviewing a murderer? But she could see that Miss Marriott was perfectly happy—in a sense—to tell Dee the whole story.

She began: 'It was nine years ago. I had come across Doris sitting in the kitchen sobbing desperately. It broke my heart; the poor child. Because you see, I had rather come to look upon her as my child—well perhaps not my own child, but something like that. She had been with me for a year or two by then, ever since she was fifteen. She was such a dear sweet child. And there was I, already an old maid, obviously I was never going to have any children of my own. So in my heart, I rather adopted her.'

Dee nodded. She had already noticed the affection they had for one another. Even Miss Didsbury had commented that they were close. 'Then what happened?'

'Oh, well, it was awful. She turned to face me, and I could see a colossal bruise across her cheek and eye. 'My word,' I said, 'what on earth have you done to yourself?' It was winter, and a thick layer of snow was upon the ground. I suppose I thought she must have slipped and bumped herself somehow. Like Sylvia today. Doris was still going home every evening at that point, and I was about to say that she should stay the night, to avoid any further accidents.' Miss Marriott halted, and taking a moment to think back, she looked down at her hands, her left hand still clutching the handkerchief.

'But no. That wasn't it at all. She told me her father had hit her. Drunk of course, he was notorious for that. One heard rumours that he hit his wife. But I had never seen the, the—what do the police call it—the *evidence*, if you like. It was so very shocking. And of course, my own father... very much in the same mould as Henry Padham, and I just thought, I can't allow this to continue. I don't want poor dear Doris to go through all that I went through. Or her mother of course. It's why I never married, really. I mean, I could have had a coming-out ball and all that sort of thing. That was what we did then. But I was too afraid of men. No, I decided at the age of seventeen that, unlike my mother, I was never going to put myself in a man's power.

'But I digress. Suffice it to say that I lay in wait for him that night to come home from the pub as usual.

And I hit him with an old walking stick from the stand. I think it had once been my father's. I hit him several times. He was caught completely off guard, and went down with something of a crash. I was younger then, only sixty-six, and stronger too in those days—or so I thought. In fact, the effort of dragging him into the house and into that passage almost killed me.

'I was already exhausted from this exertion. But I still had to go out again, to collect his hat and the walking stick. I'd left them behind as I needed both hands to drag him along. I found them, picked them up, I heard a sound, and there was Maureen Barton watching me from the bus stop. She had seen me, there was no doubt about it. There was a wide trail through the snow from where I had dragged him, and there was I, holding his hat, and my own walking stick all bloody. I know it doesn't excuse my actions, but she was a vile woman. A nagging, complaining, angry woman. Poor Clive's life was a misery. It was hardly surprising he turned to Bet for comfort. Anyway, I tried to speak to her, thinking I'd find out how much she had seen. But she wouldn't come close to me, sensibly, of course. 'I saw you hit him,' she said. 'And I'm going straight back home now to ring the police. You'll never get away with it, you horrid old bag."

Dee didn't dare to move or speak, afraid of breaking the spell. But Miss Marriott ploughed on, as if she had to purge her soul.

'She started to turn away, and I looked about me and I couldn't see anyone else around. I took a swing at her. I caught her a blow to the side of the head and she went down, oddly in near silence. But I could see right away that she was just stunned. So I finished her off with two more whacks. She was lying right beside the post box and I hoped that it would be assumed that she had slipped in the snow and hit her head, dying as a result of that. All I had to do was smear some blood on the side of the post-box. But then, I suppose I panicked. What if she wasn't dead after all? What if someone came along while I was still there? Or if they found her as soon as I had gone, and she was revived and told them about me. I froze in a kind of trance for a few seconds. I thought, anyone might see her, or me. Some idiot walking their dog, for example, so I realised I couldn't leave her there. Again, I had to drag her back to the house, and throw her into the passage with Henry. I went back one last time, just to make sure I hadn't left anything behind. A good thing I did because of the hat, of course. Henry's hat. And the walking stick that I'd already forgotten about. I was exhausted by this point and could hardly stay on my feet. I hurried home, and luckily met no one else as I went, the weather saw to that.

'But the evening took its toll on me. By the time I had got back indoors and thrown Henry's hat in with the wretched pair, and closed the opening to the passage, I was having terrible pains in my chest and arm. I knew I was having a heart attack. I knew too that I only had minutes, if that, to clear up after myself and to get help.

'I wiped the walking stick and put it away, hung up my coat that looked all right: it was black so no bloodstains showed. I knew I could get rid of it later if, God willing, I was spared. I took off my boots and my stockings which were splashed with mud and ice, and leaving the boots on the hall stand, I threw the stockings on the fire. Then—I just—rang the bell like always for Doris. Doris, bless her, immediately rang for the doctor, who ordered an ambulance, and in due course I was lucky enough to make a reasonable recovery.'

She leaned back against the sofa, her eyes closed, her shoulders softly drooping as if a heavy load had been lifted at last. 'I'm so tired. After all these years... I'd like to go and lie down, if I may, I don't feel quite well.'

But Dee couldn't leave it there. There was so much more to this story. She said, 'And so the rumours Henry had left the village began. I suppose that was fairly easy to manage?'

Without opening her eyes, Miss Marriott nodded. 'Yes, not difficult at all. Bet and Doris were just so glad he had gone, they didn't much care how or why. It's funny. A few weeks later, Doris came to me and said thank you, that she knew I had paid him to leave. She was so grateful. She hugged me. And no matter that I denied it, she sincerely believed that was what I had done. She thought I was being modest, but in all truth, such a course of action never even occurred to me. In any case, that would never have worked. That type of man, they never stay away, especially if they have been paid once. They always hope to gain more. Anyway, the police never came looking for him, and the whole village just accepted that he had gone away.'

'Just as they accepted that Mrs Barton had run away with him, that they were having an affair?' Dee couldn't help the slight bitter edge to her tone. But Miss Marriott didn't seem to notice, or if she did, it didn't offend her.

She nodded again. 'Yes, there again, I was lucky that no doubt was ever expressed, no one ever seemed determined to find out for sure. I had rather hoped that poor Clive would, in time, marry Bet, but that never happened. If he ever doubted his wife had left him, he never discussed it. At least, not to my knowledge. He seemed to embrace her absence with, well perhaps not pleasure, but certainly with an admirable stoicism.'

'But all you cared about was that Bet and Doris should be happy.'

Miss Marriott's expression softened, and she nodded. 'I should have known you'd guess.'

'I was illegitimate myself,' Dee said. 'These things happen, I suppose. William Didsbury?'

'I loved him the way a girl loves her first love. With passion, with an abandonment that would have shocked my family to the core. But oh, he was a sly villain, already engaged to be married. Full of promises until he'd had what he wanted, and then I didn't see him for dust, as they say. My mother managed everything. We kept it from my father, Mother said he would have turned me out of the house, disowned me. William was no better to his wife than he was to any other woman. Selfish to the core, and with an ungovernable temper.

'But I was able to watch my Elizabeth, or Bet as we all call her, grow up. My little baby girl. So pretty, such sweet manners as a child. A darling. As an adult, she was known to be prickly, but hard-working. Far too independent, but kind too. I wanted her to know who I was, but of course it just wasn't possible. But I loved her so much, it drove reason from my head, I always had to see her, to know what she was doing, how she was, to know everything about her. I watched her so-called family let her down time and again. And then Henry came along, and he made her life an absolute misery. I wanted to somehow make things better for her, and for Doris too, my lovely little Doris, my granddaughter. I tried, I really tried to talk some sense into Henry. I even threatened him with eviction, anything to get him to be the decent man Bet needed and deserved. In the end, there was only one way to make things better for her.'

Dee was silent, thinking about all this. Even if it was true that the families had in a sense benefitted from the departure of their relatives, that could never justify Miss Marriott's actions. And those two had not been her only victims.

'They weren't the only ones, were they? What about Tristan Summers and Serafina Rainbow? Or should I say, Sara Philpott?'

'You're angry with me, Dee dear, aren't you? I suppose that's hardly a surprise. What strong morals you have. A good thing, obviously. Though I'm saddened that you will, understandably, condemn my actions. Because yes, you're quite right. I did almost the same thing on the night of the churchyard fire. That night, I wanted to see what was going on further over, so as soon as you became distracted into helping the other young woman, I saw a chance to get away.'

'You could have been cut off by the fire. You could have died,' Dee pointed out, rather crossly.

Miss Marriott hung her head briefly. 'Yes dear, that's very true. And perhaps it would have been better that way. But as it was, again I was lucky. I happened upon Mr Summers. He had been punched in the face by Jimmy Philpott and was crawling along the ground, concussed, I should think. Philpott was quickly moved on by one of his cohorts, and there was so much happening all around, the fighting and shouting, the fire of course, that for a moment no one was attending to me. Or so I thought, and as I went by the Summers fellow, I gave him a hefty whack with my walking stick. The same walking stick had I used years earlier. Then I turned away, needing to distance myself quickly, and walked right into Miss Rainbow.

'Or rather, into Mrs Philpott as you so rightly say. She called me some vicious names and said, 'You'll pay for that, you mark my words. And for the others.' She went past me to go to Tristan's aid, I simply turned, and seeing that the coast was clear, I hit her twice with my stick. She went down heavily and rolled into the fire. I threw my walking stick aside a little further on, I thought it was time to be rid of it, and the fire seemed the perfect solution. She didn't try to get up, and hoping for the best, I—I kept going, quickly finding you and drawing you away. Mercifully the police and firemen were arriving and it seemed like the perfect moment to leave, and no one any the wiser.'

'So she was definitely Sara Philpott, Mr Philpott senior's estranged wife?'

Dee shook her head sadly. Three people not two, had been missing for the last nine years. And to think that everyone had talked about Henry Padham and Maureen Barton being missing all these years, wondering what had happened, wondering where they were. But Sara Philpott had gone unmentioned, seemingly forgotten. Except perhaps by her wayward son.

Miss Marriott nodded. 'Oh yes, Dee dear. She'd been making a nuisance of herself, telephoning me, telling me I'd pay for what I'd done, putting notes through the door when Doris wasn't about, threatening to go to the police. She didn't, I don't quite know why. Perhaps she just wanted money.' Miss Marriott shrugged. 'Whatever the reason, she knew what I had done all those years ago too. There are notes in my dressing-table drawer upstairs. She said, 'You won't get away with this like you did last time. Oh, I saw you that night. I was on my way to the bus stop; Maureen and I had planned to go to the pictures together. I went to see if I could see her coming, and that was when I saw the trail in the snow, and spots of blood. I followed it right to your house! Then the ambulance came so I left.' She told me she'd found Maureen's handbag. I'd forgotten all about it. So, obviously when I was confronted by her in the churchyard, I just—lashed out at her too. It seemed easy, necessary even.

'I know you think I am a wicked old woman. I don't blame you in the least. And I know I will face my judgment in the next life. But I'm also fully prepared to make a confession to the authorities in this life too. Dee, dear, please don't hate me.'

A tear rolled down the old woman's cheek. Dee, annoyed with herself for still caring, went to sit by her side, putting an arm about her shoulders.

*

Chapter Twenty-eight

Dee patted the old woman's hand as she clutched at her. It was icy.

'Shall I fetch you a wrap or your dressing-gown? You seem a bit chilly.'

Miss Marriott directed a gentle smile at her. 'Oh my, you're such a sweet girl. No, my dear, it's quite all right. I shall be all right now I've told my story. It's been hanging over me for so long.'

Miss Marriott was a cold-hearted murderer, Dee thought, yet she still felt an urge to protect her, to look to the woman's comfort.

'I'm afraid you'll have to tell it all over again to the police,' Dee reminded her.

Another slight smile. 'Yes, I realise that. Will it be your handsome cousin who will write it all down?'

'I expect it will be Sergeant Porter,' Dee said. 'He'll write down everything you say, then give it to you to read. If you're certain that it's what you want to say, then you'll have to sign it. My cousin will be the one who asks all the questions.'

'The inspector is a very nice man. I do hope you and he will marry. He'd be perfect for you. Though of course, many people say cousins should never marry. Especially first cousins. For the sake of the babies, of course.'

Dee leaned towards Miss Marriott and with a smile said, 'I thought you knew? He's not really my cousin. I was adopted. My real parents were completely unrelated to the Inspector.'

'Oh that's wonderful! So...?' Miss Marriott glanced at Dee and Dee nodded.

'Exactly,' Dee said. 'Hopefully, as soon as my divorce comes through, Bill and I...'

'Oh, I'm so glad for you, dear. You'll make a lovely couple. What a shame I shan't be able to come to your wedding.' She caught Dee's sorrowful look. 'Oh it's all right, my dear. I'm perfectly happy to tell him everything. I suppose I knew it was bound to come out some day, one can't keep secrets forever, you know. Do you think they will hang me?'

That took Dee by surprise. She shot Miss Marriott a horrified look, then said, 'Oh, well, I don't know. But I shouldn't think so, they don't do that anymore. I expect you'll go to prison. I doubt you'll get parole though.'

Miss Marriott laughed as merrily as if Dee had told a joke. 'My dear Dee, I doubt I'll live long enough for that! Now then, could you go and telephone to the Bird in Hand for your cousin.'

Dee said, 'He's already on his way. I phoned him earlier. I should think they will be here any minute now.'

'Hopefully,' Miss Marriott said, 'they will simply saunter along the lane to us. I'd hate it if they came in a police car with its bell jangling.'

'Don't worry, they'll walk here.' Something else occurred to Dee now. 'I suppose it was you who wrote to tell Clive Barton that his wife had died in Spain?'

Miss Marriott gave her a sheepish look. 'Yes, dear, of course it was me. After a few years of Maureen being gone, I began to see that Clive would never go back to Bet unless he thought he was a free man. So, when I was on holiday—in the Canary Islands, you know, I used to stay with an old schoolfriend and her husband. They always had a houseful, such a merry crowd, we were. Of course, the sun helps. Er—what was I saying, dear?'

'That you were on holiday in the Canary Islands,' Dee reminded her with a slight smile.

'Oh yes. And we'd been having a few drinks and a few games of whist, and someone had said something about sending postcards to her family back in England, and so it came it me: I could send a letter to Clive, make up a story about Maureen dying. My awfully quavery writing would look just like that of an elderly priest. I added in a little bad grammar and a few misspellings to make it look as though it had been written by someone whose English wasn't very good. I gave the letter to one of the other guests staying with Rosa and Archie, I asked them to post it for me from Madrid—they were going there for a few days' sightseeing on their way home.'

'But Clive still wouldn't be free to marry Bet—because *she* was still married, or so she thought,' Dee pointed out, exasperated with the old woman.

Miss Marriott looked a little crestfallen. 'That's very true. I'm afraid I forgot that part. I decided against sending another letter in case someone tried to verify the fact. I thought two letters would look rather suspicious. So I gained nothing from that exercise, I'm afraid, and sadly, neither did dear Bet.'

She leaned back in her chair. Her age was vividly etched in every line on her face. Even her eyes seemed faded and weary, the lids drooping slightly at the corners. She raised a shaky hand to her forehead.

'I'm so tired, my dear. I don't suppose they will let me go and lie down for a while?'

Dee shook her head. 'I'm sorry. I don't think they will, no.'

'Oh well, never mind. I'll have a nap once all this business is over, and they've bundled me off to prison. As Doris isn't here, perhaps I could impose upon you to make some tea, dear? I might take a little sugar in mine. As a pick-me-up. It's been rather an ordeal.'

'Good idea.' Dee crossed the room to go to the kitchen. But as she went, she glanced out of the window and saw the policemen were hurrying up the lane towards the house. About time, she thought, it felt like an hour since she'd telephoned.

'Are they coming?' Miss Marriott asked, seeing Dee looking out.

'Yes.'

'That's just as well.' Miss Marriott continued, 'I'm afraid certain things have got to be faced. By me, that is. Ah, here are our guests.'

She said this in response to the loud knock at the front door. Her voice sounded wearied, without any strength left. With a concerned look back at her, Dee ran to open the door and let the police officers inside.

Dee closed the door behind them, then took the lead, murmuring 'Come with me, I need to show you something.'

She led them along the hall to the study. She could feel their questioning looks on her but didn't trust herself to speak. She was shaking. She went directly across to the bookshelf, and as they watched in astonishment, she opened the panel, reached in for the torch, handing it to Bill who was closest to her.

She said tersely, 'Go in and take a look. I suspect it goes all the way to the church, but you won't need to go that far.'

She stepped back to wait, gnawing her fingernail, hoping they wouldn't take too long.

A moment later she heard the muffled exclamation and knew they had found the remains. As soon as the two men rejoined her, she said, in a colourless voice that had Bill glancing at her in concern, 'Come with me.'

They went into the drawing-room, and Miss Marriott put out a hand to Dee. 'You will stay with me, won't you? It will be so exhausting to explain it all again. I really ought to go and lie down.'

Dee sat beside Miss Marriott and held her hand.

Somewhat puzzled, but ever the gentleman, Porter smiled and nodded at Dee and then at Miss Marriott. He took his seat, immediately getting out his notebook and pen, and a large paper form, folded into three to create a long thin strip.

Hardy perched on the edge of the seat opposite Miss Marriott and looked at her closely. 'I understand you have something you want to tell me?'

Miss Marriott endeavoured to sit up straight. She nodded. 'Oh yes, young man, I have. But I'm only saying it all once, so you had better get Mr Porter to take it all down in full, as my formal statement.'

'Of course.' Hardy nodded to Porter, and then said, 'Miss Marriott, what can you tell me about the remains that we have just found in the passage in your study?'

She sighed and shook her head sorrowfully, whilst the others politely smiled and nodded, even now treating her like a lady, though they were clearly eager to get on with things.

'Such a terrible pity,' Miss Marriott, looking really upset. Her hands were shaking in her lap and she was breathing in odd shallow snatches.

The two men were still nodding politely, and Dee was thinking, she does actually look ill. Was that guilt, she wondered, or fear of what was to come. Or was her heart really troubling her? Dee thought perhaps she ought to send for Miss Marriott's doctor, just to be on the safe side.

As the three of them sat there watching her, Miss Marriott gave a slight convulsion and a gasp, then slid sideways onto the floor, her lorgnette bumping out of her hand onto the carpet.

Dee didn't even move. She just stared, completely unable to accept what her eyes were showing her.

Nat and Bill were on their feet and crossing to the old woman. Bill, cursing to himself, bent to place two fingers into the soft pale flesh of the neck and after a moment or two he shook his head and stood up.

'She's dead.' His tone was flat. He wrestled with a sense of disbelief. Right under his nose, too, she'd done it. Clearly it had been planned, and he hadn't the least suspicion. He was furious with himself for being so slow, caught completely off-guard. What on earth was he going to say to the chief super?

Nat ran from the room and in the strained silence, they could hear him dialling the telephone from the study, then his voice asking for an ambulance.

Bill looked at Dee. Her face was as near white as made no difference, her eyes fixed on the figure on the carpet by her feet. He touched her shoulder gently, startling her.

'Come on.' He put an arm about her shoulders and led her from the room and into the morning-room, taking her over to an armchair. He crouched on the floor beside her, taking her hand in his, pulling off his jacket to place around her shoulders.

'Deedee? Are you all right, my darling?'

She nodded. She put her head down on his shoulder for a few seconds, then found her voice. 'It's probably for the best. She'd have hated prison.'

At a little before six o'clock, feeling sick with apprehension, Dee knocked on the door and waited. This was the end of her first official case and in another hour she would be gone, home in time for dinner, in all probability never to see these people again. And she reminded herself yet again, she wasn't responsible for what had happened. She was, so to speak, just the messenger.

'Who usually gets shot,' she murmured. Then almost smiled at her foolishness. It must be a kind of stage fright, she decided.

The door opened, and she was invited in. Dee glanced around the kitchen where she'd sat twice before. This time she declined the offer of a cup of tea. She wanted to get straight to the point before the tension and uncertainty of delivering her news made her sick.

'I've got some things to tell you,' she began. 'Difficult things.'

Bet Padham grew pale, tense. This was not merely a social visit, that much was clear. Doris looked bewildered, anxious. Bet took her daughter's hand and said, 'It's probably best to just tell us.'

Dee nodded. 'Right. Well, er, in that case. Miss Marriott was about to be arrested for the murder of Tristan Summers, and that of Serafina Rainbow.'

That was as far as she got. Both Bet and Doris gasped, disbelief and shock showing plainly on their faces.

Just wanting to get it all out, Dee hurriedly continued, 'Serafina was really Sara Philpott, Mr Philpott senior's missing wife. But, just before the police interviewed Miss Marriott, she managed to poison herself with digitoxin, the medicine she had been prescribed for her heart problems. I didn't realise what she had done, and I-I'm afraid there was nothing we could do. Miss Marriott has died.' Her own eyes prickled with tears, and she had to bite her lip to keep from breaking down.

Bet's face seemed to pinch in smaller, her skin suddenly pale. She nodded. Blinking back fresh tears, her hand over her mouth, Doris glanced at Bet and patted her arm reassuringly.

Dee continued, 'Bet, Miss Marriott was also going to be charged with the murder of your husband Henry Padham and that of Maureen Barton.'

'My God!' Bet was, if possible, even paler now.

But Doris was nodding slowly. She'd always suspected her father was dead and that someone had killed him. Perhaps, when she had thanked Miss Marriott for paying Henry to leave all those years ago, she had after all guessed at the truth? Dee didn't think it was the right time to ask.

'You know,' Dee said. 'I think we could all do with that cup of tea after all.'

Doris jumped up and went to fill the kettle, Dee following behind. Doris showed her where everything was, and she put all the necessary bits and pieces onto a tray, leaving Doris to get out the tea, the teapot, and make the tea.

A few minutes later, they were once again around the kitchen table, cradling their hot cups, or stirring in sugar, and if it was still tense, at least the air of overwhelming grief was beginning to give way to acceptance.

Bet Padham said, 'Did Miss Marriott say why she had done all these terrible things?'

And almost at the same moment, Doris blurted out, 'To think she acted so shocked and upset when I told her about Tristan Summers dying in the night, she said how wicked it was. And all the time, it was her! I just can't believe it of her! How the bloody hell...?' She stopped dead when she realised what she'd said. Her mother raised an eyebrow but said nothing. Doris continued, 'Sorry Mum, it just slipped out. What I meant to say was, how on earth could a frail little old lady manage to overpower men a lot stronger than her, and even the women... They were all younger than her, after all. Apart from that Serafina woman, she was a bit older, probably my mum's age, but she wasn't *old* as such.'

Dee nodded. 'I know. But when Miss Marriott and I went to visit Miss Didsbury this afternoon, Sylvia had a fall and hurt herself, and Miss Marriott leapt to her feet and rushed to her side, all with neither stick nor a person to help her, and it was only later I realised what I'd seen. There was no hobbling, no carefully holding onto the furniture and inching her way along as she usually does. I wonder if she'd been exaggerating her frailty for some time. Of course, she knew that I'd seen her, that I'd noticed how agile she could be when she wanted to be. I mean, she was only seventy-six, it's not as though she was ninety.

'But as for the murders, well, she had the element of surprise on her side. Don't forget, when Henry was killed, Miss Marriott was a crucial nine years younger therefore nine years stronger. She said Henry was completely unprepared for her attack. As was Maureen. Although the effort of managing all that took its toll on Miss Marriott's health from that night on.'

'But why?' Bet asked again. She was understandably tearful now, Dee could see. Doris patted her mother's hand again.

Dee sighed. This next bit was going to be hard for Bet and Doris. She was concerned they would take on some of Miss Marriott's guilt, and she didn't want that. She began with, 'Well, you see, Bet, Miss Marriott was...'

'Was she my mother?'

Dee was taken by surprise. 'Yes, actually that's exactly what I was about to say.'

Bet nodded. 'I don't really know how I knew, I just... did. Perhaps because of the way she's looked after Doris over the years. It sometimes seemed, I don't know, too much for just an employer. I suppose she had an affair with my father?'

Dee nodded now. 'That's right. Yes, I'm sorry but she did. She loved him very much, she thought he would marry her. They weren't officially engaged, of course, but she believed they had an understanding. But then he left her for another woman, your mother, and some time later Miss Marriott realised she was expecting a child—you. As far as all their friends and neighbours knew, Miss Marriott's mother took her away to recover from her broken heart with joys of travelling, but in reality, she had her baby in secret, and the baby was given to your parents to bring up as their own, and they received the guesthouse as payment for that.'

Tears were rolling down Bet's face, and she nodded gently as if all made sense, as if she had always known.

Dee continued, 'Miss Marriott said she watched you grow up, always wanting to know you better, always loving you. Loving both of you. And when you married, and your husband began to treat you so badly, she couldn't bear to stand back and do nothing. She had warned him once or twice, but of course he just laughed at her. The final straw was when she found Doris weeping in the kitchen and saw the bruise from where Henry had hit her. She said she knew then that he would never change. And she had to do something about it. She really loved you, Bet. And you, Doris. I know that doesn't excuse any of the terrible things she did, but she was so desperate to help you, to protect you.'

'But what about the beatniks?' Doris asked her.

'Well, I'm afraid it was rather the same, in a way. She killed Tristan simply because he was vulnerable, and she could. She disliked him, and quite honestly, she thought he was a troublemaker. And so... But Serafina, or Sara, she had come back to the village to confront the past, to confront Miss Marriott with her actions all those years ago. At the time of Henry and Maureen's deaths, she felt she had to get away in case she was in danger herself. But it had clearly played on her conscience. She spoke to Ken Riley about it. He said she needed peace and had fallen in with the seekers for convenience and because she had started a relationship with Tristan. Miss Marriott was afraid Sara would expose her, and so, likewise seizing her opportunity that night, Miss Marriott killed Sara too.'

A little later, having said everything that she wanted to say, it was time to leave. She got a hug from both Bet and Doris.

'Let me know about Miss Marriott's funeral, won't you? I'd like to send her some flowers,' Dee said. And she gave them one of the visiting cards Monty had given her. At the door, as they said emotional goodbyes, she turned to see Clive striding towards them, completely recovered from his concussion.

'You're not leaving?' he said, seeming surprised. 'I've just heard about Miss Marriott. I can hardly believe it. What on earth's going on?'

'Bet will tell you everything,' Dee assured him. 'But, can I just ask, why did you phone ahead and warn Barry and the others to leave before taking me back to your house?'

He was clearly surprised she knew. 'Oh my word.' He was blushing, embarrassed. 'I'm so sorry. It was a stupid, stupid thing to do. I was afraid you'd tell him about Maureen not being in her grave. I'd hoped he hadn't heard about that yet. I-I'd hoped to keep it from him and Jane, tell them in my own time. As it was, they had already heard. And, well, you saw how Barry reacted, the little blighter. Though I can understand him being furious with me.'

'You could have trusted me, Clive, I wouldn't have said anything about that. But I'm glad you finally told your children the truth. Bet has a lot to tell you, and I think the police may need to speak to you today or tomorrow.'

He looked intrigued, she saw, but she didn't have the time or the energy to go into it all again. She said, 'My cousin and Sergeant Porter are still here for a day or two, tidying things up, so they can answer any questions you have. Right, er, anyway, I'm going back to London now, my train will be here soon. Take care of Bet and Doris for me, won't you?'

'I will, I promise.' He kissed her cheek. 'Goodbye dear.'

On the train twenty minutes later, she reflected that the hardest part of her investigation always seemed to be saying goodbye. She was exhausted by the emotional strain of the day. At least she'd been able to get away: Bill and Nat still had plenty of work to finish off. She didn't think she could have stayed a moment longer.

Dee reached into her bag to find one of Rob's liquorice allsorts, popping a round blue one into her mouth, and with a last look out of the window as Hartwell Priory was left behind, she opened her book.

*

Epilogue

The next morning being Monday, she presented herself at the office at half past eight precisely.

'I really must congratulate you, M'dear. You did an excellent job, I'm so very proud of you.' Monty, carried away with emotion, grabbed her hand and kissed it in his old-fashioned chivalrous manner. Dee almost giggled, so relieved that he was happy with the way things had gone on her first ever assignment.

'Oh Monty, I'm so...'

But he swept that aside. 'Yes, yes. Now look, I'd like to put you on a salary, my dear. Can you bear to do all this again, do you think? It won't always be murders or village upheavals and so forth. Sometimes it might be nothing more interesting than a missing dog or a handbag snatch or a door-to-door conman. But what do you think, M'dear? Shall we say fourteen pounds per week? And expenses of course, if you're away on a case.'

'Oh Monty, that's so...'

Again, he overrode her. 'Excellent then. You may have the weekend off!' Then he beamed at her, and she realised he was teasing her, he didn't really expect her to work at the weekend. Did he?

'No need to rush into the job, I assume you'll need a few days off to get things done at home. So I'll see you at ten o'clock on Thursday, M'dear? Is that all right?'

She kissed his cheek. 'You're a darling,' she said, and the elderly man blushed.

'Now then, be off with you. I just need your brother to take down a letter for me, for Mrs Elizabeth Padham of Hartwell Priory.'

'Bet Padham? Oh?'

'Confidentially, I can disclose that she's inherited Miss Marriott's substantial estate, and it falls to Montague Montague of London, legal services to inform the dear lady of this and to offer our assistance.'

'That's wonderful,' Dee said. 'Bet will be able to give up that vile guesthouse and live in comfort! In fact, if she's any sense, she and Clive will sell up everything and move away entirely.'

That evening, she met Bill by the front door. He was coming out as she was going in. She felt an acute sense of disappointment that he was going out for the evening, having hoped to spend some time with him.

'Sorry, must dash, might see you later if you're still here.' He was already halfway down the steps, speaking to her over his shoulder, the ample-figured blonde on his arm turning back to glance at Dee with curiosity. Dee felt dismissed, unimportant, a dead leaf on the path of his life. 'By the way,' he added.

'Thanks for your help with the Hartwell Priory case, you were pretty useful at times. But don't go thinking that I'm happy for you to keep meddling in police affairs. I shan't allow it again.'

And he was gone, seating the blonde before revving his car engine unnecessarily loudly and merging into the traffic at the corner, his hand out of the driver's window in a careless wave.

After dinner, Aunt Dottie was called to the telephone. Jenny and JJ were rummaging through the record collection to find something to put on the player. Dee, on the sofa, feeling miserable, huffed irritably and leant against her uncle's shoulder. He put an arm about her and kissed the top of her head.

'Is there anything you want to talk about? Get off your chest?'

All she said, crossly and between unexpected sobs was, 'Your son's an idiot.'

Uncle William sighed. 'I take it by that, that you mean my eldest son, and yes, if he's hurt you, my darling, he must be.'

'I love him.'

'Would it help if I told you he loves you too?'

'No.' But she smiled. She leaned back into his shoulder again. A moment later she said, 'He's still an idiot.'

'He'll learn. From personal experience, I can tell you it takes us Hardy men a bit longer than most to work things out.'

'I'm already thirty-one. It's no good to me if he waits until I'm ninety.'

Uncle William laughed. 'I don't think it'll be quite that long.'

A record was chosen, put onto the turntable, and the music started, a lively tune by the Dave Clark

Five, and JJ came over, his hand held out, and with a big grin at his father, he said, 'Come on Deedee, don't sit there with the old fossil, let's twist!'

A mile away, at the Old London Ballroom Hotel, Bill escorted the ample-figured blonde into the function room at the rear, where banners proclaimed, *Happy retirement Alf from your colleagues at the Met.*

The blonde was offered a glass of champagne, and she took one for Bill too. 'Here,' she said. 'But don't get sloshed, remember I know you're driving, and I'd have no qualms about turning in one of Dad's soon-to-be former colleagues for drunk driving.' Then she gave him a quick kiss on the cheek and wandered off to join Alf and Pam across the room.

Her place was taken a minute later by Chief Superintendent Morris Asquith.

'All right Hardy?'

'Yes, thank you, sir. How are you? Sir,' he added somewhat belatedly.

'Fine, fine. Glad to see you're obeying orders for once and making sure you're seen socialising with ladies who are a more suitable match than your married cousin.'

'Yes, sir.' Bill looked down at his feet, not particularly happy about the situation. He knew perfectly well that Dee was hurt and angry with him about all the women he'd been seen about with lately. Even his mother and his sister had taken him to one side and asked him what he thought he was playing at. *She deserves better than that*, they'd told him, which made him feel like throwing himself off a bridge. Or just getting roaring drunk, throwing his career on the fire and going straight round to her flat and demanding she run away with him to... where could they go? He couldn't think of anywhere far enough away from Asquith and the Met.

But the boss was still talking: 'Got your career to think about, my boy. Forget the girl. Can't be much good anyway if she's thrown aside her marriage vows just like that. Mark my words, you need to keep on the straight and narrow. A police officer cannot be too careful of his reputation. Got to be wholly above reproach. Right, well, enjoy your evening.' And Old Arsey Asquith took himself pompously off, having delivered his lecture, never knowing how close he came to receiving a punch on the nose followed by Bill's warrant card rammed down his throat.

He got home at the same time as his father that evening.

'Where've you been?' Bill asked William, purely out of idle curiosity.

'Oh, I took Dee home, Rob's using her car again tonight.'

'She didn't want to stay the night?'

'No.'

They came into the room his father used as a study. William immediately poured his son a scotch. 'You look like you need this. Now, then, what's going on?'

'Oh, Dad.' Bill sank into a chair. 'It's such a bloody mess.'

There was a long silence.

'Was she all right?' Bill asked eventually.

William said, 'Yes, she's fine. But obviously she's upset with you. Doesn't understand why you're seeing all these women, giving her the run-around. Thinks it means you don't love her. Am I right in assuming it's the edict from On High?'

Bill nodded and sipped his drink. 'I came very close to telling Asquith what he could do with his damned edict this evening.'

William laughed, and immediately the mood lightened. 'It'll be all right son, it's not for much longer. She'll understand.'

Bill nodded. 'Thanks, Dad. Though I'm not sure how much more I can take. You know I don't—you know—there's nothing going on with any of them. I would never... Can you get Mum and Jen off my back too?'

William drew in a sharp breath. 'Leave all the tough jobs to me, why don't you?' He poured them both another scotch. He clinked their glasses together. 'To true love. May we survive it.'

'Amen to that.'

The following morning, Rob pounded on Dee's bedroom door, telling her to get up. She turned over in bed, pulling the covers over her head. The pounding continued, and she was so annoyed she yelled back rather loudly,

'Shut up and go away! I'm having a lie-in!'

'Get up, get dressed, and make yourself look decent. Put on that blue frock you've got with the matching jacket and the hat.'

'My blue...? Why?' she yelled again over the edge of the blankets.

'Bill's here with Nat, they say we have to go with them. Hurry up.'

'What? Why?' She demanded again, falling back against the pillows, her eyes screwed shut in frustration. All she wanted was another hour or two of sleep. A glance at her alarm clock showed her it was a little before nine.

'Just get ready, Dee!' Her brother sounded thoroughly fed up with her. And immediately she heard the familiar voice of her cousin, his usual grumpy self, saying,

'Dee, we're leaving in five minutes. Don't keep us hanging about.'

She peered around the bedroom door to find the hallway clear. There were male voices coming from the sitting-room. She ran to the bathroom, had a quick wash and did her hair, put on make-up, then spritzed herself with perfume for defiance or courage, she wasn't sure which. Then she ran back to her bedroom in her underwear, glad not to meet anyone on the way.

It was more like fifteen minutes before she reappeared, coming into the sitting-room to find Nat and Bill there in smart suits, looking highly official, their expressions grave.

Nat came towards her, his hand out to her. 'I'm sorry, Miss Dee, I'm going to have to ask you to come with me.'

'Wh-what? But...' She looked back for her brother. Fear and confusion wrestled in her chest.

Bill put a hand on her shoulder and ushered her towards the door. She looked back past his grim face towards Rob, also in his best suit, but looking like a man going to his own funeral. My God, Dee thought, what on earth is this? Are we under arrest? Was it because of the recent events in Hartwell Priory? Was she under arrest for allowing Miss Marriott to kill herself instead of facing justice for her crimes?

She was escorted out of the flat, down the stairs and out into the street to where the police car was waiting. She and Rob were told to get into the back seat, then Nat drove them away.

In just a few minutes they had arrived.

Dee didn't recognise the building where they had parked. When Bill opened the door for her, she stepped out into the street with great reluctance, her heart pounding. As she got out, he looked down at her, their eyes met, and she felt the usual frisson of adoration go through her. Stupid man, she thought crossly. What on earth was going on, and why didn't he simply tell her straight? And she noted his suit more closely now—another fabulous yet obviously expensive creation. He was such a peacock, a clotheshorse. He spent more on his clothes than she did, she was certain. This inner critique saved her from the fear that was bubbling below the surface. But she couldn't ignore it any longer.

'Bill, please.'

'This way, Dee, if you will,' was all he said.

On the pavement, at the foot of a grand staircase leading up to massive double doors, they halted. Nat came up behind them, holding Rob's arm firmly. Then he released Rob's arm, and opening a box he had with him, he handed Rob a pink carnation. Bill also took one and began to pin it on the lapel of Nat's jacket, then pinned another on his own suit.

Rob helped Dee to get hers just right, then said, 'Right lads, we'll see you later.' And he led Dee up the stairs and in at the massive doors.

'Rob, what on earth...?'

And there was Violet, in a long cream dress, holding a little bouquet of pink and mauve flowers in front of her, a tremulous smile on her face.

'Do I look all right? Do you think he'll like it?' Violet asked them anxiously.

And now finally Dee understood. Promising vengeance on the three men who had tricked her, even as a smile spread across her face, she took the smaller bouquet Vi shyly held out to her. Rob came to offer Vi his arm. He kissed her cheek, and said,

'Right then, missy, let's get you married. Dee, I'm the father of the bride, obviously, and you're the bridesmaid, so get behind Vi and hold up that train of lace, and let's get going.'

He grinned at them both. Dee's eyes already glistened with tears.

'I'll deal with you later,' she informed her brother, obviously in on the secret the whole time, the wretch. 'You scared me half to death.'

She patted Vi's arm reassuringly then kissed her cheek. 'You look beautiful, Vi. And absolutely radiant. He'll love the dress almost as much as he loves you.'

She bent to lift the train of intricately worked lace from the ground. They nodded at one another, they were all ready, and with a deep breath the three of them stepped forward to walk into the room where Nat, with Bill beside him as his best man, was waiting for her in front of the registrar.

THE END

About the author

Caron Allan writes cosy murder mysteries, both contemporary and also set in the 1930s. Caron lives in Derby, England with her husband and an endlessly varying quantity of cats and sparrows.

Caron Allan can be found on these social media channels and would love to hear from you:

Instagram: caronsbooks

Twitter: caron_allan

Mastodon social: caron_allan

Facebook: CaronAllanFiction

Pinterest: caronallan

Also, if you're interested in news, snippets, Caron's 'quirky' take on life or just want some sneak previews, please sign up to Caron's blog shown below:

www.caronallanfiction.com

Sign up to my mailing list and you can read Night and Day: Dottie Manderson mysteries book 1 for FREE:

https://wp.me/P3esyI-2gQ

Also by Caron Allan

The Friendship Can Be Murder books:

Criss Cross: book 1
Cross Check: book 2
Check Mate: book 3

The Dottie Manderson mysteries:

Night and Day: book 1
The Mantle of God: book 2
Scotch Mist: book 3 a novella
The Last Perfect Summer of Richard Dawlish: book 4
The Thief of St Martins: book 5
The Spy Within: book 6
Rose Petals and White Lace: book 7

The Miss Gascoigne mysteries:

A Meeting With Murder: book 1
A Wreath of Lilies: book 2

Others:

Easy Living: a story about life after death, after death, after death

Coming Soon

Midnight, the Stars, and You: Dottie Manderson mysteries book 8

Printed in Great Britain
by Amazon

38207445R00198